The Burning Side

By Jacqueline R. Richardson

This book is dedicated to my husband, Zach, and my mom, Cindy, for their unwavering support and assistance in the writing and editing process.

Also by Jacqueline Richardson:

Dream Jumper
Beyond Reason
The Time Thief
The Time Thief: A Change of Face

September 12, 2010

...I never could have imagined that one man could destroy so many lives, even long after his death. He may have died on the burning side, but it didn't stop his reign of terror. Now I hope he goes to the burning side to which he belongs...Hell. How I wish I had known what would happen when we bought that house...

Chapter 1

Sunlight filtered through the giant oaks and maples lining the overgrown driveway, dappling the path before the truck as Bree and Jason Wilson rambled toward the house that would soon be theirs. The moment the house came into view, Bree was instantly enchanted by the air of nobility it exuded. She felt like a peasant approaching a castle. When she and Jason climbed out of the truck, they hurried excitedly to the real estate agent. She would have sprinted if she hadn't been wearing her heeled boots that disguised her short stature. As she brushed wind-blown wisps of long auburn hair from her almond-shaped, coffee-brown eyes, she looked up at the house again. This house wasn't the typical modern abode fallen victim to foreclosure, like so many of the others they considered purchasing, but rather a 19th-century masterpiece built with bricks, mortar, and muscle. It loomed over them, a massive structure of reddish-brown weathered bricks with intricate wooden accents around the windows and eaves. Bree's eye was drawn to a small widow's watch perched atop the black shingled roof, and her instant admiration for the house was intensified. The front porch was no less impressive. It was expansive with six huge columns supporting the roof above it. The porch became Bree's favorite feature of the house, and she was already imagining rocking chairs and patio furniture with which to adorn it. The backyard was quite expansive as well, though poorly maintained.

Upon entering the house, Bree was pleased to see that the interior of the home was better cared for than the yard. Though it was quite tidy and seemed structurally sound, the interior did reveal the historic nature of the home. The ceilings were unnecessarily high, and the plaster was cracking. The arches connecting the living room, kitchen, and hallways were tall and wide with bulky yet beautiful solid oak trim. The windows bore the same woodwork. The wooden baseboards on the wall along the hardwood floors were almost a foot high. The bathroom and kitchen fixtures looked antique, but still maintained a lustrous shine. There was even a massive brick chimney and evidence that a woodstove once stood in the living room. A staircase opened from the living room to the upstairs. The house had five bedrooms, two of which were upstairs, and an office. The door to the master bedroom was right at the top of the long staircase leading to the second floor, with a guest bedroom and a large bathroom off to the left. A small office was at the end of the hall across from the master bedroom. In the basement, they found an old coal shoot and an enormous fuel oil tank, evidence that this house had seen every kind of heating fuel used in the past hundred years. Instead of being deterred by the age of the home, Bree and Jason found it charming.

The house was being sold by a pudgy, grumpy accountant, Mr. Stewart, who had inherited it when his grandfather died. According to the accountant, his grandfather hadn't lived in the home, and it hadn't been inhabited for several decades. Luckily for the Wilsons, however, his grandfather had kept the home well maintained while he was alive, as he planned to someday make it his retirement getaway. Mr. Stewart didn't share the same enthusiasm for the house as his grandfather, and was eager to be rid of the burden of property taxes and maintenance. He was practically giving it away, and Jason and Bree couldn't ignore such a steal.

Though the house had already seen over one hundred fifty years of history, Bree and Jason were determined to make it a loving home for generations to come. They purchased the house and renovations began shortly thereafter. Bree and Jason spent most of their weekends there, supervising contractors and slowly moving in their belongings. Bree was in love with the place, pressing Jason constantly to make the move permanently. She loved her husband dearly, with his broad smile, big brown eyes, and handsome features, but despite his masculinity and easy-going nature she found he had an overwhelming apprehension to change. Finally, however, on a sunny spring Saturday during one of their weekend trips, he acquiesced. His company had a division in White Dove near their new home, and he was given approval to transfer. Bree was ecstatic when he gave her the exciting news. She kissed him happily and hurried off to further prepare the house for the move. She wasn't aware of how one small occurrence that same sunny Saturday would mark the beginning of the strangest time in her life.

Early in the afternoon, Bree went into the basement to store away some empty boxes. She was overwhelmed with excitement, and stopped to admire the dingy basement. It was slightly chilly and dank, but it was *hers*. She'd lived in rentals or apartments for the past 9 years, her entire adult life, so it gave her great joy to entertain the notion of actually *owning* her home. She let her eyes wander to a beautiful old piano that had been abandoned within the house.

"How could someone just leave a piano?" Bree wondered aloud to herself while fondly running her fingers along the dusty keys. She pressed down on a key, and the piano emitted a flat, off-key note. She gave a small chuckle when the key didn't pop back up but remained stuck down. As she pulled the key back up to its original position, a strong, smoky odor suddenly tickled her nostrils. It instantly became strong enough to make her breath catch in her throat. What was on fire? Her head full of disastrous scenarios, she whirled around, intending to quickly investigate. She was stopped dead in her tracks.

Before her, nose to nose with her, was the most hideous face she had ever seen, accompanied by the noxious scent of putrid, burning pork. Horror froze her as she gazed upon the floating, ashen, misshapen head gruesomely erupting with pus and fire. The orange-yellow flames danced around the lumpy, whitish face as pus and melting fat dripped sloppily to the floor. The skin on the face was waxy, pale, and had the mangled appearance of gnarly, interwoven tree roots, complete with gaps and lumps. The mouth was opened in an angry, soundless scream, exposing yellowed, cracked, jagged teeth. Stringy, wet-looking dark hair hung limply around its face, contrasting with the bright, wildly dancing flames. One eye was a gaping black hole with bubbling, off-white fluids oozing from it, sizzling as they ran down the side of the horrific face. The other eye, however, was still intact, though the bright red veins around the icy blue iris looked as though they were about to burst. This disgusting eye bulged and glared at her with a look of rage and hatred that pierced her to her very core. Lumps of melted fat and flesh plopped to the floor, sizzling as they splattered at her feet.

When Bree thought she felt a heavy mass drop onto her shoe, she was startled out of her stupor. She jumped back instinctually, her eyes diverting from the grisly gourd before her to her foot. Her shoe was clean. She looked back up and found the image of the head was gone. Bree stood frozen in shock again, unable even to blink. The suddenness of the appearance and then almost instantaneous disappearance of the abomination left her in a daze for several seconds. It wasn't until she gasped for air that she realized she was holding her breath. She also instantly noticed the absence of the smoky odor. On shaky legs, Bree walked to the steps and stumbled to the top of the stairs. She stepped out of the basement and closed the door quietly, but firmly, and then slumped down to the floor with her back against the door. She tucked her thin legs up to her small chest and wrapped her arms around herself protectively. A few strands of her long, auburn hair hung in her eyes but she couldn't seem to find the strength to lift her hand to swipe them away.

I didn't really see that. I couldn't have. It was just my mind playing tricks. Horrible, demented tricks. Her heart pounded in her chest as she tried to make sense of what she just saw. She supposed the smell of smoke could've come from the piano. Maybe it had been in a fire and still held the odor within the wood's pores. Maybe the poor air quality in the basement had affected her senses and caused her to hallucinate. Maybe she was overtired. She told herself resolutely that there had to be a logical explanation, even if she didn't know what it was. As she tried to force the experience to the back of her mind, Jason came around the corner and spotted her sitting on the floor.

"Taking a break already? I thought you'd be an unstoppable force today." He paused briefly, studying her face. His large, dark eyes showed concern. "Is everything ok? You look like you saw a rat or something."

Bree wished it had only been a rat. "I'm fine. I think there may be some bad fumes or chemicals down there, though. I feel like I need some fresh air. Why don't you come sit with me on the porch for a few minutes?"

They sat in two new patio chairs on the porch looking out over their driveway and front yard. Things were still looking quite overgrown, and the vines climbing the side of the house didn't look ready to relinquish their hold on the home. Bree wondered if it were possible that the vines were not alone in this unwillingness to let go, and immediately scoffed at herself for being so ridiculous.

Jason misinterpreted her sigh of disgust. "Upset about something, hun? We'll get things together in no time. Don't stress." He reached over and patted her hand reassuringly, a gentle breeze tousling his brown hair.

"I'm sure things will be fine," she replied. After a moment of silence, she asked, "Did you notice the piano in the basement? Why do you suppose someone would leave their piano behind? I mean, it's not the same as leaving a stove or a fridge, really. It seems strange to me."

"I can see why it was left behind. It's ugly—"

"It is not ugly!" Bree interrupted.

"Matter of opinion, I guess, but it looks like someone may have agreed with me. Besides, it probably weighs a ton, and can you imagine carrying it up all those stairs to get it out of the basement? It was probably just easier to leave the damn thing!" Jason's face took on a sudden look of horror. "Oh God, you don't want me to move it, do you?"

Bree calmed his worries. "No, no! I was just thinking about it while I was down there, and I guess the mystery of it just piqued my curiosity. That's all."

Jason was thoughtful for a moment. "I would guess that the owner probably died, and no one else wanted that ugly thing."

Bree didn't like that explanation.

Jason stood up. "Back to work."

***

After six weeks of living in their new home, Jason and Bree were happier than they had dared to hope they would be. Jason had begun work at the new location, and he was confident that making the move to White Dove had been the right choice. Bree still hadn't looked for a new job, but Jason urged her to try the housewife role for a while. She was apprehensive at first, concerned that she would grow bored quickly. With no job and no children to occupy her time, Bree spent much of her day cleaning things that didn't need to be cleaned, reading books she had already read, and making up projects for herself. Before long, however, she had so many projects underway that she barely found time to eat lunch each day. One of her latest endeavors involved the creation of a large mural on their bedroom wall, depicting a beautiful forest scene with wildlife and a lively stream. Boredom was no longer an issue.

On a quiet, early summer afternoon, Bree was engrossed in her painting when the phone rang.

"Hello?"

"Hey babe. How is everything today?" Jason sounded in good spirits.

"Great. I was just working on the forest mural. How are things at work?" She knew when he called from work that it was usually to tell her he was working overtime, so she began subconsciously scheduling back dinner and re-planning the rest of her afternoon.

"Ok, but I'll be coming home soon. I decided to take the rest of the day off. Things are kind of slow here, and it's a beautiful day out. I thought maybe we could do something fun this afternoon."

Bree smiled. "That would be a nice change from overtime! How soon before you'll be home?"

"About an hour. I have a couple things to finish up here before I take off. I'll see you then, honey! Love you."

When Bree hung up the phone, she hurried to take a shower. She'd been so absorbed in her painting that she hadn't noticed the morning slip by. She set aside her paints, not bothering to put anything away as she knew she'd be at it again tomorrow morning. She went to the closet, picked out one of her favorite summer outfits, and went down the hall to the bathroom.

The hot water felt wonderful against her skin, but she wondered if she would ever get used to the unpleasant smell the water possessed. She hated bathing in the scent of boiled eggs. Her mind wandered through other such trivial thoughts as she closed her eyes and began massaging soap over her face. As she rubbed her soapy fingers over her eyelids to remove whatever makeup may have survived last night's scrubbing, she caught a familiar, unpleasant scent that was not boiled eggs. Panic gripped her as she remembered that day in the basement, remembered that smell, and remembered that face. She hesitantly sniffed again, and the smoky, burned-pork odor was so strong it seemed like she had just opened the stove with a charred roast inside. In her panic, she opened her eyes without thinking and was instantly blinded with the stinging soap she had just applied to her face. She hissed through her teeth and swore as she turned her face into the stream of water and began to frantically rinse her eyes. Terrifying images raced through her mind. She could imagine the burning head floating inches from her face in the shower, or a charred, mangled body standing right behind her or right outside the shower curtain, staring at her, reaching for her in her helplessly vulnerable state.

It seemed an eternity before her eyes were cleared of the stinging soap, but when they were, her eyes shot open and she threw aside the shower curtain. She saw nothing. She smelled nothing. She stood there, breathing as though she had just run a marathon.

"What the hell is wrong with me?" Bree wondered aloud.

The rest of her shower was hurried, and her heart didn't stop racing until she was dried and dressed. She headed downstairs without dallying.

She hadn't realized just how anxious she was until she felt the relief wash over her when Jason walked through the front door and entered the kitchen. She rushed to him and greeted him with a hug, offering to make him something for lunch. She tried to hide her lingering anxiety.

"I'd love a sandwich. I've got to change out of these clothes, but I'll be back down in a minute." Jason kissed her cheek and walked out of the kitchen.

Bree had just finished making their sandwiches when Jason strolled back into the kitchen in comfortable jeans and a t-shirt.

"So who's the person in your painting?" He asked casually as he rummaged through the fridge for a drink.

Bree looked at him, confused. "What person?"

"The guy in the woods. Wait! Let me guess…it's Fred Bear!" Jason chuckled at his own joke, but stopped abruptly when he noticed Bree glaring at him.

"There is no man in my painting." Bree conjured up the image of the mural in her mind, and she could find nothing that could be mistaken for a human figure.

"Maybe it was just supposed to be a shadow from a tree or something, but it does look like—" Jason cut off the rest of his sentence as Bree turned and hurried upstairs. She walked into the bedroom and immediately noticed the addition to her mural. In the dark forest, lurking among the trees, was an eerie, black, human-shaped figure. She leaned closer to it and saw it was actually painted on the mural in black paint, and it looked like a shadowy apparition of a man. And the paint was still wet in a few spots.

As Jason came into the room, she turned on him, pointing at the shadow man. "Do you think this is funny? I've worked hard on this, dammit!" She was almost in tears.

"Whoa, honey! I didn't do anything! Besides, you know I can't paint!" He looked completely bewildered. When Bree stopped and thought about it, she knew he couldn't possibly have done it. The paint was mostly dried, which meant it would've had to have been painted before he even came home.

Confused, she stood silently. She then apologized. "Sorry. It's just really weird. I don't remember painting that." Jason just shrugged his shoulders and went back downstairs, mumbling something to himself. Bree stared at the shadow man a moment longer, feeling like it was somehow watching her, taunting her. Ignoring the urge to gouge it out of the wall with her fingernails, she followed Jason downstairs with her fists clenched.

"Let's take our sandwiches and go for a ride. I need to get out of this house for a while," Bree said truthfully as she grabbed the sandwiches off the counter and walked out the front door without waiting for a reply.

Chapter 2

Bree and Jason headed into town to get a feel for their new territory as they hadn't had a chance to see the sights since moving into the new house. The ride was quiet, relatively speaking, as the exhaust system and stereo in Jason's newer model Chevrolet pickup didn't facilitate conversation. Bree was glad for this silence, however, since she still needed a few minutes to compose herself after the painting incident. She hoped the ride would help clear her mind.

They began passing dollar stores and gas stations, indicating their imminent arrival upon the White Dove city limits. The truck slowed as Jason heeded the reduced speed limit signs, and Bree looked out the window at the small shops ahead with tourists poking around on the sidewalks. She loved how lively Michigan could be in the summertime, even in those tiny towns where cornstalks greatly outnumbered people. The only downside was that the abundance of tourists made you even more aware of the fact that you were *not* on vacation. Bree thought of all those Fourth of July holidays she spent as a waitress, working so everyone else could have fun. She didn't miss that.

"Want to get some coffee?" Jason broke the silence. "The guys at work said this restaurant up here—" he pointed out the windshield to a small red building—"is the best place to eat around here."

Bree thought the place looked more like a small, red barn than a restaurant, but she nodded in assent. "Maybe they'll have brochures to help us figure out where we want to go today. We still get to visit the tourist traps, right? We aren't exactly 'locals' yet."

There was no parking available on the curb, so they had to park in a grocery store parking lot down the street and walk to the restaurant.

"Blazin' Fast Burgers? That's…interesting. I hope their food is better than their name," Bree said with a chuckle. The sunshine and fresh air were doing wonders for her spirits. She walked hand-in-hand with Jason, weaving through the tourists browsing the sidewalk sales. They finally reached the restaurant and stepped inside. They found a plethora of brochures advertising local attractions at the front counter. Bree grabbed a few pamphlets that looked interesting and followed Jason into the dining room. They had no trouble finding an empty table as they were the only customers in the restaurant.

"So where are we going today?" Jason asked, eyeing the handful of brochures Bree had set on the table.

"I don't know yet. We've got one for a zoo, a county park, a local historical museum, and a gift shop of oddities. I wonder what kind of 'oddities' they could possibly sell…human eyeballs?" Bree opened the gift shop brochure as an energetic older woman approached their table. She greeted them with a smile, blue eyes sparkling, and handed them menus and silverware.

"Thanks, ma'am, but we're just going to have coffee and two of those chocolate chip cookies I saw at the counter," Jason ordered for both of them. Bree handed the menu back to the waitress and returned to her brochure. She was intrigued by the gift shop, as the photos of it showed everything from strange tea sets to jewelry, and the brochure said they sold unique books as well.

"Jason, this shop looks amazing! I think this is where I want to go today. We could use some unique decorations for the house, and I bet this shop has lots of antiques that would fit well with our ancient home. Here, take a look." Bree handed him the pamphlet as the waitress returned with the coffee and cookies. The waitress noticed the brochures.

"Are you two on vacation?" The waitress asked as she set their coffee and cookies in front of them.

"No, we actually just moved here," Bree said. "We thought we should see some of the sights and get familiarized with the area."

"Well that's nice. What brought you here?" The waitress was curious.

"My company has a branch here, and I was offered a raise to transfer to this division from our old one in Grand River. It seemed like a great opportunity." Jason divulged. Bree thought he tended to over-share sometimes. She was certain the waitress didn't care if he was offered a raise to transfer.

"So where are you living? Did you folks buy a house around here?" The waitress was full of questions. Bree had forgotten what small-town life could be like—it had been years since she had lived in one.

"We bought an old house on Williams Street. No one's lived there in a while, but we had a lot of work done to it and it's making a great home for us now. Plus we got a really good deal on it." Jason continued to disclose more information than Bree thought necessary.

"You mean that big brick house at the end of the road, near the river?" The waitress looked and sounded shocked.

"Yeah, that's the one," Bree responded. "You look a little surprised." She gave the waitress a confused look, but still tried to look pleasant.

"Oh, no! I just hadn't known it was for sale. It has sat empty for as long as I can remember." The waitress still had a strange look on her face, and she hurriedly left the table after telling them to let her know if they needed anything. To Bree, it appeared that something bothered the waitress about their house. Or maybe she was bothered by the fact that they were living in it. Bree wasn't sure, but she didn't want to pry and create an uncomfortable situation. Some things were best left alone.

They sipped their coffee in silence for a few moments before Jason whispered, "She seemed almost offended that we bought that house."

Bree nodded. "Weird, right?" They both sipped their coffee some more and were silent again, just looking at each other.

"So you want to go to the gift shop?" Jason changed the subject and began browsing the brochure.

"Yeah. It looks like it has some really neat stuff in it. Maybe I could get something pretty to put over the piano, to dress it up a bit."

"But the piano's in the basement," Jason replied, "so what's the point?"

"About that…" Bree began, but hesitated.

Jason immediately knew what she was going to say, and cut her off before she could even ask. "No. Hell no. I am not moving it up those stairs!"

"But it doesn't belong in the basement! If I cleaned it up and had it tuned, it could make a great addition to our living room décor. I could even hire someone to move it so you don't have to." Bree realized she was pleading.

"Why do you all of a sudden want it upstairs?"

"I always wanted it upstairs, but I've been trying to figure out how to convince you to let me bring it up. After that first conversation we had about it I knew it would take a lot of convincing! But I figured if we hired someone to do it, then maybe you'd let me have it in the living room." Bree was hopeful and watched Jason's expressions closely.

"I don't know. Let me think on it a little bit, ok?"

Bree could feel that Jason was starting to cave. "Ok, honey. I just want to add that I've already looked up a company who can send guys to move the piano for pretty cheap." She took a drink of her coffee and ate some of her cookie.

"I knew that damn piano would end up upstairs," Jason grumbled as the waitress returned to the table to refill the coffee cups. She said very little before placing the bill on top of the napkin holder and leaving. Jason and Bree finished their cookies and their coffee. When they went to the counter to pay their bill, the waitress was waiting at the cash register. Jason handed her the money, and on their way out the door, the waitress spoke.

"Enjoy your time here," the waitress said with an ominous tone.

Bree and Jason looked at each other and mumbled a quiet "thanks." Once the door had closed behind them and they had put several steps between themselves and the restaurant, Bree said, "Did that sound ominous, or am I just paranoid?"

"I'm not sure…it was almost like she was insinuating that she didn't think we'd be here long." Jason was quiet for a few seconds, then added, "Or maybe we are just paranoid."

They both laughed it off, even though Bree was sure they were equally bothered by the waitress's change in demeanor and parting words to them. They walked to the truck, ready to continue the day's adventure. Jason entered the gift shop address from the brochure into the GPS, and they headed off to the Gypsy's Treasure Chest.

The shop was just a few miles away, but it was set apart from all the other tourist traps by being quite out-of-the-way. The GPS led them down winding dirt roads (which were still quite muddy this early in the summer) and instructed them to make a turn at every corner. When they finally reached the Gypsy's Treasure Chest, however, they found the trip to be well worth the drive.

The shop was huge, and apparently the drive didn't deter other tourists from visiting it. The parking lot was packed with cars. Bree wondered how some of those cars made it all the way out there, especially the little hybrids and low-rider sports cars. Jason found a spot just big enough for the truck and parked. As they approached the building, Bree discovered that the shop also had a restaurant attached to it, the Gypsy's Kitchen, which explained the size of the building. She wondered how she had missed that in the brochure.

The store was much less crowded than she had expected. She thought it would be elbow-to-elbow, but the store was surprisingly spacious. She assumed the restaurant must have been the main destination for the owners of the cars in the lot. She walked through the wide aisles, with her eyes wandering over all the little trinkets and occasional gaudy piece of pottery. There was no rhyme or reason to the organization of items in the store. Jewelry, pottery, dishes, wall hangings, and even furniture were all mixed together. This place was definitely a browsing shop, and not the place to go if you were looking for something specific. She wandered from aisle to aisle, with Jason in tow, hoping her eyes would fall upon some perfect little treasure.

Bree instantly fell in love when she spotted a unique, foot-tall green and brown vase. It appeared to be made of some kind of rock, and had beautiful green, brown, and white lines throughout it, resembling agate. She picked it up and was surprised at the great weight of it. She handed it to Jason to carry, and smiled at him as he rolled his eyes.

"Come on now, that's a cool vase." Bree defended. Jason just smiled at her and continued to follow her through the store.

Bree found a strange green and black tea set a few minutes later. The cream holder looked like a tiny flower vase, and the two "tea cups" looked more like Erlenmeyer flasks than cups. She was intrigued. They had no basket or any way to carry all of the pieces, so Bree just grabbed the teapot with the price sticker on it. They would come back for the rest when they made it to the checkout. She made sure to take note of their location so she wouldn't forget where the rest of her set was.

They continued to browse for what seemed like hours, but in reality was probably only thirty minutes. Bree decided she had seen enough, and Jason didn't seem to find anything of any interest to him, so they headed toward the checkout. At the front of the store, Jason and Bree set their items on the counter, and Bree went back for the rest of her tea set. When she returned, she saw that another item had been added to their treasures. It looked like a greenish-blue blown-glass bulb that tapered to a twisting point at the top, much like the twisting point you get when you stick your finger in melted marshmallow and pull it out. The weird bulb was attached to a heavy black wooden base, and an electrical cord was wound around it.

"What the hell is that?" Bree asked bluntly.

"It's one of those lamps that you can see the electricity inside the bulb. A lightning lamp. You know, the kind that when you touch the glass all the electricity goes toward your finger. I saw it on display when you were getting your tea set." Jason looked excited about his find, and Bree had to admit that it did look pretty neat.

"It's green, too, so it'll match my tea set and vase." Bree pointed out. They paid for their items and watched the bizarre lady behind the counter wrapping them in tissue paper and placing them in a box. Bree noticed she wore old black cowboy boots over gray sweatpants. Her shirt was a bright floral pattern with reds, yellows, and greens. Bree couldn't help but think that this woman looked as though she had jumped straight out of a Dr. Seuss book. They took their box and made it out the door before a loud snort escaped Bree.

"Did you see that lady's outfit?" She whispered to Jason and giggled. "No wonder her store is so unorganized. She can't even organize her own wardrobe!"

Jason laughed. "I'm no fashion expert, and even I thought that was terrible. Maybe tomorrow is her laundry day and that was all she had left," Jason joked.

"I'd wear the dirty clothes before I wore that!"

They put the box between them in the truck, and Jason punched their home address into the GPS to make sure he could find his way home. The whole ride home was spent musing over why the lady behind the counter was dressed so crazily at the Gypsy's Treasure Chest. Bree couldn't have guessed that the next time their paths crossed, she wouldn't be laughing quite so heartily.

Chapter 3

Jason carried their box of treasures into the house and put it on the table. Bree was immediately pulling out tissue paper as soon as the box was down. She had her vase unwrapped in no time, turning it over in her hands, admiring it. Soon the vase was set aside and she went back to the box. She pulled the lightning lamp out and handed it to Jason. She was already trying to think of the perfect place to display her vase and tea set as she began unwrapping tea cups.

Once the tea set was unwrapped, she decided to place it on a ledge in the kitchen. She was fixing the spacing between the teapot and decanter when she heard Jason chuckle in the living room. She walked out of the kitchen and saw that he had his lamp plugged in on one of the end tables and was watching all the tiny lightning bolts dancing around inside the glass bulb. He was obviously delighted with his purchase. As Bree observed him and the lamp, she realized she was just as delighted as he was.

"Now let's just hope it doesn't burn the house down," Bree said jokingly.

Jason started slightly, as he hadn't noticed her enter the room. "Just don't leave it plugged in when you aren't around, like any novelty lamp. I'm not sure how old this is or where it was made, so we'll have to be careful with it. But it is awesome, isn't it?" He was smiling at her.

"Yes, dear, it's awesome." Bree laughed and returned to the kitchen to finish arranging her tea set and get dinner into the oven.

After dinner and dishes, Bree headed upstairs to face the man in the mural. Jason told her not to worry about it tonight, but he didn't understand how much it bothered Bree. She couldn't stand the idea of that shadow man watching her sleep. She left Jason downstairs to watch TV and admire his new lamp while she fixed her mural.

Reclaim my mural, she amended.

She stood in the bedroom, scowling at the man. She had brought the digital camera with her to document the strange anomaly before she erased it from the wall. She snapped three photos, then got to work. With an air of determination about her, Bree opened her paints and deposited a small amount of black, brown, white, and green on her paint palette. She painted over him completely with brown paint, just for the peace of mind that he was covered entirely in a layer of paint, before she repainted the tree trunks, leaves, and forest debris that had been there prior to his appearance. Once she was finished, she stepped back and nodded to herself in approval. No evidence remained to indicate that the shadow man had ever existed. She was relieved.

Bree returned downstairs to the living room and sat next to Jason. Now that the mural was restored, and the day was coming to a close, Bree was ready to move on to pestering Jason about the piano again.

"So honey, can we bring the piano upstairs?"

Jason gave a long, defeated sigh. "If you really want to. But I'm not touching it; you and your movers are responsible for it."

Bree was delighted, even though she had already known he would give his consent. She hugged and thanked him, telling him how happy he had just made her. As Jason continued to watch TV, Bree began planning a new living room layout, rearranging furniture in her mind to create space for the piano.

In the morning, Bree called the movers. They wouldn't be able to come out until the next day, but she thought she would begin cleaning and preparing the piano right away. She was so excited to have something new to work on that the worries of yesterday and the memory of the burning head didn't even enter her thoughts.

She grabbed an old cloth and furniture polish and headed into the basement. The piano was even dustier than she had remembered, but each swipe of the cloth seemed to be bringing it back to life and removing years of neglect. As she cleaned, she began to consider what the piano might look like in the daylight. It was beginning to look marvelous with the polish, but this observation was made in the dim lighting of the basement. For all she knew, the sunlight that filtered through the living room shades might bring out every scratch and gouge in the wood and reveal the piano as an ancient eyesore. Bree desperately hoped this wouldn't be the case. She polished with even more conviction, as though it would ensure the piano's success at beauty.

After almost an hour of nonstop polishing, Bree's tired arms were ready for a break. She went upstairs and walked into the kitchen for a drink and a snack. As she was scrubbing the tinted furniture polish from her hands, she thought she heard an unfamiliar sound. She shut the water off and stood quietly for a moment, but the sound did not occur again. She dried her hands and poured herself a glass of juice. Granola bar and juice in hand, Bree plopped onto the couch in the living room for a well-deserved breather.

It wasn't until she had finished the granola bar and was reaching for her juice that the sound came a second time. She heard it much more clearly in the absolute silence of the living room. It had come from the basement and sounded like someone had struck two notes on the piano. She froze, unsure of what to do. Her curiosity was screaming at her to go into the basement and check it out, while the rest of her was perfectly content to remain upstairs until Jason returned home from work. As she sat, contemplating her course of action, her curiosity got the best of her. She rose from the couch and walked to the door leading to the basement. She quietly pressed her ear to the door and listened, but was met with silence. The door creaked slightly as she pushed it open, and she slowly tip-toed down the stairs, making as little noise as possible. At the bottom of the stairs, she stood quietly and waited for the sound to happen again.

Bree didn't have to wait long to hear another sound. A strange metallic plucking suddenly came from the piano. Then, a note struck, and Bree started. The fall was down over the keys, so she couldn't see if they had moved. Her adrenaline was pumping at that point, and she was beginning to have second thoughts about wanting that piano upstairs. She continued to stand silently and listen, but all she heard for the next several minutes was her blood pumping in her ears.

Just as she was about to move toward the piano, she heard a scratching noise coming from inside it.

What the hell is *that?* Just as Bree was giving in to bafflement, she heard the sound that answered all of her questions. A tiny squeak came from inside the piano, and Bree was instantly relieved that something very much of this world was the cause of the strange sounds—a mouse. The relief lasted mere seconds, however, as she realized what kind of damage that mouse must have done—and still be doing—to the piano. She hurried to it and threw open the upper panel. The mouse was visible for a brief second before it ran and hid from her sight. The inside of the piano was a total disaster; nests and droppings were everywhere, and the little varmints had chewed through everything. The stench of rodent waste assaulted her nostrils. Mice had waged a war against this piano, and the poor piano had lost…ages ago, it appeared.

Though she never intended to play the piano, as she had never had lessons, she was disappointed that she no longer had the option. She would have to invest a huge chunk of money into it if she ever wanted this piano to work well again. Determined that mice were not going to get the best of her, Bree got a garbage bag and gloves from the kitchen and cleaned out as much of the mess inside as she could. What she wasn't able to pick up was then sucked out with the vacuum, the hose being shoved into every space in which it would fit. For her last assault on the mice, she took a trip to town and returned home with traps, glue paper, poison, and peppermint oil (a quick internet search had led her to the peppermint oil solution). She surrounded and filled the piano with these items, planning to keep the mouse traps, poison, and oil inside the piano for a few weeks in case any mice happened to make it upstairs with the piano. She saturated several cotton balls with the oil and placed them inside the piano. If nothing else, the scent of the oil would help cover the smell of mouse urine. For good measure, she doused the inside of the piano with an odor-eliminating spray.

Getting the piano ready to bring upstairs may have seemed more trouble than it was worth, but Bree had set her mind to it and was determined it would adorn her living room.

When Jason arrived home from work, Bree told him about the mouse ordeal. She quickly wished she hadn't.

"If you bring that thing upstairs, you'll bring all those little bastards up here! Can't you just leave it be?" Jason was disgusted.

"I put every trap and repellent in and around the piano." She explained the traps, poison, and peppermint oil, trying to convince him that they would have no mouse problems upstairs. "And if we do have problems, we can get a cat!" Bree had wanted a cat for many years, but Jason had never been keen on the idea. He took the position that pets which were trained to poop inside the house were disgusting.

"I suppose that if I tell you that I absolutely do not want it up here, it will end up in the living room anyway, won't it?"

Bree gave him a smug smile. "It just might."

Jason shook his head and went upstairs to shower.

That night, Bree dreamed of mice overrunning the house and devouring her piano. When she awoke, the digital clock on the nightstand showed 3:13 AM. She rolled onto her back and stared at the dark ceiling, thinking about her dream. Suddenly, a faint orange glow caught her attention. She sat up in bed and found the source of the glow was her mural. More specifically, it was the shadow man in her mural producing the glow. He was back, and he was enveloped in flames. The flames danced up the wall, illuminating the room with its flickering orange light.

Bree wanted to reach over and wake Jason, or jump out of bed and scream, but she found herself unable to move or speak. All she could do was watch the creepy little man burn. Oddly, nothing else seemed to be ablaze, and the fire wasn't spreading. It clung only to the shadow man, yet it did not consume him. Instead, it was as if the flames were a part of him rather than feeding from him.

All of a sudden, he started to move. The little man became animated, moving his arms and head about within his two-dimensional painted world. Bree felt instantly sick as she witnessed this trick, and grew more horrified as his little arm came out and away from the wall, no longer limited to two dimensions. His body and head followed the arm and came out of the wall as he gained mass and a three-dimensional shape, and then he fell to the floor in a blazing black heap.

Bree's throat became almost too tight to allow breath through, and her heart hammered violently against her ribcage. She wanted to close her eyes or hide under the covers like a scared child, but she couldn't tear her gaze away from the motionless, glowing black mass across the room. Then it began to stir. He slowly stood on his cylindrical black legs and turned his black spherical head, apparently observing his surroundings. Bree couldn't be sure, as the shadow man had a featureless face, but she got the impression that he stopped and stared directly at her. The burning shadow was still for a moment, seeming to stare at her. He advanced one step in her direction.

Oh God, he's coming for me! Scream! SCREAM DAMN YOU! Bree's brain pleaded with her vocal cords, but she was still in a helpless paralysis.

The tiny terror continued to move toward the bed until Bree could no longer see him over the foot of the bed. Moments later, she felt a tug on the bedding and soon saw a flame rising up and a little black head peek over the foot of the bed. Her breathing accelerated, bringing her dangerously close to hyperventilation as he pulled himself up and charged across the bed at her. He ran up her leg and stopped, standing in her lap, looking up at the terrified woman. The flames were so close and hot that Bree felt as though her skin was about to blister.

27

A deep, angry voice suddenly erupted from the mouthless face.

"She didn't die! That whore should've DIED!"

Everything went black, and Bree screamed. She was still screaming when she felt hands upon her, jarring her back and forth.

"Bree! Open your eyes. Wake up!" Jason's voice was concerned, but not frantic.

Bree opened her eyes and saw a shirtless Jason looming over her. His face was close to hers, worry contorting his features. His hands were the ones she felt shaking her. She looked around at the bedroom, dimly lit by the rising sun, and saw no angry, shadowy fiend. Her mural was as she left it yesterday, free of creepy characters.

"Honey, are you ok? Did you have a bad dream?" Jason asked as he comfortingly stroked her messy auburn hair. She choked back her urge to cry and told Jason about the awful dream.

Neither of them went back to sleep. Jason had to leave for work in an hour, so Bree made him eggs and bacon for breakfast since he had some extra time. After he left, Bree spent the morning pondering her nightmare. She wondered where "that whore should've died" came from. It didn't make any sense to her. She would have to call her mother later that day to tell her about the dream. She always shared her crazy dreams with her mother, and her mother always had some insight and suggestions as to how they might be interpreted.

Later in the day, Bree checked the traps in and around the piano. The piano appeared to have been completely abandoned by its previous tenants, for which Bree was glad. She removed the traps, poison, and peppermint oil cotton balls from the piano and brought some of it upstairs in preparation for the big move. The rest she left in the basement for the little rodents to enjoy.

The movers arrived half an hour late, but they got the job done quickly once they got there. They rearranged the living room as Bree directed, and brought up the old piano. Once in place, the piano looked as if it had always belonged there. Bree was pleased with the way it looked in the living room, and began putting the traps and cotton balls inside the piano the instant the movers were out the door.

Bree sat and admired the new addition to the living room when she was done placing traps, but was interrupted by the phone.

"Hello?"

"Hey babe," Jason's voice answered cheerfully from the other line. "How is everything today?"

"Wonderful! The movers came and moved the piano, and it looks great in the living room! What's going on with you today?" "Ok, but I'll be coming home soon. I decided to take the rest of the day off. Things are kind of slow here, and it's a beautiful day out. I thought maybe we could do something fun this afternoon."

Bree hesitated, puzzled by his response. "You just took time off the other day. Besides, it's raining outside."

"About an hour. I have a couple things to finish up here before I take off. I'll see you then, honey! Love you."

"Jason, you're not making any sense. What—" Bree was cut off by a click as the call was ended. She was completely confused and figured Jason must be up to something. She recognized the conversation as the same one they had the other day. Why would he repeat it like that? It was absurd.

Bree was bothered by the strange call for the next hour, so she polished the piano again to distract herself. Then, when Jason didn't come home early, she busied herself with redecorating the living room. She moved the lightning lamp and green vase to the top of the piano, making sure the lamp plug still reached an outlet.

Finally, Jason came home at his regular time, not a minute earlier. Bree met him at the door.

"Why did you call me to say you were coming home early? And why were you acting so weird?"

Jason looked at her as though she had "dumbass" written across her forehead. "I didn't call you today. Are you feeling alright?"

"Yes you did! I'm beginning to think you are purposely messing with me now! What the hell is going on, Jason?" Bree's confusion was breeding anger.

"I'm not messing with you! I called you two days ago, and I haven't called here from work since!" Jason's anger and confusion were also beginning to show.

"I know it was you because it said it was your office on the caller ID. You said the same things you said to me two days ago, and it didn't make any sense!" Bree paraphrased the conversation for him as she went after the phone.

"That's ridiculous, Bree!" Jason exclaimed, exasperated.

"I know!" Bree shouted, as she couldn't think of anything else to say. She scrolled through the caller ID on the phone and found the call she had received that day. "Look. It's right here. And see, it's even after the movers' number because they called about an hour before you did today."

Jason took the phone and looked at it. "Then why is it dated as June fourth? That was two days ago." Jason scrolled through the caller ID for a moment. "Wait. It's in here twice. Once after the movers' number and once before my parents called two nights ago." He scowled at the phone. "They both have the same time and date. I don't know what to say, Bree. I didn't make this call."

Bree knew exactly what to say, even if neither of them wanted to believe it. "The call was made the same time today as it was two days ago. Jason, something very weird is going on in this house."

They stood in silence, both contemplating the implications of that statement.

Chapter 4

"So what do we do now?" Bree asked Jason after a long silence.

"I don't know. I don't think there is anything we really *can* do. Strange things happen, but I don't think there's any reason to panic. Nothing else has happened," Jason said, his nonchalant attitude returning.

"What do you mean nothing else has happened? What about that creepy man painted in my mural? You and I both know, even if we didn't want to admit it before now, that no one could possibly create that shadow man by accident without noticing. I didn't paint him. He wasn't there when I got in the shower that day, but he was when you got home. Something happened in our bedroom within that hour.

"I also saw something in the basement right before we moved in. It was right after you told me you were ready to move into the house. I saw a burning head floating right in my face. It only lasted a split second, but I know I saw it. And I *smelled* it." Bree remembered the pungent odor that had filled her nostrils both that day and the day the shadow man had shown up. "So don't tell me nothing else has happened."

Jason absorbed her words quietly until she finished her tirade. Bree expected him to be shocked at her revelations, but all he said was, "Maybe this will be the end of it. I don't think we need to worry unless our furniture starts stacking itself and knives start flying at us. Everything is fine, Bree. Don't call the priest just yet."

She knew his humor was well-intended, but she felt mocked. She wished she hadn't told him about the basement incident. The fact that he had met this information with indifference made her feel like she was being silly about everything. Her face reddened.

"You do believe me, though, don't you? About the painting and the burning head?" Bree had to make sure his indifference wasn't due to disbelief.

"Of course I believe you! I just don't want to jump to any radical conclusions right now. I say we call it strange and move on. What else is there for us to do?"

Bree thought for a moment, but reluctantly arrived at the same conclusion. "You're right. I guess there really isn't anything we can do right now."

Jason and Bree didn't discuss the strange occurrences any further, and as Bree prepared dinner later that night, her mind began troubling over Jason's "do nothing" attitude. She wasn't the type of person who could easily let things go. She had finally admitted that she believed something out of the ordinary was taking place in their home, and she was ready to do something about it. But what? How do you retaliate against something you don't understand and can't definitively prove even exists? She didn't know how to explain the recent happenings, who or what was responsible, or what to do about it. This upset her. She felt like she was fighting someone or something for control of her own life, and she didn't know how to win.

Bree called her mother, Karen, after dinner. She made the call from upstairs, hoping for some privacy, as she wanted to share some of her feelings about the house without Jason overhearing. She was certain he'd had enough talk of the paranormal for today. Her mother was a little more open-minded about such things.

"Hello, Bree," Karen answered the phone. "How have you been?"

"Well…things have been interesting around here lately. The good news is that the piano got moved upstairs and I haven't seen any more mice. The bad news is that something else is becoming a problem." She told her mother about the burning head, the painted shadow man, and the phone call.

"Why didn't you tell me about any of this before now?" Karen wanted to know.

"I didn't want to overreact or make a big deal out of it, especially if it was nothing but my own imagination. But after Jason saw the caller ID anomaly after that weird phone call, I'm sure it isn't my imagination. I'm really worried about it. I'm even having nightmares about what's going on." Bree recounted her nightmare to her mother.

"That's a bit disturbing, isn't it?" Karen said.

"Where do you suppose the 'that whore should've died' part came from? What do you think it means?" Bree inquired.

Karen thought for a moment before responding. "I think maybe you feel like someone is angry with you, judging by the fire and harsh words in the dream. Maybe Jason, or maybe whatever is causing the strange activity in the house." Karen suggested.

"I'm pretty sure the dream had everything to do with the activity in the house, not Jason. Although, I do wonder if he is getting annoyed with me – if he thinks I'm overreacting about this. I get the feeling he is only humoring me when he says that he believes me. He doesn't seem worried at all, and even suggested that the phone call might be the end of it."

"You never know. It might be." Karen wasn't convincing.

"It won't be. I just know it. These things don't just stop after a couple instances, do they? I don't know anything about this kind of thing."

"This may sound silly, but have you ever watched any of the paranormal investigation shows on television?" Karen asked. "There is one I watch every week with a few guys who travel all over America and use scientific equipment to capture evidence of paranormal activity."

"Sounds stupid. It's probably all fake."

"It's possible they might spruce things up for TV, but they do have a real company. And some of the evidence they find is actually quite compelling." Karen was persistent.

Bree was skeptical. "So they just run around looking for ghosts for a living? No one would hire them if they never found anything, which sounds to me like an incentive to manufacture evidence."

"I don't know. There are actually a lot of episodes where they don't find anything paranormal. Instead they find alternative explanations for all the claims. And they're actually plumbers, so they don't do ghost hunting entirely for a living."

"Plumbers? Who chase ghosts? Are they Italian, and on a quest to save a princess by any chance?" Bree laughed. "So I suppose you are suggesting I watch this show."

"Yes. I'm not saying it will give you all the answers to your questions, but it may give you some perspective on your current situation. If nothing else, you may find it entertaining."

Bree talked a few more minutes to her mother before ending the conversation. Once she was off the phone, she thought about the show her mother had discussed with her. She knew Jason would probably laugh at her for watching it, but she wanted to see what it was all about. She might be able to learn a little about paranormal theories, anyway. She turned on the television in the bedroom and searched the guide for the ghost show. Three episodes were scheduled to come on the next night, so Bree set the DVR to record all of them.

As she teetered on the edge of sleep that night, Bree's jumbled thoughts conjured up images of fires, ghosts, and shadowy black gremlins. She didn't want to think of these things before falling asleep, but she couldn't seem to control it. Falling deeper into sleep, she began to actually smell the smoke and feel the heat of the fires in her mind. She could hear the ghosts and gremlins laughing and taunting her. She began screaming at them to stop, ordered them to go away, but they only laughed harder. The heat from the fire began to sear her skin, and the smoke burned her nostrils and filled her lungs. She opened her eyes and looked around. She found herself lying in bed with a fire raging about her. The sheets and pillows were engulfed in flames, and as she looked down at her suddenly painful hands, she discovered she was too. The skin on her fingers was blackened, but when she bent her fingers, the black skin over the knuckles tore and cracked, exposing pink flesh beneath that immediately began to sizzle and blacken as well. She brought her burning hands to her face reflexively when the searing pain was suddenly felt upon the skin of her cheeks. She heard a crisp crackling sound, like dry, fall leaves, when her fingers made contact with her cheek. A heavy mass slid down the side of her face when she pulled her hand away. She felt something plop into her lap, and her gaze fell upon a black and pink chunk of flesh that used to be her cheek resting on her burning thigh. She frantically looked to her left, afraid she'd see Jason's burned body next to her. To her bewilderment (and relief), she found Jason sleeping soundly, his side of the bed completely untouched by flames. Before finally slipping into a painless darkness, Bree prayed that Jason would remain unscathed.

Bree awoke the next morning feeling groggy and exhausted. She had a strange feeling in her chest, as though something was bothering her subconsciously. The memory of last night's dreams eluded her when she tried to recall them, so she assumed the bad feeling she had was due to last night's discovery that she lived in a haunted house. She ignored the feeling as well as she could and went downstairs to make Jason's breakfast.

At the table, Jason chuckled at her. "So how was your night on the burning side?" He smiled at her, obviously amused by his strange question.

"What?" Bree asked shortly, in no mood for riddles. She didn't understand why his words suddenly made her heart beat faster with fear.

"You were talking in your sleep last night. You kept going on and on about not wanting to sleep on the burning side of the bed. It was creepy and hilarious at the same time."

The dream came back to Bree instantly in disturbing detail. "I had a really disgusting dream about burning alive in our bed. It was anything but hilarious." Bree scowled at Jason across the table. She knew he hadn't meant to offend her, but she felt angry anyway.

"Oh. Sorry! I didn't know," Jason said defensively. "I would've wakened you if I knew you were having a bad dream." Jason was confused at Bree's anger.

"I'm not mad at *you*. I'm just mad. I don't exactly know why. I think maybe it's because I'm annoyed that I keep having these absurd nightmares."

"You only had two. I'm sure they'll stop soon. I tend to have nightmares when I'm overly tired, so maybe you just need to get to bed earlier. Don't let a couple of bad dreams bother you."

Bree was beginning to wonder if anything ever bothered Jason. She thought he would probably feel differently about things if everything that had happened recently had happened to him instead of her. He would be a little crazy and moody too. However, even though his perpetual calm sometimes irritated her, she also appreciated how his coolness kept her from becoming too agitated.

"I'm just bothered by all that has happened within the past few days. It wouldn't be so bad if the nightmares and weird activity had been more spread out. It's wearing on my nerves." Bree resumed eating her breakfast, done with the conversation. Jason understood that the conversation was over and returned to his breakfast as well.

Soon Jason had gone to work and Bree was once again alone in the house. She went about her usual business with a slight wariness. Everything had been so quiet in the house that day that she almost ignored it when she distinctively heard a cough in the kitchen. She was on the couch in the living room when she heard it, but when she peeked apprehensively into the kitchen, no one was there. Bree was relieved that nothing else extraordinary had happened by the time Jason arrived home.

When it was time for the paranormal investigators' show to come on, Bree had to do some convincing to get Jason to relinquish control of the remote.

"My mom said it was a good show, and it might give us some ideas for how to deal with our own situation," Bree persuaded.

"That's kind of like saying 'Three's Company' will help resolve roommate issues, don't you think?" Jason loved to poke holes in her reasoning.

Bree explained the show to him as best she could from Karen's description. "I just want to watch it tonight. If it's terrible, we don't ever have to watch it again."

"Who decides if it's terrible?" Jason continued to be difficult.

"I do! Now give me the damn remote." Bree reached over and snatched the remote out of his hand with a sly grin.

They sat through all three episodes. Jason couldn't decide whether he believed it was real, but he enjoyed the show anyway. Bree was quite convinced it was real, especially after the investigators were able to find alternative explanations for every claim in one case, with no evidence to suggest paranormal activity. She figured that the investigators would come up with extraordinary evidence every time if the show was faked.

Not only did Bree enjoy the show, but it also gave her ideas. In the show, the investigators used digital voice recorders to perform "EVP sessions," which stood for electronic voice phenomenon. The investigators would sometimes capture strange voices and sounds on the recorder that they weren't able to hear at the time the recording was made. Bree wanted to try this technique, as it seemed to be the cheapest and easiest way to attempt communication with whatever might be in the house. She'd have to try it when Jason wasn't home, though, because she knew he would think she was being ridiculous and try to talk her out of it. Even she felt kind of silly imagining herself walking around asking questions to an empty house. Yes, she would definitely keep this activity to herself.

In the morning, Bree was glad to wake from a dreamless sleep. She waited until Jason had left for work before she hopped in her car and ran to the nearest electronics store to purchase a digital voice recorder. It was a few hours after she returned home before she worked up enough nerve to pick up the recorder and begin her amateur EVP session.

She decided to begin in the basement. As she sat at the bottom of the stairs and asked questions like, "Is anyone here?" and, "What is your name?" to an empty room, she couldn't help but feel foolish. The basement seemed quiet, so she moved on to her bedroom upstairs where the shadow man had made his appearance. She asked the same questions she had asked in the basement, and then began asking about the mural.

"Did you paint that man in the mural? Was it supposed to be a painting of you? Why did you paint it in black, like a shadow?" She paused after the last question and listened. She thought she had heard a "thump" downstairs.

Even though she was uncertain whether the noise was paranormal, her heart began to race. If it wasn't paranormal, it could be Jason. She didn't want him to catch her partaking in such foolishness. She shoved the recorder into her back pocket and hurried downstairs. In the living room, she stood silently. No one was around, and everything was quiet. A few moments passed before she noticed the tiny bolts of electricity were dancing around inside the bulb of the lightning lamp on top of the piano. Upon investigation, she discovered it had been plugged in and switched on. As she reached up to switch it off, she heard a cupboard door bang shut in the kitchen. She froze with her hand midair and looked toward the kitchen. She heard the cupboard door shut again, only quieter this time.

Disregarding the lamp, Bree peeked into the kitchen. She was just in time to see the cupboard door swing shut on the end cupboard under the counter. It quickly opened again, about two inches, and then closed. It appeared that something on the inside was trying to get out, but was too weak to open the door all the way. Her heart thundered in her chest as she took a tentative step forward. Intense curiosity drove her on despite her fear. When she finally stood in front of the cupboard, it was still opening and closing feebly. She crouched down and pulled the door partially open.

Bree jumped back when something large and black flopped out of the cupboard, causing the cupboard door to fling open and bang into the wall next to it. She stood in the middle of the kitchen with her eyes fixed on the large black mass hanging out of the cupboard. It was moving, almost writhing. Her eyes widened when she was able to distinguish a head, arms, and a torso. It was a charred, disfigured human body. It began to slowly drag itself out of the cupboard.

Bree took a step backward. Her eyes remained glued to the creature. She couldn't believe what she was seeing, and she felt bile rise in her throat when the charred body lifted its head and looked at her with its one remaining, milky eye. It reached an arm forward and slithered its posterior half farther out of the cupboard.

This isn't just a charred body, Bree thought. *It's a corpse.*

The animated corpse continued to drag itself along the floor. Bree backed up several more steps when it began crawling directly toward her. The scene reminded her of a video she once saw of a sloth dragging itself out of the water onto the shore. The creature kept its dead gaze on her face as it slid toward her. Suddenly, it began to shudder and convulse. It flopped on the floor like a great disgusting fish, and Bree saw black pieces falling from it in much the same way burned bacon crumbles when it's dropped. The charred body's back began to bow, and a black, viscous fluid erupted from its mouth. The convulsions ceased at the same time the vomiting stopped. The corpse looked back up at Bree and resumed its advance, dragging itself right through the black goo it had expelled onto the floor.

Bree's stomach heaved. It was about to turn itself inside out when the undead corpse croaked at her.

"I'm…" It began to speak in a wheezy, choked voice, and then coughed. It never hesitated in its advance.

"…like…this…" More coughing.

Bree backed out of the kitchen and around the corner into the living room. She had moved out of sight of the corpse creature, but she could still hear it choking out its words between wheezes and coughs.

"…because of…"

Then silence. Bree couldn't hear the wheezing or dragging sound anymore. She waited what seemed an eternity before taking a step toward the kitchen. She didn't know why she wasn't running and screaming, even though that's what she felt like doing.

Thump!

Bree gasped when the mangled hand hit the floor, visible now as the creature pulled itself around the cupboards in the kitchen. It began to move around the corner and into the living room. It's one eye found Bree immediately and locked on her.

"…her!" It was more of a hiss this time when it spoke, as though the word "her" disgusted it.

A loud cracking sound emanated from the creature as its outstretched arm abruptly snapped upward at the elbow, bending the joint the wrong way. There were three more loud cracks to accompany the second elbow and both knees snapping backward. The creature rose up like a four-legged spider, and Bree turned to run. Her bravery had run its course.

Before she even moved her feet, the creature scurried past her in a blur of mangled limbs and vanished into the side of the piano. She had felt the breeze it created when it passed. Bree ran back through the kitchen and out the door. She didn't stop until she reached her car, at which point she became ill. She wiped her mouth with a violently shaking hand and got into the car, locking the doors immediately. At that point she realized her keys were still in the house. She refused to go back inside alone, so she just sat in the car and sobbed.

After about an hour, she remembered the digital voice recorder in her pocket.

Chapter 5

Bree slipped the recorder from her pocket and checked to see if it was still recording. It wasn't. The power was off. She turned it back on and saw the battery was still full. Hopeful that she had recorded the words from the charred corpse creature, she skipped the recorder back several minutes. When she pressed play, she heard her own voice asking EVP questions. She skipped ahead to thirty seconds from the end and pressed play again. To her great frustration, she heard her last few EVP questions, a long silence, and a crackling right before the recording stopped. She must have bumped the power button when she shoved the recorder into her pocket.

Tears streamed down her face once more. She didn't want to hear that thing's voice again, but she wanted others to be able to hear what she had. She wanted the proof to show Jason that there *was* a need for worry. The black gooey substance and burned bacon bits on the floor in the kitchen wouldn't be quite as compelling to Jason without the recording of the creature's voice to accompany it.

Bree tried to recall what the creature had said. She thought it had been something about how the corpse was like that because of "her." To whom was it referring? And what did it mean when it said, "…like this?" She considered the possibilities. It could have meant it was dead because of some woman, or maybe a woman was the reason it was stuck haunting her house. As she pondered the creature's words, she remembered that the angry shadow man in her dream also spoke of a woman. Could they both be referring to the same person? She knew she could be making connections that didn't actually exist, but she was trying her best to make sense of the madness that had quickly become a part of her everyday life. After all, what else was she going to do while sitting alone in a parked car?

Her attention returned to the recorder. She rewound it with shaky hands and began reviewing her EVP session. The basement session yielded nothing other than Bree talking to herself. When she listened to the upstairs session, however, she heard a whisper that was unfamiliar to her. She listened to it over and over again, trying to decipher what was being said. She couldn't tell if it was a male or female voice, but finally she understood the words. The disembodied voice was saying, "The attic." Bree was puzzled by those words. What attic? There was a widow's watch, but no actual attic of which she knew. She thought about the EVPs that were captured on the paranormal investigators' show and remembered that not all of the disembodied voices they recorded said things that made sense to the investigators. She listened to the rest of the recording but didn't hear anything else.

As time passed, Bree's fear abated slightly and she decided it was probably safe to get out of the car. She didn't know what time it was exactly, but she estimated that Jason wouldn't be home for at least another two or three hours. Her best option for passing the time was tending to the yard and flower bed. Weeds were choking out most of the flowers that had popped up around the porch, and several sticks and branches still littered the yard from the last windy day they'd had. She set to work collecting branches first, keeping a wary eye on the house each time she passed near it.

When the yard was clear of debris, she moved on to weeding the flower bed near the porch. Though she didn't want it to, her mind worked the entire time her hands did. She couldn't understand why the entity in her home seemed to be singling her out. She was the one who spent the most time in the house, true enough, but even when Jason was home the activity centered on her. Jason hadn't had one thing happen to him. He was the one who discovered the man in the mural, but it meant nothing to him when he saw it. She felt it was an attack on her and he just happened to be the one to find it first. Why was it even doing these things? What could it possibly be trying to tell her, and why? She considered that it might not be trying to communicate with her, but instead was trying to frighten her. Judging by the form of its manifestations, it seemed to her that the entity had malicious intentions. But why did it hate *her* so much?

When Bree thought Jason should be arriving home soon, she began to ponder what his reaction might be to her story. He might not believe her. After all, it *was* a completely outrageous tale. The mess on the floor was proof that something had happened, though. The black goo would be like the caller ID – tangible proof that *something* had happened. Bree suddenly had an upsetting thought: the creature had disappeared, so wasn't it possible that the black goo had disappeared as well? She had been counting on that evidence to verify her story. If it wasn't there, and she had no recording, what proof did she have to confirm that anything had happened at all? All she would have was a short EVP, which she didn't want to tell Jason about anyway because it meant she would have to reveal that she had tried an EVP session. She was unsure of what to tell Jason, if anything at all.

Within the next few minutes, Jason pulled into the driveway. Bree felt anxiety forming a knot in her chest as she stood up to greet him. She had decided to wait until she saw the kitchen before she said anything to him about today's events.

"Doing some weeding, I see. And you picked up all the branches, too? You've been busy today!" Jason smiled at her and wiped dirt from her cheek with one large, calloused thumb.

"Yeah, I guess so. How was your day?" Bree walked up the steps toward the door, leading Jason into the house as he began telling her about work. She was anxious to see the condition of the kitchen, so she barely heard a word he said as she came through the door. Her gaze fell upon the kitchen floor. To her dismay, it was clean. No goo, no bacon bits. The house looked just as it had before the creature appeared. The opened cupboard door was the only evidence remaining. It was at that moment that she realized she could tell Jason nothing without sounding insane. She wanted to tell him, to share this traumatic event with someone, but she wanted to wait until she was sure he would take her seriously. Even her mother wouldn't hear about this unless other paranormal events of similar magnitude occurred and were validated. She couldn't have the ones she loved thinking she needed mental help.

When Jason entered the living room, he noticed the lightning lamp was on. He patronizingly scolded Bree for leaving the lamp on, as if she was a small child who didn't know any better. Biting her tongue, she shut it off and unplugged it without comment. Jason went upstairs to shower shortly thereafter, so Bree took the opportunity to hide the digital voice recorder in the closet in their bedroom. While she was upstairs, she heard a noise downstairs. It sounded like the noises she had heard when the mouse was in the piano in the basement.

"Damn it! Not again," Bree exclaimed. Dashing downstairs, she went to the piano and flung open the upper panel. She saw no signs of mice, but a tiny white square of paper caught her eye. Nothing should have been inside the piano after her thorough cleaning, but she supposed it was possible that it was jostled out of some hiding place when the piano was moved. She grabbed it and gently removed it from the piano, closing the upper panel. The paper was blank on the side she first viewed and looked like it had come from a brittle old newspaper. She turned the slightly yellowed square of paper over, and her fingers suddenly lost grasp of it when she saw what was printed on it. It fluttered to the floor while she stood speechless. In neat newsprint, the paper had borne the words "the attic." It meant nothing on its own, but it became significant when paired with the EVP from earlier that day.

Bree picked up the piece of paper from the floor and brought it upstairs. She had just finished stashing it with the recording device when Jason came out of the bathroom.

"Silly question, Jason, but we don't have an attic, do we?" Bree tried to sound as nonchalant as possible.

Instead of answering, Jason asked, "Why?"

It doesn't matter why! Just answer the question, Bree responded mentally. "I just thought I might like to store some things in it."

"What about the basement?"

Oh my God, answer the damn question already! "The basement is damp. Things could get moldy. So we don't have an attic?" Bree pushed for a simple answer, hoping for no more questions.

"Yeah, we have one. I haven't been in it though, so I don't know what kind of shape it's in. I'm surprised you didn't know we had one." And just as Bree thought she wouldn't have to make up another lie, Jason added, "What did you want to put up there? I doubt it's very big."

Fighting the urge to give an exasperated roll of the eyes, Bree simply replied, "Christmas decorations and stuff. Where is the attic?"

"At the top of the house." Jason grinned, and she wanted to backhand him. She gave him an irritated look, so he added, "It's that little door to your right when you're going up the stairs to the widow's watch. Where's your sense of humor today, honey?" Jason asked rhetorically.

She feigned a smile and went back downstairs to get dinner ready in a kitchen with which she had become disgusted. Anything involving bacon was definitely off the menu for tonight, and she was especially careful to not burn the meat.

Unfortunately for Bree, Jason was in the mood for a zombie movie that evening. Scenes that ordinarily wouldn't faze her suddenly became quite terrifying to Bree because they reminded her of the events from earlier that day. She had to look away from the screen every time a zombie was crawling toward the protagonists in the film. She insisted upon watching a light-hearted animated movie before bed in an attempt to erase the zombie images from her mind. Despite the happy movie, Bree dreamed of zombies that night.

Jason didn't have to work the next day, as it was a Saturday. Bree was anxious to check out the attic, but she had mixed feelings about whether she wanted Jason to accompany her on the expedition. She didn't want him to inhibit her search for whatever she was supposed to find up there. On the other hand, she didn't want to be alone in case she encountered another entity like the cupboard dweller. She decided to bring him along, but told him it was to check out how much of a mess the attic was and if it was big enough to be used for storage. For once in his life, Jason tagged along, no questions asked.

They ascended the stairs to the widow's watch, Jason leading the way. He stopped toward the top of the stairs and worked a latch on a door to his right that Bree had never before noticed. After a bit of jostling and pushing, the small door opened. It was only about one-third the size of a regular door, making it necessary for Jason and Bree to crawl through the opening to get into the attic. Once inside, however, they were able to stand as long as they bowed their heads.

The attic was quite bare. Bree had expected a treasure trove of antiques or old newspapers, but all she could find was a small wooden crate and an old pair of what looked like ugly wedding shoes.

"It looks like you've got plenty of space to store stuff in here," Jason commented, looking around at the nearly empty room.

"Yeah, it does. I wonder what's in that box over there," Bree said as she went to the crate.

"Can I go back downstairs now? I'm getting a crick in my neck." Jason was rubbing the back of his neck, eyeing the small door.

Hesitant to remain in the attic alone, Bree picked up the wooden box and brought it to Jason. "Let's bring this out. I want to look at it."

Jason crawled backward out the door and took the box from Bree. She followed suit and latched the door shut behind her. Jason carried the box to the living room and set it on the coffee table next to the couch. Bree sat down and immediately began rummaging through the box. Inside, she found a small, porcelain ballerina figurine and several yellowed wedding items, including a veil and off-white beaded earrings. There was a newspaper folded up and shoved in the side of the box which displayed the date of August 14, 1854. Bree recalled that the house was built that same year. She set the fragile newspaper aside to be examined later. An old cookbook was the next item to come out of the box. When Bree opened it, she found handwritten recipes for many dishes of which she had never even heard. A few ancient grammar and etiquette books were at the bottom of the box. When she lifted them out, she noticed one more book hiding beneath them. It had a blank cover, but someone had sewn a piece of lace into the leather cover along the spine.

Intrigued by the customized blank book, Bree set aside the other books and picked it up. She opened the front cover and saw:

The Journal of Elizabeth Lillian Barry
March 28, 1895

Bree was excited to be holding a real piece of history, and perhaps a peak into what had gone on in this house over one hundred years ago. She turned the page and immediately noticed that Elizabeth Barry had impeccable handwriting but her spelling was terrible.

If you have discovered this journal, avert your eyes imeedietly! It is private!

The first entry was on the next page.

March 28, 1895

O, what a joyous time! I have just marryed the man I know I shall love for the rest of my life! I have decided to begin a new journal as I have enterd a new era in my life. I can hardly beleve I am now Mrs. Gregory D. Barry! Thogh I do find it unforchunate we must live under the same roof as his unsufferable mother. I am in luck that she is so ill at the time. I do hope she will pass soon so as we may go on with a private life with-out her ridicule and undesired advise. I am quite ready to have Gregory to myself and be the lady of the house. She is thretend by Gregory's affection for me as he is her favrite child and she wants for him to remain all hers. I am suprised the poor man was ever allowd to marry at all! I do feel a tad gilty for looking so forward to the passing of the woman, but she is so awful! I hardly think anyone could blame me. Gregory and I shall be so happy together, espetially once I am with child. I hope God does not delay in granting us that blessing!

The first journal entry ended there. Bree was amused by Elizabeth's outright disdain for her mother-in-law, but she thought that looking forward to her death was something Elizabeth shouldn't have put into writing. She must have been quite certain that no one would ever read her diary.

"Find anything interesting?" Jason asked, turning his attention from the television.

"Actually, yes! This –" Bree held up the diary – "is a diary from a woman who might have lived in this house. It's from 1895!" Bree was thoughtful for a while. "I wonder what it was like in White Dove in 1895."

"You should've bought that history book in the Gypsy's Treasure Chest," Jason responded as if Bree knew what he meant.

"What history book?"

"You didn't see it? It was a book about the history of St. Josephine County."

"No, I didn't see it. There was so much junk in that place that it was hard to notice everything. I wonder if it's still there," Bree hinted. She looked at Jason and smiled sweetly at him.

"We could go see if it is. I know that's what you're asking for," Jason said and smiled back at her.

Since they had nothing planned for that sunny Saturday, they decided to go for a ride to the Gypsy's Treasure Chest that afternoon. When they arrived, the parking lot was just as packed as it had been the last time they were there. Bree groaned when Jason mentioned that he was hungry, as she knew that most of the owners of these cars would be in the restaurant, not the gift shop. He seemed undeterred when she reminded him of this, so she convinced him to let her get her book in the gift shop first in case they had a long wait for dinner. She would at least have something to read.

Even though Bree knew what to expect, she was still awestruck when she walked into the Gypsy's Treasure Chest. The abundance of colorful items, candles, and incense could overwhelm even the dullest senses. They wandered through the shop with their eyes peeled since Jason couldn't remember where he had seen the history book. While searching, Bree stumbled upon a book about the paranormal that promised to reveal secrets of the spirit world to the reader. She decided to buy that book as well as the history book, hoping it would help her to understand what was going on in her house.

Finally, Jason found the book they originally sought. Bree was pleased to find it was exactly what she was hoping for as she skimmed the pages. It discussed when and how all the towns were established, and even mentioned family names of those early settlers. They brought their items to the checkout.

The woman behind the counter was dressed just as crazily today as she had been the last time. *That eliminates the "laundry day" possibility*, Bree thought, recounting the conversation she and Jason had had regarding the checkout lady's attire. Today she was wearing a bright pink bandana and a school-bus-yellow muumuu that did nothing to flatter her heavy-set figure. Bree saw that she still sported the cowboy boots.

Instead of tending to the transaction, the woman just stared wide-eyed at Bree, making Bree uncomfortable.

"We want to buy these," Bree said, pushing the books on the counter closer to the woman.

"You have an angry spirit attached to you," the woman responded ominously before looking down at the books. As Bree recoiled from the woman's revelation, the woman laughed obnoxiously. "But I suppose that's what this is for!" She gestured toward the book on paranormal activity.

"What makes you think there's a spirit attached to me?" Bree blurted incredulously.

"I can feel it surrounding you. You do not have the same aura as you did when you came the first time. Would you like to pay with credit or cash?" The woman acted as though she had only told them it might rain later that day.

After Jason told her they would pay with cash, Bree asked, "You remember us?"

"Of course. I remember everyone who comes into my shop." She made the transaction with Jason and bid them farewell. "See you next time."

Bree left the shop feeling rattled.

"Wow, that lady is just as crazy as she looks!" Jason exclaimed with a laugh as they walked next door to the restaurant.

Bree forced a smile and a laugh. She wished she could chalk it up to insanity, but after what she had been through, she wasn't about to rule anything out.

They were seated right away in the restaurant, but Bree guessed their dinner wouldn't come for a while judging by the number of people in the dining room with empty placemats. She was indecisive over which book to crack open first until Jason grabbed the paranormal book to browse through. Bree started skimming the history book after they placed their orders with the waiter. She skipped to the section focusing on White Dove. Within the first page, the family name "Barry" emerged. The Barry family founded White Dove in 1832. Bree recalled that the newspaper in the box was dated only about twenty years after that. She deduced that the Elizabeth Barry from the diary might have married one of the descendants of this founding family. After all, how many unrelated families with the same last name could have possibly been living in White Dove in the late 1800's?

Jason was much more interested in his barbecued ribs when they came than he was in the Barry family information Bree shared with him. They ate their dinner, and Bree finally understood why the Gypsy's Kitchen was always so packed. The food was incredible! By the end of her meal, Bree felt more at ease. With full bellies, they paid their bill and went home.

Bree was anxious to read more of Elizabeth's diary when she got home. She read entry after entry, fascinated by even the most mundane accounts simply because they were handwritten by someone who likely lived in her house over one hundred years ago. In each entry, Elizabeth had more unflattering things to say about her mother-in-law and rejoiced at her deteriorating condition. Finally, Bree reached the entry written on the day that the mother-in-law died.

May 18, 1895

God has finally taken home that horrible woman! I am releved that her suffering is now over, but I am even more releved that my suffering is over. I was growing quite weery of her paranoya. Lenore had the audasity to accuse me of poisoning her! In the minutes before she passed, she pointed at me and said I would never be rid of her, even upon her death. I do not understand why she hated me so, other than my steeling Gregory's affections. How silly of her to think she will continue to make my life miserable even after she is gone. I shall hardly think of her! O how wonderful life will be now. I so hope Gregory's mourning will not persist for long. I find great difficulty in hiding my joy from Gregory. He would never forgive me if he knew how I truly felt about his mother. So I am most releved to be so close to no longer having to fain affection for that horrible creeture. I do not beleve I have ever felt more gaily than I do today, exept my wedding day of corse! My life with Gregory can finally begin!

Bree was drawn to one particular sentence in the entry: *In the minutes before she passed, she pointed at me and said I would never be rid of her, even upon her death.* All along, Bree had assumed that the spirit in the house was a male. The manifestations had looked male to her, but it was possible that Lenore may have had masculine features. It wasn't unheard of.

She now began to wonder if the entity could be a woman – if it could be Lenore.

Chapter 6

As Bree read on, Elizabeth's journal entries began to take on a tone of sorrow. The entries written in the months after Lenore's death were filled with concerns regarding Elizabeth's inability to conceive.

August 29, 1895

I fear I may be as barren as a witherd old woman. Gregory and I have been attempting to conseve for five months, yet I am still without child. I am becoming aware of Gregory's frustrasions with this matter as well. It is becoming harder each month to tell him that we were unsuccessful. That burden falls upon me again this evening, but I am afraid of how he will take the news. He has been quite bitter lately since the weather has not been kind to us this season and has left us with a poor harvest. His anger fills me with fear when it is directed at me. I have tried to keep out of his way and keep as quiet as I can to avoid provocasion, but I am certain to come under his scrutany tonight when I share my disappointing news. I so hope he doesn't yell again. I know he loves me, but I know he has a great deal of responsibility resting upon his shoulders, which makes him quite ill temperd. His family is greatly respected in our town and it is not acseptible for neither him nor me to fail at anything, for if I fail, it will reflect poorly upon him. What am I to do? How long can this continue before Gregory will become so disgusted with my failure to conseve that he will refuse to even touch me any longer? I so hope his disposition improves soon. If only I could bear him a son I know he would be sure to love me forever. Please, Lord God, bring us a child!

The entry left Bree with a feeling of unease. Unable to find any desire to continue reading the diary, she set it aside and curled up next to Jason on the couch for the remainder of the evening. She felt grateful that she had such an even-tempered husband who loved her for better or for worse.

Later that night, Bree woke to the sound of piano music. She was lying in her bed in the darkened bedroom, and she looked at the clock right at the moment it blinked from 3:12 to 3:13 AM. The time registered as significant in her mind, but she couldn't think of a reason why. She sat up and listened to the beautiful notes floating into the room. Looking over, she saw that Jason was fast asleep beside her, unaffected by the music. She remembered how damaged that piano had been when she cleaned it out, and she wondered how the beautiful music she was hearing could possibly be coming from the same instrument. She nudged Jason, trying to wake him so he could experience this phantom music as well, but he only rolled over and mumbled something nonsensical about wooden skirts, obviously still asleep. Every attempt she made to rouse him from his slumber failed miserably.

Giving up on Jason, Bree climbed out of bed to investigate the sounds. She had a feeling in the pit of her stomach that she wasn't going to like whatever she found downstairs, but she knew she had to look into every strange occurrence if she was ever going to figure out who was haunting her house. The stairs creaked as she tiptoed down them, trying to be as quiet as one could be in a 150-year-old house. The music grew louder as she approached the living room through the hallway. It was definitely coming from her piano. She stopped at the end of the hallway, hesitating to go on. As the song played on, she tried to place the familiar tune. It was something she had heard before, but she didn't know where she had heard it. It was a slow, melancholy melody.

From the hallway, she could see that the living room was illuminated in a strange green light. Finally letting her curiosity get the best of her, she peeked around the corner. She could see the side of the piano and noticed that the lightning lamp was on once again on top of the piano. A bright flicker of green light could be seen every few seconds beyond the corner of the piano, but Bree couldn't tell what it was. She had no view of the front of the piano from where she was standing.

The music stopped abruptly. The silence was eerie as she stood alone in the hallway, staring at the side of the piano in the strangely lit room. A bright green light suddenly flashed around the corner of the piano as a face appeared, glaring at her as if she had interrupted something important. She could only see half of the face as it peered around the piano at her, and it was glowing with a hazy green fire dancing around it. It was somewhat decayed looking, but Bree could see it had masculine, male-like features. From what Bree could see, the face may have resembled the floating head she had seen in the basement, only this time it appeared to be attached to a body. The peering face moved back behind the piano again, and the music resumed. Had it not actually seen her, or had it just dismissed her presence?

Growing bolder, she stepped further into the living room. She could now see the profile of the apparition at the piano. It was sitting on the piano bench, entirely covered in dim green flames, and its whole body glowed a bright, almost neon green. It looked radioactive. Tattered sleeves dangled loosely from its arms as its hands moved nimbly across the keys, and its clothes were ragged. Bree thought they looked like men's clothes, but it was difficult to tell as the clothes were even more decayed than the body which they adorned. The apparition had turned its face from her when she had entered the room, so she could only see the long, dark, stringy hair on the back of its head. She watched its long bony fingers dance over the keys as it

55

continued to play its gloomy tune. Bree knew what she had to do.

"Who are you?" She asked in a quiet, shaky voice.

It kept playing, ignoring her completely. Knowing she should feel relieved that it hadn't responded, she was instead insulted by its lack of interest in her.

Speaking more loudly and with more determination, she asked, "Why are you in my house?"

The apparition stopped playing and sat still briefly.

"*My* house," it corrected her in the hoarse voice of a very aged human being. It still kept its head turned away from her.

She stood motionless, speechless. She had so many questions, but she was suddenly unable to find the resolve she'd had only moments ago.

The apparition and the bright green glow suddenly vanished, accompanied by a hiss that reminded Bree of the sound of cold water hitting a hot pan. An echoing voice quickly followed.

"Your blood...keeps me here." And then silence.

Bree stood alone in the living room, which still faintly glowed green due to the lightning lamp. The presence was gone. It was only then that Bree allowed her fear to overwhelm her. Why was this *thing* concerned with her *blood*? Shivers ran down her spine and she rushed back upstairs, climbing two steps at a time.

Back in the relative safety of her own room, she felt a little more at ease. She climbed into bed, aware of a sudden weakness in her limbs. She still couldn't believe what had just happened, but being close to Jason made her feel more secure and helped her to think more clearly. She was now quite convinced that whoever was haunting her house had lived here when he or she was alive, which added credence to the notion that the ghost might be Lenore. She was still uncertain of whether this apparition was female, though, because it had such masculine features. Regardless of who it was, the spirit had intelligence. Not only had it spoken directly to her, which it had done before when it had taken the form of the burned corpse, but this time it had responded directly to a question Bree had posed.

She may not have understood the meaning of the answer, but it had provided her with one.

Unable to even think of going back to sleep, Bree attempted to wake Jason again. She had decided to keep him in the dark about the recent activity after the cupboard creature made its appearance – and disappearance – but she couldn't keep this latest incident to herself. All she wanted to do was talk to someone about it. She didn't care if he believed her or not – at least that was what she told herself. Sharing always helped to lift some of the burden of stress and anxiety from her shoulders, and she desperately needed some relief at this point. She jostled and shook Jason to no avail. She said his name, spoke loudly, and even turned on the television. When none of these techniques succeeded in waking him, she grabbed his arm and jerked him into a sitting position. He finally opened his eyes with a start.

"Ouch, damn it! What the hell?" Jason scowled angrily at Bree, waiting for an explanation.

"Sorry, honey, but I've been trying to wake you up for a long time. Nothing else was working," Bree explained apologetically.

"Well? What do you want?" Jason demanded shortly.

Bree was offended by his tone, but went on to narrate the events of the night anyway. As she told her story, she could see his impatience growing. When she began telling him what the echoing voice had said when the ghost disappeared, he interrupted the story.

"So you woke me up in the middle of the night to tell me about another one of your nightmares? I have to work in the morning. I can't just sleep in and sit around all day," Jason said in a nasty tone, and Bree understood that he was insinuating that she was lazy.

Bree was taken aback. He had never spoken to her like this, and she could feel hot tears already welling up in her eyes.

"It wasn't a nightmare, Jason! It really happened. And you don't have to work tomorrow – it's Sunday! Why are you being so mean to me? You're the one who told me not to look for a job for a while. And I don't just sit around all day, either!

Who makes your meals? Who washes your clothes? Who cleans the house?"

"You could clean it more often than you do."

"I can't believe you!" Bree shouted through a constricted throat and then began to sob.

"I can't believe you, either! You come up with these ridiculous stories to tell me, and I don't know what to think!"

"What is wrong with you?" Bree demanded again.

"What's wrong with me? What's wrong with you?!" Jason retorted.

Bree had had enough. She fought the urge to strike him and instead got out of bed and left the room, slamming the door behind her. She locked herself in the bathroom and sobbed harder than she ever had. She imagined that this was how Elizabeth felt when she wrote that last journal entry. What the hell had happened to her husband? What the hell had she married? She had always thought he was the perfect man, with his tall, muscular physique, big brown eyes, and wonderful sense of humor. He was someone she knew she could always count on to lift her spirits and make her smile. Was Jason's behavior something he had suppressed for the three years they had been together? She knew she would have great difficulty living with him if that attitude began to present itself more regularly. She didn't know that her calm, collected, unflappable husband was capable of being a belligerent asshole. She wished she hadn't ever discovered it, either.

She found herself in a predicament. Did she spend the night on the couch, in the same room where the apparition had appeared earlier that night? Or did she crawl back into bed with Jason, even though the thought of being near him filled her with rage? Maybe she should just sleep in the bathtub all night. None of her options were ideal. She cried now not only because of the things Jason had said, but also because she had nowhere to sleep. She was even more furious with him now for putting her in this dilemma. She curled up on the thin, white bathroom rug in front of the sink with her arms wrapped around her knees and cried herself to sleep.

***

"Bree?"

The sun shone brightly in Bree's eyes when she opened them. Her entire body ached as she lifted her head and looked around, disoriented for a moment. The familiar yellow and white walls of the bathroom seemed to amplify the brightness of the sunlight and clear her head, allowing her memories of the night to return to her. She furrowed her brow when she found Jason standing in the bathroom doorway looking at her curiously.

"What are you doing in here?" Jason asked in genuine bewilderment.

"Sleeping," Bree answered curtly, looking away. She couldn't stand to look at him because all she could envision was the angry, scowling expression he had worn last night.

"Why are you sleeping on the floor in the bathroom? Are you sick?" He stretched his neck to peer into the toilet, apparently checking for evidence of vomit.

"No. Just leave me alone." Bree leaned her back against the hard cupboard door below the sink and tucked her knees under her chin, wrapping her arms around her small, slender body defensively.

"I'm confused, Bree. What happened?"

"Are you serious?" Bree asked incredulously. Jason met her question with a puzzled look. "You don't remember what you said to me last night?"

"I love you and good night? I don't think I stayed awake long enough to say much else."

"I woke you up in the middle of the night because…I was scared, and you were a total…you were really mean to me," Bree explained, choosing her words and tone carefully.

"I was mean to you? What did I say?" Jason sounded surprised.

"You said I was making up stories for attention, insinuated that I sit around all day and do nothing, and asked what was wrong with me," Bree mumbled the last part, trying to avoid letting her voice crack because she was on the verge of

59

tears. She kept her eyes down so Jason wouldn't notice the redness developing in them.

"No, I would never say that! Are you sure it wasn't just another dream?" Jason suggested carefully.

Bree nodded, still looking away from him.

"I can't believe anything like that would ever come out of my mouth! I must've been asleep still, because there is no way I would ever say those things to you. I love you!" Jason was in obvious disbelief and shock. He quickly crossed the room to Bree and crouched down over her. His arms encircled her as he said, "I'm so sorry, honey. I would never want to hurt you like that. I don't remember even talking to you last night. I had to have been sleep talking. I'm so sorry!" He hugged her tightly, and the tears finally fell despite Bree's best efforts to keep them hanging in her eyelids.

After a few minutes, Jason released her and wiped her tears from her cheeks with his thick thumbs. "Do you feel any better?" He asked gently, lifting her chin so she would look him in the eye.

"I guess. I just don't know what happened last night. It wasn't you." When those words left Bree's mouth, she realized how true they were. It wasn't him. He had been a completely different person...the same person Elizabeth described in her journal. Afraid to pursue that thought any further, Bree asked, "Can we go downstairs and get some breakfast? I don't want to talk about it anymore." Bree wiped her nose on the back of her hand and stood.

"Let me make you an omelet. Cheese and bacon?" Jason turned, leading Bree out of the bathroom.

Bree cringed. "No bacon, please."

As they entered the living room, Bree saw the lightning lamp on top of the piano was not turned on.

"Have you been downstairs already today?" Bree asked Jason.

"No. Why?"

"Just wondered," Bree replied vaguely as she moved to the piano to inspect the lamp. She knew for a fact that she hadn't shut off that light last night. It was still glowing, illuminating the living room when she had turned tail and fled upstairs. She found now that the switch was in the "off" position and the unit was unplugged, leading her to wonder if it had even been plugged in at all last night when it was giving off light.

Curious, she lifted the fall and pressed a few keys. Some of them made no sound and some created flat, out-of-tune notes. *How had the glowing man been making such beautiful music with this thing?*

Bree enjoyed her breakfast and wondered whether to tell Jason about the green pianist. She had desperately needed to share it with someone last night, but when she had, she was met with hurtful words and scorn from the man she loved. She assumed it wouldn't be like that today, but it still might not go over well. However, she felt that if she told him about the recent activity she wouldn't have to feel so alone in her battle to understand what was going on in her home.

"Jason, I need to talk to you about something, but I'm not sure how you will feel about it," Bree began apprehensively when they sat down in the living room after breakfast.

"Ok…" Jason appeared to be slightly worried.

"I've had some more experiences in this house that I don't know how to explain." Bree paused, watching for any change in the expression on Jason's face. He still looked worried, and a little confused. She continued to tell him about the apparition last night and the words it spoke. He only nodded his head and dropped his gaze to his hands occasionally. She ended her story with falling asleep in the bathroom.

"You said you locked yourself in the bathroom? The door wasn't locked when I went in there this morning," Jason sounded doubtful of the validity of Bree's story. "It wasn't even closed."

Bree frowned and thought back to this morning. Jason had been standing in the doorway when she had opened her eyes. How was that possible? Who had unlocked and opened that door?

"I know I closed and locked that door! I slammed it shut behind me because I was pissed."

61

"Maybe it didn't latch when you slammed it. Are you absolutely sure you were completely awake through all of this? I mean, I don't remember speaking to you last night, and the lamp wasn't on when we came downstairs this morning. I think maybe you had a nightmare and did some sleepwalking," Jason tried to explain away her outlandish tale.

"No, Jason. This was no dream! I was just as awake and alert when it happened as I am right now!" Bree exclaimed, becoming infuriated.

"I'm not saying I don't believe it seemed real to you, honey, but these things happen sometimes. It was the middle of the night, you've been having nightmares lately-"

"Oh really?!" Bree interrupted. "Then explain away this one! That wasn't the only thing that's happened lately." She enthusiastically rushed through her account of the EVP session, the cupboard creature incident, and finding the paper in the piano, barely stopping to breathe between sentences. When she was finished, she had to catch her breath and realized the volume of her voice had been several levels above what was necessary.

"But when you went back into the house, there wasn't any sign that it had even happened at all?" Jason had a skeptical tone that matched the expression on his face.

Bree gave an outraged grunt. "You don't believe me at all, do you? You really do think those things you said last night!"

"No, of course I wouldn't think any of those things," Jason reassured her, but Bree was aware of a brief hesitation before his answer.

"You hesitated."

"Because I'm not sure how to respond to all this. I believe that you think you saw these things, but I'm not convinced that they actually happened," Jason said regretfully, looking down at his hands.

"But what about the other stuff? The phone call that showed up on the caller ID and the man painted in my mural? And I can show you the 'attic' EVP, too, and the paper that said 'the attic' on it that I found in the piano!" Bree was running upstairs to get the recorder and paper before Jason had a chance to respond. He got up and followed her.

She was rummaging in the closet when he came into the bedroom. "The caller ID could have just been a technical glitch, and there is no reason to believe that someone else painted the man in the mural. I think you painted it without realizing it at the time. I'm really worried about you, Bree. I dismissed it before, but I can't ignore this anymore."

Bree appeared in the closet doorway with a recorder in her hand and a tiny piece of paper. Her auburn hair was disheveled and she had a wild look in her eye. She thrust the square of paper in his direction, so he took it from her. He saw it was just a small, crinkled piece of paper with "the attic" typed on it. He wasn't impressed.

"Bree, an old piece of paper in an old piano is not paranormal." He tried to hand the scrap back to her, but she was busy fumbling with the recorder.

"Explain this to me, then. Remember, I was the only one in the house at the time," Bree said with determination in her voice as she pressed play on the device and held it up to Jason's ear. He cringed away from it slightly when her voice blasted out of it, asking an EVP question. The silence that followed was broken by a faint whisper that Bree remembered as being much more pronounced. Jason seemed unimpressed again.

"I don't hear anything that couldn't be simple background noise or your own breath. Honey, I'm worried something may be going on...with you." He stroked her hair delicately, trying to be comforting. When she tried to persuade him to listen more closely to the recording, he just took it and shut it off, setting it aside. "Sit down with me, Bree. I have to discuss something with you, and you need to try to put yourself in my shoes. You need to listen to this, and you need to think about it. Ok?"

Bree's anger was slowly turning to dread. Her chest felt heavy with anxiety knowing that Jason had things to tell her that were likely going to hurt her. She reluctantly sat next to him on the bed, tears already forming in the corners of her eyes. He didn't believe any of this was real.

"Please don't be hurt by what I say. This is not meant to hurt you," Jason began. He looked at Bree meaningfully. "You know I love you more than life itself, right?" He paused, so Bree nodded, avoiding eye contact with him. "Then you should understand why I am worried. It isn't normal for people to see and experience the things you are suddenly experiencing. You're seeing some pretty outrageous things, and hearing them too. But nothing has happened to me, and no real evidence exists to indicate that these things have actually happened. I'm worried you may be having some kind of hallucinations, Bree."

Upset by Jason's assessment, Bree stood up with the intent of leaving the room. Jason grabbed her hand to stop her and continued to voice his concerns when she sat back down.

"Don't get upset, honey. This is a legitimate concern! I'm not saying you are crazy or anything, or that any of this is your fault. I just want you to consider seeing a neurologist to make sure there isn't something going on in your brain that shouldn't be. I'm not trying to insult you or tell you you're crazy. I'm just concerned about your health because I couldn't live without you. So please consider what I've said. See a doctor…for me," Jason pleaded.

The tears were again blurring Bree's vision and streaming down her cheeks. She was hurt by Jason's disbelief, but now she was beginning to doubt herself. Was Jason right? *No, of course not! I know what I saw*, Bree thought to herself. She crawled under the covers of the bed and told Jason she wanted to be alone for a while. He sympathetically obliged and left the room.

Bree spent several hours lying in bed, wondering if she really was crazy. The crazy ones never know they're crazy. They don't see their own insanity. Jason had said he didn't think she was crazy, but that he thought she had a brain tumor or something. But as far as Bree was concerned, crazy is crazy whether it's caused by a tumor or childhood trauma. Either way, he thought all of these strange occurrences were only in her head, so he must think she is crazy even if he doesn't want to call it that.

When she finally decided to get out of bed, the first thing Bree did was reach for the phone.

"Hi, Mom."

"Hey there, sweetie. Is something wrong? You sound depressed," Karen asked perceptively.

"Yes, something is wrong." She recounted to her mother the happenings of the day, including the accounts of paranormal activity that had fueled them. Karen listened intently without interruption.

When Bree was finished, she asked, "What do you think? Do you think it's all in my head? Should I see a doctor?"

"You know, honey, it might not be a bad idea. There may be paranormal activity in your home, but the possibility exists that it may be something more serious. I'm concerned about your health as well, and it might not hurt to get some medical testing done. We certainly don't want to ignore any possible warning signs that something may be wrong. And you know what? God willing, you'll find out your brain is perfectly healthy and you'll be able to rule out hallucinations. It may bring you closer to understanding what is going on in your life right now, sweetie."

Bree started to cry once more. "But I don't know any neurologists! I don't know who to call! And what do I say? 'Hi, I'm seeing crazy things. Can I make an appointment?'"

"I'll tell you what," Karen said in a reassuring voice. "Make an appointment with your regular doctor first to discuss these symptoms with him, and I'll come down so I can go to the appointment with you. I'll be there to support you. How does that sound?"

Bree felt a little better knowing she wouldn't have to deal with this on her own. She knew Jason would be helpful as well, but there's no comfort like Mom. "That sounds great, Mom. I'll call Dr. O'Brien's office tomorrow, and I'll let you know when I can get in."

After hanging up the phone and wiping away the remainder of her tears, Bree went downstairs to tell Jason of her decision. He embraced her and expressed his relief that she was taking the steps needed to make sure she was healthy.

"I can go with you, if you want. It's a four-hour drive for your mom to come down here," Jason offered.

"That's ok. I think I need my mom for this."

When Bree called her doctor's office the next day, they were able to schedule her for an appointment on Tuesday afternoon, which was the next day. She called Karen right away to let her know.

"I'll just take a couple of sick days," Karen said. "I'll come down tomorrow morning and stay tomorrow night, if that's ok."

Bree spent the rest of her Monday agonizing over her upcoming appointment. She knew Dr. O'Brien wouldn't be able to tell her much, but she knew it was the first step in actually finding out whether something was wrong with her brain. She felt almost as though she'd rather not know.

If something was wrong with her brain, it wasn't affecting her that day. Nothing unusual happened on Monday, and she didn't have any nightmares that night.

Tuesday afternoon came sooner than Bree had wanted. Her anxiety had grown exponentially since Monday, and she was thankful for the presence of her mother next to her in the waiting room at Dr. O'Brien's office. A short, plump nurse with thin, blond, curly hair finally called her name and led her and Karen to the examination room. Bree sat on the crinkly paper covering the examination table and let the nurse take her vitals. She then began the usual game of Twenty Questions: what's the reason for your visit, are you currently on any medications, etc.

For one question Bree didn't have an answer.

"When was your last period?" The nurse asked, looking at her with beady, impatient eyes.

"Um…I'm not sure. It's kind of an irregular schedule, so I don't bother trying to keep track. I don't think it's been that long ago, though." Bree tried to recall the last time she had to buy tampons, but came up blank.

"Is there any possibility you could be pregnant?" The nurse asked.

"I don't think so, but I don't know."

"I'll need you to provide a urine sample so we can be sure. Come with me." Karen waited in the room while Bree accepted a sterile cup from the nurse and headed to the bathroom. She was almost certain she wasn't pregnant. She couldn't be. She left the urine sample in the appropriate tray and went back to her room.

"This is stupid. I should've just said I was sure I wasn't pregnant. They'll probably tack an extra $50 onto my bill for this," Bree complained.

"They just have to make sure. Don't fret about it, Bree," Karen said.

A few minutes later the nurse returned with Bree's chart in her hands. "Congratulations," she said unenthusiastically. "The test was positive. The doctor will be in shortly."

Bree watched with her jaw agape as the homely gnome of a nurse turned her back and briskly exited the room.

Chapter 7

"What?!" Bree exclaimed long after the nurse was gone, addressing no one in particular. She looked over at Karen with wide eyes, resembling a deer in headlights. Karen's expression conveyed the same surprise as Bree's at first, but quickly changed to joy.

"Oh, how wonderful!" Karen said excitedly with her hands crossed over her chest. She stood swiftly and caught Bree in a strong embrace.

"Did that nurse say what I think she said?" Bree asked, still in shock.

"Yes! She wasn't very clear – or pleasant – about it, but yes, I believe so!"

Bree's whole world changed in that moment. She didn't know whether to be happy like Karen or upset because she hadn't planned this. Was she ready for it? Was Jason ready for it? Questions buzzed through her head like bees in a hive, and she had answers for none of them. As Bree sat in silence, Karen stopped fussing and returned to her seat, inferring that Bree needed to be alone with her thoughts.

Several minutes passed before Bree spoke again. "I'm having a baby...?" Then she was quiet again.

"You've got time to get ready. It may seem overwhelming now, but when the time comes, you'll be ready," Karen assured her.

"I don't know, Mom. With everything that's been going on, I'm not so sure this is the best time for me to be having kids."

"Everything is going to be fine. I'm sure things will work out in the end. Just take it one step at a time," Karen advised optimistically.

The door swung open and Dr. O'Brien entered the room. He was a tall, thin man of about forty with dark blond hair and bright blue eyes that were slightly too close together. He shook Bree's hand firmly and introduced himself since this was the first time she had been seen by him. She'd had no reason to see a doctor in White Dove before now, and she had only chosen him because most of the people Jason worked with went to Dr. O'Brien and she knew he accepted their insurance. He sat on his short, backless stool on wheels and flipped through Bree's chart.

"So, we've determined that you're pregnant...how do you feel about that?" he wanted to know.

"I don't know yet. It's quite a surprise for me," Bree admitted.

Dr. O'Brien nodded. He asked her if she had an obstetrician and offered to get her set up with one in his office, which she agreed to. He then moved on to the original reason for her visit.

"It says here that you're having hallucinations?" He indicated the chart and Bree nodded. "Tell me about them, including when they started and how frequently they occur."

Bree told him that the first one occurred about two months ago when they moved into the house and have been occurring more frequently lately. She described both the auditory and visual aspects of them as well, and told him how vivid and real they seemed to her. She finally admitted that she didn't know for certain whether they were just hallucinations.

"My family is concerned they might be hallucinations, but they seem very real to me," Bree divulged. "We just want to find out if there may be something going on in my brain that could cause hallucinations."

"Interesting," Dr. O'Brien said while scribbling in the chart. "Well, there are many different reasons one may experience hallucinations. Have you had any accompanying symptoms, such as nausea, vomiting, headaches, or dizziness?"

"No, nothing like that. I just have a short experience and that's that. I feel fine when it happens and I feel fine before and after it happens, relatively speaking."

Dr. O'Brien continued with his questions, vigorously taking notes when Bree spoke. Finally, however, he ran out of questions.

"Well, Bree, you have a couple options," he said. "I can place an order for you to have an MRI done on your brain to check for physical signs of damage or disease, or I can refer you to a neurologist. I'm not sure what your insurance covers, but both can be quite expensive. A CT scan would be less expensive than an MRI and would be less time consuming, but the fact that you are pregnant limits our options. An MRI would be safer for both you and the baby."

Bree didn't know what her insurance covered as far as specialist visits and MRI's. It wasn't something she thought she would need to know for a long time yet.

"Do I have to make a decision right now?" Bree inquired. "I'd really like to discuss it with my husband first."

"Oh, of course, think about it. Just call the office and let our receptionist, Amy, know the situation and what you've decided. I'll get you set up from there." Dr. O'Brien thanked her for coming in, congratulated her on her pregnancy, and firmly shook her hand again. Bree paid her co-pay at the front desk, made an appointment with the obstetrician, and left the office with Karen.

The ride home was a quiet one. Bree had so many things on her mind that she kept forgetting that Karen was in the passenger seat. She caught herself mouthing her thoughts and making unnecessary facial expressions more than once. She couldn't believe how increasingly complicated her life was

70

becoming, and how quickly it was happening. Would any of this have happened if she'd never moved into that house?

Jason's truck was already parked in the driveway when Karen and Bree arrived at the house. Bree had hoped it wouldn't be, as she felt she needed more time to prepare before she told Jason the news. She didn't know how he would feel about the pregnancy. It wasn't something they had talked about recently. When they got married a little over a year and a half ago, they had decided to wait to have children until they had a house of their own, financial stability, and reliable vehicles. They had all of those things now, but they also had some unforeseen troubles dumped onto their happily ever after: either a neurological issue with Bree or a terrifying entity inhabiting their home. The situation was less than ideal, and it upset Bree to think that the news she had always imagined would bring joy to Jason might now bring him dread.

"If you want," Karen said, startling Bree out of her thoughts as they sat in the quiet, parked car, "I can go watch television while you talk to Jason, or I can go up to the guest bedroom for a while to give you guys some privacy."

Bree unbuckled her seatbelt and sat quietly for a moment. "You can go ahead and watch TV in the living room. I'll bring him upstairs to tell him." Then, after another long silence, "I hope this is happy news to him."

"He'll probably be more likely to see it as happy news if you present it as such," Karen advised. She squeezed Bree's hand briefly and then climbed out of the car. Bree could tell she was still delighted with the news and wanted Bree to be delighted as well. Bree wanted the same thing.

When they came into the house, Jason was in the kitchen, snacking. He had apparently just arrived home, as he still wore his work clothes, and she had noticed that his truck was still radiating heat when she passed near it on her way into the house. The television was already on, so Karen had settled her small frame into the corner nook of the couch, waiting for Bree to take Jason upstairs and tell him he's going to be a dad.

"So, how did it go?" Jason wanted to know right away, speaking around a mouthful of sandwich.

"We have some options to discuss," Bree said hesitantly. "Come on, we'll talk about it while you change out of those filthy clothes."

As they made their way up the stairs, Bree's chest grew tighter. She felt like she had swallowed a golf ball that got stuck halfway down her esophagus. By the time they entered the bedroom, Bree knew she had to spill it immediately or explode from the anxiety.

"Jason, I'm pregnant," Bree blurted. It was so rushed that it sounded like she had made it into one word. She held her breath as she watched his face intently.

His features remained unchanged briefly as his brain processed what she had just said. When he reached comprehension, he broke into a smile – which expanded into a huge goofy grin that made his whole face light up. He swept Bree up into an unbearably tight embrace and kissed her face.

"Oh my God!" He exclaimed as he released her from his arms. "This is so…so…" and instead of finishing his sentence, Jason gave an excited shout and grabbed her for another hug.

"So this is good news?" Bree had to choke the words out because her trachea was pressed against Jason's clavicle.

"Of course it is!" Jason replied happily. He pulled away from her so he could see her face before asking, "Don't you think so?"

"Yeah, but in light of what's happened lately…it just has me a little worried," Bree admitted. "Aren't you a bit worried?"

"Well sure, but we'll get everything figured out and taken care of," Jason answered with confidence. "Quit worrying and be happy with me, honey! I'm going to be a dad! And you're going to be a mom! Isn't this exciting?"

Jason's excitement was contagious. Before she knew it, she was smiling and laughing with him, counting the months in an attempt to estimate a due date. When Jason asked about her first OB appointment, though, Bree was quickly reminded of the less joyful business at hand.

"They set me up for an appointment in two weeks. But I need to discuss our options with you regarding my neurological testing." Bree hated to change the subject to such a somber issue, but it was necessary. "The doctor can either set me up for an MRI at the hospital or he can refer me to a neurologist."

"Did he say which option he thought was best?"

"No. And I didn't ask. I was wondering if you could find out which would be better, insurance-wise, from Mandy at work." Mandy was the woman who handled health insurance issues for Jason's company. Bree knew she could call the insurance company herself, but she hated dealing with them. The representatives were always so rude to her, and she often got a different answer for the same question if she talked to different representatives. It was just easier to ask Mandy.

"I'll do it first thing tomorrow morning. Is there an option you would prefer?" Jason wondered.

"I don't know. I'd rather not have to do either," Bree replied truthfully. "It's something I have to think about, and I'd rather have all the information and know the costs before I decide...we decide," she corrected.

"Okay, I'll get that information for you tomorrow," Jason said. "Now, can we go back to being excited about being pregnant?" He asked hopefully, the smile returning to his face.

"Yes, please! But we should probably go back downstairs soon. I don't want my mom to think we forgot about her," Bree joked. Jason's delight with the pregnancy helped her to worry less about the possible neurological issues she may have. It also allowed her to be excited about becoming a mom.

When they came downstairs, Karen looked at them and smiled. "So, how do you feel, Jason?"

"I'm happy! I'm excited. Are you excited to become a grandma?" Jason asked, then added quickly, "You sure don't look like you could be a grandma."

Karen laughed heartily. "Thank you, Jason. That's very kind of you to say. And yes, I'm very excited to be a grandma! I couldn't be more pleased."

A short while later, Karen and Bree put together a nice dinner, spending the whole time discussing baby names and what Bree should expect in the early stages of her pregnancy. After dinner, Bree showed her mother the mural she had painted in her bedroom. As Karen was admiring her work, Bree suddenly remembered that she had taken photos of the creepy shadow man in the mural before painting over him. She retrieved the digital camera to show Karen.

"Wow, that is creepy!" Karen gasped as she viewed the pictures on the camera's screen.

"I know! Don't you think I would've noticed if I had 'accidentally' painted that?" Bree asked.

"Yeah...that's just strange. I don't know what else to say about it. It's weird."

Bree put the camera away when Karen was through with it and found the voice recorder. "Do you want to hear the 'attic' EVP I caught? Jason claims he doesn't hear it, but he only listened to it once."

"Sure, I'll take a listen." Karen listened to the recording carefully, asking Bree to replay it several times. "I have to agree with you. That does sound like someone whispering 'the attic.'"

"I know. I'm glad you hear it too. I think Jason just doesn't *want* to hear it. He doesn't want to believe that something strange may be going on here," Bree spoke in a low voice. Jason was downstairs and she didn't want him to overhear her talking about him.

"But can you blame him?" Karen asked. "You didn't want to believe it at first, either. It's not a comforting thought."

Bree had to agree with her mother. But the idea that she may have mental issues wasn't any more comforting.

"Can I see the stuff you found in the attic?" Karen asked.

Bree brought out the wooden crate with the books and trinkets. "I'll go get Elizabeth's diary, too," she said as she headed downstairs, leaving Karen in the bedroom with the box. When she returned, Karen was holding a thin packet of crinkled, yellowed papers.

"What's that?" Bree inquired.

"I'm not sure. It was tucked in the back of one of the grammar books," Karen replied with a puzzled look on her face. "I think it's...adoption papers."

"What?" Bree sat on the bed next to her mother and looked over her shoulder at the papers. As they looked through them, it became clear that they belonged to Elizabeth Barry. But

74

it wasn't paperwork for Elizabeth adopting a child, as Bree would've expected considering Elizabeth's journal entries indicating she couldn't conceive, but rather paperwork for putting a child up for adoption.

"Elizabeth gave up her baby? This doesn't make sense. The last entry I read in her diary said she was upset because she couldn't conceive – why would she give it up when she did?" Bree wondered aloud.

"I don't know. Her diary didn't say anything about this?"

"Not yet. I haven't finished reading it. It's like a novel. Look at this thing!" Bree held up the journal so Karen could see the size of it. "I'm only about a quarter of the way through it." Bree suddenly had a thought. "What's the date on those papers?"

Karen searched for a moment. "January 12th, 1897."

Bree flipped through the diary. The last journal entry was dated June 4th, 1896. "The journal ends before that." Bree read the entry.

June 4, 1896

I am still having difficulty coping with Gregory being gone. I still love him. I have always loved him, despite what he had become. He is still with me, of corse, as I have said before, but it is not the same. How could it be? I would rather he just move on and forget the life he had with me. His visits are becoming less frequant, I find, now that Henry has left me as well. I find little joy in this lonly life I now leed. I am damned, of course, and there is no respite for the likes of me. God has delt me this punishment for my misdeeds. I have no choice but to bare my burden with shame. I have no chance at redempshen. Gregory seems to find great satisfaction in reminding me of this every time he visits. He enjoys making me feel worthless and unclean. He refers to the child growing in my womb as an abomanation, and has told me that the child is cursed. How could anyone curse an innosent child? It is I who am cursed. I am the abomanation. I tell him not to punish the child for my sins, but he only laughs at me and tells me how foolish

I am. I hope the Lord God is more forgiving than my Gregory. I may be a foolish woman, but at least I am forgiving to those who have wronged me and remorseful when I have wronged others, which is more than I can say for Gregory. I beleve this shall be my final writing in this journal, as I no longer find any plesure in recording my life. It has become much to dark and shameful for me to have the desire to think about it long enough to put it on paper. Perhaps by the time I read this again I will be remarried to a wonderful man with a wonderful life and will have put all of this heartache and despare behind me.

The rest of the pages in the journal were blank after that. This last passage confused Bree, raising more questions than it answered. Why did Elizabeth say Gregory was gone in the beginning, but then go on to talk about him still visiting her? Had they separated, or was she speaking metaphorically, as in the personality Gregory had when she married him was gone? And who was Henry? Nothing in the last entry made sense, and Bree knew the only way to find answers was to read through the whole journal.

She gave the diary to Karen so she could read the last journal entry as well. It left her just as confused and hungry for answers as it had Bree.

"It's like a 19th century soap opera," Karen mused.

They heard heavy footsteps ascending the stairs, and within moments Jason appeared in the bedroom doorway. "What are you guys doing up here?" He looked curiously at the papers on the bed and the books from the attic.

Bree shared with him the juicy information she and Karen had just discovered. He looked bored by the time she finished speaking.

"History is great and all, but I just rented that new sci-fi movie from the TV, and it'll be starting in like five minutes...so you might want to come downstairs if you don't want to miss the beginning." Jason loved his sci-fi.

Karen and Bree put everything back in the box, save for the diary and adoption papers, and joined Jason in the living room for the two-and-a-half hour movie.

***

When Bree and Jason came downstairs the next morning, they found Karen in her pajamas, folding up a blanket from the couch. A pillow was still propped against the arm of the couch, as though she had been sleeping there.

"Mom, did you sleep on the couch last night?" Bree asked in confusion.

"Not all night. I tried sleeping in the guest bedroom, but I woke up in the middle of the night, and…well…I don't think you need a neurologist," Karen stated ominously. "You aren't hallucinating."

Jason beat Bree to the question. "You saw something too?"

"I not only saw something – it actually touched me. There is definitely something unnatural in this house," Karen stated, looking around as though she thought the entity might have overheard her.

"What happened?" Bree wanted to know. She went to the couch and sat down, indicating that Karen should do the same.

"I woke up because I felt cold. I looked over at the clock, and for some reason I still remember that it said 3:13 AM."

Bree recalled that 3:13 AM was the same time she awoke to music and saw the ghostly pianist. She filed that bit of information away in her brain and let Karen continue her account uninterrupted.

"I felt like I was being watched, so I looked around the room and saw a black shadow standing in the corner of the room. It was a human shape and quite tall. I could see it had a head, arms, body, and legs. It was very distinctly outlined, but I could see through it a little bit – it wasn't solid. As soon as I noticed it, it spoke to me in a whispery, hoarse voice. It said something like, 'You aren't Mother. Get out of Mother's room!'

"I was too scared to move at that point, so I just sat there in shock, staring at the figure. It then started to slide sideways, like it was on a conveyer belt or something, and dissolved into the wall. Within seconds, I felt something cold bump against my arm. When I looked over, I saw a white head was pushing through the wall, like the wall was made of thin latex. What I felt touching my arm was the nose. I jerked away from the wall and screamed, but it was one of those hoarse, almost soundless screams. Then two hands started pushing out of the wall from either side of the head, and it continued to come out slowly, like the wall was giving birth to it. The shoulders and chest, the torso, and eventually an entire human-shaped body had pushed its way out of the wall, and it looked like it was covered in white latex. I had jumped out of the bed by that point and was backing toward the door as its feet came loose from the wall. It then started jerking around and convulsing on the bed. Right when I reached for the doorknob behind me, the thing's head suddenly snapped up and it started crying like an infant at me. I fumbled with the door handle for a second, but finally got the door open and backed out of the room as the thing flopped onto the floor with a loud thud. I shut the door behind me and ran down here. I turned on every light in the living room and waited. When nothing else happened, I got one of your spare pillows out of the closet and slept on the couch." Karen looked a little ashamed when she added, "I still haven't been back in that room yet."

Instead of feeling frightened, Bree felt enraged and guilt-ridden that her mother had to go through that in her house. It was one thing to harass Bree, but this entity was crossing the line by terrifying her loved ones. No one should have to experience such things, especially as a guest in someone else's home.

"Why didn't you come get us?" Jason demanded. He seemed to be just as upset as Bree.

"I didn't want to bother you guys. I knew Jason had to work today, so I thought it was important to let you sleep. Besides, what could any of us have done?" Karen pointed out.

"Still, Mom, we could've helped you calm down and feel less frightened."

"Yes, dear, I know. But it's all over and done with for now, and I'm fine. More importantly, you're fine. It's this house that has something wrong with it, Bree, not you." Karen looked around uneasily. "Now we just need to figure out how to fix it."

"I've been trying to figure out that one for a while now. I don't even know where to begin! How do you get rid of something you don't understand or know anything about?" Bree was frustrated.

Bree suddenly remembered the book on the paranormal that she bought at the Gypsy's Treasure Chest. Then she remembered what the crazy woman had said to her.

"I just remembered I bought a book on the paranormal over the weekend at the Gypsy's Treasure Chest, but I haven't had a chance to really look at it yet. It might have some answers for us. Hopefully it'll be more helpful than the crazy woman who sold it to me." Bree told Karen about her encounter with the strange woman.

"Oh yeah, I remember that," Jason let out a small laugh. "I thought it was pretty ridiculous – at the time." Bree could sense that Jason was finally beginning to believe the house might be haunted. Jason glanced up at the clock hanging over the television. "I've got to get ready for work. Do you guys need me to do anything before I leave this morning?"

Bree asked Jason to check out the guest bedroom quickly before he took off for work. He did so after eating a quick breakfast and reported that nothing appeared to be amiss.

"Take care of our baby today," he said with a smile as he walked out the door.

Bree and Karen returned to their discussion of the entity after Jason left. They perused the paranormal book and found it was divided into sections: Types of Entities and Hauntings, Why Spirits Stay Behind, Investigation Techniques, Living without Fear, and Reclaiming Your Home. They began to read the final section, but soon found that they needed to first determine what type of entity and haunting with which they were dealing. As they flipped to the first section and browsed the entity descriptions and capabilities, they became confused.

"This thing has power and behaves kind of like an inhuman entity, yet I am quite certain it was once a living person." Bree frowned. "I had been thinking it was Lenore, Elizabeth's mother-in-law, but after what it said to you about its mother, I'm now thinking it might actually be Gregory. Maybe the guest room was his mother's room, because she did live with them until she died. But who knows – I could be way off. I don't even know for sure that Elizabeth lived in this house. I just assumed so because her diary was here." It bothered Bree to realize that all she had learned and inferred could be completely off-base. She had just been accepting her own assumptions as facts.

"I think it's important to figure out as best we can who this spirit could be," Karen opined. "It might help us to discover what it is that keeps it here and what it wants. It was the one who led you to the attic, right?" Karen asked, and Bree nodded. "Then I suspect we should be able to find answers in the things you found up there. I think it may be a good idea to finish reading that diary, because that seems like the most logical place to start."

Bree had to agree with Karen's conclusions, but couldn't overlook one minor problem. "We don't even know if Elizabeth definitely lived here. That diary could've been brought here and left by a different family who lived here before us."

Karen pondered that for a moment. "Was there anything else in the box that could've indicated that she lived here? Oh!" Karen suddenly exclaimed. "The adoption papers! They might have some location information on them!" Karen disappeared up the stairs, clearly on a mission.

Bree continued to read the paranormal book, looking at the investigation techniques section while Karen was upstairs. She came across a paragraph discussing electricity and how entities can use electrical energy to fuel their activity and manifestations. Bree thought about the lightning lamp, which always seemed to be on when something paranormal was taking place. Could the entity in her home be drawing power from that?

The book suggested using an energy source, such as a Jacob's Ladder, to help the entity manifest itself while performing an investigation. Bree considered trying to use the lightning lamp next time she mustered the courage to attempt communication. It was a long shot, but it was worth a try.

Bree realized her mother had been upstairs for a long time, so she went to see what was keeping her. "What did you find out?" Bree asked when she walked into the bedroom.

"Well, the adoption papers show that Elizabeth lived in White Dove," Karen answered without looking up. She had the ancient newspaper from 1854 spread out on the floor in front of her. "I also found your house in this newspaper. Take a look." She waved Bree over to her.

Sitting on the hard floor next to her mother, she noticed the black and white photo of her house immediately. It hadn't changed much, at least on the outside, in one hundred fifty years. She saw the short article next to it and read through it:

On August 2nd, construction of the future Barry family home was completed. Gregory J. Barry began construction of the house on March 12th, the day after asking Edith White, daughter of Mr. and Mrs. John W. White, for her hand in marriage. Upon her acceptance of his proposal, he promised her a new home on their wedding day, and has been true to his word. Gregory and Edith were joined in marriage on August 9th in the presence of close friends and family. Congratulations, Mr. and Mrs. Gregory J. Barry.

Another Gregory Barry? Bree grabbed Elizabeth's journal and flipped back to the beginning. She found the place where Elizabeth wrote Gregory's full name in her first entry, but it wasn't an exact match. Elizabeth's husband was Gregory D. Barry, whereas the builder of the house was Gregory J. Barry. It had to have been a relative of Gregory's. It probably wasn't his father, Bree thought, as his mother's name was Lenore, not Edith. Elizabeth never wrote of Gregory's father, so Bree didn't even know what his name had been. The article was written forty-one years before Elizabeth and Gregory were married, so Bree wondered if it could be Gregory's grandparents. She grew more confused the longer she tried to figure it out.

"So what do you think of that?" Karen startled Bree out of her thoughts.

"I don't know. I guess it's another strong indicator that Elizabeth probably lived here."

"I wonder how this Gregory was related to the Gregory from the diary. It couldn't be the same person, I wouldn't think." Karen said. "He would've been like sixty years old in 1895."

Something occurred to Bree. "Edith and Gregory were probably his grandparents, and the house probably was passed on to his father. That would make sense. But if that were true, then Gregory's mother would've died at only about forty years old. That seems quite young to me." Bree's mother was already beyond forty, and Bree couldn't imagine losing Karen any time soon.

"Who knows. People didn't live as long a hundred years ago, and she could've had any number of illnesses or diseases that weren't well understood at the time. It doesn't seem completely unreasonable to me that Gregory's mother could've died at forty years old in 1895." Karen glanced at the clock in the bedroom. "I should get going soon. I didn't leave anything for your father to eat for dinner, so I should probably try to get home to prepare something. Are you going to be okay here by yourself if I take off soon?"

"Of course. I've survived this long in this house. Besides, I've got a lot of reading to do," Bree gestured toward the diary.

Bree and Karen went into the guest bedroom together to gather Karen's things. As they carried her overnight bag downstairs, Karen suggested that Bree might not want to make that room into a nursery.

"Oh God, no! I'm not sure where we'll put the nursery, but it definitely won't be in that room!" Bree was horrified by the thought of a similar occurrence happening while her baby was in the room.

Bree saw her mother off shortly thereafter. She immediately immersed herself in the diary once Karen was gone, hoping to find the answers she sought. As she read through the passages, Elizabeth depicted an increasingly ugly and verbally abusive Gregory. Their inability to conceive infuriated Gregory month after month, and he blamed Elizabeth entirely. The words Bree read were the words of a defeated, emotionally battered woman.

Suddenly, Elizabeth began mentioning Henry in her writings. It was usually just to say that Henry helped Gregory with something that day – nothing detailed. Bree soon understood that Henry was Gregory's younger brother.

Finally, Bree reached a passage that revealed more about Henry, and hinted at why he may have been important enough for Elizabeth to mention him in her last entry.

December 1, 1895

I can lie to myself no longer. The feelings I harbor for Henry are far from innocent. I hardly understand how he and Gregory can be of the same blood, as Henry is so hansome, charming, sweet, and always smiling. Gregory has become so horribly unrecognizible from the man I married not so long ago. I fear I may have married the wrong Barry boy. I do still love Gregory, but my heart is growing fonder of Henry every time I see him. I am quite sertin he feels the same fondness for me. Unforchunately for both of us, we are bownd to another and our coy smiles and quiet looks to one another are completly forbidden. O but how am I to ceese this behavior? I feel it would be like trying to tell an apple tree to not blossom, or a songbird to not sing if I were to tell my heart to ceese feeling such fondness for Henry. I know it would not listen. My love for Gregory will have to sustane me, however, as I have no choice but to be faithful and loyal to my dredful husband. Nothing can ever come of my feelings for Henry, and knowing this fills me with great regret. Had only I met Henry first!

When Bree finished reading the entry, she grabbed the phone. Her mother would likely still be on the road, so she dialed Karen's cell phone.

"Is everything okay?" Karen asked when she answered the phone.

"Yeah, everything's fine, but I just found out something from Elizabeth's diary. Henry was actually Gregory's brother, and I think Elizabeth and Henry may have had an affair. How's that for a 19th century soap opera?"

Chapter 8

"I knew it!" Karen exclaimed. "And then Gregory left her, and that was why she kept talking about her misdeeds and being damned, I'll bet."

"That could all very well be true, but we don't know for sure yet. I still have quite a bit of reading to do."

"Keep me posted," Karen requested.

Bree returned to the journal when she hung up the phone. The next interesting, scandalous passage was dated from mid-December.

December 16, 1895

I am forchunate that Henry was around today. I was in the washroom scrubbing the greese out of Gregory's clothes when I caught one of his shirts on the corner of the washboard and tore a hole in it. He and Henry had just come in from the barn, and unforchunately for me, he walked into the washroom right at that moment. He heard the taring sound and became inraged. He started screaming at me, telling me how useless and foolish I was, and how he would have been better off marrying Mr. Stanley's deaf daughter with the withered arm. In my anger, I lashed out and told him that

I wished he had married her instead of me as well. His face turned red and his eyes grew wide in disbelefe that I would say such a thing to him. He began to shake with anger and bellowed at me, calling me an ignorant wench, and then he did something I never knew he would do. He struck me. I was in shock at first and just stood in silense until I tasted the blood upon my tounge. I started to sob loudly, unable to control myself. This only infuriated him more, and he struck me again, yelling at me to stop crying because I was emberressing him and myself. When I could not stop, he raised his hand to strike me again and I dropped to the floor, holding my arms over my face to protect myself. Henry rushed in and grabbed Gregory's arm, stopping him from striking me again. They argued breefly before Gregory stormed out of the room, and then out of the house. Henry came to me and helped me to my feet, asking if I was all right. When he saw the blood on my mouth, he dabbed it jently with a damp cloth and then wiped the tears from my cheeks. And then the most wonderful, horrible, confusing thing happend. He lightly kissed my cheek, very close to the corner of my mouth. When I gasped in suprise at his behavior, he quickly appoligized and left the room. I am now more confused than ever before! I think I may love Henry. It felt so nice when he kissed me, and it left my knees feeling weak and my heart leeping in my chest. Is it just the fasination that a schoolgirl has for a schoolboy, or is it real love? It feels so real to me. He ocupies my mind throughout the day, and I know he shall haunt my dreams tonight. O what am I to do? I know I should feel gilt-riddin for my indiscresion, but I do not. I feel invigerated. I wish for it to happen again though I know it is wrong. What if Gregory finds out? What if Henry tells him? And why am I not disgusted with myself? I know not how to feel or what to do!

December 17, 1895

Gregory hasn't spoken to me at all today. He acts as though I do not even egsist. The strange thing is that this does not bother me in the least. I rather enjoy being ignored by him, as I do not have to worry about him saying disgraceful things to me. It also allows me to ponder my delimma with Henry. He did not come around today, and I do not know when I shall see him again. I do hope it is soon, though! I am begining to wonder if I have put to much significanse upon Henry's kiss. Perhaps it was ment to be innosent, only as a means to comfort me in my time of sorrow. Am I placing to much meaning upon it? If it was innosent, then why would he appoligize as though he knew he had done something wrong? And why would he leave the room so quickly without explination? I have been contemplating his intentions all day, but I have come to no grate conclusion. I have also been wondering how to behave around Henry now that this has happend. I assume I should pretend nothing has happend, but I despritely want to find out what compeled him to kiss me. I wish I could talk to him about it. If only I could get him alone again, I could stop torchureing myself with these questions and just find out the answers from him. But what if he were to say that it was as meaningless as a kiss on a child's forhead, ment only to comfort? I would have my answers, but I would also be emberressed and broken hearted. Though I am not sure how I would respond if he were to tell me that he ment the kiss the way I thought he did. It would delight me to hear this, but it would also leave me in a strange position. I suppose confronting him directly with my quearies would only resalt in more confusing feelings, and is not a good idea. I hope I do not have to go on like this for much longer! I wish my heart had not cast me into this situation! I must admit, however, that it has made life a great deal more exiting as of late!

The next few entries were more of the same. Bree was just getting into the January entries when Jason came home from work.

"Did you call Dr. O'Brien to let him know that we aren't going to do anything right now?" Jason inquired.

"No," Bree replied sheepishly. "I kind of got sucked into this journal today, and my mom and I were researching the paranormal. I want to get this thing out of the house before the baby is born."

"I know, but we should notify Dr. O'Brien's office soon, just as a courtesy." Jason started rummaging through the cupboards for an after-work snack. "So did you and your mom find out anything?"

Bree told him about the newspaper article and how they'd decided to try to find out who was haunting the house, as it would help them to determine the proper course of action. She told him that they thought it might be Gregory since the ghost talked about "Mother."

"So why do you suppose he's haunting our house?" Jason wondered.

"I don't know yet. I don't even know if it definitely is him. From what I've read in her journal, it appears Elizabeth may have had an affair, but I still have a lot to read before I know for sure. I think most of our answers may be in that journal."

"Is there anything I can do to help out?"

Bree considered his offer, and quickly thought of a use for his services. "Maybe this weekend you and I can conduct an investigation, like the ghost chasers on TV. I've been wanting to do something at night, but so far you haven't been very open to the idea of paranormal activity, so I haven't wanted to ask. How would you feel about an investigation?" Bree was hopeful.

"I suppose we could do that. But what do we do? Just walk around with the sound recorder? We don't have any video recorders or infrared cameras or anything cool like the guys on TV," Jason sounded slightly discouraged and doubtful.

"That's okay. It's not like we're trying to capture evidence to share with others – this is just for us. We're just trying to get it to answer our questions and communicate with us. We don't necessarily need cameras for that."

Jason mulled it over for a minute before replying. "We can try it and see what happens. We have to do *something*, anyway." He headed upstairs to shower.

While Jason cleaned up, Bree thought about the upcoming investigation. She began to plan out what techniques they would use, and where they would focus their efforts. Also, she set the DVR on the satellite receiver to record the paranormal investigators' show, which was scheduled to come on the next night. She might be able to get some ideas, learn new techniques, and gather more information about the paranormal. In the meantime, she would have to finish reading the section on investigation techniques in the paranormal book. She would also have to keep at the diary.

When Jason returned downstairs, he had questions about the investigation. "We aren't going to try to use a Ouija board for this investigation, are we?"

"No! From what I've heard, Ouija boards are dangerous. Apparently, they can open the door to even worse things than what we already have in our house! Non-human, powerful entities. Absolutely no Ouija boards!" Bree said firmly. She had read in the paranormal book to never use Ouija boards as an inexperienced, amateur investigator. The paranormal investigators on television had relayed that same warning as well.

Jason seemed relieved at Bree's intense objection to the use of a Ouija board. "Good. I've always heard those things were bad news, and I didn't want to have to try to talk you out of using one if you had your mind set on it. And I definitely don't want to have to go out and buy one." He suddenly changed the subject. "So have you been taking care of my little one today? Making sure not to overexert yourself?"

Bree laughed. "I hardly think reading is overexerting myself. But just to be safe, maybe we should go out for dinner tonight so I don't overexert myself by lifting pans and washing dishes."

Jason thought that sounded like a great idea. "Want to try Blazin' Fast Burgers again? They're pretty close by and we never did get to try their food. Well, other than cookies."

The restaurant was much busier at dinnertime than it had been at lunch when Jason and Bree were there last. They were seated by the older woman who had waited on them before, and she recognized Jason and Bree immediately.

"You're the couple who moved into that house on Williams Street, right? I waited on you once before," the waitress reminded them as she handed them menus.

"Yes, that's us. We thought we were due back for another visit," Jason replied politely.

The waitress said she would be back to take their order shortly. Bree wondered if she would act as strangely toward them as she had the last time. She had hoped they would have a different server this visit, but it appeared that the woman was the only server in the restaurant. Watching her buzz from table to table, Bree observed that she spent more time than necessary at certain tables, and concluded that their waitress must be quite a gossip queen. They had quite a delay in placing their order because she was busy giggling and chatting with a table of old hens. Bree shared her observation with Jason.

"Small town service, dear," Jason replied good-naturedly. "You get a little gossip with your meal."

The waitress finally made her way back to their table to take their order. After they told her what they wanted, she asked, "So how do you like living in White Dove so far?"

"It's fine. We're doing alright," Bree answered vaguely.

"How's the house been treating you?"

Jason and Bree exchanged surprised glances. "Okay, I guess," Bree said, hesitant to reveal their paranormal problems with a stranger.

"Doesn't the story of the place bother you guys at all? I think it would bother me," the waitress asked, being intentionally ominous.

Bree frowned at her. "What story?"

They heard a bell ring from the kitchen, and the waitress quickly excused herself, promising to be back to chat in a while.

"What is with that old lady?" Jason whispered. "She acts like she's the popular girl at school trying to make the new kid feel uncomfortable."

Bree had to agree. "She's succeeding. Has she been talking to people about us I wonder? And why didn't she tell us this 'story' the first time we met?" They kept their conversation to a whisper.

"Maybe she hadn't heard about it either until she started telling people someone moved into the house. Who knows. Like I said: small town. People talk about *everything*," Jason reminded her. "You can't fart without somebody talking about it."

"You have such a way with words, Jason."

"I'm a classy guy," Jason joked.

Bree returned the discussion to the waitress' story. "So do you think the story about the house will help us figure out what's going on there?"

"It might, but it's more likely just a bunch of exaggerated details put together into a ridiculous rumor. That's usually the case," Jason said matter-of-factly, as though he was the rumor expert.

The waitress returned with their drinks and rushed off again without a word. As Bree sipped her coffee, she felt watched. She looked around discretely and found that several patrons had their eyes turned toward her and Jason. They quickly looked away when she made eye contact.

Jason seemed oblivious of the stares. "Should you be drinking coffee while you're pregnant?" He asked.

"One cup is fine." She dropped her voice to an even lower whisper. "Did you notice all those people staring at us a second ago?"

"No, but it doesn't surprise me. Our waitress has been making her rounds, and she probably has pointed us out to everyone as the new people in town who live in the old house on Williams Street." Jason smiled at Bree and added, "Or maybe they were just wondering what such a beautiful woman was doing with a guy like me."

Bree laughed at his attempt at flattery. They sipped at their coffee and critiqued the restaurant's décor, then moved on to its patrons.

"They're all so *old*!" Bree commented in a quiet whisper.

"I know!" Jason agreed. "They must all be part of the waitress' posse," he joked.

When the waitress came to their table to refill their coffee cups, she was obviously ready to chat. "I mentioned to a few people that you two had moved into that old house there, and I was told that a woman killed her husband in that house a long time ago. Had you heard that yet?" She had leaned in so close while she was talking that it made Bree lean back in her chair. Close-talkers made her uncomfortable.

"No, we hadn't heard anything about the house," Jason replied.

"Well, I heard it happened back when the house was first built," the waitress elaborated her story. "The wife caught her husband cheating on her, so she drugged him and burned him alive in his sleep. I also heard that she killed herself in the house shortly thereafter because she couldn't take the guilt. My husband says he heard the place was haunted and no one has lived there since the first owners died." She looked from Bree to Jason, and back to Bree, who was gawking at her. The waitress seemed pleased with the disgusted and surprised expressions on their faces. "Now, I don't know how much of that is true, but I thought someone should let you know that the rumor exists." Another bell rang from the kitchen. "That'll be your dinner. I'll be right back." She hurried off to the kitchen.

Jason sat forward in his chair. "Well, that left me feeling ravenous – how about you?" He asked sarcastically.

"I'm still trying to decide whether that whole conversation was really appropriate for the time and place. I'm leaning toward not." Bree realized she was scowling and had to make a conscious effort to relax her face. The waitress returned to the table.

"Here you go," the waitress said cheerfully as she placed their plates in front of them. They mumbled thank-you's and the waitress pranced off, probably looking to ruin someone else's dinner.

Bree poked at her grilled chicken, unable to recover her appetite. She forced a few bites down when Jason urged her to eat, reminding her again that she was now eating for two. Her mind mulled over the disturbing story the waitress had disclosed to them. Some of it didn't make sense in light of what Bree already knew – or thought she knew – about the house's history. People had lived in it since the first owners, as it seemed to have been passed down through the Barry family until Gregory and Elizabeth inherited it. Did Edith kill Gregory J. Barry and then commit suicide? Is that why the house was haunted? Or did the story of Elizabeth, Henry, and Gregory's love triangle become misconstrued and embellished? She supposed either could be true. She knew nothing of Edith and Gregory J. other than their part in the creation of the house and that they were probably related to Gregory D. Barry. She felt she was even farther from discovering the truth than she had been before, and she knew she would have to read more of Elizabeth's journal once she got home.

By evening's end, Jason had found his appetite and cleaned his plate while Bree needed a carry-out box for the rest of her dinner. She put it in the fridge when she got home, knowing it would probably sit there untouched until it went bad. She never liked restaurant leftovers, but
couldn't bring herself to throw out food while it was still good. Jason sat in his usual spot on the couch and turned on the television, so Bree grabbed the journal and curled up next to him.

January 8, 1896

Henry came by today while Gregory was in town. He came alone, which was strange because his wife usually acompneys him when they visit when Gregory is away. I imeedietly knew something was amiss, but I was overjoyed to see he was alone. When I greeted him and told him Gregory was out, he told me he knew that and he was here to see me. He wanted to talk about Gregory. He asked me if he had been treating me any better than he was before. I did not lie. I told him that indeed he was, but only because he was hardly speaking to me or acknoledging my egsistense. I told him I perferred it that way. I would rather be ignored than hollerd at. He was upset by my revalation, saying that a woman like me should not have to live like that. He started talking about his wife, and how he wished she were more like me. He spoke of their union as a marriage of convenience, not of love. His wife's parents had five daughters and no sons. Cecilia, his wife, is the eldest daughter, and at the time of their marriage, she was the only daughter old enough for marriage. Cecilia's mother had died in childbirth many years earlier, and her father had fallen deathly ill. He wanted to marry off Cecilia so there would be a man to take care of the farm and the rest of the girls when he passed. He had called on Henry and asked him if he would take Cecilia in marriage. Henry told me he agreed because he grately respected Cecilia's father and because he knew that Gregory would inherit their own parent's farm, so it was a good opertunity for him to obtane his own land. I shared with him how wonderful and charming Gregory had been when I met him, and how we married because we thought we loved each other. I told him that I was not so sure of that any longer, as Gregory had become a diffrent man from the one I married. I asked Henry if Gregory had been a nice young man before now, or if he had always had the potenshal to be a dredfully miserable bastard. Henry said Gregory was always quite tempermentil, but was also very good at faining grace and charm when required of him. Apparently, I had fallen in love with what he pretended to be, not who he actually was, and am suffering the consequenses of that mistake. Henry comiserated with me, as we are both in joyless, loveless marriages. He even confided in me that Cecilia seldom has relations with him, and this is why they have yet to be blessed with any children. I found it strange that he would share such intimate details about his relationship with his wife with me. Becoming emersed in the conversation and not considering propriety, I mentioned that Gregory and I had tried to conseve, but failure after failure led Gregory to become disgusted with me. I revealed that he now refuses to touch me in any way, wether it be intimately or not. I think we both realized at that moment that the conversation was highly inappropriate for a married man and a married woman to be having with each other. I appoligized for being so crude. He told me he had not ment to say some of those things, but he felt so comfortable talking with me that the words came out anyway. I felt the same way, and told him as much. Then *he made a peculiar request. He told me not to tell Gregory that he had come by. He wanted to keep it a secret. He then said that he would like to come over and talk with me again sometime, just the two of us, as he enjoyed our talk today so much. I agreed that the visit had been a lovely one, and said that I would love to get together again as well. I felt a terrible loneliness heavy my heart when I bid him farewell today. I had been able to share things with him that I haven't disgust with anyone but myself through this journal! Talking with him did wonders for my spirits and lifted some of my burdens, but it also made me fall more deeply in love with Henry. Being alone in the house with him and talking of intimate matters made me realize that my body was just as suseptable to his charms as was my heart. I tred upon dangerous ground by having such thoughts and feelings, but there is naught I can do to stop it! I know not yet when Henry will visit again, but I do so look forward to it with egarness!*

Bree read through several more passages before Henry made another "secret" visit.

January 21, 1896

Henry came by alone again today! It has been so long that I had begun to worry that he had been insinsere about his promise for another visit. Gregory was gone to the Dickson's place to help Emery fix his barn since a tree fell on it in the last ice storm. My heart lept in my chest when I saw Henry standing at the door. I brewed some coffee for him and we sat at the table and began to talk like old friends. He then pulled a flask from his shirt pocket and poured some of the contents into his coffee. When I laughed, he said it was to help take the chill off after being out in the snow. He offerred some to me, and I declined. He leaned over and poured some in my coffee anyway! I voiced my concern that Gregory would smell it upon my breath when he came home, but Henry reminded me that it wasn't likely since Gregory seldom speaks to me anymore. I told him he was probably right, but I drank little of my coffee after that.

It is not a drink of which I am particulerly fond anyway. We talked of Cecilia and her sisters, as most of them still live with Cecilia and Henry in the house Cecilia's father bilt. He complaned that it was like living in a henhouse at times and he could not wait to have them all married off. As he drank more and more of his coffee, he began to speak of more inapropriate things just as he had last time. He mentioned that he and Cecilia could hardly ever have relations, even if she had let him, because there was so little privacy in a house with so many women. He then commented that this house was so quiet and private that one could get away with anything here. I am not sure of his meaning, but I got the feeling it was crude. He said he enjoyed his time with me because it was so relaxing and peaceful compaird to his time at home. I invited him to come and visit any time he liked. He asked if things were improoving between Gregory and I, and I told him they were not. We were in a constant state of muchual disdain for each other it seemed. I said that it was not the life or marriage I would have picked for myself had I known any better. I told him how it filled me with greef to know that this unhappiness would be my life until my death. He tried to comfort me and tell me that things might not always be this way. He told me not to despare, and said that everyone can find happiness even in the direst situations. He reminded me that visiting with me was one of the things that made him happy even though he had a miserible home life. I told him that he made me happy as well. He then said that he could make me happier than I'd ever known if only he had the chance, and he grabbed me and pulled me close to him. I almost fell out of my chair when he did that. That would have been so emberressing, and it would have ruined what happend next. Henry kissed me again! Only it was a real kiss this time! Even though I could taste the whiskey on his breath, it was still more amazing then the last time we kissed, and definately more passionite than any kiss Gregory and I ever shared. When I came to my senses and pulled away from him, he looked hurt. I told him that I liked the way it felt when I kissed him, but that I knew it was wrong. He asked how it could be wrong when we both enjoyed it so much. He reminded me that we were both in loveless marriages with spouses who dispised us, no children to speak of, and the only thing that made us happy was spending time together. He had a point, but I still knew it was wrong not only in the eyes of society, but in the eyes of God. I told him this, and he argued that God would not give us such feelings if they were unholy. I know how wrong he is, but I want so badly to beleve him that I actually do a little. I even let him kiss me again because it felt so wonderful. I just keep pretending that it isn't wrong. God forgives His children for their sins, and I think He would understand that I have been driven away from Gregory and have no one else to turn to but Henry. God has seen all the wreched things Gregory has done to me, and heard him curse His name, yet he is not punished for his behavior. I should be entitled to the same liberties Gregory is given. Gregory deserves to be deseved and betrayed for all he has put me through. Wrong or not, Gregory deserves this. Henry left shortly after our kisses, anxsous to be gone before Gregory returned home. I asked him to return as soon as he could for another private talk. I think together Henry and I will bring the punishment to Gregory that God will not.

Bree was surprised at the sudden change in tone of that last journal entry. She told Jason about it.

"In the course of one entry, she has convinced herself that cheating on Gregory is the right thing to do," she recounted. "At first she said she knew it was wrong, but then justified it by saying that Gregory is a horrible man who deserves to be punished by her and Henry."

Jason raised an eyebrow. "Maybe that story the waitress told us tonight isn't as far off as we thought. Maybe Elizabeth and Henry took that 'punishment' too far," Jason suggested.

"You think they murdered Gregory? I don't know. I don't think that's what she meant." Bree thought about it for a moment. "Then again, she did go from believing cheating was wrong to believing it was basically necessary in a very short time. It's almost like her affair with Henry is turning her into a psycho."

"Love will do that to people," Jason commented.

"So will manipulation," Bree added, referring to Henry's behavior. She returned to the journal.

January 22, 1896

After I wrote my last entry, I began to wonder if I really meant that Gregory deserved to be punished because God was not doing it. I realized I was just upset that I felt as though I was the one who was being punished for Gregory's abominible behavior. Why should I be so miserible when I had done nothing wrong? I had begun to doubt the resolve I had last night when I wrote in this journal, until today. Today Gregory reminded me just how severely he needs to be punished. I made him a dilisous, hearty stew for dinner, and he became inraged when I served it to him. He asked if that was all I made, and when I told him yes, he slapped my face with all his might. When I asked what was wrong with it, he grew even angrier and slapped me again. He bellowed that my stew was not fit to sustane a field mouse and demanded I make him something heartier. Through my tears, I asked him what I should make, and he shoved me to the floor and kicked my side with his boot. He said I should know by now what to make a man for dinner. He kicked me again and called me a useless wench. He sat down and said he would suffer through the stew because I was to incompitent to make a decent dinner anyway. When I started to get up, he dumped some of his stew on the floor in front of me and told me to stay on the ground and eat there like the dirty mongrel I was. He said if I cried he would beat me and give me a reason to cry. After that, I was reminded why he needed to be punished. And what grater punishment is there than deseet and betrayal by your own spouse? Why should I remain faithful and loyal to such a beast of a man? God must understand. How could he not?

Bree soon came upon the entry recounting the next visit from Henry.

February 4, 1896

    Henry and I have reached a point of no return. I feel both ashamed and invigerated. Henry made his private visit today while Gregory was delivering firewood to old Mr. Ferguson. Henry insisted upon brewing the coffee himself this time when he came into the house, and I allowed him to. He brought me my cup instead of allowing me to pour it myself, and when I tasted it, I quickly discovered he had added whiskey to it again! He then wagerd me that I could not drink it all. I feel foolish for it now, but I exepted his wager. By the time I reached the bottom of the mug, I felt very silly indeed! He then poured me another cup, with the whiskey, and insisted I drink that intire mug as well. So I did. I could not think clearly by the end of that mug of whiskey coffee, but I felt happier than I had in a very long time. Henry must have been feeling the same way, as he kept laughing and saying the silliest things! I do not remember much of what we said to each other, but suddenly I remember kissing Henry. I do remember him asking how much longer Gregory would be out, and I think I told him Gregory would be gone for at least another hour. He then made a strange request to see the rest of the house, to see what I had done to change it since his mother died. I thought it odd, but I now know he only made the request so he could lure me to the bedrooms. The next thing I remember, we were in Lenore's old room, and he was removing my undergarments, laughing about how Lenore must be so ashamed of him, her least favrite child. I know we made love then, though I remember little of it. After an undetermined amount of time, I woke up alone in my bed, fully dressed. I felt less inebriated than previously, but I was still quite dizzy. I looked about the house, but I found I was alone. I went to the washroom to clean away some of my shame. I felt ashamed of what I had done, yet I was not sorry it had happened. I was not so much ashamed of the deed as I was of the manner in which it was carried out. I then returned to bed and fained illness when Gregory returned home. His only words to me when I told him I felt ill were "not as sick as you make me." I just smiled at him, thinking of what I had done to thouroughly disrespect him earlier.

Bree felt a little queasy herself after reading that passage. Elizabeth wasn't only disrespecting Gregory, but she was completely disrespecting herself. How could she not see that Henry was not a good man either? Bree hoped it turned out that Elizabeth did murder Gregory. And Henry.

Chapter 9

The next day, Bree called Karen to share with her the story the waitress had told them and what she had read in the journal.

"That's a pretty incredible story," Karen commented after Bree relayed the waitress' story. "It's probably not entirely true, but there may be *some* truth to it. I wonder if your local library would have any old records or newspapers that might help you find out if the story was true."

"I wouldn't know where to begin. If it came down to it, I'd have to hire someone to do the research. I have no experience in anything like that," Bree said.

"Speaking of research, did you find out anything more from the diary?"

Bree read a couple of the more interesting passages to her mother. When she finished narrating the last entry she had read, she said, "So apparently evil runs in the family."

"I'd say!" Karen agreed. "Gregory's an abusive asshole and Henry is a sleazy manipulator. Elizabeth should've seen a huge red flag when he told her he only married Cecilia so he could have his own land." Karen paused for a moment and then added, "But I guess it may have been more acceptable back then to marry under those terms."

"Even so, he's still sleazy," Bree stated. "I hope Elizabeth figures it out soon in the journal because I'm tired of reading about how wonderful and charming she thinks he is, and how she is sure she's in love with him."

"To her he probably does seem wonderful compared to Gregory. Gregory ignores and abuses her, while Henry actively pursues her and makes her feel important and desirable. She probably ignores all the warning signs with Henry because Gregory is so terrible to her that she'll cling to any kind of positive attention, even if it isn't genuine," Karen deduced.

"Gregory gave her a complex, and Henry uses her insecurities to manipulate her. What a couple of swell guys. I hope Elizabeth did kill Gregory. I may never know if she did, but I'm going to believe she did unless I find out otherwise. It just makes me feel better. Henry deserved to meet an untimely end as well! I wonder if the entire Barry family was that bad." Bree was surprised at how upset she could get over something that happened more than a hundred years ago to someone she didn't even know. Although, as she plunged further into her diary, Bree was beginning to feel an inexplicable bond with Elizabeth.

"Don't get so worked up over inconsequential things," Karen chastised. "Stress is not good for someone in your condition. Just focus on keeping that baby healthy and finding out what's going on in your house so we can get rid of it."

"Yes, mother," Bree replied sarcastically. She got off the phone and returned to reading the diary.

February 5, 1896

I am feeling much less confident in my choices today than I felt yesterday. Without Henry here to reassure me, I am questioning whether I have done what is right for me. Will God forgive me for what I have done? If it happens again, will He forgive me for that? I am only human, and I have needs and desires like any other woman. Why should I be denied my most basic need for love and exeptance because I made an ill thought out promise to be faithful to Gregory? Had he not hidden his true nature from me and deseved me in the beginning, then I would not have even married him! I promised to love the Gregory I once knew, and I do still love that Gregory, but he is dead! All I have now is the biligerant counterpart to that old Gregory, and I do not want it! I should not be expected to keep a promise that was based on a lie. I was deseved! I was tricked! Does God see that? I hope He does, for I do not know if punishing Gregory and fullfilling my need for love are worth eternal damnation. I hope Henry comes by again soon to reassure me that my desicions have been the right ones. I need to talk to him about other things as well. I do not know what transpired after we made love yesterday, as I recall nothing between the time we made love and the time I woke up alone. I also want to know where our relationship stands. I know not if he plans to make love to me again, but I would assume he does. I just have so many questions that only he can answer! He must come by soon!

As Bree read through the next several passages, she came across more accounts of Gregory's violent abuse and Elizabeth's yearning for Henry. Henry continued to avoid her for over three weeks after their illicit encounter. Elizabeth even wrote that one day he came to help Gregory with something, and he completely ignored her the whole time he was there. Elizabeth began to write about feelings of rejection and of being used. She was confused about where she stood with Henry. Finally, Henry made a secret visit in early March.

March 2, 1896

All of my previous worries and concerns were for naught! Henry made a speshal visit to see me today while Gregory was in town. I chastized him thouroughly for not coming to see me sooner and for ignoring me intirely when he came to help Gregory down some trees out back. He explaned that he could not get away from the house because Cecilia and her sisters kept finding things for him to fix around the house in addition to his usual chores. As for ignoring me when he was here, he said he did not want to do

103

anything to rouse Gregory's suspishions, as he had asked Henry a few strange questions that day. He said Gregory asked him if he had ever noticed any unfimilar carrages or people around our house, and if I had said anything strange to Cecilia lately. He said he denied seeing anything or hearing that I'd been speaking to Cecilia. He said Gregory did not actually admit it, but Henry thinks he may suspect something is going on with me. He asked if Gregory has voiced his conserns to me. I assured him he had not, but I admitted that I felt it served him right to have those worries. I asked Henry if he would still visit me, as I did not want this to be his last visit. He promised he was not going to stop seeing me. He then confided that he had a difficult time staying away for as long as he had last time because he wanted very badly to make love to me again. I felt my cheeks warm when he said this and know I blushed. I asked him what had happend after our lovemaking last time, and he laughed. He said he had not realized I was that inibriated. Apparently I fell asleep next to him, so he dressed me as best he could and put me in my own bed and left me alone to sleep off the drink. I asked him if I had made a fool of myself, and he assured me I had not. He was then very forward and told me he wanted to make love to me again today, so we did. It felt so wonderful to be in his loving embrace. Henry is a much more tender and giving lover than Gregory ever could be. After Henry left today, I felt much better about our union than I had the first time it had happend. Nothing about it felt dirty or shameful this time. We were just to people, deeply in love, sharing our love for one another. I cannot wait to see him again!

"Can't you see you're just a booty call?" Bree cried out loud in exasperation. She continued talking to the diary in the empty house. "I know Gregory is a complete asshole, but have some self-respect!"

A loud bang resonated through the empty house, startling Bree. It sounded like a door upstairs had slammed shut.

"Hello?" Bree called out stupidly. She knew Jason wasn't home, so if someone was upstairs, they were either uninvited intruders or not of this world. Either way, they weren't likely to respond to "hello."

Bree closed the journal and quietly went to the hallway. She saw and heard nothing, so she continued on to the bottom of the stairway. There was no one at the top of the stairs or in the hallway upstairs. She climbed the stairs, realizing halfway to the top that she had nothing she could use as a weapon. She pushed on, knowing that the source of the noise wasn't likely to be something against which a weapon would be useful anyway. At the top of the stairs she saw that the only door that was shut was the guest bedroom where her mother had stayed. She knew that she and Karen had left that door open yesterday after Karen left, and Bree hadn't touched it since. Images of pale creatures crawling from the walls flashed through her mind as she reached for the door handle. It was cold. She quickly pulled her hand away, and her fingers stuck to it slightly the way they do when touched to a frosty metal pole on a winter day. When she looked more closely at it, the handle was covered in a thin layer of frost. She felt the door itself, and it too felt cold.

Feeling a strong rush of anger and determination, Bree confronted the spirit in the house. "I know this is your doing!" she shouted, looking around. "I'm coming in! This is *my* house!" She grabbed the handle again and tried to turn it. It didn't budge. She tried to wiggle it back and forth, but it still would not come free. Bree became infuriated and, without thinking, shouted, "Open this damn door right now or I'll burn this God-damned house down!" She heard the sound of ice cracking and the door handle jerked free. Stunned that her threat had not gone unheeded, she pushed the door open slowly. A blast of chilled air rushed across her face, but the air temperature seemed to quickly return to normal as she entered the room.

The guest bedroom was empty. Nothing seemed out of place until Bree noticed that the bedding was slightly rumpled, as if someone had sat on the bed. She quickly smoothed the comforter and walked back out of the room. She contemplated whether to shut the door or leave it open, and she finally decided to leave it open because it seemed to be the opposite of what the entity wanted. She returned to the living room with a smile on her face. *It's on now, asshole*, she taunted silently.

When Jason came home that night, Bree told him about the guest bedroom.

"It appears to respond to threats," she concluded.

"Threats from you," Jason pointed out. "You're scary when you're mad!" He laughed, making light of her discovery.

"Be serious for a minute, please. We could be on to something here."

"Like what?" Jason asked, his jovial demeanor diminishing.

"If something weird starts happening, we might be able to stop it by being firm and threatening. It's just a hypothesis, of course, and might not work in all situations. I think it's worth a shot, though. It worked today."

"Sounds good. Whatever we can try, right?" Jason replied.

While they watched the paranormal investigation show that evening, Bree took notes on what equipment they used, what questions they asked, and anything important they discussed about paranormal activity. By the end of the show, she was already planning out the investigation she and Jason would conduct over the weekend. She thought their best bet would be to focus their efforts in areas of the house where she had experienced the most extreme paranormal activity. They would investigate the whole house, but they would spend more time in the guest bedroom and in the living room near the piano. As for equipment, she was limited to the digital voice recorder. She wanted to have the lightning lamp on as well while they investigated, just because she thought the entity might be able to draw some energy from it to help it manifest and interact with them. She also wanted to use it because that lamp always seemed to be on whenever something paranormal happened. After watching the show and developing her strategy, she was feeling optimistic about the weekend.

Bree had a strange dream that night. In the dream, she was hovering above herself in the bedroom, and immediately recognized that it was the night Jason had said those awful things to her in his sleep. She couldn't hear what was being said - everything was silent to her. She saw herself get out of bed and followed as the "other" her stomped to the bathroom and slammed the door. The "other" Bree locked the door and cried on the bathroom floor. Suddenly, Bree floated through the wall and into the hallway, down the stairs, and into the living room where she saw a man sitting still on the piano bench. She realized it was daytime now, as sunshine was streaming in through the curtains. The man was dressed in dirty brown pants, worn-out black boots, and a white, long-sleeved, button-front shirt. He had long brown hair that was pulled back in a disheveled ponytail. He had no facial hair that Bree could see. She recognized him as the glowing green pianist she had seen the night she had slept in the bathroom – the night she was reliving right now. This time, however, she could tell that it was definitely a man, and he looked very much alive.

The man at the piano suddenly stood, looking toward the stairs. When he turned his head, Bree could see that his eyes were reddened, as though he had been crying, and he had a look of deep sadness on his face. She floated above him as he ascended the stairs and stopped outside the bathroom door. Bree felt panicked because she knew the "other" Bree was in the bathroom crying and was afraid the strange man would hurt her. She then remembered that the door was locked and felt a little relieved. The man stood outside the door for several minutes, standing quietly with his head bowed. He then reached for the door and opened it, as though the door had never been locked. Bree floated through the wall to get into the bathroom, and was shocked when she found it was not the "other" Bree in there. Instead, a young woman in a pale blue, old-fashioned dress with long sleeves and a long skirt was sitting where the "other" Bree had been, and she was also crying. She had beautiful long, blond, curly hair that shielded her face from Bree's sight.

"Elizabeth," the man said, still standing in the doorway. His voice startled Bree, as the dream had been silent up to that point. She understood now that the woman was Elizabeth Barry and the man was either Gregory or Henry.

The crying woman ignored the man in the doorway. He lingered only a moment longer, then walked away, disappearing into the hallway. Bree did not follow him, but stayed with Elizabeth, who continued to cry on the floor in the bathroom. Elizabeth stopped sobbing and looked up, directly at Bree.

"You know little yet," she said to Bree. "The worst is yet to come." Elizabeth began sobbing again, and Bree was suddenly hurled up through the ceiling. She woke with a gasp.

She shared her dream with Jason at the breakfast table.

"That might explain why the door was unlocked and open when you woke up that morning," Jason conjectured.

Bree shuddered. "I don't like the idea that someone or something opened the locked door and stood in the doorway while I was sleeping. I don't even care if it could see me or not. It's just creepy!"

"If something like that happened, where an entity was just going through the motions from some past event, that would be considered a residual haunting, right?" Jason asked. After Bree nodded, he added, "Can you have a residual *and* intelligent haunting in the same house?"

"It seems so. A lot of the places the ghost chasers investigate have claims of both intelligent and residual activity. I just wish I could know for sure whether what I saw in my dream had actually happened in the past or if my mind just created it because I've been reading Elizabeth's diary a lot lately." Bree's instincts told her that her dream wasn't a creation of her own.

"It's kind of scary that Elizabeth warned you things would get worse," Jason said as he stood up to clear his dishes from the table.

"I don't know if it is actually scary or not. She could've been talking about her diary entries, telling me that things got worse in her life after the date of the entry I last read," Bree offered.

"Or she could've been warning you that the activity in the house is going to get worse," Jason contended.

"Or she could've meant nothing by it because she was just a creation of my mind." She didn't think that was the case, though.

Jason sighed from the kitchen. "Regardless of what she meant or didn't mean, I want you to be careful. Remember that you've got more than just yourself to worry about now."

"Trust me," Bree shot back, "I haven't *forgotten* that I'm pregnant."

After Jason left for work, she found herself thinking about her baby. She knew she was pregnant because the nurse and doctor had told her so, but she didn't feel pregnant. Her body hadn't changed outwardly, and she hadn't experienced any morning sickness or other unpleasant pregnancy symptoms other than occasional moodiness. It was hard for her to believe that in just a little over eight months she would be bringing home a new addition to the family. Now that she'd had time to get over the initial shock and had gotten used to the idea of having a baby, she was excited about it. She still worried about whether the house would be entity-free by the time the baby came, but she was happy nonetheless. Her heart was filled with a warm feeling every time she thought about the tiny person growing inside her. She didn't know what gender the baby was yet, but she had already begun to think of it as a "he." She didn't know if it was motherly instincts or just wishful thinking. Jason said he didn't care if it was a boy or girl, but Bree hoped for a boy. Regardless of the gender, she knew that little baby would be well-loved and protected by her and Jason.

She began to consider what kind of a father Jason would be. His patience was great, almost to the point of being irritating to Bree. Would that last with a child? She hoped so, because her patience left a lot to be desired. She knew he would be a very loving and accepting father because it was in his nature to be that type of man. What she didn't know was whether he would be the type of father who was deeply involved in the parenting or the type of father who left mom to do most of the work. She hoped he would interact with the baby just as much as she would. And she hoped he would change diapers once in a while, too.

The phone rang and interrupted her thoughts. It was the receptionist from Dr. O'Brien's office, saying that Dr. O'Brien wanted to know if Bree had come to a decision regarding her recent visit. Bree explained that she had decided to take no further action at this point, but she thanked the receptionist for contacting her. When the call was concluded, Bree reached for Elizabeth's diary.

March 3, 1896

Gregory was in a very strange mood today. I caught him staring at me a number of times, though I do not know for what reason! I hope he has not figured out that Henry and I are in love and meet secretly while he is away. When Henry told me yesterday that Gregory had been asking him strange questions and thinks that Gregory suspects my infidelity, I was at first a little worried. However, there is a part of me that wants him to know because it would be humiliating and shameful for him to know that he had been betrayed, disrespected, and deseved by his own wife and brother. On the other hand, there is a part of me that doesn't want him to find out because I know not what he will do. He is of a violent nature, and I fear the beating he might deal me if he knew I was unfaithful. Also, I would likely never see Henry again, which is my gratest fear. I know not how I would go on without Henry in my life. He is what gives my life meaning and purpose now. He saved me from the wreched lonliness and heartache that Gregory has caused me. I do not know what is ment by this strange behavior from Gregory today, but I hope it does not mean that he thinks I am overdue for a beating. O I should not have to live like this!

March 5, 1896

Gregory's strange behavior persists. Yesterday he tried having a conversation with me! I was so stunned and afraid I would say something to displease him that I only nodded and gave brief, sucsinct answers. When I failed to provide the nesissary dialog to maintain a normal conversation, Gregory became very gloomy. He looked at me with disappointment in his eyes, which left me very confused. For what reason should he be sad? For so long he has ignored me or treated me unkindly, never saying or doing

110

anything plesent for me. He has refused to touch me for many months. How can he expect me to suddenly begin being his companien again after all he has put me through? As if this behavior was not strange enough, he tried to inishiate relations last night! I pretended I had already fallen asleep, so he let me be. I do not understand why his demeaner has changed so drasticly! What am I to do? I cannot lay with two different men! I have already crossed moral bounds and do not wish to dive any deeper into imorality. I cannot give up my Henry, but how long can I deny my own husband what is rightfully his? I never thought I would say this, but I wish Gregory would begin dispising me again as I do him. He has been outside most of the day today, so I know not how he is behaving yet on this day. I think I may retire to my bed shortly after dinner tonight, faining a terrible headache to deter him from trying to lay with me again.

In the subsequent passages, Gregory continued to try to rekindle his relationship with Elizabeth, and Elizabeth continued to resist because of her current relationship with Henry and because of Gregory's past behavior. Bree wasn't sure how to feel about Elizabeth's situation. She knew that Elizabeth shouldn't have gotten involved with Henry in the first place, but now that she had, what was the right course for her to take? She tried to put herself in Elizabeth's shoes, but found it difficult as she had never been in an abusive relationship or been the kind of woman who was unfaithful. She felt for Elizabeth, but she also disapproved of her actions.

As for Gregory, his behavior puzzled Bree as much as it did Elizabeth. Was he affected by some type of mental illness, such as a mood disorder? Bree wondered if he had something like an extreme form of seasonal affective disorder since he was horrible all fall and winter but seemed to be recovering as spring approached. She was no psychologist, but she felt that mental illness was the only explanation for such confusing and contradictory behavior. Of course, at that time mental illness was even less well-understood than it is today and Gregory might have lived the rest of his life without even understanding why he felt the way he felt and did the things he did. *Then again,* thought Bree, *maybe he's still an asshole but is pretending to be nice again because he can see that he's losing his wife and doesn't want to end up in a situation that would bring shame to his name.* If that was the case, he was too late. Bree then wondered if it was possible that he already knew about Henry and Elizabeth, and his present actions were simply to try to end the affair quietly before it could become public knowledge. She wished Gregory had left a diary as well!

She continued reading and finally came to something interesting.

March 30, 1896

Gregory confronted me today about my lack of interest in him. He wanted to know who had stolen my attention from him. I assured him that he still held my attention and interest, but that it was difficult for me to get over the way our relationship had been all winter long. He admitted that it had been a tough winter, but he did not appoligize for his cruelty toward me in these past months. He instead said that he was feeling like his old self again and that I should forget the things that happend because they were not going to happen again. I told him I could never forget his cruel words and hard blows, and that I still needed more time for my heart to heal. He then asked me why I seemed to be so fond of Henry. I was taken aback by his question and fear my face may have reddened. I told him I knew not his meaning. He said that he had noticed I watched Henry with a great deal of interest whenever he was around the house, and that he knows that at least on one accashon Henry had come to the house when he was away. I should have vehemantly denied his accusashions, but the question that escaped my mouth first was where he had heard such a thing. He told me that the night I had been ill in bed (which was the day that Henry and I had first made love and I had to sleep off the drink) he had stopped to Henry's house on his way home and Cecilia had told him Henry told her that he had gone to see Gregory at our house. He said he passed

Henry on his way to the house and Henry told him he had stopped by for a moment, but had left imeedietly since Gregory was not home. Gregory then told me that when he came home, he noticed that coffee had been made as he could smell it, and he saw that two mugs had been dirtied. He asked if I could explain why he should find these things only coinsidental. I had to think quickly, so I gave the excuse that I was feeling ill that day and had tried some coffee, but when that failed to make me feel better I used a second mug to make myself some tea. I acted as though I was thouroughly offended at his insinuashions. He told me he worries because he knows things were bad between us for a while, but he still loved me and did not want someone else to steel my heart from him. I agreed that things were very bad between us, but I lied to him and told him that my heart could never be stolen from him. I reminded him, however, that my heart needed time to heal after what we had gone through, so I hope that will be sufficcent to end his advances for a while until I figure out what I am to do. I hope he beleved what I said to him today. Henry and I will have to be exeedingly careful from now on.

Bree couldn't believe Elizabeth planned to keep the affair going even after Gregory voiced his suspicions. She was going to get caught – it was just a matter of time! As Bree read on, she expected to see "Gregory caught us today!" However, after reading through the entire month of April, she still hadn't come upon those words. Elizabeth continued to fool around with Henry and reject Gregory's attempts at seduction. Bree was beginning to feel badly for Gregory despite his past behavior, until he started turning into Mr. Hyde again toward the end of April. Elizabeth's journal entries described the onset of his mood change as rather sudden.

April 29, 1896

Gregory's foul mood persists. I think he has once again become the man I hated so this past winter. I somewhat welcome this change, however, as it makes it easier for me to continue loving Henry. Gregory has completely abondend his attempts to lay with me, which has brought me much releef. I no longer have to make excuses. His demeaner is a bit different, however, than it was over the winter. He is still distant and foul-mouthed, but where he was full of anger and venom before he is now more sorrowful and loathing. Perhaps it is different because my rejection has caused his foul mood this time, whereas last time there were many things contributing to it. I do not know for certain, though. I feel a great deal of gilt for causing his unhappiness to return, as there is still a small part of me that loves him, but I think things are better this way. If he resumes his indiffrence toward me, then he will be less likely to try to catch me being unfaithful. It is easier to be with Henry when I know Gregory does not care about me.

Bree knew Elizabeth meant two things when she said "easier" in that last line. It was easier for her emotionally because she felt less guilty about it, and it was easier for them to meet because Gregory wasn't paying much attention to what she was doing. In Bree's opinion, the entire situation had turned Elizabeth into someone no better than Gregory or Henry. It made her sad to realize that, as she had sympathized with Elizabeth since the beginning of the journal and had developed a fondness for her. She was being completely poisoned by her relationships.

Within the next few entries, Bree finally found the passage that promised to answer some of her questions.

May 6, 1896

I have been so completely foolish! This cannot have happend! I have not menstrated this month, and I was ill suddenly once yesterday and again this morning! I know what all of this means, but I know not why! I thought I was barren after Gregory and I failed to conseve, but now I fear I am with child! O God, what do I do now? I have not lain with Gregory in many many months, and it will be obvious to him that it is not his child! Why

114

did I not have relations with him when he still wanted me? At least then there would have been the possibility that the child was his. I would try to seduce him now so as he would think the child his when my belly begins to round, but I know he will have nothing to do with me. And what of Henry? How do I tell him that he has fathered a bastard child? O what have I done! I fear Gregory already suspects something is amiss. After I was ill this morning, I knew what was wrong with me and was overcome by tears. Gregory came to the door, but I was too ashamed to even respond when he called my name. I know he watched me cry on the floor for a while before walking away, but I had no control over myself. I could not stop crying or even stand for almost one hour. He has said nothing more to me today, but he has given me several curious glances through out the day. If I cannot maintane my composure, he will be asking questions of me before I am ready to answer them. But when will I ever be ready to answer them? How will I be able to answer them? I wish I were dead! I cannot face this!

After reading the entry, Bree's forehead felt tight, and she realized she'd had her eyebrows raised and her eyes widened as she read. The baby Elizabeth gave up for adoption was Henry's baby, and the scene she had witnessed in her dream had really happened. She now knew something else as well: the man at the piano definitely was Gregory, in both her dream and the night she woke to music.

Chapter 10

Since Gregory was the glowing green pianist she had seen the night she slept in the bathroom, he was also probably the reason the bathroom door had been unlocked and opened sometime before the morning. Bree was confident that she now knew who haunted her house. She'd suspected it was Gregory before, but she was certain now.

She set aside Elizabeth's diary and began writing EVP questions to ask Gregory during her and Jason's paranormal investigation. When she was finished, she read the list over:

Is your name Gregory? Why do you remain in this house? Do you know you are dead? Did you die in this house? How did you die? Is there something you've been trying to tell me? Did you know Elizabeth had an affair? Did you know Henry impregnated her? Why did you treat Elizabeth so badly? Did she die in this house? Why did your mother not like Elizabeth? Why do you only show yourself to me and my mother, but not to Jason? Is the piano in the house special to you? Was it yours? What did you want me to find in the attic? Is it something in Elizabeth's diary? Do you just want me to know what happened to you? Why do you always appear to be on fire or burned? Are you the only spirit in this house?

After reviewing her list, Bree was somewhat surprised to see how much she still didn't know. She had felt like she'd figured out so much by the time she finished the May 6th diary entry that she couldn't believe she still had this many unanswered questions. Would Gregory answer them for her? She knew he was able to speak, manifest in different forms, and manipulate objects, but she didn't know if he would cooperate when she asked him to do these things for her. He had interacted with her that night at the piano, but it was brief and his answer was unclear. She added *"What did you mean when you said my blood keeps you here?"* to her list of questions.

When Jason came home from work later that day, he had a surprise for her. It was a video camera that had night vision capabilities.

"Where did you get this?" Bree asked, excitedly looking it over.

"I put the word out at work that I needed a night vision video camera because something was emptying our birdfeeder every night and we wanted to find out what it was. I knew you'd like to have one of these for our ghost hunt this weekend, but I couldn't tell everybody I needed it for that." Jason was obviously proud of his treachery.

Bree interrupted him before he could continue. "We don't even have a birdfeeder."

"Nobody needs to know that. Anyway, Howard from the front office does a lot of hunting and has a lot of hunting related gadgets, and he said I could use his camera he puts up at his bait pile. Pretty nice camera, isn't it?"

"Why doesn't he just use one of those motion sensor cameras that just take a picture?" Bree wondered.

"Because he's Howard and he has to have the best of the best of everything," Jason replied simply.

"Ah, one of *those* people," Bree said, wrinkling her nose in disgust.

"Hey, his frivolousness means we have a great camera for this weekend, so don't turn your nose up too high," Jason scolded.

"Ok, ok. Do you know how to use it?"

"He showed me the basics on it. So when do you want to do this investigation?" He said "investigation" as though he wasn't comfortable using the word. "Ghost hunt" sounded much better coming from his mouth.

"We could either do it tonight or tomorrow night. If it's all the same to you, I was hoping for tonight, but we can wait until tomorrow if you're feeling tired tonight. I'm just excited to see what will happen."

"*If* anything happens," he corrected. "Don't be too disappointed if nothing does happen. Our ghost doesn't seem to perform when I'm around."

"You should be thankful for that. Could we investigate tonight, then?" Bree prodded.

"Yeah, that's fine. Now go make me some dinner, woman!" Jason demanded jokingly.

Bree narrowed her eyes at him. "You're lucky I love you so much," she warned, roughly bumping his shoulder with hers as she passed him to get into the kitchen.

After dinner, Bree watched a couple of the recorded "ghost chasers" shows to get her into the ghost hunting mindset. By the time it was dark outside, she was ready to get started. They had a difficult time deciding where to set up the camera, but finally settled on placing it on a shelf that overlooked the living room and the piano. Bree fetched her digital voice recorder from upstairs while Jason got the lightning lamp off the piano.

"Well," said Jason, with the lightning lamp tucked under his arm, "shall we go 'lights out?'"

"Yes sir," Bree affirmed. She quickly switched on both the voice recorder and the video camera before shutting off the standing lamp in the corner of the living room, which was the only light on in the house.

Jason clicked on his flashlight and pointed it toward his chin, illuminating his face. "Where do you want to begin?" He smiled a creepy smile, stretching his mouth wide and bulging his eyes.

Bree went to him and took the flashlight from him. She had hoped he would be more serious about the investigation. "Let's start in the basement and work our way up."

The basement was basically no more than a huge storage room. They kept boxes in the basement full of things that probably should've been thrown out, but neither of them had had the heart to do it. Instead, these things, such as graduation gowns and clothes that didn't fit anymore, sat in their boxes waiting to get moldy and mildewy enough to be deemed garbage. A large freezer also occupied the basement, but it was mostly empty. Bree only used it when Jason had a successful deer season, and that hadn't happened this past year. Several old lawn chairs were leaned against the back wall, and Jason unfolded two of them and placed them in the middle of the large, mostly empty basement for him and Bree.

Bree sat down next to Jason and shut off the flashlight. The instant darkness was overwhelming for a moment, and seemed to envelop her like a huge black amoeba. It reminded her of the darkness she experienced when she took a cave tour in the South and the guide shut off his light deep in the cave. Her eyes slowly began to adjust, and she could make out the outline of Jason's head and shoulders.

"So what do we do now?" Jason whispered, startling Bree.

"We ask questions," she responded. She checked her digital voice recorder and saw that the red light was on, indicating that it was recording. Her list of EVP questions had been left upstairs in the living room, so she decided to wing it until they moved their investigation upstairs.

"Who are you?" Jason asked first.

Bree waited a moment before asking, "Is your name Gregory?"

"Why are you here?" Jason followed.

"Are you the man I've been seeing around the house, or are there others?" Bree waited for Jason to take his turn at a question, but he remained silent. She continued, "Do you have some attachment to the piano that was down here?"

Jason chimed in again. "Why don't you ever show yourself to me? Why do you only appear to Bree and Karen?" Before Bree could ask a question, he added, "Are you intimidated by other men?"

They continued their questions for the next fifteen minutes, and then decided to sit quietly and listen. Bree plugged in the lightning lamp at that point, hoping to energize the basement. After about ten minutes of silence, they heard a bump overhead coming from the living room or kitchen.

"What was that?" Jason wondered aloud and began to rise from his seat, grabbing the flashlight.

"I don't know. Let's go see." Bree unplugged the lamp and followed Jason upstairs with it.

They searched the kitchen and living room but found nothing out of place. Bree set up the lamp on the kitchen table and sat down to begin their investigation of the kitchen area where she had encountered the cupboard dweller. She checked her recorder to make sure it was still on and began asking questions.

"Why did you crawl out of the cupboards in here?"

Jason nudged Bree. "Should I ask some of the same questions I asked in the basement, or just assume that it already heard me when I asked them the first time?" He whispered.

"You can repeat your questions as often as you want. I don't know any better than you whether it heard us in the basement or not."

Jason nodded and began asking the same set of questions he had used earlier. Bree had picked up her question sheet from the coffee table when they were investigating the source of the "bump" sound, so she began to ask those questions.

A sharp gasp suddenly escaped Jason and he bolted up out of his seat. His gaze was directed behind Bree in the living room.

"I just saw a shadow appear in the middle of the living room and then in an instant it looked like it was sucked down through the floor!" He exclaimed excitedly. He turned on the flashlight and hurried into the living room. Bree got up and followed him. The beam from the flashlight darted all about the room, but Jason and Bree saw nothing unusual. "It was right here," Jason pointed the flashlight beam at the floor two feet in front of him. "It just suddenly appeared – a solid black mass in the shape of a person – and within a fraction of a second it just – woosh!" Jason indicated the movement the apparition had made by holding his hands up in the air and then quickly letting them fall down. "It looked like it was sucked into the floor!"

Jason's excitement was contagious. Bree felt energized and hoped to have more strange things happen. She was ecstatic that Jason finally got to see something.

"I hope the camera caught that!" He said as they both looked up at the video camera. The camera seemed to be pointing right at them, so Bree thought it was a good possibility that they caught the occurrence on film.

"Me too! Let's move our investigation to the living room," Bree suggested. She had Jason place the lamp on top of the piano again and turn it on. They sat on the couch and resumed their questioning.

"Why do you remain here? Are you waiting for someone to right the wrongs that were done to you?" Bree inquired.

"What wrongs were done to you, Gregory?" Jason used Gregory's name for the first time since the investigation began.

"Elizabeth's diary says you also wronged others – especially her. Do you want to right those wrongs as well?"

The tiny lightning bolts in the lamp suddenly became concentrated to one area on the glass.

"Are you seeing that?" Bree pointed to the lamp.

"That's weird…it's like somebody has their hand on the glass." Jason watched the lamp in awe. "I wonder if it's somehow drawing energy from it."

The concentrated beam of electricity began to slowly migrate around the glass, as though the invisible "hand" was sliding around on the glass bulb. Jason and Bree were mesmerized by it, but they tried to keep their eyes and ears open for anything that might be happening elsewhere in the house.

As suddenly as the lightning lamp had begun its strange activity, it stopped. The electricity spread out to the rest of the bulb again and the lamp resumed its normal functioning. They waited for something else to happen, but the house was quiet.

"Do you think he was absorbing energy from the lamp?" Jason asked, his eyes still keeping watch over the lamp.

"I hope so. If that's the case, then maybe we'll see and hear some strange things soon," Bree responded with an eager tone. "I have to go to the bathroom, so I'm going to go take care of that before things get too exciting. Be right back." Bree hurried to the first floor bathroom. She hardly used that bathroom because it was quite small and cramped, and her knees were only about four inches from the cupboard door under the sink when she sat on the toilet. She could almost wash her hands and use the toilet at the same time. Tonight she was in a hurry, though, and didn't want to waste time by running up the stairs to use the good bathroom. She didn't even bother to close the bathroom door.

As she washed her hands after using the toilet, the mirrored door on the medicine cabinet in front of her suddenly swung open about six inches. Startled, Bree looked up from her hands and gave a short yelp when she saw the reflection of a ragged man in the mirror. The mirror had swung open just enough to give her a full view of the bathroom doorway to her right, and she saw Gregory in its reflection. He was in his decomposing form, leaning against the doorjamb. She turned her head quickly, but found he was no longer there. She looked back at the mirror and saw the doorway was vacant in the reflection as well.

A relieved sigh escaped her lips as she reached up to close the medicine cabinet. As her own face came back into view of the mirror, she let out another startled gasp and dodged to her right. In the mirror, she had seen the reflection of Gregory's rotted face in profile only a few inches from the side of her face, as if he were getting ready to whisper a secret in her ear. After dodging away, she could see that no one was next to her. There wasn't even room for anyone to be standing next to her.

"Jason! Come here!" She called out the door.

Within seconds, Jason was next to her. "What's wrong? What happened?"

She told him what she had just experienced. She was pleased that he had appeared to her, relatively speaking, but she was also disappointed because the experience wasn't captured on their equipment. She wished Jason had been there to experience it with her and that she'd had a chance to attempt communication.

"I'm no expert, but I get the feeling he's just getting started. We've still got a long night ahead of us," Jason pointed out.

When they returned to the living room, Jason noticed the fall on the piano had been raised. "I know it wasn't like that a few minutes ago. Should I put it back down?" He wondered.

"Yeah. Put it back down and let's see if we can get him to lift it again," Bree suggested. She looked over her shoulder at the video camera on the shelf. "That one *has* to have been caught on camera."

Jason lowered the fall and they sat down on the couch to resume their investigation. They asked Gregory to move the fall again. Jason was polite at first, but then began calling Gregory a sissy when they failed to see results.

"We all know you can do this shit, Gregory. Quit playing games like a little kid! Be a man! Come talk to us. Come move something. Quit hiding like a sissy!" Jason provoked.

Upstairs they heard the sound of heavy footsteps, like someone wearing boots was walking around over their head. The steps sounded like they went from the back room, which they were using as a computer room and was on the opposite end of the upstairs from their bedroom, to the top of the stairway in front of their bedroom. Bree held her breath, waiting to see if the steps would continue. She was not disappointed. One heavy footstep sounded like it hit the top step, then paused. After a brief silence, another loud footfall was heard. The footsteps slowly descended the stairs in this manner, getting louder as they got closer. Bree tried to imagine what those feet carried. Anxiety tightened her chest as she and Jason sat motionless, waiting for the maker of the sounds to come into view.

The steps finally sounded as though they had reached the bottom of the stairs, as the next step didn't create the familiar creak that the stairs produced. The pace had quickened, as well, as the footsteps echoed down the hallway toward the living room. Bree could feel the vibration of each footfall through the floorboards under her feet.

When the footsteps came out of the hallway and were quite obviously in the living room, no one appeared. They heard someone walk into the middle of the room, but saw nothing. Then all went silent. Jason clicked the flashlight on and shined it around the room even though the light was unnecessary as the lightning lamp still illuminated the entire room. They were the only ones in the living room.

"Where is the bastard?" Jason asked in frustration.

"I don't know. Maybe he's right there, where the footsteps stopped, but we just can't see him."

"Show yourself!" Jason demanded. When nothing happened for several minutes, he tried to provoke the spirit again. "Gregory, we've been reading about what a whore your wife was. It must really piss you off that your brother went and knocked her up after you couldn't do it."

"Jason!" Bree chided.

"I'm just trying to get him to do something. Chill out," he said as he patted her knee.

"Fine. But do you think he even knows what 'knocked up' means? I don't know that they used that phrase in the 1890's," Bree pointed out.

"Well, he seems to be aware of things going on around him, so maybe he's picked up some slang."

Bree took a more civilized approach as she began to question the spirit again. She felt like she and Jason were playing good cop/bad cop. "Why did you treat Elizabeth so badly? She really seemed to love and adore you when you first married her."

"Are you still here because of unresolved issues with Elizabeth and Henry? Did one of them murder you? We heard a rumor that Elizabeth might have murdered you."

"Is there anything we can do to put your spirit to rest – to help you move on and leave our house?" Bree asked. Almost instantly she felt a breath on the back of her neck and heard an angry whisper in her ear.

"*My* house!"

She jumped up and whirled around. She imagined the scene she saw earlier in the bathroom mirror with Gregory's decaying face only inches from her ear, but she saw nothing was there.

"What, what?" Jason asked with alarm.

"He whispered in my ear. He said '*My* house,' and he sounded pissed." Bree shuddered and added, "I even felt his breath on the back of my neck."

"Ew. Corpse breath," Jason joked, trying to calm Bree's nerves.

"Haha," she said sarcastically. "Just quit ruffling his feathers for a little while because I know he'll just take it out on me. Now I think I know how Elizabeth felt." Bree then directed a question to Gregory. "Why do you single me out? Why do you seem to like to frighten and abuse women?"

"Pick on me for a while, Gregory. I'm the one who keeps saying all the mean things. Bree's just trying to help you."

"Leave me alone," Gregory whispered from across the room. Jason and Bree looked at each other with their eyebrows raised.

"You heard that too?" Bree asked.

"Yeah. It sounded like it came from over there by the piano," Jason answered, pointing toward the piano bench.

"I'm sorry, but we can't leave you alone, Gregory. We live here now, and we need to know why you are still here too. Let us help you," Bree coaxed. There was no response.

After an exciting start to their investigation, everything suddenly quieted down. They sat in the living room for over an hour trying to get Gregory to interact with them again, but to no avail. Jason was becoming discouraged. He tried provoking again, but there was no reaction.

"I guess he's done for the night," Jason concluded.

"Not necessarily. Maybe we just wore him out and he'll be ready to go again in a little while," Bree suggested hopefully.

"That sounded unbelievably dirty," Jason laughed.

"Pervert," Bree scolded and gave him a nudge. "You know what I mean."

"Of course I do, but what kind of man would I be if I hadn't pointed that out and laughed?"

Bree ignored his excuses and moved the conversation back to the investigation. "I think it's time to move on to another area of the house. Should we check out any of the other bedrooms down here, or do you want to head upstairs?"

Jason contemplated the options for a moment. "Has there even been any activity in the rooms down here?" He asked Bree.

"Not that I know of, but I never go into them."

"Let's just go upstairs then. Maybe we'll save the downstairs rooms for another night," Jason decided. He left the lightning lamp on the piano and he and Bree took their investigation upstairs. Bree headed straight for the guest bedroom, which she had come to think of as 'Lenore's room.' While the two of them sat on the bed and took turns asking EVP questions, Bree kept glancing at the wall behind her to make sure there weren't pasty-white hands stretching toward her. She still couldn't understand how her mother could have taken that incident so calmly and not even bothered to wake her or Jason. Bree would've run either straight for Jason or straight out of the house like she did when she encountered the cupboard dweller.

"Gregory," Bree asked, "what was the creature that crawled out of the wall in here the night my mother stayed in this room?"

Jason went with her line of questioning. "Was it you? And why did it make sounds like an infant crying?"

"This was your mother's room, wasn't it? In her diary, Elizabeth said that your mother was overly fond of you. Is that true? Did you know that Elizabeth thought your mother was jealous of her because she stole your affections from your mother?" Bree paused so Jason could participate in the questioning.

Jason jumped at the opportunity. "Were you quite attached to your mother? Is that why you turned into such an asshole after she died?"

Bree made a connection in her mind. She knew it was a stretch, but she asked, "Was the creature that crawled out of the wall in here a form of yourself, and were you crying like an infant because you missed your mother?"

"Did you know Elizabeth and Henry had sex in here? Probably in the very bed your mother used to sleep in? Maybe even died in?" Jason asked in a disgusted tone.

"Wow, way to be blunt," Bree chuckled.

"Well, it's true, isn't it?"

Bree returned to the questioning. "Why didn't you want me to come in here yesterday? Are you protective of this room?"

The sound of piano music could suddenly be heard from downstairs.

"He's back," Bree said in a sing-song voice.

The music continued as they rushed down the stairs to the living room. When they saw the piano, the fall was still down over the keys.

"Should I lift the cover?" Jason whispered to Bree, just loud enough to be heard over the music.

Bree nodded. "Go slow, though."

Jason slowly reached over and gently lifted the fall. They saw the keys were being depressed, but they couldn't see the fingers that were playing them.

"How are you making this piano work, Gregory? And what are you playing?" Bree asked. She recognized it as the same song she had heard him playing several nights prior.

"Was this your piano when you were alive? Do you still consider it to be your piano?" Jason walked around the piano bench as if he thought that he could see Gregory if he tried a different angle.

"When I spoke with you the other night, you said my blood is what keeps you here. What did you mean by that?" Bree wanted clarification.

The keys suddenly stopped moving as the music ceased.

"Your blood...is *her* blood...is *his* blood...and *its* blood," Gregory whispered into her ear, and at the same time she felt a brief, icy cold touch on her stomach.

"What are you talking about?" Bree shouted, wrapping her arms around her belly protectively. The thought of him touching her filled her with horror and anger.

127

"What's going on, Bree?" Jason asked with concern.

"You didn't hear that?"

"Hear what?"

She told him what Gregory had whispered to her and that she thought he had touched her. "But what the hell is he talking about? Whose blood is 'hers' and 'his'?"

"Maybe by 'blood' he means relatives or family. Is he saying you are related to someone – maybe Elizabeth?" Jason suggested.

"That's impossible. I'm not related to any Barry's as far as I know. Are you?"

Jason shrugged his shoulders in response to Bree's question, indicating he hadn't a clue. "He said it was *your* blood that was her blood, not mine."

"What the hell would Gregory know about me or my family? He's probably been dead almost a hundred years!" Bree was feeling defensive. She didn't like the idea that Gregory thought she was related to Elizabeth. He couldn't really know anything, though, could he? "I'm going to have to tell my mom about this later," she decided.

Jason turned his attention back to the investigation. "Are you suggesting that Bree is somehow related to Elizabeth? And therefore, so is our child?" No response.

Jason asked most of the questions from that point on, as Bree was distracted by Gregory's revelation. When she realized the battery was dead in the voice recorder, she notified Jason and wondered how long the recorder had been off before she noticed it.

"Are you ready to call it a night?" Jason wanted to know.

"Yeah, it's getting pretty late – or should I say early. It's 4 AM. I'm tired." They made their way to bed after turning off the video camera. Bree was so worn out she didn't even brush her teeth. She was out the minute her head hit the pillow.

Bree had her most frightening dream yet that night. In the dream, her baby had already been born, and for some reason she and Jason had made Lenore's room into the nursery. She dreamed that she woke up in the middle of the night to a horrible screeching sound coming from the hallway outside her bedroom. She scrambled out of bed and ran out into the hallway, and immediately encountered something that made her blood freeze. Standing outside her baby's bedroom door was the blackened, rotting corpse she recognized as the cupboard dweller. Its eyes blazed iridescent red like the eye shine of a cat as it looked up at her. It stood on bent, feeble looking legs that had bits of blackened flesh hanging from them, and she saw it had something cradled in its disgusting arms. Terror gripped her when she realized it was her baby that it held, and the baby suddenly began to scream in a way she had never heard a baby scream. It was the scream of pure terror.

"Give me my baby!" Bree screamed and lunged at the creature.

The horrible thing screeched and moved in a flash, shooting into the nursery with unimaginable speed. The door slammed shut in Bree's face. She grabbed the door handle, but found the door was frozen shut again as it had been the day she'd threatened Gregory in order to make him open the door. Her baby screamed and cried from inside the nursery while the creature screeched. Bree was insane with terror for her little one, and her heart felt like it was in a meat grinder.

Her fists slammed against the door painfully as she screamed to Gregory to open the door. "I know it's you, Goddamn it! Let me in! Give me my baby! Don't you dare hurt my baby, you asshole!" She screamed until her voice went hoarse and pounded until the blood from her hands spattered the door, but she couldn't stop. She could still hear her baby screaming, which at least meant that it was still alive.

"You wouldn't burn the house down with your baby inside, would you?" Gregory's laughing voice entered her head. She knew he was referring to the threat she made the last time he had held that door closed.

"Leave my baby alone, you fucking bastard!"

"I'm afraid I can't do that. I told you – your blood is her blood, is his blood, and therefore its blood too. The bloodline will *not* live on," Gregory said in a cool tone, as if he were stating a simple fact.

The nursery went silent, and she heard Gregory laugh.

"Do you still want to help me?" He taunted as his voice faded away.

Bree awoke with tears streaming down her face. She curled into a ball and cried. The dream left her completely shaken and terrified. She had been totally helpless to protect her precious little child, and her heart wrenched every time she thought about its terrified little screams and the silence that followed.

Jason woke up and asked her what was wrong. She told him the disturbing dream she'd just had, and he held her while she continued to cry.

"I want him out *now*!" Bree choked out between sobs.

Chapter 11

Bree didn't sleep at all the rest of the night. Even after breakfast was eaten and the table was cleared, her heart ached. She had never been as terrified in her life as she had been for her baby in her dream last night. It stuck with her, and she knew it would for a long time.

"Do you want to start reviewing the video and voice recorder data today?" Jason asked her as they relaxed on the couch after breakfast.

She honestly didn't. The last thing she wanted was to hear that terrible voice again, even if it was through a pair of headphones. However, she knew she had to go through the data sooner or later as it might contain some of the answers she so desperately sought.

"Honey?" Jason prompted when she failed to answer.

"Yeah, let's start it today and get through it as quickly as possible. Then I want to start looking into getting rid of the nuisance," Bree responded, her tone full of disgust.

"Do you want to take the voice recorder and I'll review the video?"

"That's fine I guess. I take it you want to get moving on it right now?"

Jason had an eager expression in his eyes. "Yeah. I'm excited to see if we caught some of that craziness on film." He reached over and patted her leg before rising from the couch. "I'll be upstairs analyzing the video if you need me." He snatched up the video camera and bounded up the stairs like a little boy with a brand new video game.

Bree's dread matched Jason's excitement in magnitude. She didn't bound up the stairs to retrieve the recorder like Jason did; she trudged. Her motions were slow as she changed the battery in the device and dug out the headphones in the bedroom. On the opposite end of the second floor she could hear Jason tinkering around in the computer room. She didn't want to sit alone to review the recording, so she went across the hall to join him. He was just finishing his setup.

"Well, here we go," he said as he clicked the playback button on the computer screen. Bree pulled up the metal folding chair and sat next to him, declining his offer to switch her metal chair for the computer chair. She stuck the headphones in her ears, exhaled a deep breath, and started the recording from the beginning.

As she listened, her eyes were drawn to the computer screen. It wasn't exact, but she knew the video was playing back at about the same point in time as the recording she was listening to since both were turned on at about the same time at the beginning of the investigation. Therefore, if she heard a noise on the recorder, like the bump they heard while they were in the basement, she should be able to see if anything happened on camera at that same time. Reviewing in this manner would be quite convenient, she concluded.

She got to the part in the recording where they heard the noise upstairs from the basement. She couldn't hear the noise on the recording, but she could hear her and Jason responding to it. She watched the screen intently, but nothing happened on camera. A short time later she and Jason came into view, and she determined there was about a thirty second delay on the video compared to the audio recording.

When she heard Jason gasp in the recording at the point in the investigation where they were both sitting at the kitchen table, she sat forward in her chair to better see the screen. In less than a minute, she and Jason might see the apparition of Gregory. She wasn't disappointed. As they watched intently, a black shadow figure appeared on the screen and Jason let out an involuntary yip of excitement. Keeping his eyes glued to the screen, he reached back and shook Bree's leg to get her attention, unaware that she was already seeing the footage. The shadow had disappeared by the time he withdrew his hand from her leg.

He whirled to face her. "Did you see it? We caught it!" He exclaimed.

She paused her recording. "Yeah, I saw it. Can we rewind it and watch it in slow motion?"

"I can rewind it, but I don't think there is any option for slow motion on our basic media player."

Jason skipped the video back and they watched the appearance of the shadow figure again. It looked as though it appeared instantly, started to take a step forward – toward where Jason and Bree had been sitting in the kitchen at the time – and then sank quickly into the floor. It was just as Jason had described it last night. Jason rewound the video and watched it repeatedly for the next five minutes, and since Bree wanted to keep her recording in sync with the video, she kept her device on pause as well and watched the many replays with him.

"I can't believe we caught it on camera! This is just as good, if not better, than most of the stuff the ghost chasers catch on TV! That's amazing," Jason said, his excitement slowly turning into awe.

"That is really cool. I still haven't gotten anything on the recorder yet," Bree commented. "Shall we move on now? There's probably more to see." She was anxious to move along the analysis.

Jason agreed and they both continued reviewing their data. A short time after pressing play, Bree heard the first EVP from the investigation. During the investigation, they had moved to the living room after seeing the apparition and had begun to ask questions regarding why Gregory was still present in the house. They had asked if he wanted to right his wrongs or have the wrongs righted that were done to him, and he had apparently responded.

"I have done no wrong," the voice of Gregory whispered in the background of the recording.

"Pause that, Jason. I've got something," Bree said as she removed her headphones. She handed them over to Jason and let him listen to the recording. "Do you hear it?"

"'I have done no wrong'?" Jason raised his eyebrows questioningly. "How can he honestly believe that?"

"I don't know. I think we've already established from the diary entries that he's got some major mental issues, though," Bree offered as an explanation.

Jason was thoughtful for a moment. "Can a ghost be crazy? If he had some kind of mental illness in life – some malfunction in his brain – would that actually carry through to the afterlife? And what if he had been put on medication to control it? Would his symptoms return in the afterlife because that was like his 'default' mode?"

Bree had no answers for those questions. "Those are interesting questions. I never really thought about any of that before."

"Me neither, not until now." He handed back her headphones and returned his attention to the computer screen. Bree hurried to get the headphones back in her ears and pressed play on her recorder at the same time Jason resumed the video playback.

In the audio recording, Bree soon heard the two of them commenting on the strange activity with the lightning lamp. She nudged Jason and told him to watch the lamp in the video. Unfortunately, the tiny bolts weren't very visible in the video. They could see themselves pointing at the lamp from the couch, but the lamp wasn't clear enough to make out what was happening to it.

"That sucks," Jason stated simply and kept the video rolling.

Bree nodded in agreement even though Jason wasn't looking at her and resumed her audio review. She heard nothing unusual for a while, even through the bathroom ordeal, but the thought of the bathroom made her realize she needed to go. She started to stand up, reaching a hand toward Jason to tap him on the shoulder to notify him of her quick break, when Jason made a startled sound. Bree had looked away from the screen momentarily and had thus missed whatever Jason saw.

"God, did you see that, honey?" He asked as he paused the video and turned to look at her. She saw his eyes were wide.

"No, I was just getting up to go to the bathroom and I looked away. Play it again," she said.

Jason hesitated. "You may want to go to the bathroom first," he suggested ominously.

"Oh, come on. I'm not going to pee my pants. Just show me."

"I almost did, and I don't even have to go! But suit yourself." Jason moved the video back several seconds and pressed play.

The screen showed the empty living room, as Jason had just gone to see why Bree had been making a commotion in the bathroom. Immediately, a faint shadow drifted up from the floor in front of the piano, and as it rose, the fall on the piano was lifted. Bree's first thought was that the footage wasn't any more shocking than the footage of the first apparition, but just as she was thinking that, she discovered what had startled Jason. After the fall had been lifted, the shadow figure hesitated for a second and then shot directly at the camera with unnatural speed. A disturbing face suddenly filled the screen. Patches of long, stringy hair clung to the scalp in the places where it appeared that flesh still remained. The piercing eyes were sunken in hollow-looking sockets with missing eyelids, and they expressed a deep, violent hatred. Its mouth was opened impossibly wide in what appeared to be an enraged scream. The head suddenly began to tremble and then shot to the left off the screen.

The entire scene only lasted about three seconds from the time the apparition drifted up from the floor to the time its face shot off the screen, but Bree felt like those hateful eyes had stared at her for several minutes. She had cried out unwillingly when the apparition flew at the camera, just as Jason had, and when it was gone, she had to sit back down in her chair. She was reminded of how she felt the first time she saw Gregory as a burning, floating head in the basement. The expression on the face from the video was very similar to the silently screaming, flaming head.

"Pretty intense, wasn't it?" Jason commented.

"He looks so *angry*. I don't want to live with such a violent, hateful thing anymore," Bree complained. She suddenly felt like crying, but didn't know if it was due to a true emotional reaction or just her pregnancy hormones causing her to be overly sensitive.

"We'll get rid of him. Don't worry," Jason reassured.

"How? What's our plan? I'm tired of saying we'll take care of it without actually having any idea how we're going to do ·it."

"I'll tell you what. When we get done reviewing these recordings, we'll go online and look up paranormal investigators in our area that can help us with our problem. Does that sound like a good start?" Jason waited for her approval.

"Yes, that sounds like a great start. Let's finish this analysis." Bree used the bathroom and returned to the audio analysis.

The next paranormal event from the previous night was caught on the recorder, but nothing showed up on the camera. The footsteps that traveled from the room they were in presently to the middle of the living room could be heard clearly on the audio recorder, yet the creator of those footsteps was absent in the video just as it had been to the naked eye. The recorder also caught Gregory saying, "Leave me alone," which both Bree and Jason had heard with their own ears that night, but it failed to pick up Gregory whispering, "My house," in Bree's ear. The sound of Gregory's voice made Bree feel queasy.

Next, the recording yielded an EVP from the upstairs guest bedroom. Jason and Bree had been asking Gregory about his mother and he had evidently been listening. All he said in the EVP was, "Mother…" in a sad, regretful tone. His voice was as clear and loud in the recording as Jason and Bree's voices were. "Mother" was the last paranormal evidence on the recorder, however, because the playback stopped right before they heard the piano music coming from the living room. Bree hadn't realized that the recording had shut off *that* early in the investigation, but she was relieved that it had because it meant she didn't have to hear Gregory's bloodline speech again.

She and Jason watched the remainder of the video together. Jason was greatly disappointed that the keys moving on the piano couldn't be seen on the video because Bree had unknowingly blocked the camera's view of the piano. She began to apologize when a loud voice came blaring from the computer.

"It'll be over soon," Gregory's voice predicted ominously.

Jason and Bree both gasped and jumped out of their seats, taking a quick step back from the computer.

"That's impossible! That camera doesn't even record sound!" Jason exclaimed, perplexed.

"Maybe it wasn't actually on the recording...maybe he was just talking through the computer just now. Rewind it," Bree suggested.

Jason skipped the video back and played it again. The voice blared out at them once more, making them both jump again.

"How the hell did his voice get into the video when we were using a camera that doesn't record audio?" Jason wondered aloud.

"He's full of amazing tricks," Bree answered with disgust.

The rest of the video revealed nothing extraordinary. While Jason copied the video to their computer's hard drive and erased it from the memory card, they pondered what Gregory meant when he said it would be over soon.

"Maybe he knows we're going to get rid of him and he won't be here much longer," Jason suggested.

"I'm sure he knows we want to get rid of him, but I doubt that's what he's talking about," Bree said. "He sounded menacing when he said it, like it was a threat. Whatever it is he's referring to, I have a feeling we aren't going to like it. I think maybe he's going to try to get rid of *us*."

"Do you think he would try to get rid of us before we found out what happened to him? He seems pretty adamant about giving us hints to help us learn about the events of his life," Jason pointed out.

"That's true, but it could just be because he's a narcissistic asshole who thinks his life was the most important and interesting thing anyone could learn about. I just don't know. A lot of the things he says and does don't make sense. I think he's just as crazy now as he was when he was alive."

"Did you ever finish Elizabeth's diary?" Jason asked.

Bree shook her head. "Still working on it, but I'm almost through it. I should be able to finish it either today or tomorrow," Bree answered, and then changed the subject. "Can we look up paranormal investigators now?" She was anxious to begin the search for help.

"Sure," Jason replied simply and opened the internet browser on the computer.

"Would it bother you if I let you get started while I put this recorder away and give my mom a quick call to let her know what we found?" Bree asked.

"That's fine, honey. Go ahead and I'll see what I can find."

Bree kissed him on the cheek and went into the bedroom. She stuck the recorder in the closet and sat on the bed with the phone. She wondered what her mother would think of the evidence they'd gathered the night before as she dialed Karen's number.

"Hey, Mom," Bree greeted when Karen answered the phone.

"How is everything there? I haven't heard from you in a couple of days. How are you feeling?" Karen was full of questions.

"I'm feeling alright physically, but I'm getting worn out emotionally by all this paranormal crap. Jason and I are looking into getting a paranormal investigation group to help us get rid of Gregory because he's starting to become exceedingly threatening." She told Karen about last night's investigation and how Gregory had insinuated that she was related to Elizabeth –

or at least that was what they had concluded. She also told her about the terrifying dream she had that same night after the investigation. "We went over the evidence today and got some really creepy footage," Bree added and went on to describe their findings, ending with the scary close-up and the mysterious audio recording on the video.

Karen was concerned. "It sounds like things are escalating out of control. I'm worried about you being in that house by yourself so much, especially with these new threats from Gregory. Why don't you come up and stay with us until things calm down there?"

"I'm not going to run away from him," Bree replied resolutely. "Besides, I don't want to be four hours from Jason. Don't worry. We're going to get this taken care of before something bad happens."

"It's a mother's job to worry. You know how you felt about that helpless little baby in your dream? That's how I feel about you. You're my only child, and I'll be damned if I'd let anything bad happen to you. Please consider staying with us," Karen pleaded. "I know your father would love to see you."

"I'll think about it," Bree lied. "You know, I didn't call you to worry you. I called because I wanted to know your thoughts on Gregory thinking I'm related to Elizabeth." She hesitated for a moment before asking, "Do you think it's really possible?"

"Well, I suppose anything could be possible if you look back far enough, but I don't think it's very likely. I don't know much about our family history or your father's family history, to be honest with you," Karen admitted. "I only know about immediate family. I don't even know that much when it comes to your great-grandparents because I never met any of them. They all died before I was even born. Did you want to talk to your dad about it? I can have him call you when he gets back in from the garage," Karen offered.

"No, that's ok. I just really wish I could find out more about our ancestry so I won't have to wonder about Gregory's claims." Bree was frustrated. "I want to know if he actually does have any reason to target me the way he does. And what makes

139

him think that hurting me or my baby will 'end the bloodline', as he puts it? Hasn't he ever considered how much a family tree branches over time? Hell, Dad has eleven siblings who all had children who had children."

"On the other hand," Karen began as though she had just figured out a piece of the puzzle, "I am an only child. You are my only child, and my mother was an only child. I don't know about my grandmother, but as far as it goes for you, my mother, and me, we don't really 'branch.' Interesting…" Karen trailed off and grew silent, obviously absorbed in her own thoughts.

"So if any of what Gregory said is true, then I would have to be related to Elizabeth through your side – is that what you're saying?" Bree was beginning to worry that there was an increasing possibility that Gregory could be right.

"That would be the only possibility if you and your little one are the 'end of the bloodline.'"

The line was quiet for a minute while Karen and Bree thought about what to do next.

Karen broke the silence. "I guess I'll have to give your grandfather a call and see what he knows about our ancestry – my mother's side, particularly. I don't know how much he'll know, though."

"It's worth a shot, anyway," Bree encouraged. She wished her grandmother was still around to share what she knew.

Before they ended their conversation, Bree posed an unrelated query to her mother. "Do you think spirits can be crazy?"

"What do you mean, exactly?" Karen sought clarification.

"Well, we've kind of assumed that Gregory had some kind of mental disorder from the diary entries, and I'm just wondering if it would be possible for his disorder to continue to affect him in the afterlife," Bree explained. "I mean, if mental disorders are caused by chemical imbalances and brain malfunctions, would the symptoms still persist if the cause no longer existed?"

Karen had a thoughtful reply. "But isn't personality and emotion and all human intelligence basically dependent on chemical reactions, interactions, and electronic impulses in the brain? If his personality and memories and intelligence are still intact, then I would say the fact that the brain no longer exists doesn't seem to affect the behavior of the entity. Perhaps there is something more to our existence than physiological functions – perhaps we have an inherent essence that is molded by our lives and experiences, or how we have perceived them. Therefore, if one has a mental illness in life that alters one's perceptions, his or her essence could be molded by these inaccurate perceptions. Then, in death and the afterlife, this person's essence may no longer use brain activity to function, but would forever feel the effects of being created with faulty equipment, if you will. In short, they would still seem insane," Karen concluded.

Bree had no response for a minute. She hadn't expected such a long, well-thought-out answer. "That actually kind of makes sense in a weird way. I hadn't thought about it like that before. The way I was looking at it was that mental illness was a sickness that affected the brain and body, like cancer or Alzheimer's. Once you die, it doesn't seem like you would be affected by those diseases anymore because you have no physical body for them to affect. I thought maybe in death you would be cured – blind can see, paraplegics can walk, et cetera."

"That's an interesting view too," Karen commented. "The concept of mental illness carrying on into the afterlife is something that I've considered before, especially after watching some of the Ghost Chaser's episodes when they investigate old mental hospitals."

"I wondered how you just came up with that whole 'essence' concept. I couldn't believe you just came up with that off the top of your head." Bree said, and Karen chuckled. "It's just not something I had ever thought about until Jason brought it up today. I haven't really had time to ponder it or come up with a theory of my own yet, but I think I like your idea."

"I'm sure there are lots of theories out there on the subject. But I'd rather you focus your time and energy on removing the spirit from the house now instead of figuring out if he's still insane," Karen urged.

141

"We're working on it. In fact, I should probably let you go. I left Jason to search for local paranormal investigators and I should get in there and help him. I'll let you know what we find out." Bree promised Karen that she would be careful and hung up the phone.

When Bree returned to the computer room, she saw a photo of a familiar woman on the computer screen. She recognized the odd attire immediately.

"Is that the crazy lady from the Gypsy's Treasure Chest?" Bree asked in disbelief.

"Sure is," Jason replied. "She runs her own paranormal group. The MichigIndiana Paranormal Society. I know she may seem a little out there, but I thought you might be interested in trying someone we are at least a little familiar with. Plus, it says that they offer their services for free. The other two I looked into charge for each 'house call.'"

They perused the MichigIndiana Paranormal Society's website to learn more about the group before making a decision. MIPS, as they called themselves, had been together for eight years and consisted of nine members. The Gypsy's Treasure Chest lady, whose name was Cora Schaeffer, was a medium. There was a demonologist in the group as well, but the rest of the members were just regular people interested in the paranormal who conducted investigations in their spare time as a hobby. They were mostly technological professionals.

"What do you think?" Jason asked. "Should we give them a call?"

Bree considered it briefly before replying. "Might as well. We need to do something ASAP." She waited to see if Jason would go get the phone to make the call. She really didn't want to have to do it. When he didn't get up, Bree asked, "Could you be the one to call? I hate making phone calls to strangers."

Jason sighed. "So do I. But I guess I can do it. What do I say to them?"

"Just say that we looked at their website and wondered if they would be able to help us drive a malicious entity from our home. I'll get you the phone."

142

When Jason placed the call, he found it went through to the Gypsy's Treasure Chest store. A young man answered the phone. He put Jason on hold when he said he needed to talk to someone about the MichigIndiana Paranormal Society. Actually, he wasn't exactly put on *hold*, rather, the young man sat the phone down on a hard surface with a "clunk" and yelled, "Ma! Someone's on the phone asking about MIPS!"

A few minutes later there was a shuffling sound on the other end of the line and a woman asked, "Are you still there? This is Cora."

"Yes. My name is Jason Wilson, and my wife and I have been having some disturbing interactions with an unwelcome entity in our home. We saw the MIPS website and wondered if you could help us to rid our home of this entity?" Jason told her where they lived and mentioned that he and Bree had been into her store a couple times.

"I know I'll recognize you when I see you. I never forget a customer. We would be glad to help you, but we won't be able to drive out the spirit in our first visit. We need to assess the situation first, and it can sometimes take two or three visits before we can determine the best method for removing the spirit from the house," Cora explained.

"That's fine. We just need to have someone help us with this because things are really starting to get out of hand. He's becoming increasingly threatening, especially to my pregnant wife," Jason conveyed his concern.

"You said 'he.' You think it's a male spirit?" Cora asked.

"We actually know quite a bit about him and have even communicated with him. He tends to focus all of this attention on my wife, Bree, and mostly tries to communicate with and harass her."

"I see. It sounds like we're needed right away, then. Would tomorrow night be ok for you, around eight o'clock? We can come and check things out at that point, and you can share your experiences with us, if that works for you."

143

"That sounds great. We've even got some video and audio recordings you might be interested in seeing," Jason added. He said goodbye and shared his news with Bree.

"I wish they would come tonight," Bree complained.

"We've survived this long. I think we can make it one more night," Jason encouraged.

That afternoon, Bree decided to spend the rest of her day trying to finish Elizabeth's journal.

May 7, 1896

Gregory still remains silent. I was forchunate today that he was out of the house when I became ill from the smell of the brewing coffee. I have yet to decide how to handle this dire situation. Last night I made an attempt to convince Gregory to lay with me, but he only grumbled at me and pushed me away as if I were some annoying cat seeking attention. I have not decided wether or not I will make another attempt tonight, though my despiration to remady the situation is great and will likely drive me to make another attempt. I have also considerd the possibility of attempting to end the pregnancy by means of long, vigerous rides on our spirited filly, Buttercup, or perhaps by taking an "accidental" tumble down the stairs. I suppose I could also provoke Gregory, as a beating like the one he delt me the night I made him stew for dinner would likely bring an end to my current condition. On the other hand, I would never be able to forgive myself for destroying the life of an innocent child, even if it isn't yet out of the womb. It is also possible that these actions could result not in the ending of the pregnancy, but only in disfigurment and damage to the child. I simply know not what I am to do! I still have not revealed my situation to Henry, either. But what will he do? He is married to another woman and surly will not claim this child as his own. Gregory will likely leave me when he learns of my condition. It is possible that he may not leave and just tell everyone that the child is his in order to avoid public dishonor and embarrassment, but I feel that is a very slight possibility. I beleve he is more likely to abandin

144

me and reveal me for what I am. I would then be cast out of my home with my bastard child and no hope of ever having a man want me again. I doubt even my own father would take me in and give me shelter. I would be left with nothing! O what a stupid, foolish harlot I have been! Damn me for giving into the devil's temptation! Damn Gregory for making me feel the need to find companionship outside of our marriage! Damn Henry for tempting and seducing me! And damn the miracle of life!

Bree was startled to see different handwriting when she turned to the next page in the journal.

May 7 – Never assume that a man has no interest in what his wife writes in her journal. – Gregory

"Oh my God!" Bree exclaimed involuntarily. She would've bet her life savings that Elizabeth had the same reaction when she found out Gregory had read her journal.

Chapter 12

"What?" Jason inquired from the opposite end of the couch in the living room where they were both lounging. "Is something wrong?"

"Look!" Bree shoved the opened diary at Jason. "Gregory found Elizabeth's journal when they were alive!"

Jason took the journal and looked it over. "That must've been a real kick in the nuts to find out his wife was pregnant by his brother by reading it in a diary. You'd think that she would've hidden this diary well considering the scandalous things she disclosed in it." He handed the diary back to Bree.

"Maybe she did, but he found it anyway because he was suspicious of her and was snooping around. Although, from what he wrote, it sounds like she just left it out assuming he wouldn't read it."

"I'm inclined to think the latter, based on what he wrote," Jason opined. "What happened next?"

"I don't know. I haven't read past his entry yet. I'm almost afraid to! I feel nervous for Elizabeth," Bree admitted sheepishly. "I know it doesn't affect me directly, but just knowing that this really happened to someone – someone who once lived in our house – makes it more real to me."

"Let me know what happens…happened," he corrected.

Bree read on apprehensively. The next passage wasn't entered until fourteen days after the last one.

May 21, 1896

I fear I may be up all night recounting the events of the previous fortnight. My life is in shambles. So many horrible things have happend that I have had neither time nor the desire to record any of them until now. My husband is dead. My former companion seems to have forsaken me. I am still secretly carrying a bastard child. I am tormented by visions of Gregory's putrid corpse, and fear I have gone completely mad. So where do I begin?

After writing in my journal last time, I spent the afternoon outdoors as it was a gorjous day. I weeded and worked in the garden, fed the chickens, and even brought the washboard outside to wash the clothes. I paid little attention to Gregory's whereabouts that entire day. When I came in and put dinner on the table, he did not come to eat. I went out and rang the dinner bell four seperate times, yet he never came. I ate and cleaned the table and dishes and still he stayed away. Growing concerned, I rode around the farm to find him, but he was nowhere to be found. I sat down with my sewing bag and worked on patching some of Gregory's clothes while I awaited his return from wherever he had disappeared to. Long after darkness had fallen, Gregory finally came through the door. He appeared dishevelled and reeked of liquor. He had a bottle of moonshine in his hand and a ciggarret between his lips. I knew something was horribly wrong, as this was not Gregory's usual behavior. I asked him what had happend to him, but he only looked at me with hollow, glassy eyes. His face was wet and his eyes red as though he had been crying. He stumbled his way through the house to the piano he had inherited from his rich Uncle. I followed him at a distance, not wanting to provoke an outburst, but curious of his condition. He sat at the piano and prepared a ciggarret with great difficulty. I had never seen him smoke tobbacco before, and know not if he ever had. When he tried to light the ciggarret, he kept

147

dropping the matches on himself, the piano, and the floor. His ciggarret finally caught flame and he sat and played the piano, stopping only to drink his moonshine and make more ciggarrets. He ignored me compleatly while I stood and watched him play. I was amazed at his talent, and I do not know where he learnd to play. The longer he played, the more intoxicated he became, and soon his clothes were soked with whiskey since he sloshed it on himself sevral times in his deteariorating condition. I decided to go to bed and leave him for the night, and chose to sleep in Lenore's old room to make sure I stayed out of his way compleatly. I fell asleep to the sound of piano music that grew worse the longer Gregory drank and played.

In the morning, I went downstairs to find his boots still sitting near the piano. I assumed he was still passed out in his room, sleeping off his drink, and chose not to wake him. I made breakfast and coffee and was thankful to not have an upset stomach that morning. When Gregory still had not come down to eat when his breakfast was sitting on his plate at the table, I went up to check on him. The horror I found when I opened the bedroom door was incomprehendable. A terrible stench of burned flesh and hair and wood made me ill right there in the doorway. I then saw a large black mound on the half-burned bed and knew it was Gregory. I stood frozen in the doorway, and in my stupor I thought I imagined I saw Gregory – alive and well – standing next to his charred body. He even spoke to me, saying a ciggarret fell out of his mouth and ignited his liquor-soaked clothes while he slept. He said he did not even wake. He said it was my fault, and the devil would drag me to hell for what I had done. Then he was gone, and I was alone in his room with his dead body.

I began to wonder what would happen if I notified the Sherriff. Would he think I did this to him? As his wife, I should have been in the same bed as him, but I was not. I did not want him asking questions regarding that matter. He would find that suspicious. I noticed that only Gregory's side of the bed had burned.

My side of the bed had not burned, and I would not have burned even if I had been sleeping in that bed. But I know the smell and heat from the burning side would have roused me from my slumber. There would be a lot of questions raised by Gregory's death, of this I was sure. Questions I do not wish for everyone to know the answers. I could not – cannot – have anyone looking into my life right now! So instead of sending for the Sheriff, I rode to Henry's house. He was outside when I arrived and I told him quietly that something terrible had happend to Gregory, but I needed him to come see for himself and discuss some things with him before we told anyone. He went inside and told his wife he was needed for a short while at our farm, but I do not beleve he told her any more. When we came back to the house, I quickly told Henry about Gregory's behavior the previous night and showed him the horror in the bedroom. I shared my concerns with him about having secrets uncovered by an investigation, as I knew these secrets would ruin his reputation as well as mine. I then revealed to him that I was carrying his child in my womb. He became very upset and panicked after hearing and seeing all that he had, and he quickly devised a plan. He wanted to bury Gregory's body out in the back of the farm and then have me claim that Gregory just did not come home last night. Then he would be considered missing, but not necisarily dead, and it might put less suspicion on either of us and could result in fewer questions for us to try to answer. I liked the idea, but was afraid that it could be risky to try to move the corpse from the house. If someone were to come by and see us, it would be worse than if I had just gone to the Sheriff from the beginning.   We decided to bury him in the cellar. Together, we carried him out of the room and to the cellar, and I will never forget the horror of that task. I do not wish to describe it. As we dug the hole, we discussed our story. I would tell the Sheriff that Gregory had not come to dinner last night, and that I began to worry then. I would then say that I fell asleep in the chair waiting up for him, and in the morning I had discovered that he still had not come home. I knew the men at the tavern would say he had been there (Luckily, I had correctly assumed that was where he had been), so that would prove that he had not been home with me. I would tell the Sherriff that I had not seen him since right after breakfast, and that he had told me that he was going into town. The fewer particulars, the fewer lies to keep straight, the better. I would then say that I found Gregory's horse outside the stable with its saddle still on in the morning, so I went to Henry's house to see if Gregory had been there. When I found he had not been there, I asked Henry to come help me look for Gregory around the farm. We looked for him everywhere, thinking he may have come home late and perhaps fallen off his horse somewhere on the farm, but found nothing. That was when we would say we decided to get help. Then the Sherriff would find out from the men in town that Gregory had been at the tavern and everyone would assume he fell off his horse somewhere in his inebreated condition. Henry and I felt confident that this story would keep us clear of suspicion and questions.

When the hole was dug, we bundled Gregory's putrid body in the burned bedding. We then broke and ripped the bed to pieces and buried it with Gregory's body, as well as his boots that had been near the piano. Finally, we moved Lenore's bed to the master bedroom to replace the burned, destroyed bed. Henry and I then both went back to his house to tell his wife our rehearsed story, and she insisted upon accompanying us to town to console me. I was grateful for this as it would look less suspicious than if it were only Henry and I together. I put on my best act for Cecilia, pretending to be worried sick about Gregory, and she seemed to beleve it. The Sherriff did as well. Little did they know, I was upset because he was dead, not because he was missing. The Sherriff gathered a few locals and they searched the farm and nearby roads for any sign of Gregory. They looked for him for three days, and in that time, I found his entry in my journal. I now had the answer to why he had been out drinking that day. He knew everything. Or did he? How much had he read? How long had he been reading it? And why did I leave it in the nightstand drawer!

Needless to say, Gregory was not found. They assumed he injured himself by falling off his horse, then wandered into the woods in a drunken stupor and died. The coyotes probably got to him by now, they think. When it was determined that Gregory was probably dead, Henry's family and I decided to hold a small funeral ceremony for him. We had it yesterday, and after the funeral, Henry told me that he was likely going to be put in charge of the farm now that Gregory was gone. I am concerned by this news, because Henry has had an air of indifference toward me lately. He has not mentioned my pregnancy since I told him of it. Of course, I would never tell anyone that the child was his, and can now say that Gregory is the father without anyone being the wiser. And if I had not always assured Henry that I was not laying with Gregory, I suppose I could have even lied to him and claimed it was Gregory's child. O is there any part of my life that I have not irrepirably damaged? I do hope Henry will find the time soon to come see me and share his plans for the farm and to discuss where we stand. I am lost right now, unable to even fathom what will become of my life. I despised Gregory, but I despirately needed him. I daresay I even loved him still, despite what he had become. Without him, I am an autumn leaf, dangling perilously, about to be wrenched from my sturdy tree by a gust of wind, destined to float aimlessly with the currents before tumbling wildly to the ground to begin my decay. If I am lucky, my father and mother will shelter me again if Henry spurns me. I have not much confidence that he will make an effort to aid me in my time of need. What unforchunate decisions I have made.

Now there's the understatement of the century, Bree thought after reading the last line of Elizabeth's entry. In her mind, an unfortunate decision was choosing to sit on a black leather seat in bikini bottoms on a hot, sunny day. Having an affair, getting pregnant by your husband's brother, and lying about the death of your husband seemed to Bree like decisions that were a few steps beyond unfortunate.

151

"Gregory burned to death while passed out drunk in his bed," Bree blurted to Jason. "And he may still be buried somewhere under or near the house."

"What?!" Jason looked at her with wide eyes.

She began to explain to him what had happened, but then just handed him the diary and told him to read it.

When he was through, he shook his head. "No wonder he's still here. He's probably *still here*," he said while pointing at the floor. "It's even worse to know that he died here too, probably in the same room we sleep in!" He tried to shake off the thought.

"I know, but knowing what happened to him might help us in our attempt to get rid of him," Bree suggested. "So do you suppose the 'vision' she 'imagined' when she found Gregory's body was actually his ghost and not just her imagination?"

"It probably was him. I wonder if he appeared to her again after that."

"He must have. Remember when my mom and I read the last page of the diary? Elizabeth talked about Gregory's 'visits' in that entry, so she would have had to have seen his ghost again. And from the way she made it sound in the final entry, she saw him on a regular basis," Bree said.

"So I wonder how we're supposed to find out if his body is still buried here. If it is, I want it removed," Jason said decidedly.

"I don't know. I don't know where the cellar was – whether it was under the house or just nearby. We have a full basement that I'm assuming was put in more recently. If the body was buried under the house, you'd think it would've been dug up when the basement was done. I just don't have a clue where to begin with that," Bree admitted. "Maybe MIPS will have some advice for us when they come tomorrow."

"I hope so. It creeps me out to think we might have a dead body buried around our house."

"Creepier than having its angry spirit *inside* the house?" Bree pointed out.

"I don't know about creepier, but it definitely adds to the creepiness of the situation."

152

Bree agreed with that statement and returned her attention to the journal. She wanted to have it finished before MIPS came the following night.

May 22, 1896

I saw Gregory today. I saw him many times today. His body is dead, but his soul remains in the house, and he will not leave. He told me so. When I opened my eyes this morning, he was standing next to the bed, looming over me. I screamed and crawled to the other side of the bed, but he still stood there, his eyes following me. He looked the way he had when I found him on that fateful morning. He was burned and blackened and even emitted a nausiating odor. The only recognizable features were his cold, hateful eyes. He spoke in a hoarse whisper and said I would never be rid of him. It reminded me of Lenore's final words to me. I sat in silence, only staring stupidly at him. He suddenly vanished before my eyes, but when I turned to climb out of bed, he was there behind me. I started and fell back onto the bed with a yelp, and he let out a hidious laugh. He said I should be more careful with the disgusting abomination growing in my womb, and then disappeared again. I immeedietly ran to the window and vomitted. I was badly shaken by this encounter, but I feared it would not be the last. I was correct. He came to me again this afternoon while I was preparing a pie to bring over to Henry's family. He appeared in the entryway, and this time he looked like his usual self before his death. He was much less frightening that way. I said to him "You are dead. You need to move on to wherever it is God wants you." He scowled at me and said that there was nowhere else for him to go. He then told me that I would have somewhere special to go when I died, though, and God had no love for me after the things I had done. Before vanishing again, he crudely requested that I ask his brother how he liked having Gregory's used, lousy goods. I was stung by his words. They bit just as hard as they had while he was alive. I did my best to ignore my sore feelings and brought the pie to Henry's.

Henry still was uncertain about the farm. He is considering the possibility of leasing the fields to other farmers since he does not have the time to work them himself and giving me a portion of that money. However, he also mentioned that I might want to have someplace in mind to go to in case he decides to just sell the house and the farm. I do not even know if he can do that to me, as I have little knowledge of legal matters, but I would not be suprised if he did it and got away with it anyway. I think he wants for me to disappear like Gregory supposedly did. It has become obvious to me recently that Henry never was nor ever will be a decent man. I should have known better – he is a Barry boy, after all. He is just as despicable as Gregory, if not more so. He would not think anything of putting me out on the street to become a beggar. How could I have been so wrong about Gregory and Henry? I must be the most foolish, ignorant woman in the entire world!

I was in a foul mood when I returned home, and I walked to my chair with the intention of sitting down and having a good long cry. Unforchunately, as I moved toward it, Gregory appeared in the chair, looking quite grousome again. I screamed at him in frustration and outrage, telling him to leave me alone. He only laughed. He said he would be here with me forever, to remind me every day of what a whore I was and to wait for the day the bastard child was born so he could punish it for even existing. He said he would be my curse, and he would be my child's curse. I told him that I would never let him do anything to an innocent child, and he told me there was nothing I could do to stop him. To distract him from the subject of my unborn baby, I asked him why he talked to me more now that he was dead than he did when he was alive. For some reason, this question seemed to upset him and he growled at me and disappeared. I saw him once more after that while I was brushing out my hair in the mirror just a few moments before sitting down with this journal. I saw him standing behind me in the mirror, but when I turned, he was not there. I wonder if he shall make these visits a regular, daily event. Though I do not care for his demeanor, I must admit that his presence makes me feel much less alone than I would feel otherwise. It is still difficult knowing that I _am_ alone, and though Gregory may visit me in spirit form, he will never truly be here again. I suppose I do still love the miserable bastard.

May 24, 1896

Gregory made several appearances again yesterday and today. He was being very abrasive and ugly toward me yesterday just as he was the day before, but today he was more somber and almost remorseful. Though he may be dead, his spirit is just the same as it was when he was alive, and I still do not understand his strange moods! He has taken to waking me by standing near the bed and staring at me in the morning, as this is how I have awakened each morning for the past three mornings. I can feel his eyes upon me just as plainly as I can feel the warm sunshine passing through the curtains. I must admit, however, that the sunshine is a much more pleasant feeling than Gregory's stare. Today at least he was in his normal form instead of the hidious burned form he sometimes takes. He did not talk to me straight away, but only stared at me as I went about my usual morning routine. It was not until I was preparing my midday meal that he spoke to me. I did not see him this time, but only heard his voice as though it came out of the walls. He asked me why I did not love him. I replied that I had loved him, espeshally when we were first married. He asked why I stopped loving him, and I told him I never stopped loving him. I said that he was the one who pushed me away and treated me horribly, and asked why _he_ stopped loving _me_. Gregory told me he could not change the way he was and oftentimes an unexplainable misery overtook him and made him lash out at those around him. He said that it did not mean that he did not love me. He said that my indifference toward him in the previous months made him feel even more miserable and sour, espeshally when he made an attempt to rekindle our relationship in early March. I asked him why he refused my advances in the days before his death if he still loved me and was bothered by my previous indifference. He said he was retaliating for the times I refused him in March, and he was becoming suspicious of my strange moods. His suspicions were what drove him to peek at my journal. He was quiet for a few moments, and I noticed he had appeared at the kitchen table. I went and sat near him, wishing I could touch him to comfort him. He looked so forlorn. He said that he read several journal pages while I was outside on the last day he was alive, and that he was completely sickened and heartbroken by what he discoverd. He could not stand the knowledge he held after reading my journal, so that was why he went to the tavern to drink until he could forget what he had learned. I asked him why he did not confront me, and he responded that there was nothing he could have said to me that would have changed anything, and the last thing he wanted to do was talk about it. I asked if the vision I saw of him on the morning I discoverd his body was really him or if I had imagined it. He said it was he, and he said that he watched his body burn after he died. He then looked up (he had been staring down at his folded hands the entire time he spoke) and told me my lover was coming. He warned me that I should be nice to Henry if I wanted him to let me keep living in this house. Then I heard a knock at the door and Gregory disappeared.

When I answered the door, it was Henry. I was uncomfortable about letting him in the house knowing that Gregory was watching, but what could I do? He came in and acted as though nothing had changed between us. He mentioned that he had a couple of young fellows interested in farming the fields on the property, espeshally since Gregory had done a lot of the work in the fields already this season. He told me that he probably wouldn't have to sell the house this year if the deal goes through with those young farmers. I fained the most gracious smile I could though I was not at all comforted by his news. I do not like uncertainty. He then came very close to me and said that it would be much easier for us to meet now that we did not have to worry about Gregory discovering us. He then tried to kiss me. I was disgusted by his actions. It had become blatently obvious to me that Henry cared for no one other than himself and cared only to satisfy his own needs and desires. He did not care how I felt about losing my husband, and he did not care that I was carrying his child in my womb. He just wanted to satisfy his own carnal urges and assumed that I would be more than willing to lay with him. When he tried to kiss me, I turned my head away and stepped back. He asked what was wrong. I asked him how he could even think of propositioning me after the events that had transpired recently. He said there was nothing we could do to change the past and that it was no reason to deny our desire for each other. I asked him what he planned to do about the child I carried. He looked at me as though I was mad and speaking nonsense. He said it wasn't his child to worry about. As far as anyone was concerned, it was Gregory's child, he said. He told me he was not responsible for his brother's children, or his brother's wife, for that matter. I knew he meant this as a threat, and it took all I had to not wallop him right then. I was furious! However, I was able to keep myself calm and told him I had no desire to make love because I was still feeling upset about Gregory's death and my current situation. This seemed to upset him greatly. He said he could get much better than me anyway and stormed out the door. I have not seen Gregory again since Henry left. I still feel his presence, but I have not seen his ghost or heard his voice. I'm sure he will be there next to the bed in the morning, though. I hope his mood is more like it was today than it was yesterday. It is easier to remember why I loved him when he is not being a balligerant pig.

May 27, 1896

I have had nothing happen lately about which is worth writing. Gregory is back to being angry and unkind after his breef spell of sorrow of which I spoke in my last entry. I have not seen Henry since he stormed out after I refused his advances. I know not what is happening with the farm, but no one has notified me that I need to leave. I cannot help but wonder what will become of Gregory if I am forced to leave our home. Will he still remain here? Is it possible that his spirit would follow me to my new home? I might enjoy time away from his harsh words, but I know I still would miss him if I left and he did not come with me. Only the Lord knows why. Love is a very strange thing. I think it would surely be better for Gregory if he moved on, out of this world and into the next, even if it did leave me lonely. I hate his demeaner and his words, but I crave his company to drive away my loneliness. I suppose I am a very confused woman!

May 29, 1896

I visited my parents today. I had to get out of this house for a while, as my loneliness was driving me mad. I had not seen Gregory at all yesterday or today, and I am wondering if he has abandoned me compleatly just as Henry has. I needed some kind of company, so I spent the afternoon with my mother. Father was out working, so I did not see him at all. I told my mother about my pregnancy, claiming it was Gregory's child, of corse, and discussed with her my uncertain situation with the house and farm. She first assured me that I was welcome to come back home and live with them until I found a new husband if I was forced to leave, and then she began to insist that I come back home regardless. She said she did not think it was safe or proper for me to be staying in this house all by myself with no man to look over me. I told her I was fine for the time being, but appreshiated her concern. I know she will discuss it with my father and will push the issue until I give in and move back into their house. I do think it might be a good idea to do so if Gregory continues his absence, as I do not like how lonely it is in this house by myself. I have been terribly lonely since I came home from my father's house. I remember when I thought I lived a lonely existance when Gregory began ignoring me and treating me badly. How I wish to have those days back again! It was nothing compared to this! I keep calling out to Gregory, but he doesn't respond. I've even tried complaining about how miserable my pregnancy is making me feel in order to provoke his anger and ellicit some kind of reaction, but still nothing. I do think he is still here, but I cannot be certain. Maybe he has moved on, which would probably be for the best.

May 30, 1896

I saw Gregory today. He made me feel compleatly worthless with his words today. He told me the only thing I was able to do was lie on my back and that I was compleatly useless for anything else. He said I could not even get conception right. He said I was a failure at everything – being a wife, being a woman, keeping promises, having some intelligence – I have failed at all of those tasks. He even told me he knew I would fail as a mother, as well. Before disappearing, he suggested I take my own life and save myself and the rest of the world from the disaster my life has become. I was going to hell anyway, so he said it did not matter if I committed suaside. I did not see him again for the rest of the day, but his words have stuck with me. They swarm my thoughts like angry bees, stinging me over and over again. Part of me thinks Gregory is right, but the other part of me wants to beleve that he is not. I must admit that I am feeling more miserable and hopeless as each day goes by.

When Bree flipped the page, she saw that the next journal entry was the June 4th entry, the final entry, of which she had already read. She had completed Elizabeth's diary, and she felt she had almost all the answers she had sought in the beginning. All she needed to know now was why Gregory seemed to despise her so much, if his body was still buried on the premises, and how to remove his spirit from her home. She could not – would not – bring a baby home to a house haunted by such a malevolent entity. She wondered if that was why Elizabeth gave up her child, since Gregory had been threatening to punish it once it was born. It comforted her to know that MIPS was coming to their home tomorrow to help them in this struggle.

Jason saw her close the diary and toss it on the coffee table. "Did you finish it?" He inquired.

"Sure did. Apparently Gregory harassed Elizabeth a whole lot more than he does to me. He had entire conversations with her almost daily, sometimes several times a day," Bree said.

"I wonder if his spirit has grown weaker over time, because he doesn't interact nearly as much with us as he did with Elizabeth in the weeks after his death."

Immediately after the words left her mouth, the television channel changed on its own. It went to a Christian church station, and the man on the television was in the middle of a sentence. The very next words from his mouth were, "You give me strength. You make my spirit stronger…" and then the channel changed back to the original programming Jason had been viewing.

"I wish I could say that was a strange coincidence," Bree confessed.

"Me too," Jason agreed.

The phone rang a short while later, and it was Karen. Before Bree could begin telling her mother about Elizabeth's final journal entries and the odd television incident, Karen said she had some very interesting news.

"I talked to your grandpa today," Karen began excitedly. "He said he didn't know much about your grandma's ancestry, especially since her mother was adopted. Your great-grandma – my grandma – was adopted and grew up about ten miles from White Dove in Three Lakes." Karen was quiet while Bree absorbed this information and realized what it might mean.

"So my great-grandma could possibly have been the child Elizabeth gave up for adoption," Bree said slowly.

"That's what I'm saying," Karen confirmed.

"Now there's one hell of a coincidence."

Chapter 13

"I hardly know what to do with that information," Bree confessed. "Is there any way we can find out whether my great-grandmother was Elizabeth's child?"

"I don't know how hard it would be to find definitive evidence of that, but it would help tremendously if we could find out when her birthday was. If her birthday matched up with the birthday on the adoption papers, I think that would be all the proof *I* would need to believe that my grandma and Elizabeth's child were one in the same," Karen said.

"Yeah, me too. Do you have anything that might have her birthday on it? Like a newspaper obituary or funeral program?" Bree asked hopefully.

"No," Karen replied. "And I asked your grandpa if he knew when it was or if he had any documentation with her birthday on it, but he didn't. I didn't want to dig too much because I'd rather not get him involved in this. You know how he is." Bree imagined her mother probably rolled her eyes with that last comment.

"Overly gung-ho, yes. He does like to be helpful. He didn't ask why you wanted to know about grandma's family?"

"He asked, but I lied and told him I needed some information for my passport. I told him not to worry about it, but

I'm sure he'll send me a bunch of information about our family history anyway." Karen sighed. "Bless his heart."

Bree laughed. She asked, "So how are we going to find out her birthday, then?"

"I know where my grandma is buried, so I had the idea that I could take a trip to the cemetery to see if the full date of birth is on the grave stone." Karen sounded proud of her sleuthing skills.

"That's a great idea! When are you going to do that?"

"I'll probably go tomorrow. Your dad and I can stop there when we take our usual Sunday drive." Karen and Jerry, Bree's father, always went sightseeing on Sundays. They had done so for as long as Bree could remember. She figured it was something they did to get away for a while when she was young, and it just became a weekly tradition.

"I'll get out the adoption papers to look up the birthday again. When you call me tomorrow we can make comparisons, and this way we'll both learn the truth at the same time. It just wouldn't be fair if you found out before me," Bree teased.

"Ok, I guess that's fair," Karen agreed.

"Now that you've shared your interesting news with me, it's my turn." Bree told her mother about Elizabeth's final journal entries depicting Gregory's death and subsequent haunting. She then told her about MIPS coming the next day to investigate their home.

"I'm glad you guys are getting help." Karen sounded relieved. "Things do seem to be getting a little out of hand for you. I'll make sure to call you before eight tomorrow so I don't interrupt their investigation."

The rest of the night was quiet for Jason and Bree, and the next morning Bree woke from a dreamless sleep, which she welcomed these days. She and Jason tried to have a relaxing Sunday afternoon, but it was difficult with the anxiety they were both feeling regarding the impending MIPS investigation.

"So do you think MIPS will do any actual investigating tonight, or just ask a lot of questions and look over our evidence?" Bree asked Jason as they lounged on the couch, still in their pajamas even though it was almost 4 PM.

162

"I hope they do an investigation. Cora seemed to understand how serious we felt the situation was becoming and that we wanted to resolve it as quickly as possible."

"But what if they don't? Should we ask them to do one? And you have to work tomorrow. What if the investigation will take all night?" Bree was beginning to fret.

"Relax. We'll cross that bridge when we get there. I can always call into work if I'm too tired in the morning," Jason replied. "Maybe you could focus your energy on preparing for their visit so you aren't busy worrying about it," he suggested.

Bree took a deep breath to try to calm her nerves. "You're right. But you're going to help me."

They went up to the computer room. She instructed him to mark all the places in the video that showed paranormal activity so they didn't waste time trying to find them when the investigators were there. She would do the same for the audio by writing down the time of each occurrence on the recording.

As she skipped through the voice recordings to find the EVP's, she began to consider some of the questions she had for the investigators. She set aside the recorder for a moment and began a list:

- How would we go about figuring out if there are any remains buried under or around our house?
- What methods have you used to expel spirits from other homes?
- Have you ever had a case similar to this one?
- If worse came to worse, would destroying this house and building a new one solve the problem?

Remembering the strange occurrence with the TV yesterday, Bree added:

- Is it possible that my interactions or even my presence could somehow be fueling the spirit's manifestations and giving it more power?

She put down the list and resumed her work with the audio recorder. As she found each EVP, she was unsurprised to discover that Gregory's voice still made her feel nauseous. Each time she heard him speak, she thought of his terrible laughter and psychotic cruelness from the dream she'd had two nights ago. She was able to finish tagging the EVP's, however, and she smiled at Jason as she removed her headphones. He had finished with his video long before Bree was done with the audio, but she wouldn't let him leave the room until she was done. It was bad enough that she had to listen to Gregory's voice again, and she wasn't about to do it alone. Jason ceased picking at his fingernails and hopped out of his seat, appearing relieved to be able to resume his Sunday lounging.

When they returned to the living room, Bree noticed that it was almost 5 PM.

"Damn, honey, we need to get showered. Look at the time. I need to start thinking about dinner!" She was already beginning to feel stressed and anxious again.

"Hotdogs and mac'n'cheese are good enough for me," Jason stated. "Let's eat first, then shower."

By 6:30 PM, Bree was finally in the bathroom, undressing for her shower. As she waited for the water to run hot, she weighed herself and stepped up onto the toilet so she could get a full view of herself in the medicine cabinet mirror. She really didn't know why she almost always did those two things before or after her shower because nothing ever changed. She always weighed 121 lbs., and her small, slender body always looked fairly toned. But as she stepped down from the toilet, she realized that over the next few months things *would* start to change. She climbed up and looked into the mirror again, this time with a more critical eye. She thought that perhaps her breasts did look slightly larger already, but nothing dramatic. Turning to the side, she tried to distend her belly to resemble a pregnant one – well, *more* pregnant one – and smiled at herself as she pictured how funny she was going to look with a huge belly perched atop her skinny legs.

Eventually she realized she was wasting hot water and quickly began her shower. Lost in her thoughts of babies and parenthood, she disregarded the quiet cracking sounds coming from the ceiling above the shower. When she closed her eyes and tipped her head back to rinse the shampoo from her hair, however, she felt something lightly tickling her face. She opened her eyes and found herself staring at Gregory's putrid face. His hair was dangling down, with his gooey-looking locks grazing her face. His body was hanging down from the ceiling, like a bat, except he was only visible from the waist up. The rest of him seemed to be inside of or a part of the ceiling. He was hanging down so that his face was only about twelve inches from Bree's head.

Bree screamed and jumped out of the shower, never taking her eyes from Gregory. The shower continued to run with the curtain wide open, and Gregory continued to hang from the ceiling and watch her with his unblinking, hateful eyes. She startled when she suddenly felt the floor vibrating, but she quickly realized that it was Jason's footsteps as he raced up the stairs.

"A slip in the shower," Gregory hissed menacingly, "is all it would take…" He was quickly sucked up into the ceiling as Jason burst through the door.

"Are you ok?" He asked breathlessly. He had obviously run up the stairs as fast as he could when he heard Bree scream. His eyebrows were pinched together in concern as he looked at the vacant, running shower and saw that Bree's skin was still dripping wet and covered in goose bumps. "What happened?"

"He scared me while I was in the shower. He hung upside down right in my face and said that a slip in the shower was all it would take. Then he disappeared," Bree described the incident with a scowl. She felt tears welling up in her eyes. "Jason, I don't know how much more of this I can take. He's really beginning to mess with my mind. I'm afraid he's going to try to hurt me and the baby soon. Why can't he just let all this hundred-year-old bullshit go?" Bree exclaimed in frustration. She looked up at the ceiling where Gregory had been and shouted, "Get over it, you dick!"

Jason pulled Bree to him and held her in a close embrace, trying to soothe her nerves and calm her fury. "I won't ever let him hurt you or the baby, sweetie," he declared.

Bree knew there was little Jason could do to stop Gregory if he did try something, but she was comforted by his words anyway. She asked him to stay in the room while she finished rinsing off and he kindly obliged. As she dressed afterward, he changed his clothes, as his had gotten damp when he hugged her wet body a few minutes earlier.

The phone rang shortly after Bree was finished getting ready. She worried that it might be MIPS calling to reschedule and was relieved when she saw her mother's cell phone number on the caller ID.

"Have you got the adoption papers nearby?" Karen asked excitedly.

"Damn, I forgot. I'll get them now." She ran upstairs to the bedroom and found the papers after minimal searching. "Ok, what have you got?"

"January 11, 1897."

Bree looked down at the papers. "The papers were dated for January 12, 1897, and the date of birth for the child was … January 11, 1897." Bree and Karen were both quiet for a moment. Then, "Huh," was all Bree could say. She had rocks in her stomach.

"Yep," Karen answered.

"What a completely unlikely coincidence this is. It's strange how things unfold sometimes, isn't it?" Bree mused, still unsure how she should feel.

Karen agreed.

"Wow. Well, I hate to do this," Bree said, "but MIPS could be here anytime so I'm going to let you go for now. I'll call you tomorrow and we can talk more about how weird this is."

"Ok sweetie. Good luck and *be careful*!"

Eight o'clock finally came, bringing with it the arrival of the MIPS team. When Bree saw two large vans and a truck pull into the driveway, she remembered that she had something she wanted to discuss with Jason before the investigation. She quickly addressed it now.

"Should we tell them everything we know about Gregory and Elizabeth right away, or let them try to figure it out first to see if they get it right? I mean, if Cora's a medium, she'll probably be claiming that she's communicating with Gregory, and I want to make sure she's the real deal before I invest too

166

much confidence in her." Bree spoke quickly, hoping to get an answer from Jason before MIPS came to the door.

"Uh," Jason fumbled, obviously caught off guard. "I guess that makes sense, but we should be open and tell them what we know before *too* long. We'll want them to have all the information they need to help us get rid of him. It took us a long time to find out the real story, and we don't want to wait that long for them to figure it out on their own."

Bree nodded as the investigators knocked at the door. She wanted to tell them everything, but she didn't want to be deceived or tricked by frauds. Even though MIPS didn't seem to be out for financial gain, she still felt wary.

She and Jason greeted Cora and her crew of misfits graciously and invited them inside. Upon crossing the threshold, Cora stopped and closed her eyes, standing completely still. Bree had to fight her urge to giggle as she noticed how silly the woman looked, standing there with a serious look of concentration on her face while her clothes conveyed a message of whimsy. She wore turquoise green leggings that no one her size should ever own, a billowy, flowered shirt straight out of the sixties, and of course, the ugly cowboy boots. It was hard for Bree to take someone seriously who looked that ridiculous.

As Bree struggled to keep the smirk from her lips, Cora opened her eyes and spoke. "There is a very bad energy here. Something terrible inhabits this home." She sounded almost in awe of its dreadfulness. She suddenly looked at Bree and Jason and smiled, then, as though they were old friends she hadn't seen in a long time. "Ah, yes. I remember you two! Thanks for calling us," Cora said as she extended her hand to each of them. "We look forward to assisting you with your problem." She paused momentarily, looking around ominously, and added, "And I think it may be a real doozy of a problem!"

Bree and Jason invited their guests to join them in the living room for the consultation. Kitchen chairs and seating on the floor were needed to accommodate the entire crew in the slightly under-furnished living room. Bree noticed someone even took a seat at the piano bench.

As everyone settled into their seats, Cora spoke to Bree. "I remember the last time you came into my store. You bought a book about paranormal phenomena, and you had a menacing energy surrounding you. I could see something very dark had attached itself to you. Now that I am here, I can feel that same unpleasant presence, only greatly magnified." When she was done speaking, she looked at Bree and appeared to be waiting for Bree to respond.

Bree wasn't sure how to respond to that, and the reply that left her lips was less than clever. "Um, yeah. It's pretty bad." She instantly felt like a dimwit, but for some reason she couldn't think of anything with which to follow it up. Her nervousness befuddled her brain.

Luckily, Cora didn't look at Bree as if she was dimwit. Instead, she tried to move the conversation forward. "Tell me about some of the things that have happened, but refrain from disclosing too much about the assumptions and discoveries you've made about the spirit's origin or purpose until after we've conducted the first investigation. I don't want to have any bias. When and how did all of this start?" She seemed to be speaking directly to Bree, not to Jason.

"It started before we even moved in permanently. We had some renovations done and had been staying at the house over the weekends to clean and prepare it for inhabitation. It was during one of these weekends – I believe it was the weekend that we decided the house was ready to move into – that I saw a bodiless head floating in front of my face when I was in the basement." She told her about the experiences she and her mother had in the house and described what she had seen in the shower earlier that day. She purposely left out any dialogue from the encounters, deciding that she would reveal it later when she was more confident with Cora's abilities. She also only referred to the spirit as "he" instead of divulging his name.

"Amazing," one of the crew members said in awe when Bree had finished sharing her claims.

"Indeed," agreed Cora. "Does he ever try to communicate with you verbally?"

Bree hesitated, so Jason chimed in. "We have some recordings of his voice and some interesting footage you would probably like to see." He told them vaguely about their amateur investigation.

The entire team filed up the stairs behind Jason and Bree to the computer room to view the evidence. After a little cramming and jostling, everyone made it into the room. That was when Jason discovered that the computer had somehow been turned off.

"I did *not* touch it," Bree announced, unprompted. She didn't want Jason to even get a chance to try to pin it on her.

Frustrated, he tried to switch it back on. "Now all the marking I did on the video is gone. I'll have to go through and find it all again." He was apologizing profusely to MIPS when he realized that the computer wasn't booting up. He tried several times to turn it on, but nothing happened.

One of the tech professionals in the group suggested that maybe the unit wasn't receiving any power. When Jason looked at him in confusion, the fellow responded with the typical arrogance characteristic of any company IT worker.

"*Is it plugged in?*" He asked with is eyebrows raised and his jaw slightly slack, even shaking his head slightly as though he were speaking to a small, foolish child. Bree didn't know his name yet, but she mentally tagged him as Mr. IT.

Jason was about to dish out a smart-ass reply when Bree stopped him. "Hey look, Jason. How the hell did it come unplugged?" She pointed at the electrical cord on the floor.

"That is *never* unplugged," Jason said, putting emphasis on each syllable. Bree knew he felt foolish, and like most people, would probably spend the next several minutes trying to explain that he wasn't stupid by reiterating that they never touched the computer's power cord, so he couldn't have expected it to be unplugged. And she was right.

Once the computer had power and began to start up, a black screen greeted them with a message about an error in their hard drive and displayed a code.

"You've got to be shitting me." Jason's anger and frustration were palpable.

Mr. IT offered to take a look, so Jason moved from the computer chair. After a few moments, Bree and Jason were informed that their computer needed a new hard drive and possibly a new motherboard. They had likely lost everything on their computer.

"How could that have happened?" Jason was beginning to sound of despair. Bree knew how he felt, as she was fighting back tears herself.

"Static, a power surge – a lot of things can damage a computer and its components. It's just part of owning a computer," Mr. IT explained.

"Well there goes all of our video evidence." Bree let out a defeated sigh. "At least we still have the audio recordings, though they aren't nearly as impressive."

The digital voice recorder was passed around the room. Once everyone had heard the EVP's, Cora suggested that Jason and Bree describe the video evidence to her. They told of the apparition slipping into the floor, the close-up face, and the loud "It'll be over soon" anomaly.

"That would've really been something to see, I'll bet," Cora said. "Do you feel that any of this computer malfunctioning business could be paranormal in nature? Do you think the spirit is the one who caused it?" Cora asked Jason and Bree.

Bree answered, "I'm inclined to think he has something to do with it, considering the circumstances and timing. But what do you think? You're the expert."

Cora corrected Bree's assessment. "Well, I wouldn't consider anyone in the field of paranormal research to be an 'expert,' but I have seen a lot. And I agree that the computer coming unplugged and crashing could possibly be paranormal. I don't find it absurd that he would try to hinder our investigation in any way he can, especially if he knows of our intentions. I don't think he wants to leave this house," Cora announced.

Everyone stood quietly for a few moments, waiting for Cora to decide their next move.

"Let's all go back downstairs," Cora suggested. "You guys can relax for a while," she indicated the team members, "and Jason and Bree can give me a walkthrough to help me get a feel for the place. I want to find out if there are certain areas or objects that he is more strongly tied to than others."

Cora's tour began in the basement. Bree showed her where the burning head had appeared to her and where the piano had been. Cora said little, so they moved onto the main floor. Cora was presented with the piano and spent a long time running her hands over the wood, keys, and bench with her eyes closed. Occasionally she would freeze and stand motionless for a moment, then continue her strange procedure. When she finally backed away from the piano, Bree asked her if she discovered anything. The only response she got was, "In due time." Cora didn't show a lot of interest in any of the other rooms on the main floor, even the kitchen where the cupboard dweller had made his appearance or the tiny bathroom where Bree had seen Gregory twice in the mirror the night of her and Jason's investigation. The upstairs rooms, however, proved to be more intriguing.

When they led Cora upstairs, she immediately was drawn to the master bedroom at the top of the stairs. She walked into the middle of the room and stood quietly with her eyes closed. She remained that way for what seemed like an eternity to Bree. As they watched her, Bree saw her lips move slightly and heard her faintly speak the words "burning side" with her eyes still closed.

Apparently, Jason had heard the whisper as well. "Just like your sleep talking," he commented in a whisper. When he saw Bree's confused expression, he knew she wasn't following. He explained, still whispering, "Remember that night when you had the nightmare about burning alive in our bed? You got mad at me in the morning because I was teasing you about your sleep talking." An expression of recognition spread across Bree's face, so Jason continued, "In your sleep, you kept saying that you didn't want to sleep on the *burning side*."

"You know what's weird about that?" Bree began, also whispering so Cora wouldn't hear her. "Only the side of the bed that Gregory was sleeping on was the one that burned. Elizabeth's side was untouched, according to her diary. So his side of the bed was the 'burning side.'"

They looked at each other, wordlessly agreeing that it was weird. They noticed that Cora had begun to walk around the room.

"Oh, this is lovely!" She exclaimed, admiring Bree's woodsy mural. "Is this the painting that had the shadowy figure appear in it?"

"Yes," Bree replied, and she pointed to the place where it had been. "He was right here, but I painted over him. I found him to be unnerving."

"As would I," Cora agreed.

After a few more minutes, Cora was ready to move on to the next room. She didn't feel the need to see the computer room again, as she had already experienced that room, so she went into the guest bedroom. When she suddenly gasped and brought her hand to her chest, Jason rushed to her side.

"Is everything alright?" He asked with concern.

"It's ok; that happens sometimes. I just felt a very strong reaction is all. I'm fine." She gave him a reassuring smile and walked away from him, further into the small room. Her large frame made the dimensions of the room appear to be even slighter than they actually were. She closed her eyes and stood in the middle of the room just as she had in the master bedroom. When she finally opened her eyes again, Bree asked her a question.

"So what are you picking up?"

"We will sit down and discuss it shortly, I promise. I just like to do the entire walkthrough first," Cora explained.

She spent less time looking around the bathroom than she had in the other two rooms, which surprised Bree. She'd had a few experiences and had seen a vision of what had transpired in that room over a hundred years ago. She wondered if Cora had seen any visions in that room as well.

The next place they brought Cora was the attic. Bree had serious concerns about Cora fitting through the tiny door into the attic, but thankfully Cora didn't even try. She only poked her head in momentarily and was ready to move on again. She took a quick glance in the widow's watch, but seemed unimpressed with what she felt in the room. Bree then informed her that this concluded the tour of the house.

"Well, kids, we have got a lot to talk about," Cora announced as they returned to the living room.

They found the MIPS team lounging quietly when they entered the room.

"Are you ready for us to set up?" asked a pretty young brunette with black-painted fingernails.

Cora turned to Jason and Bree. "Would you like us to do a full-fledged investigation tonight? It usually takes several hours and we wouldn't be out of your hair until probably about four o'clock in the morning, just to warn you."

Bree and Jason looked at each other and nodded in unison.

"Yes, we were hoping for that," Bree answered. "We really want to get this...thing...taken care of as quickly as we can."

Cora instructed the crew to begin setting up the equipment, directing the specific placement of each instrument in particular locations. As the team worked, Cora sat down with the concerned couple.

"I'm not going to sugar-coat this for you," Cora began. "There is someone or something here who wants to do harm. I haven't honed in on exactly who this spirit is or why they want to cause harm yet, but that will come in the investigation. The team will run their investigation first, and then we will sit down together and I will try some direct communication with the spirit. I don't think we will be disappointed tonight because I get a very strong feeling that this entity *wants* to speak and be heard. It definitely seems to have a message."

Those last words made Bree's blood run cold, as she already knew what that message would likely be: *watch your back, Bree*.

The medium then asked if they had any questions for her. Bree went back upstairs to get her question list from the computer room. When she returned, Jason asked the first question from her list before she even had a chance to speak.

"If we believe that there may be human remains buried around or under our house, how would we go about figuring that out?" It obviously bothered him greatly to know that Gregory's bones could be right under their feet.

Cora was quick with a response. "We know an archeologist, Perry Anderson, who has equipment that can detect such things in the ground. It's called a ground-penetrating radar. He mainly works with Native American burial grounds and remains, but he's helped us in the past. I'll contact him as soon as I can, but he does charge a fee for the use of his equipment."

"It would be worth it to finally know," Jason replied. Bree felt the same way. The worse things got with Gregory, the less she worried about how much it would cost to eradicate him from their home.

"Anything else?" Cora wanted to know.

"Yes," Bree replied quickly. "I have a list of questions here. First, what methods have you used to expel spirits from other homes?"

"We've tried a number of techniques, all successful under the right circumstances. We've had the family sit down together and order the spirit to leave their home. We've had a priest bless a few homes. In rare cases, we've found remains, and after the remains were removed from the premises, the haunting ceased. If you think there may be remains on your property, this method may be the one we'll need to use first."

Bree was in agreement. She asked her next question. "Have you ever had a case similar to this one?"

Cora thought for a moment before responding. "We've had a few cases involving angry and violent spirits, yes. But I've never felt the presence of a spirit with the client *outside* of the home like I did with you. I don't yet know if that is significant. We won't know the full extent of your problem until after we investigate."

Cora's answer worried Bree. Instead of moving on to the next question on her list, she asked, "What do you mean? You think the spirit is attached to *me*, not the house?"

"No, I don't know if that's the case. I just found it odd that I could feel it outside of the home. It may be nothing important. We'll know more soon."

Bree still didn't feel comforted, but she asked her next question anyway. "If worse came to worse, would destroying the house and building a new one fix our problem?"

"Like I said, I'm not sure yet. We've never had to go that far before."

Bree was feeling more and more worried with every answer. "Is it possible that my presence in the house and interactions could be fueling the spirit's manifestations and giving it more power?" She was afraid to hear Cora's reply.

"We have found this to be the case before. Once we had a situation that seemed to escalate as the client interacted with the entity more and more, but when we instructed him to ignore the entity, the activity slowed and eventually stopped altogether. We haven't encountered this but once, though."

"I have just one more question," Bree said. "If we have learned certain things about the spirit's life and possibly why it may be haunting this house, when should we share this information with you?"

"After tonight, if I make contact, you can tell me what you know. I will leave it up to you, though, if you want to tell me right away or after another investigation. Sometimes the information helps, but sometimes it isn't accurate and can cause for confusion. If you aren't very confident of your information, you should sit on it for a while," Cora advised. "I like to conduct my investigations with as little bias as possible, especially in the first visit. I don't want to misinterpret something because I'm expecting a specific response."

Bree and Jason acknowledged that they understood. They were fairly certain that the information they had gathered was factual, but they didn't say as much.

The MIPS team reconvened in the living room where Bree and Jason were sitting with Cora. They had completed their setup and were ready to begin investigating.

"What do you want us to do while you investigate?" Jason wondered.

"You can join us, if you want," one of the crew members suggested.

Cora thought that was a fine idea. "We may have more success if you two are with us. It seems that Bree's presence may fuel the activity."

Excited for the chance to be part of a real investigation, Bree jumped at the opportunity without bothering to consult with Jason. She assumed he would feel the same as she did. The MIPS crew split into three teams in order to control the group size during the investigation. The first team took Jason and Bree with them while the rest of the MIPS crew gathered in the kitchen to sit quietly and wait their turn. Bree's team consisted of Sarah, the pretty brunette with the gothic taste in nail polish; David, a tall, slender computer information systems analyst with ruddy hair and the thickest glasses Bree had ever seen; and Sam, a chubby, curly-haired, online computer game enthusiast with a knack for numbers.

Their investigation began in the living room. The typical EVP questions were asked, regarding the spirit's name, reason for being there, et cetera. When offered a chance to ask questions, Bree declined because she felt self-conscious. A few of the MIPS members seemed like they could be a bit judgmental and she didn't want to be criticized for having poor investigation skills.

Jason, however, didn't seem fazed in the least. He jumped right in with a question. "How do you feel now that we've brought a whole team in to flush you out?" His tone was aggressive, challenging.

When things remained quiet, the team decided to move the investigation upstairs. As they headed toward the guest bedroom, Lenore's room, the door forcefully slammed shut, right in front of Sam's bulbous nose.

"Holy shit!" He exclaimed, jumping backward. "Did you see that?"

Everyone but Bree and Jason were excited. They were glad something happened for the team to see, but slamming doors was small biscuits for Gregory. Sarah stepped forward and opened the door, which swung open easily. They tried to get the door to slam shut again by walking by it and jumping up and down near it, but they couldn't debunk the incident. The investigation continued.

In the guest room, David asked the spirit to slam the door again to prove that it was really there. Everyone thought they heard faint laugher shortly thereafter. Bree recognized and hated that laugh, but she said nothing. The rest of the time spent in the guest room yielded no other strange activity.

The next paranormal occurrence happened in the master bedroom. Sarah asked the spirit to knock on the wall to let them know it was present. They heard a loud bang on the mural wall in response. Bree even noticed that the wall was hit with such force that the floor shook. Then David and Sam both claimed to smell smoke in one area of the room. It was confined to a small area, and everyone had a chance to experience it before it suddenly dispelled. They then decided it was time to let the next team have a go at it and headed down to the main floor.

On the way down the stairs, Sam suddenly stumbled and lurched forward. Bree was directly in front of him and quickly dodged to the side to avoid being knocked over by Sam's overweight body. He managed to catch himself at that point, fortunately, and saved himself from taking out the entire group.

"Something grabbed my foot, I swear!" Sam shouted shrilly. He shone his flashlight at the stairs off of which he had just come. They were bare, with nothing to trip over. He continued to puzzle over the incident as they went down the stairs.

Bree felt frightened after that event. Sam had almost knocked her down, which could have been catastrophic for both her and the tiny person growing inside her. She decided to sit out the rest of the investigation for fear of what Gregory might try next. There was no doubt in her mind that he was behind Sam's fall.

A couple long hours later, at 1 AM, the first part of the investigation was complete. It was now time for Cora to try to speak with the spirit directly, which was the part that Bree dreaded the most. She didn't want to hear his threats, but she knew it was a crucial aspect of MIPS's procedure. Reluctantly, she sat next to Cora at the dining room table.

Everyone gathered around the small table, sitting on whatever they could find as there was again a shortage of chairs. Jason was seated next to Bree, holding her hand under the table to offer her comfort.

Once everyone was settled, Cora began to explain how her session would be held. "I want you to forget everything you've learned from the entertainment industry about mediums. We are not going to try to summon spirits who have already passed into another world. All I am going to do is use my gift to hear and feel the spirits that have stayed behind and remain in this house. I only wish to communicate enough to discover what they want, why they are here, and figure out what we need to do to send them on to the next world. I don't follow a script or say any special chants other than a short protection prayer before beginning the session. I just do whatever comes naturally. I won't open myself to the spirits to let them use me as their puppet, and if I feel that there is any danger of this – or if anyone is in imminent danger from the spirit – I will draw back and end the session to avoid any more provocation. With that, I feel we are ready to begin."

Cora instructed everyone to join hands while she led the group in a prayer for protection against any malevolent spirits. When she was finished, only Bree and Jason continued to clasp each other's hands.

The medium sat quietly for a long time with her eyes closed. The only light illuminating the room came from the lightning lamp on the table, which Bree had suggested using to help draw Gregory to them. Unfortunately, the green glow made the whole scene seem creepy to Bree.

After several agonizing minutes of silence, Cora spoke, keeping her eyes closed. "There is a man here in the room. I can feel the anger and resentment emanating from him." She was quiet for a second, then continued, "He says his name is Barry. No, wait. Gregory? It's Gregory, I think. He is feeling a great deal of hostility toward someone seated to my left."

178

Bree already knew she was the one to Cora's left whom Gregory was targeting.

"He wants to take something from that person…from Bree…something that is strongly a part of her. He keeps saying 'blood.' I don't understand. He wants to take her blood?" Cora remained still with closed eyes. "He says I'm stupid. He's angry with me for being here and for not understanding his meaning. He wants to know if all women are so useless." Cora turned her head toward Bree and Jason, eyes still closed, and said, "Go ahead and ask him your questions. He's still ranting, but he may hear and respond."

Bree wasn't expecting to be able to speak to Gregory directly during the session, so she was caught off guard. Her brain fumbled for a question, and finally she knew what to ask.

"How do you know I'm related to…her?" She asked, purposely refraining from using Elizabeth's name as she hadn't yet told the medium about her.

Cora responded quickly. "He says he can tell. It's almost like he can smell her on you, is how he describes it. He seems disgusted by this."

"Is your body still buried here?" Jason spoke up.

"He's not answering that. I can feel that he doesn't want you to know the answer to that."

"Don't you want a proper, respectable burial?" Jason asked. "We can give you that if you let us know where to find your body."

"He feels suspicious. He doesn't want to discuss this anymore. Wait, he has a question for you. He wants to know why he can't harm Bree. I can't tell if he's actually asking this or if I can just feel his strong curiosity at this."

"You can't harm me because I didn't do anything to you! What kind of a stupid question is that?" Bree exclaimed incredulously.

"He says you misunderstand. He tries, but is unable to harm you. Some force always…blocks…him?" Cora sounded confused with the last sentence. She went quiet and seemed to be trying to concentrate. Suddenly she inhaled loudly, like she had just learned a juicy secret. She smiled slyly.

179

"There is another spirit here...a woman," she revealed, smiling widely.

Chapter 14

Cora seemed surprised, but pleased with her discovery. She said, "The man's presence was so overpowering that I almost missed her completely. She was like static in the background."

Bree was shocked. *Another* spirit? Her mind raced with questions. Was it Elizabeth? Was it Lenore? Why was this woman here? Was some of the activity actually from the female spirit and not Gregory? It took an extraordinary amount of will power for Bree to keep from blurting out every question that entered her mind. She waited in anticipation for Cora to continue, but the medium sat silently again, leaving Bree in suspense.

Finally, Cora spoke again. "She doesn't venture far from Bree, it seems. I'm still surprised I didn't notice her sooner. She's very good at hiding her presence."

Bree was instantly curious about the spirit's reason for staying near her. Why would it want to follow her around? Was *she* the reason that Gregory was so drawn to Bree?

"She's finally speaking to me," Cora interrupted Bree's thoughts. "She says her name is Liz, or Lizzy." Cora then gave a short chuckle. "She says she doesn't like it when Bree calls her by her full name."

Elizabeth. She was here. She'd been listening. Bree instantly felt embarrassed for some of the things she'd said about Elizabeth – Liz – out loud while reading the diary.

"She protects you, Bree. She keeps the angry male spirit, Gregory, from causing you physical harm. I've never seen this before," Cora confessed, apparently in awe. She asked the spirit, "How do you do it, Liz?" After a brief pause, she relayed the answer to the group. "She says she can't explain it to us in a way we would understand, but she can hide her presence from the other spirit. He didn't know she was here – but he does now. He's trying to interrupt my connection with Liz right now. Bree, she has a message for you: she wants you to be warned that it's getting more difficult for her to protect you from Gregory. He is very strong. Run while you still can, she says." Another long pause. "She's closed herself off from me, now. I think she's trying to hide from the other spirit. He is very angry that she's here."

"Elizabeth! I mean, Liz," Bree called frantically. "Why are you here? Did you die here, too? Did you know you were my great-great grandmother? Why did you give up your baby? What happened after your journal ended? Please don't leave yet; I have so many questions for you!" Bree pleaded.

"I'm sorry, Bree, but she's gone. Gregory is coming through again. He said she didn't die here and she shouldn't be here. She should be in Hell with the other prostitutes. He has a strong hatred for Liz. It's actually making me feel a little ill." Cora began to take controlled, deep breaths, apparently trying to calm herself.

Bree took the opportunity to lash out at Gregory. "You don't belong here either! You should be in Hell! You should've continued burning for eternity!"

Cora gasped suddenly, as though a light bulb just went on in her brain. "That's what you meant! I heard you in the bedroom, Gregory, when you tried to tell me about the burning side. I didn't understand then, but I've just now seen the vision of what happened to you. The burning side of the bed! You burned to death in your bed, but your side was the only part of

182

the bed that was consumed in flames! Bree, were you aware of how he died? He says that you knew this."

"Yes," she replied simply.

"He blames Liz. He says that if it weren't for her, this wouldn't have happened to him. He says this is why he must…end the bloodline…because it is saturated with evil…and the continued existence of it brings him dishonor." Cora relayed Gregory's message with obvious confusion in her voice. She didn't seem to understand why Gregory felt this way.

For a moment, Bree didn't understand why Cora was so confused. She then remembered that Cora didn't know any of the history between Elizabeth and Gregory, as Bree hadn't shared any of it with her. She knew she would have to fill her in on the details after the session was over. She no longer had any doubt that Cora was legitimate.

"Oh my, we need to end – right now," Cora said urgently. She concentrated in silence for several minutes.

Bree looked around the table at the faces of Cora's crew. They appeared only slightly concerned. Bree deduced that this sudden end to the session was something that had happened a few times before. She returned her attention to Cora just in time to see the medium open her eyes for the first time since the beginning of her session.

Cora immediately turned to Bree, her brows furrowed in concern. "Bree, it is not safe for you to stay here. I could feel the boiling hatred this entity has toward you, and I saw that he wanted to – *wants* to – hurt you. Well, more specifically, he wants to terminate your pregnancy. Did the activity in the house pick up after you got pregnant?" Cora wanted to know.

Bree reflected on the past couple of months before giving a response. "It's possible. I mean, things started to get really bad just a couple weeks ago, so I suppose that would have been soon after I had conceived. I didn't know I was pregnant yet, but maybe somehow Gregory knew. He seems to know a lot about me before I even do."

"I think it is your pregnancy that is driving his violence. He is a violent spirit by nature, I believe, but it seems to me that your condition is what is making him more angry and violent than usual. I would strongly suggest you consider finding somewhere else to stay until we can rid your home of his presence."

With stubborn resolve, Bree replied, "He will not run me out of my own home. I will not be bullied by him. And what about Liz? Didn't she say she was protecting me?"

"Yes, but she also suggested that you 'run while you still can' because he is becoming more difficult to stop," Cora reminded her. "I'm not trying to scare you or suggest that you are weak, but I'm afraid this situation is more dangerous than you realize. You shouldn't be thinking of him as a schoolyard bully, but as a serial killer hiding in your closet."

Those words worried Jason. He squeezed Bree's hand gently to get her attention. When she turned to look at him, she knew he could see the anger and fear in her eyes. He pleaded with her, "Please, honey. Please don't knowingly put yourself in harm's way just to prove your bravery. Gregory doesn't seem to care. He *wants* you to stay, so he can hurt you. It isn't a game, Bree, so please don't try to 'win.'" He looked at her with love and deep concern in his dark brown eyes. He only wanted her to be safe; she understood that. But she also wasn't the type of person to back down from a fight, especially in her own home. Conflicting feelings consumed her as she tried to find the right words to say to Jason. She didn't want him to have to worry, but she couldn't swallow her pride just yet. She wasn't ready to hide under the covers like a scared child.

"I appreciate everyone's concern, I really do. But I'm afraid if I leave now, he's going to think I'm weak. If he thinks I'm weak, wouldn't it just make things worse?" Bree tried to reason.

Cora countered her argument. "He doesn't care how strong or weak or determined you are. No matter what, he's going to continue to attack you. Standing up to him isn't likely to make a difference. Now, I can't *make* you leave, but I will advise you that it would probably be the safest route for you to take right now."

Bree was reminded of one of her encounters with Gregory. She argued, "Standing up to him has worked before.

When he caused the bedroom door to freeze shut, he released it when I threatened to burn down the house. My threat worked." Bree was trying to convince everyone that it was logical and necessary for her to stay and fight. She couldn't win with an argument based solely on having pride and determination.

Jason stepped in. "But that was the only time it ever worked, wasn't it? He gets more violent and relentless each day. I think it's gone beyond the point where empty threats and standing our ground will be effective. We need to step back and let the professionals take care of this. If not for me, do it for our little one growing inside you. If you stay in this dangerous house, the baby has to stay too. Is that really what you want?"

Jason's logic chewed at Bree's resolve. She didn't want to put the baby in danger, especially while it was so small and fragile. It might not look like a baby yet, but she knew that right at that very moment it was working on growing a little heart, a little brain, and all the things that would someday make it into a fuzzy-headed, sweet little person who would look a little like her and a little like Jason. She'd only known of the baby for less than one short week, but already she loved it. She loved that it was made from both her and Jason, and she loved what it was going to become. When she thought of someday holding that baby in her arms and watching it grow, she realized that swallowing her pride was no longer an issue. There was no way she was going to put herself in danger while carrying such precious cargo.

"Bree?"

Jason startled her out of her revelation. She hadn't noticed how much time had elapsed since Jason had last spoken to her, but she had apparently been lost in her thoughts for some time.

"Sorry. I was just thinking about what is really important now. Re-prioritizing," she explained quietly. "I seem to say this all the time anymore, but you're right...again. I shouldn't risk it, especially when I'm not the only one taking the risk." Bree was apologetic. "But where do I go? What do I do?"

"Do you have any family or friends nearby who know about your situation?" Cora inquired.

"Not nearby," Jason answered for Bree. "We're still new to the area and don't have any close friends here yet. The only people we've told about this are Bree's parents, and they live four hours away. Maybe we could just stay in a hotel for a while, until this is over. How long could that be?" Jason wondered.

Cora wasn't supportive of that idea. "It can be a lengthy process, particularly when it comes to powerful entities, such as this one. It would be best if you could stay with family or close friends so you have a support group to help you through this. You wouldn't believe what a difference it can make just to have others around you who love and care about you. It makes the whole ordeal that much less stressful."

"Yeah, but even if Bree's parents would take us in for a while, I have a job. I can't just up and leave for a spell without proper notification," Jason stressed. "It takes at least a week to get vacation time approved."

Cora replied to Jason, "Please don't take offense, but it isn't you that I'm worried about. The entity doesn't seem to care as much about your presence. He's after Bree and the baby. Granted, it would be best if you could both vacate the house, but I think it's most important to get *Bree* out of here right away. If it takes a week for you to get your vacation time, so be it. But we should get Bree out of here sooner than that and you could join her when you are able."

"Jason and I are obviously going to have to talk about this," Bree said with slight irritation at Cora's relentlessness, "but there isn't much we can do at…" she glanced at the clock, "…two-fifteen in the morning. I'll see what kind of plans I can arrange and what will work for *us*. What's the next step for you guys? When will you be back?"

"It will be soon, hopefully within the next couple of days. We have to work around everyone's work schedules. This is a very serious case, though, so we'll definitely do our very best to be back as quickly as we can. I'll get a hold of Perry to see about checking the grounds for remains, and let you know what I find out right away."

"What will you do in your next visit?" Bree was curious.

"We'll do another investigation, much like the one we did tonight. I want to hear more from Liz. I don't understand the animosity between her and Gregory. There's a lot of this puzzle missing," Cora acknowledged.

Bree sighed. "Oh, we can fill you in on all of that, if you're ready to hear it. I've read the entire journal that Liz – I've been calling her Elizabeth – wrote over a hundred years ago. It explains a lot of this."

Cora agreed that Bree should share this information with her now. Bree gave her the cut-and-dry version of the events that preceded and ultimately led to Gregory's death, and mentioned that Gregory had even haunted Liz while she was alive. Cora sat attentively and showed great interest in the story Bree told.

"I don't know when or how she died, though, because the journal ends long before she even had her child...which I recently discovered was most likely my great grandmother. I have a lot of questions for Liz myself," Bree admitted.

"We can address them at the next investigation. This is a very interesting case, with quite a history of dysfunctional behavior. Such strong emotions, such great pain can be the perfect catalyst for a truly monumental haunting. I think we may try to ask the spirits to leave the home at the end of our next visit, but I don't know how effective that course will be in this case. It's the first step we always take, though," Cora explained.

"Is there any way we can get Gregory to leave without affecting Liz? I don't want to make her leave if she doesn't want to."

"It's best if we try to make both of them move on. For all we know, her presence could be helping to keep him here as well."

"Maybe that's what he meant when he told me that my 'blood' keeps him here. She is my blood, in a sense. She's my great-great grandmother." When Cora didn't respond, Bree added, "I don't know though. He talks in such riddles that it's hard to follow his meaning sometimes."

Cora nodded in agreement. "I definitely understand your frustration with that!" She looked around the table at the MIPS team. "Are you guys ready to pack up and head out? I can finish up here with Jason and Bree if you want to start breaking things down." With that, the team disbursed. Cora returned her attention to her clients once all of the members of her crew had left the table. "Is there anything else I can do for you before we go? Do you have any more questions for me?"

"How long will it be before we hear back from you?" Jason asked. "I know you said you'd like to get back here within the next few days, but when will we know for sure? Are you going to call us?"

"Yes, I'll call you tomorrow night, right after I call Perry. I'll have a better idea of what will work for my team then as well. Sarah can do some research tomorrow, and I'm hoping Sam and Chris will be able to analyze the data we collected tomorrow as well." Cora leaned forward and whispered conspiratorially, "I'll bet they've got nothing better to do anyway. That is, if they can put aside the computer games for one day." She chuckled at her own cattiness.

Once MIPS had all of their equipment packed into their vehicles, Jason and Bree went out on the porch and thanked them all for coming. Bree assured Cora that she would find a place to go as soon as she could. They watched MIPS drive away before they went back into the house and turned off the porch light.

As they wearily headed up the stairs to bed, Jason asked, "So are you really going to go stay with your parents, or were you just saying that to pacify Cora?"

Bree couldn't tell from Jason's tone whether or not he liked the idea of sending her to her parents' house. She knew he wanted her to be out of the house and safe, but she didn't know how he felt about her being four hours away from him for an undetermined amount of time. He probably wanted to go with her instead of staying alone in this hostile house.

She replied, "I really do want to leave, for the baby's sake. It really made me think about it when you pointed out that the baby had to stay as long as I did. I wanted to discuss with you, though, where I should go. Do you want me to go all the way to Tandish to stay with my parents? Or do you want me to try to find somewhere closer?"

Jason took so long to respond that Bree was about to ask him if he'd heard her. He finally said, "I want you to go wherever you will feel the most comfortable and safe. Of course I want to have you nearby, but I don't know how we could swing that without having to stay in a hotel. We don't have any close friends here. What do *you* want to do?" Jason asked as he undressed, preparing to climb into bed.

As Bree slipped into her pajamas, she answered, "None of our options are ideal. I don't want to be so far away from you, but I think my parents' house is where I would be most comfortable. I still have to talk to them about it, but my mom did offer to have me stay with them a while ago. The other thing that kind of sucks about that arrangement, though, is that I'll have to make a lot of trips back and forth for the investigations. Ugh, everything is such a mess." She sighed wearily.

"We'll make it work. It's worth it to know that you and Junior will be safe. You'll both be far away from him and the house, way out of his reach. That's enough for me. Besides, I can put in for my vacation time and join you before too long," Jason said supportively. He rubbed his hand over her belly as she lay down next to him in bed.

"There is one more thing that kind of worries me, though," Bree said with furrowed brows. "Cora mentioned that she found it odd that she could feel Gregory's presence with me even when I was outside of our house. I hope it doesn't mean that he can *follow* me. What if I bring him into my parents' house by accident? What if he just follows me around, torturing me forever?" She was beginning to get an uneasy feeling in the pit of her stomach. Finding out that she couldn't even run from Gregory as a last-ditch effort to save herself and the baby would leave her feeling completely hopeless.

Jason was already shaking his head dismissively. "No, no. Stop that. I can't imagine that it could be possible. You know what I think? You know how people who smoke in their homes always smell like smoke, even if they haven't been smoking recently? How that odor just sticks to their clothes and everything in their house? Maybe Gregory is like the cigarette smoke. Cora could just 'smell' him on you, if you will. Can you try to think of it that way?"

Bree wondered if he actually believed that was possible, or if he was digging for any explanation just to calm her. It was an interesting theory, she had to admit, and she desperately wanted to believe it was true. She had come to believe that anything was possible. Unfortunately, that mentality also meant that she had to believe it was possible for him to follow her, as well.

"Thank you, Jason. Sometimes you know just the right thing to say to help me feel better," she said with a smile.

"Sometimes? Only sometimes?" He pretended to be offended. "At the very least, I would say *most* of the time I know the right thing to say." He smiled at her.

"Oh, shut up," she chided playfully. She kissed him and snuggled in next to him, already feeling sleep pulling at her eyelids. Jason reached over and turned on the alarm before settling into a comfortable position. Bree took it to mean that he was still planning to try to make it into work in the morning. Poor fool.

As they lay in bed, Jason's breathing slowed and evened out, indicating that he was fast asleep. Bree tried to match her breathing with his. It was something she often did when she was lying next to him, as it calmed her and helped to lull her into sleep. She began to doze, teetering on the brink of stage two sleep, when a soft "thud" brought her back.

"What the hell," she whispered to herself with a tone of disgust rather than curiosity. She had trouble lifting her heavy eyelids and had to blink lazily several times before her eyes began to focus properly. Looking around the room, she saw nothing out of place. The sound she thought she heard had seemed like it was far away, perhaps in another room. She wasn't about to go investigate the origin of the sound because at this point she was just too tired to care.

Bree closed her eyes again to make another attempt at sleep. She found that Jason's breathing was still slow and deep as she nuzzled into his shoulder once more. He had obviously been unaffected by the bump in the night. Just as she started to match his breathing, she heard another thump. With an exasperated groan, she pulled the covers up over her ears.

Thump...thump.

Irritated, Bree climbed out of bed and went to the bedroom door. Had this happened a week ago, or even a couple of nights ago, she might have left the bedroom to see what was going on. Tonight, however, she intended to shut the door and drown out Gregory's nonsense. As she began to swing the door closed, she heard another few thumps. She realized that they were footsteps, and they sounded like they were coming up the stairs. They began to pick up speed, as if Gregory was now hurrying up the stairs, heading straight toward her. *Thump, thump, thump, THUMP THUMP...* Bree slammed the door the rest of the way shut and tried to pretend that she wasn't beginning to feel frightened. To prove her courageousness to herself, she leaned her back against the door with her arms folded casually and listened. The footsteps thudded quickly to the top of the stairs, stopping right outside the door against which she leaned. The ensuing silence was eerie. Bree wondered if Gregory might be standing behind her, just on the opposite side of the door from her.

Suddenly, the door upon which she was leaning shook violently as if it was barraged with a flurry of pounding fists. Bree leapt away from the door with a shout. Her fatigue made her clumsy, and her body wasn't entirely prepared for her reflexive action. She tripped on her own feet and fell hard. Her knee hit the floor first and she continued to propel forward onto her right side, landing with her elbow and forearm under her ribs. Somehow, she managed to keep her head from hitting the floor.

As the pain shot through Bree's body, the door continued to rattle and shake under the pounding fists of an angry spirit. She looked up at the bed just in time to see Jason spring up out of it.

"What the hell is going on?!" He demanded in a tone full of anger and fear. He rushed to Bree's side, watching the door the entire time. "Are you ok? What's going on?" He asked again.

The banging on the door suddenly ceased. In the quiet, Bree could hear her heart beating in her ears.

Instead of answering Jason's questions, Bree first addressed Gregory. She sat up, looked at the door, and shouted an angry, "Fuck you!"

"Are you ok? What just happened?" Jason asked again impatiently.

Bree described the footsteps and how she slammed the door on Gregory. "I was leaning against the door, listening for the footsteps. He came right up to the door and started pounding on it! It startled me, and I fell when I tried to jump back." Her voice was cracking, warning of imminent tears.

Jason was almost panicked when he heard this. "Did you fall on your stomach? Do you think you're ok? Is the baby ok?"

She shared in his panic. As soon as she had begun to fall, she'd automatically tried to avoid landing on her belly. Whether or not it mattered how she landed, she didn't know, but protecting her belly was her immediate response. She didn't know if a fall like the one she had just taken could trigger a miscarriage or not, and she was deeply worried.

"I fell on my side, but I don't know if that even makes a difference. It wasn't the hardest fall I've ever taken, but it was still jarring. God, why didn't I just stay in bed?" Bree reprimanded herself angrily as her distress grew in magnitude. "What do I do now? How do I know if I'm ok? I really need to talk to my mom, but it's three o'clock in the god-damned morning!" Bree cried, still sitting on the floor with her legs crossed beneath her. She crossed her arms and buried her face in them, leaning forward to rest her elbows on her knees.

Jason hated how small and defeated she looked, all folded up on the floor and in tears. He gently grabbed her by her elbows, trying to coax her up from the floor. "Let me help you get up, sweetie. Let's take it slowly and carefully, though. Come on, honey." He guided her into a standing position and slowly walked her to the bed. "Lie down and take it easy while I get the phone."

"Who are you calling?" She asked.

"*You* are calling your mom. A mom is still a mom, even at 3 AM," he declared. He switched on the bedside lamp and handed her the phone.

Karen's answering machine picked up after several rings, but just as the recorded message began to play, a groggy, barely recognizable female voice said, "Hello?"

"Mom?" Bree said, then began to cry all over again.

"Bree, what's wrong?" the grogginess was quickly fading from Karen's voice. She was switching into the protective "mother bear" mode.

For the second time that night, Bree managed to choke out the words to describe what had happened. "What do I do now? Am I going to be ok?" She hoped for reassurance.

"Are you getting any cramping or pelvic pain?"

"Nothing but a sore knee, hip, and arm, but my fall happened only a few minutes ago."

"Good. Just lay on your back with your feet elevated tonight, and take it *super* easy for the next few days. I would spend most of my time lying down with my feet up if I were you, and watch out for any pelvic pain or heavy spotting or cramping," Karen advised.

Bree began to calm her crying. "Thanks, Mom. I don't know what I would do without you."

"I'm always here for you, sweetie. Now, get some rest. I'm sure everything will be fine. Maybe tomorrow you can call me if you're up to it and tell me how the MIPS investigation went," Karen suggested.

"Yeah, I've got a lot I need to talk to you about, so you'll definitely be hearing from me tomorrow. I love you, Mom."

"I love you too, honey."

Bree placed the handset on the nightstand. Jason immediately wanted to know what Karen had advised her to do, and after Bree told him, he vowed that he would call in sick to work and spend the day catering to her every whim. He grabbed some extra pillows to prop under her feet, and then shut off the light. He crawled into bed beside her, being careful not to jar her too much.

As they lay there, both awake yet exhausted, they felt the gravity of the situation weighing down on them. Bree stared at the ceiling in the dark, trying to form one coherent, complete thought. Her stress and exhaustion, however, only allowed for fragmented thoughts, which bumped around and mingled like drunken singles in a noisy nightclub. She felt defeated and afraid, and her inability to contemplate the situation clearly only magnified those feelings. She wondered if talking would help to organize her thoughts.

"This is really happening, isn't it," Bree said as more of a statement than a question. After Jason mumbled a "Mmm-hmm," she continued with, "I wish I would just wake up tomorrow and find out that this had all just been one long dream – that none of it was real."

"But then the baby wouldn't be real either," Jason pointed out. "Someday soon, this will all be over. Maybe in time it will seem like it was only a dream...well, nightmare," he corrected. He was quiet for a while before he spoke again. "When things get really bad, just remember that there is always someone out there who has got it even worse than you do. Be thankful that things aren't any worse than they are."

Even with her slow thinking and fragmented thoughts, Bree found a hole in his logic. "Someone has to have it worse than anyone else in the world. There always has to be a bottom rung."

"Not necessarily, if you consider relativity and perspective..." Jason trailed off, apparently too tired to articulate his thoughts as clearly as he wanted to. He hastily finished with, "Whatever. Just be glad we aren't that bottom rung!"

She smiled, knowing that his words were true. Closing her eyes, she finally drifted off to sleep, ending one of the longest, most stressful days of her life.

Jason woke up to his alarm in the morning. After calling in to work and fabricating a story about severe gastrointestinal distress, he returned to bed. He and Bree then slept the entire morning away, not rising to meet the day until well after noon. Jason kept his promise to pamper Bree all day, letting her do nothing for herself other than use the bathroom. She had no worrisome symptoms that afternoon. Her worry slowly melted away as the day progressed uneventfully.

By dinner time, she wanted to call her mom. Jason used the phone briefly to order a delivery pizza, then brought the phone to the living room couch upon which she had been lying all afternoon. (He had wanted to make her stay in bed, but she'd insisted upon going downstairs to save him from having to spend his day running up and down stairs.) Jason gave her the phone and instructed her to check the caller ID if the call waiting beeped at her, as he was hoping to hear from Cora tonight. She gave him a "yeah-yeah" and dialed her mother.

After a brief update on Bree's condition, Karen asked, "So what happened with the investigation last night?"

Bree told her about every detail she could think of up to the point right before Cora discovered Elizabeth's presence. "Cora said that Gregory claimed some force was keeping him from hurting me. That was when she realized there was another spirit in the house, trying to hide its presence. It's Elizabeth!" Bree revealed excitedly.

"What? She's been there this whole time?" Karen was flabbergasted.

"Apparently so. She's been protecting me from Gregory. And I also found out that she prefers to be called 'Liz,' which I'm having a hard time getting used to. She's always been 'Elizabeth' to me." Bree then shared with her mother the concerns Cora had for her safety. "She thinks I should vacate the premises for a while until they can expel Gregory – and Liz, probably – from the house…"

Before Bree had a chance to ask, Karen demanded that Bree stay with her and Jerry. "As soon as you feel up to making the trip, come home. Jason is welcome to stay as well, of course, if he can. Do you want me to come get you?"

"No, no. I'll need to have my own vehicle so I can travel back and forth. I want to be able to help with this investigation as much as I can. I want to know that I had a hand in kicking Gregory's ass out of my house." She told her mother that she'd have a better idea of how to plan the week after Cora called them. "We still don't know when they're coming back. If they'll be here tomorrow, then I won't leave until the next day, after the investigation. If they aren't coming until later, then I'll leave tomorrow, assuming all is well with the baby." Bree felt anxious to get away from this house, especially after the previous night's scare. He was becoming far too aggressive for her to feel that she and her baby were safe.

Karen instructed Bree to keep her informed on her plans, and they said goodbye.

"Still no Cora yet?" Jason inquired once he realized Bree was no longer on the phone. He was growing impatient, as he always did when awaiting an important call. But Bree couldn't blame him. When Bree shook her head, he sighed noisily. "If she doesn't call soon, I'm calling her," he asserted.

Long after they received and ate their pizza, at a quarter to eight, they finally heard from Cora.

"How have things been since we left?" She asked Jason, who had been the one to answer the phone.

"Not so good," he replied. He told her about the violent banging on the door and Bree's fall.

"She needs to get out of there soon. Has she made any plans to stay somewhere else yet?"

Jason said she would be staying with her parents, and that she would be leaving within the next couple of days. Cora seemed relieved to hear this.

"I talked with Perry," Cora said. "He's willing to work with us, but he wants to talk with you to discuss a price. He said he could go out there as soon as tomorrow if you guys can strike a deal before then." She gave Jason Perry's phone number and said he should call him as soon as he gets off the phone with her. "Also, I just wanted to let you know that the boys aren't done with the analysis yet, but they will be by tomorrow. Sarah is still researching the place, but she hasn't come up with much yet. It seems that the house has been uninhabited for quite a long time. If you and Bree are open to it, we can come out to investigate tomorrow around the same time as before, along with Perry if possible. Some of the team members won't be able to make it, but we can get along fine without them. I know how urgent this case is. It has gone to the top of MIPS's priority list."

196

"We sure do appreciate it, I hope you know. It would be great to get everybody here tomorrow. I'll give Perry a call right away. Hopefully I won't have to take out a loan to employ his services," Jason jested. In truth, though, he was slightly worried about the cost.

"Oh, no. He's pretty reasonable," Cora assured him, though he never trusted the word "pretty" in that context. She asked if Bree was available to speak to her.

"Cora wants to talk to you," Jason said as he handed Bree the phone. "MIPS will be coming tomorrow, and I've got to call Perry tonight too," he quickly filled her in before she spoke to Cora.

Bree nodded to Jason and said "Hello?" into the phone.

"Hi, Bree. How are you feeling?"

"I'm doing alright now, thanks. So what's up? You guys are coming tomorrow, I hear."

Cora gave her the details. Then she asked, "Will you be joining us, or are you going to be at your parents'?"

"Oh I'll be here. I'm not leaving until the day after tomorrow. Anyway, I plan to commute to make every investigation and meeting."

"That's wonderful. I've always felt it was best to have everyone involved, especially those who are most affected by a haunting. I admire your courage, kiddo," Cora praised. "I'll see you tomorrow at eight."

As soon as Bree ended the call, Jason was busy dialing the number he had received from Cora. He was only on the phone briefly with Perry before they had come to an agreement. She wasn't exactly pleased with the price she heard while she was eavesdropping, but she was grateful that they could at least afford it.

Jason and Bree went to bed shortly thereafter. Jason wanted to get as much sleep as he could, since he knew he wasn't going to be able to call in again after the next investigation without raising questions at work.

Bree spent Tuesday alone in the house. Jason called her several times from work to check on her, though, so she didn't feel quite as lonesome. Her mother called her from work once as well just to see how she was feeling and to find out when she would be making the trip to Tandish. When she wasn't on the phone, Bree spent her time lounging on the couch, watching television, and snoozing. The lack of activity made her feel lazy and groggy, but she didn't want to take any chances by overdoing it.

After Jason arrived home from work, he waited on her hand and foot. They had leftover pizza for dinner and waited for MIPS and Perry to come. Since Bree had been alone and confined to the couch all day, she had grown incredibly bored and craved some kind of entertainment that didn't originate from the television. She found herself talking Jason's ear off. Either he didn't mind or he was just tuning her out, because he didn't complain. She didn't care which it was anyway, as she was just happy to have some company.

At eight o'clock, Perry was the first to arrive. He wasn't at all what Bree had expected. She thought he would be yet another short, scrawny, glasses-clad tech wiz, but was surprised to see a tall, burly, handsome man at the door. He had thick brown hair, bright blue eyes and a deep tan, probably from spending so much time outdoors in the sun searching for remains and artifacts. He had a large white van parked in the drive that had "Anderson's Ancient Artifacts Recovery Company" printed on the side in huge red letters around the image of a Native American headdress.

When Jason went outside with Perry to survey the backyard, MIPS pulled into the drive. Everyone convened out in front of the porch, so Bree slipped on her sandals and went out to join them. Jason scolded her immediately.

"Honey, you should be resting on the couch. We'll be inside in just a minute."

Bree hated being left out, but she also hated having arguments in front of other people. She gave her best "Yes, dear" smile and went back in the house. Everyone but Perry came in a few minutes later. Perry was apparently setting up his equipment and getting started so he could get to work while he still had some late summer evening light with which to work. The MIPS team also wasted little time in beginning their equipment setup.

Meanwhile, Cora and Sarah sat down with a laptop and a folder of papers to speak with Jason and Bree about what was discovered in research and analysis.

"On the research end," Sarah began, "there wasn't much I could find about the house that pertained to our particular case. I did find that it was built in 1854 by Gregory and Edith Barry, and was passed on to one of their sons, James Barry, and his wife Lenore. It then went to Gregory D. Barry, and his wife Elizabeth. Henry W. Barry then obtained it, and Samuel J.D. Barry inherited it. It was then sold to Edward P. Miller in 1956, who sold it to Michael Beechum. His grandson, David, inherited it and sold it to you. It appears that after Henry got the house, the property was mostly used for farming and the house wasn't inhabited until Mr. Beechum bought it. He was from Florida, and apparently had it fixed up in 1976 and likely used it as a vacation home. That was all I found," Sarah concluded.

Bree had a question. "When did Samuel Barry inherit the house from Henry?" She wanted to see how long Liz might have been living in the house after Gregory's death.

"Let's see," Sarah said as she looked through her folder. "Samuel got the house in…" More shuffling. Finally, "1928."

That information made Bree happy. She was glad to know Henry hadn't sold the house out from under Liz, at least not for a long time after Gregory's death.

"Is that information significant?" Cora wanted to know.

"Not to the case. Just curiosity," Bree said with a casual wave of her hand.

"Well, are you ready to see what we found in analysis?" Cora asked.

"Definitely," Jason answered.

It wasn't until she and Jason were watching Cora click and type on her laptop that Bree noticed the ridiculous outfit Cora had chosen for today. Bree wondered if she had tried to dress up for this visit, perhaps because she knew the handsome Perry would be there. She was wearing a low-cut, ruffled, bright red blouse with puffy sleeves that belled out at the wrist. She wore a pair of faded black jeans with extremely tapered legs that Bree guessed she had probably bought sometime in the early

90's, and holey yellow socks. She had removed the ugly black cowboy boots at the door. Bree noticed she even had her big toe sticking out of one sock hole, revealing the long, dirty, yellowed toenail adorning it. She wished Cora had just left the boots on rather than wave her fungus-infected toenail all over her house.

Cora finally got the first piece of evidence ready to show them. "This camera was pointing to the guest bedroom door when the group you were with approached it for the first time. You can see it slam right in Sam's face." She played the video, and sure enough, the door slammed on the laptop screen. "Next, we've got a voice from the guest room." The audio clip was Gregory's faint laughter that everyone had heard during the investigation. After that, Cora played a clip of the loud bang that was heard in the master bedroom.

Bree wasn't interested in the things she and Jason had already heard and experienced firsthand during the investigation. She wanted to see what they found after she had decided to sit it out.

"Chris' team caught this, also in the guest room," Cora introduced the next bit of audio evidence. Bree heard a whispery, menacing voice come from the laptop. It sounded like it said, "Where's Bree?" in a sarcastic tone. "I'm especially impressed by that piece," Cora said. "It's so clear, and you can even hear the sarcasm in his voice. Unfortunately, he seemed to stop responding to us after that, because nothing else was caught until we began the direct communication session. This is an audio recording taken right after I discovered the presence of Liz." Bree heard Gregory's voice again, and this time he sounded like he was seething.

"Bitch!" He hissed.

"I hope she is still able to hide herself from him even though he knows she's here now," Bree worried. "I would hate to think that she spent this whole time protecting me from him, and I repay her by helping to reveal her presence to Gregory."

"I think she's gotten pretty good at hiding," Cora assured Bree. "I can't feel her at all right now, but I'm sure she must still be here. Try not to worry about her, Bree. It's you we need to be the most concerned about when it comes to Gregory."

Once Cora had finished showing Jason and Bree the evidence, the MIPS team reassembled in the kitchen. Setup was complete, and they were ready to begin the second investigation. Cora asked if Jason and Bree would be joining them again, but they declined since Bree was still recuperating from her recent fall. The first team went off to investigate while Jason, Bree, Cora, and the few remaining MIPS members sat quietly at the table in the kitchen.

Bree had a few questions for Cora, but she didn't want to disturb the investigation by speaking out loud. She grabbed a nearby notepad and pen and wrote down one of her questions: *Are we going to try to speak to Liz tonight, even though you don't feel her presence right now?* She then passed the notepad and pen to Cora. Cora read the note, wrote a reply, and passed it back to Bree. It reminded Bree of when she used to pass notes to her friends in high school.

Bree read Cora's response. *Yes. Is there something you would like to ask her?*

Bree wrote down several of the questions she had for Elizabeth. *Did she die here? Why did she stay or come back here when Gregory's spirit was here? Has she ever tried to interact with me? Does she know she is my great-great grandmother? Why did she give up her child?* She hoped Liz would answer at least a few of her questions.

As she was passing the notepad back to Cora, Perry came to the door. He quietly motioned for them to come outside. Jason, Bree, and Cora all went out to see what Perry wanted.

Once everyone was out on the porch with the door quietly closed behind them, Perry said excitedly, "I think I've found something."

Chapter 15

"It could be remains," Perry declared.

At first, Bree felt sickened. She looked at Jason and found him to be pale, apparently taking the news as well as she.

Perry explained his findings in greater detail. "Now, it might *not* be remains, but it is large enough and at a depth that allows for the possibility that it could be remains. I've flagged the location," Perry said as he turned and gestured for them to follow him into the backyard.

When they rounded the corner of the house and the backyard came into view, Bree didn't see anything immediately. Perry had led them out across the middle of the yard before Bree finally saw the little yellow flag. It was at the far end of the yard, right on the border between the grass and the trees. When she saw the flag's location, she knew the item Perry had found couldn't be Gregory's remains. Elizabeth had clearly stated in her journal that she and Henry had buried him in the cellar, and from her description of events, it didn't sound like the cellar was any distance from the house.

"That isn't right," Bree blurted as they approached the flag. "They didn't bury him this far from the house."

Perry replied defensively, "Well, there's definitely *something* here worth taking a look at."

Cora interjected. "Bree, we can't dismiss possible evidence just because it doesn't match exactly with what you read in the journal. That's what you're going from, isn't it?"

"Yeah. The journal said they buried him in the cellar because they didn't want to parade his body around outside where someone might see them burying him. I don't think they would've hauled Gregory and all the bed pieces this far away from the house and risk being seen," Bree explained doubtfully.

"But does the journal specifically say where the cellar was located?" Cora questioned.

"Well, no, but aren't cellars generally under the house? I know they can have outside access, but I thought the cellar itself was under the house."

"Often times, yes," Perry informed her. "But not always. I've encountered cellars dug into hillsides as well. Regardless of whether or not this is an old cellar location, there is something buried here. Now, shall we start digging?" Perry already brandished a spade shovel.

"Hell yes!" Jason exclaimed. "I'll get my shovel out from under the porch and help you. I'll be right back." Jason sprinted off and quickly returned with a shovel similar to Perry's. "Let's get to it! Now, how far down are we going?"

Perry sunk his shovel into the grass next to the little yellow flag. "About four feet down. I don't know if we'll be able to get down to it before we lose daylight, but I can come back tomorrow."

The men started digging up earth without saying anything more to Cora or Bree. The two women looked at each other and Bree shrugged.

"I guess we'll go back inside and resume the investigation, if that's ok," Bree said.

"Yep, that's fine," Jason answered absentmindedly as he concentrated on the excavation.

Cora and Bree quietly entered the house and sat at the kitchen table again. Bree noticed that the next team must have begun their investigation because there was a different group of MIPS members sitting at the table when she and Cora returned. Cora looked over the list of questions for Liz that Bree had written on the notepad. She scratched a quick reply and slid the notepad to Bree.

Great questions! Anything else?

Bree contemplated whether she wanted to add any more questions to her list. If she wanted to, she could have written pages and pages of questions for Elizabeth and spent an entire night conversing with her. However, she knew this was not possible and tried to keep her questions limited to those most important to her and to the case. She looked up from the notepad and shook her head to answer Cora's question. Cora nodded in acknowledgement and held out her hand, indicating that she wanted the notepad again. Bree passed it back to her, watched her write for a few moments, then read what Cora had written when the notepad was returned to her.

Things are very quiet tonight. Subdued. The spirits seem to be hanging back for some reason, even Gregory. I doubt the team is having any luck right now in catching anything.

Bree didn't know how to feel about this. Since when was Gregory prone to shyness? Was he afraid that he would finally be cast out of the house? Was he saving up his energy for something else? She wondered if he could just be waiting out the MIPS investigation, hoping they would leave so he could have her all to himself again. His behavior was incredibly confusing sometimes. She couldn't wait to be rid of him and his mind games.

Within the next hour, daylight had gone completely and Jason returned to the house. Perry had headed out, telling Jason that he would return the following day. The men had not been able to dig to the object in the ground before they ran out of light, but they had gotten a lot accomplished. Jason had suggested that they just use flashlights to finish the excavation, but Perry had insisted that they wait for daylight. He had told Jason that a flashlight wouldn't provide them with sufficient light to ensure that they didn't miss anything or accidentally damage something with the spade in the process of digging.

Jason felt Perry's excuse was a crock and thought Perry was probably just ready to be done for the night so he could go home. He shared all of this with Bree upon his return to the table through the use of the notepad.

She was disappointed that they hadn't been able to uncover the possible remains in the yard. She desperately wanted to find out what was buried back there and entertained the idea of staying in White Dove a short while longer just to see what was recovered. She thought that perhaps she could still leave tomorrow, only later in the day than originally planned. Of course, that would mean spending another lonely day in the house with the ghost of a man who wanted to extinguish the life blooming inside her.

By midnight, the investigators were through with the first phase of the investigation, and seemed to be thoroughly bored by the lack of activity in the house that night. When they sat around the table with Cora, they told her that absolutely no one had a personal experience. It was nothing like the first night. They wanted to know her thoughts on the sudden quietness.

"Well," Cora said uncertainly with a shrug of her shoulders, "I'm kind of stumped. I can feel that Gregory and Liz are still here, but their presences are…well, faint. I'm wondering if perhaps Gregory is attempting to hide himself the way Liz does, but I have no idea why he would do that. We already know he's here, and we know he isn't shy!" She exclaimed with a chortle. "In all honesty, I don't know exactly why this is happening."

"Maybe he's getting weaker from our interference. Maybe our presence is helping to drive him out," Sam suggested as an excited expression spread across his pudgy face.

"It's hard to say, Sam." Cora shrugged again. She looked around the table. "Let's get ready for a direct communication session. I want to try to make contact and see if anybody can tell me anything."

Jason set up the lightning lamp in the middle of the table, and then sat next to Bree. He found her hand under the table and clasped it in his. She always loved how her small hand seemed to get lost within his much larger, rough, calloused one.

It made her feel like even if the whole world came after her, she could always find safety and shelter in that hand. She looked at him and smiled. He had his head turned away from her, but it didn't matter. She wasn't smiling *at* him so much as *because* of him.

When Cora asked everyone to join hands for a short prayer, Bree mentally prepared herself for an unpleasant encounter. She looked down at the table while she waited for Cora to inform the group that she had connected with someone after the prayer was finished. Several minutes passed, yet all was silent. Curious, Bree looked up at Cora. Cora was sitting calmly with her eyes closed, appearing to be in deep concentration. Bree saw that the rest of the MIPS team looked bored and tired. She wondered if her and Jason's case would remain at the top of MIPS's priority list if Cora was unable to make contact tonight. She didn't want them to assume that one quiet night meant that the danger had dissipated.

Finally, Cora exhaled loudly, sounding relieved. "Liz has come to us. She says she won't stay long, but she knows Bree has some questions for her. Would you like to ask them, Bree?" Cora offered.

"Yes! Thank you. Liz, I wanted to know if you knew you were my great-great grandmother," Bree asked first.

"She says that she did know that. That's why she's tried so hard to protect you. What else would you like to know?"

"Have you ever tried to interact with me?"

"She says she has. It was she who led you to the attic, to her journal. You heard her on your audio device and you found her clue in the piano."

"Oh, wow. I thought—," Bree began, but was interrupted.

"Wait, Liz says she has to go now. Gregory is looking for her again. Bree, she wants you to know that you shouldn't worry about her when you drive Gregory from this house. She would leave willingly anyway if she knew he was no longer here and no longer a threat to her family."

"But wait! I have—," Bree tried again, but was cut off once more.

"Sorry, Bree. She's severed the connection. I'm going to try to find Gregory."

While Cora concentrated in silence, Bree stewed. Not only did she hate being interrupted, she was upset with Elizabeth for leaving her with so many questions. There would be very few, if any, opportunities for Bree to speak with her again, so it wasn't likely that she would ever learn the answers she sought. She knew she shouldn't be upset with Liz, especially after discovering that she had helped Bree find the journal and had been protecting her from Gregory's hostility, but she was. Sometimes having a few answers made the curiosity even more frustrating than it would be with having no answers at all.

Cora broke the long silence. "I know he's here, but he's avoiding me. He doesn't seem to want to speak with us tonight, and I can't make him." After a few minutes of further silence, Cora opened her eyes and looked at Bree. "Did you want us to ask the spirits to leave the house tonight? I'm not overly confident that it will work, but I'd still like to give it a shot if you are willing."

Bree considered her options. If they were successful in casting Gregory from the house, then Liz would probably leave as well, taking with her all possibility of ever finding out about the child she gave up and what happened to her after June 4th, 1896. However, Gregory needed to go. It took Bree mere seconds to weigh the options once she had them on the table. Getting rid of Gregory was the first and foremost important thing given the current situation. She could live without having Elizabeth's full story, but she couldn't live with Gregory any longer.

"Let's do it. I'm ready," Bree replied confidently.

Jason nodded. "Hell yes. Whatever we can try, we should."

"Excellent. Everyone join hands, please. I will lead. Concentrate on my words. You can even repeat them mentally if you would like, just to keep you focused. Let's begin."

Bree closed her eyes and listened to Cora's appeal to the spirits. She repeated each word in her mind, imagining that they were nails being pounded into Gregory's eternal coffin to keep him locked away forever. She didn't know if it helped to give power to Cora's words or not, but it gave the words more meaning in her mind.

Cora repeated her demands several times, and she wasn't finished until Bree was sure at least half an hour had passed. Toward the end, Bree began to lose her focus and wonder how many times Cora was going to "order the spirits to vacate this house, to move on to the next realm to face their judgment." She didn't think that Cora's phrasing could possibly entice anyone to leave.

MIPS took down their equipment while Cora spoke with Bree and Jason. "He hasn't left yet, but Gregory's presence seems to be weakening. I can hardly feel him right now. Things could go either way at this point. We'll have to see what happens over the next few days with Bree out of the house. We'll have to see what comes out of the ground tomorrow, too, when you and Perry finish your dig. Please call me when you unearth the object, if you would, to let me know if there are remains. We can discuss our next step at that time." Cora reached over the table and squeezed Bree's hand lightly. "Have a safe trip to your parents' place tomorrow. You should be able to rest easy there."

Jason and Bree thanked Cora and the MIPS team and sent them on their way. The two then plopped onto the couch in the living room to unwind before heading upstairs to bed.

"What time are you leaving tomorrow?" Jason quizzed while looking at the ceiling, lolling his head back until it was resting on the back of the couch.

"I'd like to stay long enough to see what you uncover in the backyard. I think I can brave one more day alone in this house."

Jason gave a short laugh, finding humor in his thoughts, then fell silent, failing to share these thoughts with Bree.

"What?" It annoyed her when people did that. *If you laugh out loud,* she thought, *you might as well share the damn story because someone will always ask "What?" if you don't.*

"How irritated would you be if you waited around the whole day just to find out that the object in the yard was somebody's dead dog?"

208

"I fail to see how that's funny," Bree said reproachfully, developing an attitude with her growing weariness.

"It would be a little funny," Jason retorted, closing his eyes and smiling sleepily. "So you'll still be here when I get home tomorrow afternoon?"

"Yep," she answered. She then changed the subject. "Tonight's investigation was kind of weird, wasn't it?"

"Define weird," he replied sarcastically.

"Well, relatively speaking. Don't be a smartass. What's going on with Gregory? Why is he…disappearing, I wonder?"

Jason mumbled, "I don't know," without using any real words.

Bree continued as if she hadn't heard him. "And why can't Liz just take a second to answer my questions? I didn't even have an opportunity to ask her the most important question. I may never get another chance to find out what happened to her, and it bothers me. Doesn't that bother you?" Bree's question was met with silence. She looked over at Jason and found he had passed out while she was speaking to him. She gave an exasperated grunt. "I hate it when you do that! Hello! Hey!" She shook him until he groaned at her. It took several more shakes and one threat involving a cold glass of water before he finally opened his bloodshot eyes. "Why don't you go up to bed," she told him. "I'll wait to turn this light off until you get upstairs." She knew that none of the lights were on upstairs, and knew he would probably trip in the dark in his current state. She assumed he would turn on the bedroom or hallway light when he got to the top of the stairs so she could have some light by which to find her way.

As soon as she heard his footsteps reach the top of the stairs, she clicked off the lamp. She mumbled a few choice words to describe her husband when complete darkness filled the house. He hadn't turned on a light for her. She began to ascend the stairs in the dark, and could see a tiny crack of light was coming from the closed bathroom door upstairs.

"Jason, could you turn a light on for me?" She shouted. No response. *He is so dead if I fall and bust my face,* she thought.

She slowly made her way up the stairs, holding the railing tightly and feeling for the next step to make sure it was completely supporting her entire foot before lifting herself and moving on to the next step.

As she carefully felt for the next step after making it halfway up the staircase, a terrified scream tore from her throat. Cold, sticky fingers had suddenly wrapped themselves firmly around her bare ankle. She could feel them squeezing her leg painfully, and she tried to pull herself free from their grip. She screamed again when she discovered that they held her with a strength that greatly surpassed her own. Reacting so quickly that she hadn't the time to feel apprehension at what she might see, she looked down at her ankle. The darkness was too complete to reveal her assailant. She whipped her head around quickly to see if there was anything behind her. Nothing caught her eye immediately, but a moment later her eyes adjusted enough to make out a vague, dark shape lying on the stairs behind her. She heard it wheezing. An agonized cry escaped her and she tried frantically to wrench herself free to flee from this mysterious, wheezing thing, but to no avail. She was trapped. Terrified, she shouted Jason's name as loudly as her vocal cords would allow.

In an instant, the bathroom door was flung open at the top of the stairs, spilling light into the darkness upstairs. The light was faint by the time it reached the staircase, but she saw that it was sufficient to make out the stairs in front of her, and bright enough to reveal the grotesque, grey, bony fingers that clasped at her ankle. She inhaled sharply and instantly turned her head to look behind her.

What she saw would forever be seared into the darkest part of her brain. Lying on the stairs, on its belly, was a pale grey, naked, hairless, deformed human body. It appeared to be in the early stages of decomposition. The revolting head, which was much too large for the body, was lumpy and misshapen, and it was looking up at her. One milky blue eye pointed off to the side, apparently unable to focus. The other eye appeared to be almost entirely black, like a large pupil, but the outer edges, where the whites showed, were bloodshot. This eye was focused directly on her eyes. The tiny, bloody red lips, which sat beneath a nose bearing oddly porcine qualities, parted, revealing broken, jagged teeth embedded within bloody, receding gums. A strange, deep, yet childlike voice came out of the repulsive mouth.

"Carry me, Mama." It began to reach for her with the hand that wasn't holding her ankle.

Bree closed her eyes tightly and tried to scream, but her vocal cords failed her. All that came from her was a wheezing sound that oddly resembled the wheezing of the creature on the stairs. She suddenly felt hands on her arms and she began to flail. Her eyes shot open and she ceased her struggling instantly when she realized she was trying to fight off Jason. She looked down again. The creature was gone. Her ankle was free, though she thought she could still feel the fingers wrapped around it.

"Whoa, relax – it's me, Bree! What's the matter?" Jason no longer appeared to be half-asleep as he had been the last time she'd seen him. He was trying to establish eye contact with her, but she was looking around the staircase frantically.

"That *thing*! Didn't you see that horrible *thing*?!" Bree cried out.

"What thing?"

"The giant, deformed baby thing! It had my ankle! It called me 'Mama!' It actually had a hold of my ankle – I couldn't get away from it!" She was shouting. Suddenly, her head began to spin, and the edges of her vision blurred. Jason was speaking to her, but it sounded like she was hearing him from under water. Her stomach flopped, her legs buckled, and everything went black.

***

"Bree, baby, are you alright?" Jason fretted.

Bree opened her eyes and found that she was in bed. Jason was sitting on the edge of the bed, leaned over her, looking at her with wide, worried eyes.

"What happened?" She wanted to know.

"You passed out," Jason told her. "You were hysterical when I met you on the stairs, breathing too fast and even shaking a little. You were yelling about some deformed thing and how you couldn't get away, and then you got a weird, glazed-over look in your eyes. I knew you were going to pass out when I saw that look, so luckily I was ready to catch you when you went down." He stroked her hair and kissed her forehead. "You need to do a better job of staying on your feet," he chided gently. "How are you feeling now?"

"Queasy," she replied. "But I don't know if it's from passing out or from the horrifying experience I just had. Jason, you wouldn't believe how terrifying that was."

"What happened, exactly? I had to have been in the bathroom for only two minutes before I heard you screaming for me."

She relayed to him the series of events that led to her hysteria on the stairs. She then went on to ask, "What the hell happened with you? Why didn't you turn a light on for me? And why didn't you come to my rescue sooner? I screamed like ten times!" She exaggerated.

"I honestly didn't hear anything except you screaming my name, and I came out as soon as I heard it! I had the water running in the bathroom, and it probably drowned you out. No pun intended." Jason gave her a wry smile, knowing that the situation wasn't right for jokes but lacking the willpower to refrain from making them. When she looked at him with disgust, he added seriously, "I couldn't have been in there for more than two minutes. It's not like I was purposely ignoring you while I sat and read the newspaper," he replied defensively.

"Why did it take you so long to get to me after you heard me scream your name then?" She asked accusingly.

Jason was puzzled by her question. "It didn't take me long at all. I threw the door open, ran to the top of the stairs, and switched on the hallway light. That was when I saw you standing in the middle of the staircase, gripping the railing. I came right to you. From the time I ran out of the bathroom to the time I got to you, no more than five seconds could have passed. Honestly."

"Oh." She believed him, but to her it had felt like several minutes had passed. She thought she had been looking at that nasty creature for quite a length of time rather than mere seconds. "I'm sorry. It seemed like a long time to me. It was so horrible! You should've seen that thing! It was proportioned like a baby, with a head much bigger than what fit the body, but it was the size of an adult. And the way it gripped my leg – nothing in this house has ever touched me like that. I felt a coldness from Gregory once, and my mom felt something touch her arm once, but there has been nothing like this before. I wonder if it left marks," Bree wondered as she drew back the covers to inspect her bare leg. She and Jason leaned in closely, but saw no discernable abrasions.

"So, was it Gregory?" Jason asked.

"I don't know. It didn't *look* like him, but not every creature that appears in this house does. I don't know how, but it seems that he can appear in a number of gruesome forms," Bree surmised.

"Are you sure you still want to stay in this house until the dig is completed?"

"Not after that experience!" Bree exclaimed. "I'm going to get up a little before you do so I can get everything packed up, and then I'll be out the door at the same time you leave for work. I'm not spending one more minute alone in this house until Gregory is gone."

"Good. I'm glad you're doing this. It makes me feel a lot better knowing that you and the baby are going to be safe," Jason said as he headed toward the bedroom door. "I'm going to shut these lights off. I'll be right back." When he returned a moment later, he had a question. "Don't you have your first prenatal visit coming up soon? What are you going to do about that?"

"Yeah, I think it's early next week, but I don't remember exactly when it is. I'm not sure if I should reschedule it or just drive down and go to the appointment. I hate to put it off, especially after my fall. I don't know. I'll cross that bridge when I get there," Bree decided as she moved over to her own side of the bed so Jason could climb in.

"So you're alright now? I can go to sleep?" Jason asked.

"Yes, of course," Bree confirmed. "Though I know *I* won't be getting much sleep. I'm still too freaked out to be able to relax."

Soon Jason was lost in dreamland, leaving Bree alone with her thoughts. Try as she might, she couldn't stop thinking about the incident on the stairs. She didn't know an entity could grab her like that and hold on to her so firmly for so long. It wasn't the brief touch that she'd heard described on television. She had never been physically seized by the evil in her house until now, and she couldn't figure out what had changed to allow that to happen. Cora had said that Gregory's powerful presence was waning, so why did he seem more powerful than ever tonight? Was he retaliating for their attempts to expel him from the house? And how was it possible for him to manifest in so many different forms? He had been the crispy cupboard dweller, the convulsing white creature that her mother had seen, and now the giant deformed baby. Or at least she assumed they were all him, just in some form of morbid disguise used to incite terror in her very soul.

Bree thought of something else. Hadn't Liz claimed she was protecting Bree from Gregory? Where was Liz tonight? She hoped that Elizabeth hadn't left already, assuming that Gregory was on his way out as well. If Cora sensed that Gregory's power and presence were dwindling, then Liz might have sensed the same thing. Whatever happened, she knew Liz was either in the process of losing the power struggle with Gregory or she was no longer able to protect Bree at all.

Something was changing, of that Bree had become abruptly aware. What she didn't know was what was changing, and what it meant for her and her unborn child. She prayed that the situation would turn in her favor, and that MIPS would be able to finish Gregory off once and for all. He had no business hanging around in this world anymore. It was time the devil brought him back to Hell where he belonged.

Bree slept very little that night and was out of bed before Jason's alarm sounded. She quickly packed her clothes, but waited until Jason was up before venturing from the bedroom to collect her toiletries from the bathroom. Jason gave her a long hug and kiss as they stood outside, about to part ways.

"I'm going to miss you, honey," Jason confessed. "Please be careful, and take care of my little one."

As Bree pulled out of the driveway and honked one last farewell, she cried. She had never spent more than one night away from Jason since they had been together, and she already knew it was going to be tough for her. She also felt terrible about leaving him to sleep alone in that house of horrors. Would Gregory go after him now? She couldn't wait until Jason's vacation request went through and he could join her in Tandish. Or, with any luck, MIPS would have Gregory out of the house by this time next week. Regardless of what happened, she took some comfort in reminding herself that these arrangements weren't permanent.

The trip was long and boring, but finally Bree pulled into her parents' driveway. Her mother came out to greet her as she began unloading her luggage from the vehicle. Karen ordinarily would have been at work at this time of day, but she had taken the day off when Bree notified her of her early morning departure.

"Here, honey," Karen said as she snatched Bree's bags from her hands. "You don't need to be messing with all this in your condition. I'll get the bags." She ushered Bree into the house. Before going after the rest of the luggage, Karen mentioned that there was a kettle of hot water on the stove and instructed Bree to pour herself a cup of herbal tea.

"Thanks, Mom," Bree called to Karen as her petite frame disappeared out the door.

As she sat down at the kitchen table with a hot cup of chamomile vanilla tea, Bree felt a comforting calm envelop her like a warm, cozy blanket. Being home reminded her of simpler times, when her greatest worries concerned boys and gas money for cruising in her mother's car. Of course, back then those were serious issues for a high school girl. She was glad that she hadn't known then what she knew now. *Hell, I still wish I didn't know what I do now,* she thought. *Sometimes ignorance really is bliss.*

Karen joined Bree at the table with her own cup of tea after lugging all of Bree's bags into her old bedroom. "It's so nice to have you home," she said with a smile. "And it's lovely to have our grandbaby here as well. Do you have names picked out?"

215

"It's still a bit early. We haven't had a whole lot of time for that, especially with…well, you know."

Karen gave an understanding nod. "So how are you feeling? I trust you've been trying to take it easy."

"Yeah, I'm doing ok, but last night was a very trying night." Bree told her mother about the previous night's investigation.

"So does Cora think he's losing his hold on the house?" Karen wondered.

"I don't think she's sure what's going on, but I'm certain Gregory hasn't lost any of his power." She shared her experience on the stairs with Karen. Karen's eyes were as big as saucers by the time she was finished with her story.

"That's the most disturbing thing I've heard yet!" Karen exclaimed. "You poor thing!" She reached across the table and took Bree's hand comfortingly. "But you're safe now. There are no psychotic boogeymen in our closets, I can assure you. God, I'm so glad you are out of that house."

"Me too, believe me! I just hope Gregory doesn't decide to go after Jason since he has no one else to harass and torture. I feel badly that he has to stay there all by himself for the next week."

"He'll be fine, I'm sure," Karen assured her. "That man's got biceps bigger than my head. He can handle anything," she added with a laugh.

"I just wish I knew what the hell was going on with Gregory now. I want to believe that he's being forced out, but I don't. After what happened last night, I *can't* truly believe that. A few minutes of repetitive chants aren't enough to drive out an evil that can physically attack a person. There's no way," Bree declared.

"That was only the first step, though. I'm sure MIPS has other methods that they'll try, and I'm sure one of them will work. I pray for your relief from Gregory every day, so I'm certain God will give you and MIPS the tools you need to get rid of this spirit. Have you been praying?" Karen asked.

"No. It's not something I often do anymore. It isn't that I don't believe in God, it's just that I don't feel like He's ever listening to me."

"It still doesn't hurt to try. If there was anyone who could take care of Gregory, I would think He would be the one to do it," Karen said.

Bree nodded, looking down at her tea. "You know, this whole situation has really changed my beliefs about the afterlife. All throughout school, I believed in Heaven and Hell. Then in college, I decided that it was probable that there was nothing at all after death. In recent years, I had become completely undecided. Now, I'm beginning to think that maybe you get some kind of choice."

"A choice?"

"Yeah, like whether you want to stay behind and wander as a 'ghost,' or go on to get placed in Heaven or Hell. Maybe some people stay behind because they're worried that they have a good chance of being sent to Hell. Maybe some stay because they think that they can somehow change something they weren't satisfied with before they died." Bree looked at Karen. "If you were given a choice, would you stay or move on to have your fate decided?"

"I would move on, definitely. I would think that wandering around Earth alone for eternity would be a type of hell in its own right. What would you do?" Karen asked.

"I don't know. I like to think that I'm a decent person, but I've done things that are considered sinful according to the Bible. I don't know how anyone could live in complete accordance with the Bible's laws, especially in this day and age, so I would have worries about whether I would be admitted into Heaven. And what about all the other religions of the world? Who's to say that Christianity is the *right* one? What if I took my chances and found that the god of some other religion was the one passing judgment? And for that matter, what about all the Greeks and Romans and pagans before them? Would they have been sent to Hell for worshipping many gods? There are just so many unanswered questions that would make me afraid to leave this world."

217

"We are only human, and we do err," Karen said. "We cannot be blamed for that. But almost all religions reward kindness, honesty, and morality. My belief is that being a good, loving, moral person will get you into the 'heaven' of any religion."

Bree quietly drank her tea and wondered if she was a "good" person. She certainly wasn't as bad as Gregory. If anyone should be sent to Hell, it was him.

"What do *you* think happens to us when we die?" Bree asked Karen. "Why do you think some souls stay behind?"

"I think the spirits that are left behind are stuck. I don't think they made a conscious decision to stay, but they have such damaged souls or a strong feeling of having unfinished business that they literally *can't* move on. Their inability to let go of something that happened to them during their lives binds them to this world. Until they find a way to cope with it or find some kind of closure, they won't even see the so-called 'light,' or whatever they're supposed to walk into to enter the next life. I think of it as if the traumatic event was a blindfold, inhibiting their ability to see where they're supposed to go," Karen explained. "I think that if we were given a choice outright, then there would be a lot more ghosts around."

"Maybe there are," Bree countered, "but they just don't have the ability to make themselves known. Perhaps only a small percentage of ghosts can actually move objects, show themselves, and communicate with the living world."

"Interesting. But what would give those few the ability to interact while most couldn't?"

"It could be something inherent, like other human talents. Only a small percentage of people can naturally solve complex math equations in their heads. Maybe it's something like that. Some have the ability, and some just don't," Bree reasoned.

"What about residual haunts? Why would someone choose to stay behind, then choose to do the same thing over and over again?"

Bree was again quick with an answer. "Don't we do the same things over and over again each day? If you spent all your

218

life adhering to a certain schedule, don't you think some people would continue to follow that familiar pattern? They might not even realize that they are visible to anyone in the living world while they go about their routine. Or maybe with residual haunts there isn't even a real ghost there at all, just the energy left over from their life. Or, better yet, they've somehow fallen into a *Groundhog Day* effect in their afterlife. Hell, I don't know," Bree said with a shake of her head.

"You have some intriguing ideas, but I'm still sticking to the belief that it isn't a conscious choice because it seems to me that a lot of hauntings are caused by ghosts of people who were unhappy in this world and experienced a great deal of suffering in their lives. Why would people who hated this world so much *choose* to stay here? I don't think they would," Karen concluded.

"You have a valid point," Bree admitted. "But what if they chose to stay behind because they thought maybe they could exact their revenge on those who made their lives miserable? Like Gregory. He didn't seem to be happy in his life, but when he died, he stayed. I think he chose to stay so he could make Elizabeth pay for what she did, and he is still trying to take his revenge."

"But, Bree, if staying behind is a choice, then how could a spirit be forced to move on? In Gregory's case, it seems that he would never decide to leave of his own free will, especially if you continue to live in that house."

Bree deliberated before giving an answer. She thought about human free will and considered what would make a living person leave a place that they didn't want to leave. Then it came to her: laws. Enforcement. If someone were evicted, they couldn't just stay in the home indefinitely just because they refused to leave. That was why we had laws.

"Who's to say that the spiritual realm doesn't have some kind of law? MIPS has had success in the past in ridding homes of unwanted spirits. If there were no rules governing spirits, you'd think that exorcisms, blessings, cleansings, and all other methods of deterring and eradicating spirits wouldn't work. The spiritual laws could even be like our physical laws. You know, for every action there is an equal and opposite reaction. If people in the living world perform a certain ceremony to command a spirit to leave its current quarters, then maybe the spirit *has* to leave, whether they want to or not. Like if I were to push you, you would move forward even if you didn't want to. You would have no control over it. Some people are larger and stronger, so you would have to push them harder to make them move. Maybe it's like that, but you just have to use the right force, or ceremony, to push the spirit to make it move.

"On the other hand," Bree continued enthusiastically, "these laws could be like our legislative laws. Either they comply or the proper authorities, say God or angels, take action. When spirits 'misbehave,' we often perform rituals to call upon God or some savior or other higher being to step in and take control of the situation – to enforce the laws and punish those who have broken them. Maybe Gregory is breaking the laws of the afterlife and we just need to figure out how to get somebody up there to come and take care of him." Bree felt winded by the time she finished speaking. She had risen from her chair at some point during her speech and had been pacing about like a mad scientist zealously explaining how he had discovered some secret of the cosmos. She sat back down and took a long drink of her tea, which was beginning to cool, while Karen quietly considered her postulation.

"I do imagine there are laws that must be followed. God has given us laws to follow in the world of the living, so I'm sure he must have similar laws in place for the world of the dead. I would think that causing harm to others, as Gregory is attempting to do, would be a violation of the laws. I am confident, though, that God will take notice and free you from Gregory's torments," Karen assured her.

"Then why didn't He free Elizabeth from him, I wonder? He tormented her as well," Bree pointed out.

"Maybe she never asked Him to," Karen retorted.

Bree couldn't refute that. Elizabeth had revealed in her journal entries that, though she resented Gregory's abhorrent behavior, she was too lonely to want him to leave permanently.

After a long silence, Karen invited Bree to join her in the living room to enjoy her cozy new couches. Once comfortably seated, Karen asked Bree what she wanted to do while she was in Tandish.

"Enjoy being able to truly relax for once," she replied.

"As you should," Karen agreed. "Right now you need to just focus your energy on growing that little baby." After a brief pause, she asked, "So how do you feel?"

"I feel fine, but I'm pretty sure you already asked me that."

"No, I mean how do you feel about your pregnancy? Have you and Jason had time to get comfortable with the notion of being parents yet?"

"Oh, yes," Bree said with a smile. "We're excited about it now. I know I was pretty worried at first, and I still am, but I was surprised at how fast my feeling of general acceptance of the situation turned to a feeling of excitement and joy. I hate to get all gushy, but I get such a wonderful 'warm and fuzzy' feeling when I think about the little person growing inside me that Jason and I created. It's like nothing I had ever felt before." Bree became embarrassed when tears began to blur her vision. She quickly changed the subject before they could swell enough to escape her lower lids.

"So, do you want to watch a movie or something?"

***

All afternoon, Bree waited anxiously for Jason to call and let her in on what was dug up in their backyard. Finally, as Karen was setting the table for dinner, he called.

"Did you dig it up yet?" Bree asked excitedly when she answered the phone, not even bothering to say hello.

"Hey, now. A 'hey how are you, I've missed you today' would have been nice," Jason chided playfully.

"I figured we could get to that later, but I'll admit that I do miss you. Now, please tell me, did you find anything?"

"Oh yeah. We found something alright."

Chapter 16

"We found bones," Jason revealed. "Perry says they're human bones, and they're old. Well, not that the person the bones belonged to was old, but the bones have been in the ground for a long time. We found something unusual, though. The bones were buried alone, with no other items, and they were placed in a burlap sack. Perry said it was obvious to him that they had been moved from their original burial location and placed in the sack long after the flesh had decayed. He thinks what might have happened, based on the events described in Elizabeth's diary, was that there was a cellar under the house, and that was where the bed and body were buried. Then, when the basement was dug, someone must have come across the remains. For whatever reason, they decided to put the bones in a bag and rebury them in the backyard. This is all just speculation, of course," Jason pointed out, "but it's the best explanation we have for what we found."

Bree's stomach was doing flip-flops. Those *had* to be Gregory's remains, and they had been right there in her backyard the whole time they'd lived there. Real, tangible pieces of the man who was tormenting her and her unborn child were now in their possession. Or were they?

"What did you do with the remains?" Bree wanted to know.

"Perry took them with him back to his office. He's contacted the local authorities, and I guess they have some process they'll go through so he can demonstrate to them that the bones are over a century old and that we didn't disturb any actual gravesite. Whatever needs to be done, he knows what to do and has apparently done it many times before."

Bree, being the penny-pincher that she sometimes was, immediately asked, "Are we paying him extra for this?" She felt completely ridiculous the moment the words were out. Who asks something like that at a time like this?

"No," Jason answered, sounding slightly put-off. It passed quickly, however. "If everything checks out, the bones should be buried in the city-owned White Dove cemetery. There probably won't be a name displayed, though, because it's not likely that anyone will be able to prove that the bones actually belonged to Gregory Barry. It should still be enough to be considered a proper burial, I would think. It's the best we can do, anyway, and at least his body won't be on our property anymore," Jason said with obvious relief.

"So his whole skeleton was in the bag? There's no chance that something might have been missed and could still be under or around our house?"

Jason didn't answer immediately, causing Bree to worry. Then he said, "I think so, but we didn't lay it out piece by piece. He'll do that later, I'm sure, while he's examining the remains. I'm sure he'll let us know if it isn't all there. But can we please not worry about that right now and just be happy that we're doing something that should help our situation?"

Bree tried to repress her worries for Jason's sake. "Of course, honey. I'm sorry I worry so much. I am glad that we're doing something, and it does make me feel quite a bit better. Have you called Cora yet?"

"No. I wanted you to be the first to know. I'll call her a little bit later tonight."

Bree talked to Jason for a few minutes longer. When she walked from the living room, which was where she had taken his call, to the kitchen, she found that her parents were sitting at the dinner table and had been patiently waiting for her before starting dinner. She quickly ended her conversation with Jason and joined them at the table.

"Sorry about that," Bree apologized. "I didn't know you were waiting for me."

"Oh, no, it's fine," Karen assured her. Before serving herself, she asked Bree what Jason and the archeologist had found, apparently more hungry for details than for dinner.

"They found bones." She told them what Jason had shared with her.

"That must be a relief to know that the body is off your property now," Jerry, Bree's father, said.

"It is, but I hope they got *all* of the remains off the property."

"I'm sure your ghost wouldn't stick around just because a finger bone got left behind somewhere," Jerry reasoned.

"I wouldn't be so sure of that," Bree argued. "I think he would find any stupid reason to stay in that house and continue his reign of terror."

"Who knows," Karen chimed in. "Maybe he's already gone now that his body is gone. When are MIPS doing their next investigation?"

"I don't know. Jason still has to call Cora and tell her about their findings. He's supposed to call me back later and let me know what they decide to do next."

When Jason called back late in the evening, he had news to share. "I talked to Cora, and she said that she's been in contact with Father Francis Gates. He has done work with them in the past, and he's interested in helping us. Cora's in the process of setting up a day when he can come and perform a house blessing."

"That would be great," Bree said. "Let me know when it is and I'll be there for it. They do want me there for it, don't they?"

"Of course. Cora wants you to be involved as much as you can be."

"So how do you feel about sleeping alone in that house tonight?" Bree wondered.

Jason gave a grunt of indifference. "I'm not too worried about it. You know me. I can sleep through anything. Even if he did try to scare me, I would probably just mumble something unintelligible and roll over, snoring. I'm more worried about shutting off my alarm in the morning and falling back asleep. I won't have you there to nudge me out of bed."

Bree laughed. "Yeah, you are pretty notorious for doing that. Do you want me to call you in the morning to make sure you get up?" Bree offered.

"No, no," Jason chuckled. "You just go ahead and sleep in and relax. Don't worry about me. I'll move my alarm across the room and set the alarm on my cell phone, too. I'll be fine."

Bree and Jason talked for almost an hour before they noticed how late it was getting. They said their I-love-you's, and just as Bree was about to take the phone away from her ear and terminate the connection, she heard one last request from the other line.

"Come home."

"Jason?" She heard nothing but silence. "Jason, are you still there?" She waited until the phone began to make that obnoxious noise that let her know the line was dead on the other end. She hung up and went into the living room to talk to her parents.

"The weirdest thing just happened," she began, then corrected herself. "Well, not the *weirdest* thing, but something pretty strange just happened." She told her parents about the strange ending to her phone call with Jason.

"Was it Gregory?" Karen asked.

"It was so quiet and whispery that I really couldn't recognize the voice. Hell, it was so faint that for a second I thought I might've imagined it. But it had to be Gregory, right? It wouldn't be Elizabeth. She was the one who wanted me to leave the house in the first place. I know it wasn't Jason."

"Did you hear the voice after Jason hung up or was it just before he hung up?" Karen inquired.

"I'm not sure," Bree replied as she tried to remember if she even heard a noise to indicate that Jason had ended the call. She didn't think she had. "But I think I would be even more disturbed if I knew that the voice had spoken after the connection had ended...Oh no," she said as a lead brick dropped in her stomach.

"What?" Jerry and Karen both asked in unison.

"Remember back when things first started happening in the house? I got a phone call from Jason one day that was basically an exact recorded message from a call he had placed a few days earlier – do you remember that?" Bree waited until they both nodded before continuing. "That obviously had to have been Gregory trying to scare me and get my attention in the beginning, which I've realized by now but never gave any more thought to – until now. What if he can still harass me here by using the phone? What if he calls me?" Bree felt sick.

Karen looked uneasy. Trying to calm Bree, she suggested, "Maybe he could only do that to the phone in your house. He probably can't actually place calls."

Bree wasn't satisfied. "He's manipulated objects much more substantial than a phone, so I don't see why he wouldn't be able to push 'Talk' and 'Redial.' What the hell do I do if he starts calling me?"

"Why don't you sit down for a minute. You're getting yourself all worked up before anything serious has even happened," said Jerry.

Bree obeyed her father and sat in the couch recliner closest to her. Deliberately lowering her voice to sound more calm, she said, "Even if he can't actually make calls to this house, he's already proven that he can talk to me when I'm on the phone with Jason. I cannot give up my calls with Jason! It's bad enough that I have to be so far away from him, but to not be able to talk to him would be torture!"

"Then don't give up your calls with Jason," Jerry told her. "You've dealt with worse things than Gregory's voice. Have your usual conversations with Jason, and if Gregory tries to cut in, just ignore him and pretend you don't even hear him. He may have made it unsafe for you to be at home with Jason, but he can't hurt you from 300 miles away, even through a phone line. Don't let him keep you from speaking with your husband."

The tone of Jerry's voice let Bree know that he was giving her an order, not a request. It was his way of trying to be strong for her when he could see she was beginning to lose her resolve.

"Your father is right, Bree," Karen agreed with a nod. "This is one case where I think you can safely stand up to his bullying. And if worse came to worst, Jason could even call you from his cell phone outside the house. There's no reason you should have to give up communication with your own husband."

After speaking with her parents, Bree felt some of the fight return to her. Just because she'd had to run for her own safety didn't mean she had to go belly-up from now on with every confrontation with Gregory. What could he possibly do to her over the phone? Call her names? Make threats? She was hundreds of miles away from him. Of course, she still worried in the back of her mind that he would somehow find a way to follow her, but Cora and Jason had both helped to mostly ease those worries.

Two uneventful days passed before Bree received news from Jason regarding the scheduling of the blessing. She had spoken to him on the phone many times in those two days, but Gregory hadn't again joined their conversation. She wondered if he was listening in as Jason told her about his recent conversation with Cora.

"Cora set up the blessing for this Sunday afternoon, and she suggested we bring any family to it that is currently aware of our situation and supportive of us. She set it up for 3 o'clock in the afternoon. She wanted to make sure to set it for a time that would allow you and your family to come for it and still be able to make it back to Tandish in the same day so you wouldn't have to spend the night here," Jason said. "Are you sure you'll be up for such a long day?"

"I can handle it. I'll have to do it again on Tuesday, too, for my prenatal appointment. It sucks to have to travel so much, but I suppose it's a necessary precaution to make sure I don't have to stay in that house. Did you get your vacation time approved yet?"

"I just got the green light today, so I'll have all next week off. Unfortunately, I'll have to do one week off, one week on, then one week off again. They can't afford to have me gone for two weeks in a row this time of year. But at least I'll get to be with you. That's all that really matters. I'm thinking of heading up there Friday after work. That way, when Sunday rolls around, we can make the trip together and split up the driving and I won't have to spend Friday and Saturday night alone. I'll be able to go with you to your doctor's appointment as well," he said. "I can't wait to see you. I really miss you."

"I miss you too. I'm not used to being away from you for this long. I can't wait for things to go back to normal. Have things still been pretty quiet around there?" Bree asked.

"It's like he's not even here. I haven't seen or heard one thing since you left. I take it nothing else has happened with the phone?"

"Not yet. I've got to tell you, it has been really nice to be able to relax. I haven't been this at ease in weeks! Even if he were to butt in on our calls once in a while, it still wouldn't compare to the crap I had to deal with when I was there. I'm glad I did this, despite the time apart," she admitted.

"Me too. Are you enjoying your time with your parents?"

"I am. In fact, my mom and I went shopping today after she got off work and bought a few little baby outfits and a bassinette. I can't wait until we find out the baby's gender so I can start buying pink or blue things instead of just yellow and green. That'll be so much fun!"

Jason laughed. "Then we can get things that say 'Daddy's little princess' or 'Daddy's little tough guy.' As silly as it may sound coming from a guy, I'm looking forward to that too."

A few minutes later, Bree asked about the remains. "Have you heard from Perry?"

"Oh yeah, I forgot. He called me on my cell phone this morning. He finished looking over the bones, and it appears that everything is intact. He also mentioned that there didn't appear to be any signs of damage to the bones to indicate foul play, if you were interested. That's probably a good thing for when the cops or coroner or whoever it is takes a look at them."

Bree breathed a sigh of relief. "Well at least I don't have to worry about pieces of him still being buried around our house."

"I thought you'd be relieved to hear that. I know I was."

"Well, honey, I suppose I should let you get to bed," Bree said reluctantly as she heard the grandfather clock chime nine times. "I'll have to talk to my parents about the blessing to see if they'll be able to come to it. I love you, and I'll see you Friday night!"

***

Bree was overjoyed to see Jason's pickup pull into the driveway early in the evening on Friday. She had just been browning some hamburger for the enchiladas she had planned for dinner when she happened to glance out the window and see it. Dropping her spatula onto the counter, she ran out the front door to greet her husband. He climbed out of the truck and scooped her up in a tight embrace.

"I've missed you so much!" He said with his face buried in her hair and neck, muffling his voice.

As they kissed and hugged and shared words of endearment, Bree suddenly heard a loud beeping coming from the house.

"Oh shit! The hamburger!"

Running inside the house, she was met with a hazy cloud of smoke and the ear-piercing alarm of the smoke detector. Karen had just run into the kitchen and quickly snatched the pan from the burner. Seeing that her mother had taken control of the burning hamburger, Bree hurried to the smoke detector and pulled the battery from it, silencing its awful shrieking.

Karen, as unflappable as always, laughed and shouted, "Dinner's ready!" She was doing her best to salvage the hamburger that hadn't already burned to the pan.

Bree took the table fan from the living room and set it up in the kitchen so it was blowing out the front door in an attempt to blow the smoke out of the house. When she looked up, Jason was standing in the doorway with the fan blowing on him. She hadn't realized that he had been there the whole time. He shook his hair as he stood in the wind from the fan as if he were modeling.

"Oh, Bree, you know how I like to make an entrance," he joked.

Jason brought his bags in and everyone sat down for a dinner of burned-beef enchiladas. It wasn't exactly the "welcome" dinner Bree had planned, but she was thankful that no one complained. She did notice, however, that no one asked for seconds.

The evening was a happy one for Bree, full of laughter and conversation, until the phone rang. Karen looked at the caller ID on the handset before answering it and hesitated.

As it rang in her hand, she said, "You're not going to like this, Bree. It says it's coming from your house."

"Don't answer it!" Bree cried.

Everyone sat without speaking as the phone continued to ring. When the answering machine picked up the call, Bree held her breath.

"I hope I dialed the right number. This is Bob Hughes," the voice said from the answering machine, and Jason laughed. "I was calling to let Jason Wilson know that everything is fine with his house. Have him call me back on my cell phone when he gets a chance." Click. Beep.

Bree looked with chagrin at an amused Jason, waiting for an explanation.

He gave a sheepish grin. "I told Bob from work to keep an eye on the house for me this week. I didn't think he would actually go inside and use *our* phone to call me, and I didn't think he would go there to check it *tonight*."

"How did he get *this* number?" Bree demanded.

"I gave it to him. I told him to call it if he couldn't get a hold of me on my cell phone…which I left in the truck," he remembered.

"Dammit, Jason! That scared the hell out of me!" Bree scolded. "You need to tell me if someone is going to be calling us from our vacant house so I don't just assume it's Gregory!"

Karen got up and erased the message from the answering machine. "Well, thankfully it wasn't Gregory. Let's just leave it at that," she said calmly in an attempt to halt any squabbling.

***

After a relaxing and enjoyable Saturday, Bree and Jason prepared themselves for a stressful Sunday. Karen was able to join them for the blessing, but Jerry, as usual, had things to take care of at work. Bree, Jason, and Karen left Tandish early Sunday morning, and were annoyed to find that everyone else seemed to be heading south as well. Despite the heavy traffic, they made it to White Dove an hour before the blessing was to take place. Bree made a couple of frozen pizzas for a late lunch as they waited at the house for Cora and the priest to arrive.

"So what happens at a blessing?" Bree asked Jason around a mouthful of pizza.

"How should I know?"

"You're the one who's been talking to Cora. I thought maybe she would've explained it to you."

"She did, somewhat, but I don't remember now. I think he just comes in and says a prayer."

Bree and Karen were less than satisfied with Jason's answer, but decided to let it be. They would find out soon enough.

Just as Bree was throwing out the greasy paper plates from lunch, Cora and the priest appeared at the door. She greeted them and ushered them inside. She saw that Father Francis Gates carried a black briefcase with him and wore the traditional black garb and white collar of the Catholic priests. He was a man of about sixty with gray hair and a potbelly. He wore a pair of small-framed glasses which had lenses that made his gray eyes look too small for his round face. He held one stubby-fingered hand out to Bree as she introduced herself, her mother, and Jason.

"Wonderful to meet you. I'm Father Francis Gates. I've heard all about your struggle," Father Gates said as he shook everyone's hand. "Cora told me what has been happening here, and I knew I needed to come out here and bring the power of God into this battle."

"We are very thankful, Father," Jason said sincerely.

Cora stood next to Bree and Karen and made small talk while Father Gates opened his briefcase and began removing its contents onto the kitchen table. Bree watched him as she spoke with Cora, and saw him take out a plain, white bowl, a beautiful glass bottle filled with what must have been holy water, a Bible, and an aspergillum, which looked like a small whisk broom.

"I can feel that Gregory is very apprehensive about what is going on," Cora suddenly spoke, appearing to have become aware of his presence. She looked at Bree with a hopeful smile. "I think that's a good thing."

Father Gates poured the holy water from the bottle into the bowl, then made the sign of the cross and mumbled a prayer quietly. After gently returning the bottle to the briefcase, he turned and asked if there were any unholy or tainted items within the house.

"Any pornography, drugs, or other sinful objects should be removed before I bless this house. Also, if you have any, it would be beneficial to place a crucifix over both the front door and the side door," Father Gates advised.

Jason and Bree looked at each other, wracking their brains to try to remember where they might have had a crucifix.

"Grandma's necklaces!" Bree exclaimed. She ran upstairs and rummaged through her jewelry box. She had inherited a few large cross necklaces from her grandmother when she passed and hoped that they would serve the purpose. They didn't have the little Jesus on them, but they were all she had at that house. Most of her other religious items had been left at her parents' house when she left for college, and she'd never reclaimed them. Bree grabbed two of her grandmother's old necklaces from the tangle of necklaces in the jewelry box drawer and rushed back downstairs.

"Will these work?" She asked Father Gates as she dangled the necklaces in front of him.

He nodded and instructed her and Jason to hang them over both doorways, from the inside. They had to dig out two nails from the miscellaneous drawer in the kitchen and get the hammer from the basement, but they finally got the crosses hung.

When they returned to the living room where Cora, Karen, and Father Gates all waited, the priest just looked at them as though he were waiting for something.

"I think we're all set now," Jason said uncomfortably under Father Gates' unnerving stare.

"Are you sure? Have all sinful items been removed from the house?" The priest asked accusingly.

"There's no need to remove anything," Bree replied with a slight edge to her voice. "We lead a pretty simple life. The most sinful thing you'll find in this house is in a cardboard carton in the freezer and bears the words 'Triple Chocolate' in its name." Karen laughed at Bree's ice cream joke, but the priest didn't seem amused.

"Ah. Very good then. Let's all step outside," Father Gates said as he led everyone out the front door to the porch.

Bree, Jason, Cora, and Karen assembled on the porch behind the priest. Father Gates asked Cora if she could carry the holy water for him throughout the blessing so he would have his hands free to carry and read from the Bible. She quickly obliged, taking the bowl from him and standing off to his side. The priest opened the Bible to a book-marked page and began reading. As he read, he dipped the aspergillum into the holy water and flicked his wrist, spraying droplets of holy water upon the house and front door. He then led everyone inside. He followed a similar procedure for each room in the house, reciting different prayers and reading different passages from the Bible for each room. He ended the blessing by blessing the kitchen and side entrance.

After returning all of his items to the briefcase on the table, Father Gates shook everyone's hand again and urged Jason and Bree to attend his mass the following Sunday. They gave him an indefinite "maybe," though neither of them thought that they would. Cora thanked Karen for being present at the blessing and told her that she wished she could stay and visit for a while, but she had driven Father Gates here and needed to drop him off at home. Before she left, Bree wanted to ask her something.

"Do you still feel Gregory's presence? Is he still here?"

"I still feel his presence, but it seems to be fading quickly. I can feel it diminishing even as we speak." She smiled. "At this rate, he may be gone by the time I am able to return for our next investigation!" She looked jubilant as she promised to be in contact with them within the next few days to set up the next investigation. She then left with the priest, and on her way out the door she urged Bree to keep her time in the house brief until they could establish that Gregory had gone.

Leaving the house exactly as it was, Karen, Bree, and Jason went back to Tandish, feeling optimistic about the blessing.

***

Two short days later, Bree and Jason had to make the trip to White Dove once again for Bree's first prenatal appointment. After an exceedingly long wait in the waiting room, they were finally called in by a tall, thin, plain nurse with long blond hair. Bree was glad to see that it wasn't the haughty, plump nurse whom she'd seen when she'd had her appointment with Dr. O'Brien. The tall nurse introduced herself as Marsha while she led Bree and Jason to the scale. She was much more pleasant than the other nurse had been. After recording Bree's vitals and weight, Marsha brought them into a small room with a desk and two chairs. Bree answered an endless list of questions about her health, Jason's health, their family's health histories, and so on.

Finally, forty-five minutes after being called from the waiting room, Bree met the obstetrician, Dr. Horton. He was of average height and weight with kind brown eyes and brown hair that was beginning to gray. His face and demeanor suggested he was younger than his hair let on. He performed the physical after

Bree told him about her concerns regarding her recent fall, and finally asked her the question she had been waiting for.

"Do you want to do a quick ultrasound to make sure that everything looks as it should? You don't have to, since you haven't had any bleeding or other issues since your fall, but we could check anyway if it would make you feel better," Dr. Horton offered.

"I would like to do the ultrasound, please," Bree replied quickly. She didn't want to have any doubts.

Dr. Horton dispensed a large quantity of gel from a tube onto Bree's belly and began the ultrasound. Bree and Jason watched the screen on the machine, but couldn't make out anything recognizable.

"There it is," Dr. Horton said, looking at the screen.

Bree still didn't see anything. "Where?" She finally asked when the doctor failed to point anything out to them.

"Right there," he said, pointing to a tiny, peanut-shaped object in the middle of the screen. "That's your baby. And it looks like everything is just fine right now."

Bree stared at the peanut on the screen. It was hard to believe that the tiny blob was her baby and would grow to six, seven, maybe even eight pounds inside of her. She looked at Jason and smiled.

"According to this," Dr. Horton informed them as he pushed buttons on the machine, "your estimated due date is March 2nd, based on the baby's size and development. Does that sound about right to you?"

"Sure, I guess," Bree said. "I had no idea how far along I was."

The doctor printed a picture of Bree's "peanut" baby for her and Jason to take home. Dr. Horton congratulated them and instructed Bree to make an appointment for next month. After setting up her appointment, Bree and Jason drove back to Tandish.

On the drive back to Karen and Jerry's house, there wasn't a quiet moment in the car. Bree and Jason spent the entire four-hour trip discussing names, wondering which features the baby would inherit from whom, and, finally, which room would become the nursery.

"I refuse to make Lenore's room into the nursery," Bree declared. "After what we've experienced in that room, there's no way I'm putting an infant in there, regardless of whether Gregory is there or not."

"That's fine. I agree with you one hundred percent. Maybe we could use the computer room," Jason suggested. "We could easily put the computer in another room, maybe even the guest bedroom. That way our rooms can still all be upstairs."

"I like that idea. I hadn't even thought about the computer room. I've always just thought of it as an office and hadn't even considered that it could make a nice little nursery. I like that idea," she repeated. "We'll definitely have to invest in a baby monitor, though, since it is all the way on the other side of the house."

"Well, yeah. But it is directly across from our room, so we should be able to hear the little one easily enough if it cries anyway."

"I suppose we don't have to worry about all that too much right now, though," Bree said. "The baby will sleep in the bassinette in our room with us for the first couple months anyway."

Jason reached over and held Bree's hand before he spoke again. "We need to talk about something that I know you don't want to talk about, but we need to. What are we going to do if we start approaching your due date and we're still having problems with Gregory?" He gave her a meaningful look briefly before turning his eyes back to the road as he drove.

"We won't be having problems with him by then," Bree stated confidently, offering no suggestions or alternatives.

"I would like to believe that too, Bree, but what if that isn't the case? Shouldn't we have some kind of back-up plan?"

Bree sighed heavily. "If we absolutely needed to, we could probably find a place to rent. We can't afford to buy another house, and I can't live with my parents indefinitely. I guess if push came to shove, we would have to put the house up for sale and rent in the meantime. Whatever happens, I will not raise my child in the same house with Gregory, and that's that," Bree said with finality.

Once back in Tandish, Bree shared what they had learned at the appointment with her parents. Karen marveled over the barely discernable peanut-shaped baby in the ultrasound picture the way only a grandmother could. She was also excited to hear that Bree finally had a due date.

"It gives you a sense of legitimacy to finally have that due date, doesn't it?" Karen said.

"Yeah, it kind of does," Bree agreed. "I have an actual time line now, and know that at or around that time, Jason and I will be bringing home our very own little person! Now we can't wait to find out if it's a boy or a girl! I hate saying 'it' or 'the baby' when I want to say 'he' or she.'"

"Soon enough. Believe it or not, this time will fly by," Karen informed her.

Jason came into the room, looking down at his cell phone. When he was sure he wasn't interrupting, he told Bree, "I have a voicemail from Cora. She wants to set up another investigation for this weekend. How does that sound to you?"

"Sounds great. Go ahead and call her back and tell her to pick a time, and we'll be there."

Jason set up the investigation for Saturday night at 8 PM. Minutes after ending his call with Cora, his phone rang again. It was Perry. Bree tried to glean information by eavesdropping on Jason's side of the conversation, but wasn't successful in figuring out much. She waited eagerly for him to share with her what Perry had said when he flipped his phone shut.

"The police want to talk to us about the remains," Jason said casually.

"What? Why?" Bree began to panic.

"We're not in trouble or anything. They just want to see where we dug up the bones and get our side of the story regarding their discovery. Perry said it's routine and we've got nothing to worry about. He said he passed my cell number on to them and I'll probably be hearing from them within the next few days." Jason seemed unconcerned.

"We better not be in any trouble," Bree mumbled.

***

The rest of Bree and Jason's week together passed more quickly than Bree had wanted. Jason received a call from an Officer Wilks and had set up a time on Saturday before the MIPS investigation to speak with him regarding Gregory's remains.

"Are we going to ride together tomorrow? Are you coming back with me to spend one more night at my parents' before you have to go back home for work?" Bree asked Jason on Friday night before they went to sleep.

"Of course! I want to spend every minute I can with you. Besides, it's not like it would cost us any more in gas to do it that way than if we were to drive separately and then have you come back to Tandish alone," Jason pointed out.

"I wish you didn't have to go back to work yet. It's stupid that they wouldn't give you two weeks of vacation in a row," Bree complained.

"Any other time of year it would have been fine. Summer is always hectic around the plant. That's when we have the highest numbers in production," Jason explained. "But don't worry. I'll be back again on Friday to spend another week with you, and hopefully everything will be taken care of by then. I don't want to only be able to see you on the weekends after that."

"Whatever happens, we'll make it work," Bree assured him.

Jason and Bree made it to White Dove in the early afternoon on Saturday. When they walked into the house, Bree noticed that the phone wasn't in its cradle, but was lying in the middle of the floor, as though someone had knocked it from its perch on the wall. She was immediately on edge.

"That was not on the floor when we left here on Sunday," she said suspiciously, pointing to the phone on the floor for Jason to see. The time of the blessing had been the last time they had been in the house. They hadn't even stopped in on Tuesday when they came for Bree's prenatal appointment.

238

"Yeah, but Bob has been here since then. He called me from the house phone on Thursday to say that everything looked fine. He might have set it in the cradle haphazardly and it fell," Jason reasoned. "To me, it just looks like it fell. I wouldn't look too much into it. Everything else seems to be in order."

"What is with Bob, anyway?" Bree asked, trying to get her mind off the phone as she put it back onto its perch. "Did you *tell* him to come inside and check everything over every other day?"

"No. I gave him the key and told him to keep an eye on the house for me. That was all I said. I just assumed that he would know I meant to drive by it occasionally and that the key was only to be used if he thought something seemed amiss. I was obviously wrong."

"Please tell me you won't have him watch the house again," Bree requested. "That whole thing with him coming into the house so much weirds me out."

"Oh, definitely not. I'll keep my key and take my chances next time."

They walked through the entire house, checking every room to make sure nothing seemed out of place. They even checked the fridge and cupboards for evidence that Bob had been snacking on their food. Fortunately, everything was as it should be. Everything except for the phone, that is, which nagged at Bree though she tried to forget it.

An hour after the agreed upon time, Officer Wilks finally came to the house to interview Jason. Jason and Bree took him to the backyard to show him the location where the remains were found. They then tried to give him the sanest sounding explanation for why they hired an archeologist to search for remains on their property.

"Just so I have this right," Officer Wilks said with skepticism, "you hired Mr. Anderson to look for remains because you were having paranormal activity in your house?"

"That's right," Jason answered, unfazed by Officer Wilks' tone. "We've had the MichigIndiana Paranormal Society come to investigate, and they were the ones who put us in contact with Perry Anderson. We thought it might be a good idea to see if maybe there were ancient human bones on our property, and there were. Now we just want to make sure they get the proper burial they should have – in a cemetery."

Apparently satisfied with Jason's statement, or simply not caring, Officer Wilks thanked them for their time and left. He gave no indication as to whether they could expect to hear from him again or not. Bree hoped they wouldn't. She just wanted the remains to be buried and be done with all of it.

As Bree watched the clock change from 7:54 to 7:55 PM while she and Jason waited for MIPS, she thought about how tired she and Jason were going to be on the long drive back to Tandish.

"I hope this investigation doesn't take too long. I don't want to be just hitting the road at 3 AM," she said.

"I know," Jason agreed. "We should've planned this better and at least brought overnight bags, just in case." Jason glanced out the window. "Oh, good. They're here."

They went out onto the porch to greet the team and help them carry in equipment. Bree saw that the whole team was present for this investigation. When she saw Cora approaching the steps to the porch, she had to bite her lip to keep herself from bursting into a laughing fit. The outrageous woman was wearing a cornflower blue headband with the most obnoxious, huge, floppy, polka-dotted bow that Bree had ever seen. She didn't even know where one could buy an accessory like that. *Oh, wait. Yes I do. The Gypsy's Treasure Chest!* she thought to herself. Instead of laughing, she managed to give Cora a big smile. She knew Cora would think that she was smiling so widely because she was happy to see her. She wouldn't have a clue that it was actually because Bree was greatly amused by her ridiculous head gear.

Cora greeted Bree with a big, unnecessary hug, giving Bree a faceful of giant bow. "Wasn't that blessing just wonderful?" Cora asked.

"Indeed," she replied as she led Cora into the house.

The moment Cora stepped over the threshold, she froze. She looked around with her brows furrowed in confusion.

"Something's changed," Cora said in wonderment.

240

Chapter 17

Bree stared at Cora with her heart in her throat, waiting for her to elaborate. Cora closed her eyes as she always did when she was concentrating and stood like a statue for several minutes. As she stood, blocking the doorway, the MIPS crew assembled behind her on the porch. Everyone was silent. All Bree could hear was her pulse pounding in her ears as her heart raced. She wanted to scream, "What?! What's changed?!" Yet she remained silent. When Cora finally opened her eyes, her face remained unchanged. She still looked perplexed.

"Could I take a walk around the house?" Cora requested, failing to reveal what she thought she'd discovered.

"Yes, of course. What's going on?" Bree asked with concern.

"I don't want to say yet until I've gone through the whole house. This won't take but a few minutes," Cora said as she walked away from Bree and headed toward the basement.

Bree hung back with Jason and the MIPS team, inferring that Cora wanted to do her walkthrough alone. She looked at everyone, trying to read their faces, but found that they all appeared to be just as confused as she was.

"Does this happen often?" Bree asked Sarah, who was standing closest to her.

"No. I'm not sure what's going on. She must have discovered something she hadn't expected," Sarah stated the obvious.

No one put down the equipment they held as they continued to stand at the door and wait for Cora's return. Bree gave Jason a worried look, and he came over to her and put his arm around her waist.

"I don't think this is a good thing," she whispered.

Jason gave her no reply, but pulled her closer to his side. She could tell that he was worried as well. A few of the MIPS members whispered among themselves, but the group remained relatively quiet as they watched Cora come out of the basement and walk through the rooms on the main floor. She then headed upstairs, still not saying a word to anyone as she moved through the house with deliberation. Five minutes later, she came down the stairs, smiling. She came directly to Bree and put her hands upon Bree's shoulders, preparing to share with her something of great significance.

"He's gone, Bree," Cora said as happy tears welled up in her eyes. "I don't feel any trace of his presence anywhere in this house. He's gone!"

Cora pulled Bree into a powerful embrace. Bree's knees felt weak as she tried to absorb what Cora had just revealed to her. Tears began to form in her eyes as realization set in. She hugged Cora back and started to cry. She was free!

"Oh my God! I...I...this...," Bree stammered, unable to find the right words. She let go of Cora and turned to Jason, who had a relieved smile on his face. "We're free!" She finally exclaimed with exuberance.

Everyone cheered and applauded, as though their team had just won the Super Bowl. After the initial excitement died down, Cora presented Jason and Bree with the option of conducting a final investigation.

"We found nothing in the analysis from the previous investigation, and I am sure nothing would show up with this investigation, either, but I want you to know that the option is still available if you want to do it," Cora offered.

"What do you think?" Jason asked Bree.

"I think we should take everyone out for dinner instead," Bree suggested. "Why waste our time investigating an empty house?" She laughed, overjoyed to be able to say those words.

The MIPS crew repacked the equipment and they all drove out to the Gypsy's Kitchen, upon Cora's insistence. She wanted to give them all a free dinner in celebration of their success.

"You two have been through hell – wouldn't a free meal with friends be a great end to this? Besides, I hear the food there is great!" Cora had said with a laugh before they'd left.

At the Gypsy's Kitchen, they all sat at a huge back table and laughed and conversed about everything except Gregory. The subject that had initially brought them together never came up the entire evening. Bree had never felt so relieved and carefree as she did that evening. When everyone finally began to reach for their purses and belongings as closing time approached, Cora offered Jason and Bree one last hug.

"I am so happy for you two," Cora said warmly. "Please feel free to call me for any reason. You two are no longer my clients, but you are my friends. I do expect you to let me know when that little one finally makes its arrival!"

Bree was still elated as she and Jason made their way back to Tandish in the dark. She couldn't stop smiling. Knowing that she no longer had to be fearful in her own home filled her with great relief. It was an enormous burden off her shoulders to know that now she would be bringing her baby into a safe home. She couldn't wait to share the wonderful news with her parents, but she couldn't decide whether to wait until she could tell them face to face or whether to call them right away. Finally, about two hours from Tandish, her excitement got the best of her. She grabbed the cell phone and speed dialed her mother.

"Mom," Bree said excitedly when Karen answered. "I have some fantastic news. He's gone! Gregory is gone! I can move back into my own house again!"

"Oh, Bree, that's wonderful!" Karen cried. She quickly relayed the news to Jerry, who was nearby, before continuing her conversation with Bree. "So are you staying there tonight?"

"No. We didn't bring any clothes or anything with us, so we're on our way back to Tandish. I was going to wait to tell you the good news when we got back to your house, but I just couldn't keep it to myself any longer! I'm so happy I could explode!" Bree exclaimed.

"Me too! Oh, this is such a relief! How did they determine that Gregory was gone?"

Bree told her about Cora's revelation. Karen congratulated Bree on their success and promised that she would wait up for them to get home so she could speak more in depth with her. When Bree flipped the phone shut, she looked over at Jason's face, which was bathed in the pale green light from the dashboard. She was surprised to see that he looked troubled.

"What's wrong, Jason? I can't think of a better time to be happy, but you don't look it."

He hesitated. "This may sound silly, but just now, when you said *his* name out loud, it made me feel anxious."

"Gregory?" Bree said without thinking.

"Yes, *that* name," Jason said with slight perturbation. "I just think that it may be best if we don't mention his actual name anymore. Call me superstitious if you want, but I don't want to unwittingly invite him back into our lives."

"Who do you think he is? Beetlejuice? I don't think that saying his name a few times is going to bring him back."

"I would just feel better if we could refrain from using his name, especially inside the house. Can we do that, please?" Jason pleaded.

Bree could see that he was genuinely concerned. "Yes, honey. When we are in the house, we won't say his name or discuss him in any way if you think that's best. I can see where you are coming from. In fact, we don't even have to discuss Elizabeth, either," she added.

"Thank you. Maybe we should put her journal back in the attic, as well, and just try to forget this whole mess ever happened."

"There's about a snowball's chance in Hell of ever forgetting that this happened, dear," Bree said.

"But we don't need reminders."

"The whole house is a reminder! The piano, the lightning lamp, the stairs, the mural – all reminders! We can't erase the fact that it happened. It's not something you can forget. But what we can do is move on and remember that we made it through this together. When things get stressful, we will know that it isn't as bad as it could be because we've been through worse. We can put it behind us, where it belongs, and we can refuse to talk about it, but we can't ever forget it," Bree said with finality.

Jason couldn't argue with that.

Upon entering her parents' house, Bree was greeted by Karen with an enthusiastic hug. Karen already had wine glasses and a bottle of white wine out on the counter in preparation for a celebratory drink. She poured a glass for everyone, giving Bree just a splash, and they retired to the living room to discuss Bree and Jason's plans now that they were freed from Gregory's torment.

"I can't even put into words how happy I am," Bree said, smiling. "I am so glad that we finally have a home that I'll feel comfortable and safe in. I won't have to worry about my baby being harassed. I'll be able to take a shower in peace. I won't have to look over my shoulder every time I'm alone. It's such a wonderful feeling to finally have peace of mind!"

"Well, after the baby comes, there will be no such thing as showering in peace," Karen pointed out with a chuckle.

"So Gregory's bones didn't even have to be properly buried to get him to leave your house?" Jerry wondered.

"I guess not," Jason replied. "As far as I know, his remains are still somewhere in Perry's lab. It must've been enough just to get them off our property and have the house blessed."

Bree could sense that Jason felt uncomfortable with speaking about Gregory. She agreed with him that it was best not to mention his name or talk about him within their own home, just to be safe, but she didn't see the harm in speaking about their experiences outside of the house. She decided to ask Karen for her opinion, but chose not to disclose Jason's standpoint to avoid putting him on the spot.

"Mom, do you think it would be safe for Jason and I to mention Gregory's name or talk about what has happened to us after we go back home? I mean, now that he's gone, do you think it might draw him back if we talk about him?" She knew her mother didn't know any better than she did, but she always valued her opinion and found her ideas to be intriguing.

"I don't know. I think that would be a question for Cora. I guess if it were me in your situation, I would probably avoid talking about him in the house, even if it does sound superstitious. Of course, you are talking to someone who still actually knocks on wood," Karen divulged.

"I feel the same way," Jason admitted. "I just don't want to take any chances."

"Well then, we don't have to talk about it anymore." Karen raised her glass and toasted, "Here's to new beginnings."

***

Bree's first week back home was less relaxing than she imagined it would be. Instead of feeling at ease because she knew Gregory was gone, she found herself worrying that she would suddenly discover that he had come back. All of her fears were sparked by a strange dream she had the first night home. She dreamt that she was standing at the bottom of the stairs in her house, intending to ascend. As she lifted her foot to the first step, Gregory suddenly appeared in front of her, blocking her way. She tried to move around him, but he kept getting in her way. Finally, he disappeared momentarily, then reappeared at the top of the stairs.

"I'm not going anywhere. You'll never get past me," Gregory taunted from the top step, right before Bree awoke.

Bree had shared her dream with Jason. He told her that she shouldn't worry about it and urged her not to even think about him. When she had called and asked her mother about it, Karen suggested that the dream meant that Bree was worried that she wouldn't be able to get over what Gregory had put her through. Bree had somewhat accepted Karen's interpretation, and since she felt apprehensive about discussing Gregory within the house, she had dropped the subject completely. However, she still felt uneasy in the days that followed.

Three weeks passed before Bree was finally able to let herself again believe that Gregory was gone. Her days had been quiet and uneventful, and she had slowly let her guard down a little each day until she finally felt there was no reason for apprehension. Once she had reached that point of comfort, it was as if her life began anew. The house in which she lived was not the same place of terror it had been, but instead had transformed into a cozy, happy home within which wonderful new memories were made each day. These happier, more recent memories slowly overwrote Bree and Jason's memory of Gregory and the hell they had endured. They did not speak of him again, finding no need to rehash that part of their life. When Perry called them to notify them of the reburial of Gregory's remains in the White Dove cemetery, they thanked him for his help in the matter but did not visit his grave. They had washed their hands of it all. By the time Bree's pregnancy had reached twenty weeks, and she was scheduled for an ultrasound, she and Jason had all but forgotten about Gregory.

As Bree sat on the couch the morning before her ultrasound, drinking the huge glass of water she had been instructed to drink to ensure a full bladder at the time of the procedure, she felt the light flutters of the baby's movement within her.

"Jason! I can feel the baby moving again!" Bree shouted to her husband, who was in the kitchen.

Jason rushed to her side and placed his hand over her swollen belly. "Is it still doing it?" He asked eagerly, waiting to feel something.

"I don't think you can feel it from the outside yet. It's more of a tickle inside my belly than a kick. I think we still have a few weeks before it'll really start kicking," Bree informed him.

He seemed disappointed. "I can't wait to feel that first big kick. And I can't wait to finally be able to say 'he' or 'she' instead of 'it.' It makes me feel like I'm talking about a piece of furniture or something when I say 'it,'" he said with a chuckle.

"We'll know whether to say 'he' or 'she' within the next few hours, hopefully."

By the time they got to the hospital, Bree felt like her bladder was going to explode. Luckily, she didn't have a long wait before her name was called and she was led to a small room with barely enough room for the bed and ultrasound scanner. A short woman with eyes so dark they were almost black and long, dark, curly hair was sitting next to the bed, preparing for the ultrasound. She greeted Bree and Jason, and as Bree got on the examination bed, the woman asked her if she was sure she had a full bladder.

"My back teeth are floating," was Bree's reply.

When the ultrasound began, Bree had a hard time biting her tongue as the radiologist pushed the transducer around her belly with force, putting an enormous amount of pressure on her bladder. *If you make me piss my pants, I'm going to kill you*, Bree thought. All of her hostility melted away, however, when the woman showed them their first view of their baby's profile.

"It actually looks like a baby now," Jason marveled. "It's definitely not a peanut anymore."

Bree had tears in her eyes through most of the ultrasound, which happily weren't due to bladder control troubles. The radiologist took pictures and measurements of the baby's body parts while the baby moved, kicked, and rolled around on the video display screen. She pointed out everything to Jason and Bree as she worked. As she was taking measurements on the legs, she asked if they wanted to know the baby's gender.

"Yes, please!" Bree blurted.

"It looks to me like you've got a little boy," the woman revealed.

"A little boy!" Bree cried, looking at Jason. "We've got a little boy!" She laughed.

"I knew it!" Jason said.

"Time to start buying blue," Bree said with a smile.

***

248

Over the next few weeks, Bree spent much of her time shopping and decorating the nursery as her belly continued to grow. They had converted the computer room into the nursery, as planned, and it now had blue walls with a sea-life themed wallpaper border near the ceiling. The room was furnished with a crib and a matching changing table and dresser, which was already full of clothes. The bassinette was also set up in the nursery, waiting for the day when it would be moved into Bree and Jason's room. By the time Bree was seven months pregnant, everything was ready for the baby, save for one thing.

"So have you decided which name you like best?" Bree prodded Jason. They had narrowed the choice to three names: Russell, Brady, and Daniel. The middle name they had already decided would be James, which was Jason's middle name.

"I can't pick one. I like them all. Why don't you pick?"

"I like them all too, but I think I'm beginning to grow partial to Daniel. I really like Brady, too, but I wouldn't want to open him up for *Brady Bunch* jokes when he starts school," Bree said.

"Then let's go with Daniel. Daniel James Wilson. I like it." Jason tried out the name a few times, then gave a nod of approval.

"Perfect!"

On the morning of January 11th, Bree was startled out of her sleep. When she sat up, she couldn't place her finger on what it was that had roused her. She climbed clumsily out of bed and waddled to the bathroom, which was something she had to do with increasing frequency as the baby grew heavier upon her bladder. As she walked back to the bedroom after using the bathroom, she heard the television downstairs. She thought Jason had been in bed when she left the room, so she peeked into the room and saw that there was still a mound under the covers on his side of the bed.

That old tingling of the spine she hadn't felt in months was beginning to work its way up her back, causing the hairs on the back of her neck to stand on end. She quickly tried to quell her fears by reasoning that she or Jason must have accidentally activated the automatic turn-on timer on the television. That was the logical explanation. She didn't even dare to think about what else could have turned on the television.

Telling herself that she had nothing to fear, Bree began to descend the stairs. She would simply shut off the television and return to bed with Jason. After she had carefully gone down the first three steps, however, she stopped. Why should she have to haul her pregnant butt down the stairs when she could get Jason to take care of the television?

As Bree turned to go back up the stairs, three things happened in rapid succession. First, she felt her balance begin to waver, as is common when one has their weight distribution thrown off by a huge pregnant belly. Next, Bree thought she heard a quick, faint whisper say, "Watch your step." Then, she felt herself being pushed backward off the step upon which she stood. It all happened so quickly that she had no time to react, and couldn't catch herself. She went crashing down the stairs and didn't stop until she reached the bottom.

Bree was in agonizing pain by the time her body came to rest at the base of the staircase. She was gasping for breath, but wasn't sure why. Had she actually gotten the wind knocked out of her? She tried desperately to call for Jason, but was unable to produce more than a raspy wheeze. She placed her hand over her belly, hoping to feel some movement from the baby. She didn't. Panic set in, causing her to take rapid, shallow breaths. She began to feel the same dizziness she had felt before she had passed out the night she saw the creature on the stairs. When she tried to sit up, the dizziness became more intense and she felt herself beginning to slip out of consciousness. Just before her world went black, she saw Jason appear at the top of the stairs, a look of horror on his face. For some reason, she was briefly reminded of her last dream of Gregory.

"Bree! Bree! Wake up! Come on, baby, wake up!" Jason was shouting at her.

Her vision was quickly restored, and she realized that her eyes were already open. She was still on the floor at the bottom of the stairs, and Jason was at her side, lifting her torso onto his lap. She must have only been out for a moment.

Looking up at Jason, she cried in panic, "The baby's not moving, Jason! What if he's hurt?!"

"Everything will be ok," Jason tried to assure her, but the alarm in his voice and eyes betrayed him. "Are you hurt? Can you stand?"

Bree evaluated her body mentally, but other than aching abrasions, she thought she seemed fine. "I don't think anything's broken, but it's not me I'm worried about!" She grabbed onto him and slowly raised herself off the floor. In that instant, she realized her initial assessment had been wrong. "Oh my God. I think my water broke." Her sweatpants were soaked. Her panic was renewed. "No, it can't break yet! It's too early! Jason, help me to the bathroom and call the hospital!" she barked.

They gingerly made their way to the tiny downstairs bathroom. Bree managed to get her pregnant belly around the sink so she could sit down on the toilet. There she waited for Jason to get through to someone in the maternity ward at the hospital. When he finally had a nurse on the phone, he handed it to Bree. She shot daggers at him.

Covering the mouthpiece on the phone, she angrily hissed, "The whole point of you calling was so that *you* could talk to someone to find out what to do! The last thing I feel like doing right now is talking on the phone!" When he reached to take the phone back from her, she waved his hand away impatiently and put the phone up to her ear. She knew she was being a raging bitch, but at that point, she really didn't care.

Without greeting the nurse on the other end, Bree began to tell her the situation. "I'm seven months pregnant, and I fell down a long flight of stairs, which resulted in my water breaking. I haven't felt the baby move since it happened, which was about five minutes ago, and I don't know what I should do."

After answering a few questions about her current condition, Bree was advised to get to the hospital as soon as she could. Jason helped her into some clean pants, put down a few towels in the passenger seat, and helped her out to the car. On the way to the hospital, Bree began to feel contractions.

"No, no! This is all wrong!" Bree shouted as another, slightly stronger contraction began. "It isn't time for him to come yet! He's not ready!" Bree finally let the tears come. She sobbed all the way to the hospital entrance.

Jason was left at the registration desk to fill out paperwork while a nurse brought Bree to the maternity ward. She was quickly helped into a hospital gown and put into a bed next to an ultrasound scanner. A nurse informed her that they were trying to contact her obstetrician, but since he wasn't available yet, she would be examined by a different doctor. She didn't retain his name, even after he introduced himself and performed a pelvic exam.

"You have a preterm rupture," the doctor said in a thick Indian accent. "This is a very serious matter. You are at 30 weeks, is that correct?"

"Yes. I fell down the stairs at home and my water broke immediately afterward. When will I find out if the baby is all right? What's going to happen?" Bree fretted.

"We'll give you a medication to try to stop your contractions, we'll put you on some antibiotics to prevent infection, and we'll give you corticosteroids to speed along the baby's lung development. At 30 weeks, the baby's lungs aren't fully developed yet and will need a little help. We'll take a look at the baby in a moment on the ultrasound to see if it has suffered any injuries from the fall. I'll be able to tell you more once the ultrasound is done." The young Indian doctor left the room.

Jason soon came into the room, accompanied by a nurse. He looked as frightened and haggard as Bree felt. He rushed to her side and kissed her forehead. She reached for his hand and told him what she had learned from the doctor.

"I've called your mom," Jason told her. "She needs to get someone to cover her at work, and then she'll be on her way."

"I'm scared, Jason," Bree confided with new tears in her eyes. She still had salt dried on her cheeks from her last bout of tears.

"I'm scared too, honey. But we'll be ok. Daniel will be ok. We can make it through anything, remember?" Jason tried to instill confidence in her, though he had little to spare himself.

Jason's words reminded her of all they went through with Gregory. When that had been over, she thought nothing worse could ever happen to them. She now knew how wrong she had been. If anything were to be wrong with Daniel, or if he didn't survive this ordeal at all, it would be infinitely more traumatic than any stupid little thing Gregory ever could have done.

Bree suddenly had a flashback to her fall that morning. She had been so preoccupied worrying about Daniel that she hadn't even revisited the fall itself until now. She remembered hearing the faint whisper, warning her to watch her step, then a feeling of being pushed. A surge of adrenaline rushed through her body as she considered the implications.

"Oh my God, Jason. Gregory is back! He came back!" Bree shouted frantically, pulling Jason closer to her as if to make him hear and understand her better.

Jason furrowed his brow. "What are you talking about? Why would you say that?"

"I didn't fall this morning. I was *pushed*! I didn't remember it clearly until now, but I remember being pushed and hearing someone whisper 'watch your step'! It was him! It had to be him! He's back!" Bree sobbed, choking out the last few words, "He came back."

Jason contested her conclusion. "No, Bree, that can't be. He's been gone for six months! Nothing has happened in the house this whole time. Are you sure that's what really happened? Maybe it just felt like you were being pushed when you lost your balance."

Bree was infuriated with Jason's disbelief. "Don't give me that shit! I know what I felt, and I know what I heard!"

"Why didn't you say something sooner? You're just remembering this now?"

"A lot happened right after the fall, and I even blacked out for a second when I hit the bottom of the stairs. I was too busy worrying about what was *going* to happen to even think about what *had* happened. Like I said, I didn't remember it clearly until just now. And now I'm certain that it was Gregory who pushed me down the stairs and caused all of this! You need to call Cora. NOW," Bree demanded.

Their conversation was interrupted by the entrance of a woman into the room. Bree recognized her as the radiologist who performed her twenty-week ultrasound. The woman looked apprehensive upon entering the room.

"Is everything all right in here?" The radiologist asked timidly.

"We're just worried," Bree replied. "We want everything to be ok with our baby."

"I understand. We're going to take a look right now," the woman said calmly.

Bree squeezed Jason's hand and held her breath when the image of Daniel came up on the ultrasound scanner's screen. The radiologist looked him over thoroughly before saying a word. As each second ticked by in silence, Bree grew exponentially more anxious.

Finally, the woman bestowed upon them the most wonderful news they had heard all morning. "The baby appears to be unharmed." She then added a caveat. "But much of the amniotic fluid has been lost, and the amount remaining is decreasing as we speak." She looked at Bree empathically. "He can't stay in there for very long without any fluid. I'm going to get the doctor."

Just as the woman began to stride toward the door, Bree gasped. When the woman stopped and looked at her, Bree said, "I'm having another contraction. You might want to hurry."

The doctor arrived quickly with a nurse in tow. The nurse inserted an IV into Bree's arm, through which she was given several medications.

"We're going to try to drag this out for just a little while, Bree, to give the steroid time to work," the doctor told her. "It's going to be an uncomfortable couple of days for you, but I promise you that it is what is best for your baby. Unfortunately, there are greater risks when babies are born prematurely, but we don't have much of a choice at this point. Your water has broken, which increases the chances of infection, and there is little amniotic fluid left. Luckily, though, the baby is uninjured

254

from your fall. We will do our best to help you deliver a healthy baby. Do you have any questions for me?"

"What if I still go into labor, despite the medications, before the steroids have time to work?"

"We're going to try to make sure that you don't, because it could be very dangerous for the baby if he is born before his lungs are ready," the doctor replied softly.

Bree didn't ask any more questions, as she was afraid to hear the answers. When the doctor left, Bree and Jason sat alone in the room, expressing their despair in privacy with tears and sobs.

Bree continued to get contractions throughout the day, but due to the medication, they were inconsistent and weak. In the evening, Bree finally persuaded Jason to call Cora.

"Cora wants to come out to the house as soon as possible," Jason told Bree when he returned from the lobby. "She also wants to come here to see how you are doing. I hope you don't mind, but I told her that would be alright."

Bree wanted visitors about as much as she wanted a kick in the teeth. However, she knew Cora meant well and thought that perhaps her getup could help to lighten Bree's mood. That woman had obviously never heard the term "fashion faux pas." Bree nodded to Jason in consent.

"Good," he replied, "because she's already on her way. Would it be alright if I took off for a quick minute after she's visited so we can go out to the house and she can have a look around? She'll be able to tell us if he's back." Jason's tone of voice conveyed his skepticism regarding Gregory's inexplicable return.

"By all means. I'm not going anywhere. But do try to hurry back, ok? If something does happen soon, I don't want to have to deal with it without you," Bree stressed.

When Cora made it to the hospital a half hour later, Bree wasn't disappointed by her outfit. Cora looked like a giant, walking bottle of Pepto-Bismol wearing cowboy boots when she strode through the door. Her skin-tight pink leggings were matched with a huge, puffy, retro-style pink winter coat. Bree assumed the coat had been in Cora's wardrobe since the 1980's.

On her head, Cora wore a pink stocking cap with a huge pom-pom dangling at the tip. And, as always, the ratty old cowboy boots brought the whole outfit together.

"Oh, Bree! You poor thing! How are you feeling?" Cora fussed as she moved to Bree's side.

Like a dog turd. What the hell do you think? Bree wanted to say. Instead, she replied, "Not so well. I keep having painful contractions, but since they want to keep me from going into labor for a few days, I basically have to sit and endure the discomfort. I don't even know what all they've injected into my IV so far, but it seems like they've come in to inject something into my system every couple hours. There are so many uncertainties right now that I'm going crazy with anxiety. So I guess when I said 'not so well' just a second ago, I was being conservative."

Cora shook her head with sympathy throughout Bree's complaining. "Aw, that's terrible. I'm sorry you have to go through this. Do you have other family coming? Will your mother be here to help you through this?" Cora wondered.

"She's on her way," Bree said. She looked around for a clock, but couldn't find one. "I think she should be here soon. I *hope* she gets here soon, anyway." Bree decided to cut to the chase with Cora, as she had already grown weary of the idle chitchat. "So you and Jason are going to go check out the house now?"

"Yes. If anything is there, I'll find it. Jason told me the gist of what happened, but if you don't mind, I would like to hear exactly what you experienced."

After giving Cora a detailed description of what had happened to her that morning, Bree sent Jason and Cora on their way to get some answers. She felt incredibly alone once Jason had left the room. Again, she felt the urge to cry, and indulged that urge. She turned onto her side and curled up as much as she could around her pregnant belly, tucking her hands under the stiff, white hospital pillow under her head. She stared at the tray next to the bed, then at the plain, pastel pink wall behind it. Despair was sinking its claws into her, and she felt more hopeless than ever. No one could tell her with certainty that her baby would survive this. She loved this baby so much already, and had gone to great lengths to ensure his safety. But now she stood the chance of having him ripped away from her, despite her efforts to keep him safe. She began to plead with God.

Please don't take him. You can't take him from me. He's not just a fetus, an unborn thing. He is my baby boy, and I love him. He has a name. He has a room, with a crib and a dresser and a changing table where I will change his tiny clothes. He has a home to explore. He has grandmas and grandpas that are excited to meet him. Please don't take that away from them. He has a loving father who already carries a picture of him around in his wallet. He has a loving mother who can't bear the thought of leaving this hospital without him. God, he has a name. He is Daniel James Wilson, and you can't have him back yet. Please let me keep him. Don't deprive the world of the light he will bring it. You can't take him, not after all we've overcome!

"Bree? Are you ok, sweetie?"

Karen's voice brought instant comfort to Bree. "Mom!" She exclaimed as she turned toward the door. When she saw her mother's face, it was pale and lined with worry and fatigue. Karen hurried to her bedside.

"Are you and the baby still ok?" Karen inquired, concerned.

"So far, I think. Mom, I'm so scared," Bree choked. Her voice was becoming hoarse from her incessant crying.

"It'll all be ok," Karen said. Bree took solace in those words even though she knew Karen didn't know any better than she did how everything would turn out in the end.

Bree sat with her mother in the cold, disinfectant-scented room and awaited Jason's return. When he finally came into the room an hour later, Bree's chest tightened with anxiety. She was afraid of what news he might bring.

Jason greeted Karen and made small-talk with her before he noticed Bree staring at him with bugged eyes.

"Well? What did Cora find?" Bree wanted to know.

"Nothing. She didn't sense anything in the house, Bree. I don't know what happened to you on the stairs, but Cora is quite confident that he isn't there," Jason said.

Bree was relieved, but confused. If it wasn't Gregory, then why had she heard a whisper and felt herself being pushed down the stairs? Was she just mistaken? Had her brain just misinterpreted the noise from the television as a whisper and her loss of balance as a push? She still wondered about the television, but knew that there were plenty of other plausible, logical explanations for why it had been on.

Over the next couple of days, Bree's contractions grew more uncomfortable. Jason left her side only to get coffee and use the bathroom, and Karen was at the hospital every day. At night, Karen stayed at Bree and Jason's house, but returned to the hospital early each morning. Bree was thankful for their unwavering support and positive attitude.

By nightfall on her third day in the hospital, Bree was ready to give birth to Daniel. She endured hours of the most excruciating pain she had ever felt, surrounded by doctors and nurses and hospital equipment. She tried to focus on Jason, who was at her side through it all, but the drugs they had given her for pain made it difficult to focus on anything. Finally, she felt all the pain vanish as Daniel entered the world. She heard a strange whimper at that moment. She tried to see what was going on, but nurses blocked her view of her new child. Suddenly, one of the doctors, followed by a handful of nurses, whisked the small bundle from the room before Bree could even see him.

"Wait!" Bree cried. "I want to see him! I want to see my baby!" She tried to sit up, but was instructed to stay put. She looked at Jason, heartbroken. "They wouldn't even let me see him," she sobbed.

Jason squeezed her hand, and tears were already running down his cheeks. "I saw him. He was tiny, but he was perfect. He was perfect, Bree."

Chapter 18

Bree was allowed to take a quick shower while the nursing staff changed the linens on her bed. When she returned to her bed, she asked Jason if anyone had told him anything about Daniel.

"All I've been told is that someone will let us know about his condition soon," Jason relayed to her. His face had already traded its expression of joy for one of anxiety. Bree was glad that he had at least been able to enjoy a brief moment of happiness, as it was more than she had experienced.

As they anxiously awaited news regarding their child, Jason paced the room while Bree stared at the door with Karen seated by her side. When Dr. Horton finally entered the room, Jason froze in his tracks, much like Bree's heart.

"Daniel is resting in the neonatal intensive care unit right now. He is stable, and everything appears to be functioning normally so far. Bree, are you feeling up to a short trip to the NICU to meet your son?" Dr. Horton offered.

"Yes! Let's go. I'm ready," Bree declared as she tried to scramble out of bed.

Dr. Horton quickly stopped her. "Wait just one moment. A nurse will be along soon with a wheelchair. You have to take it easy for a little while, which means you can't be doing a lot of walking around."

The nurse arrived on cue and helped Bree into the wheelchair. Bree was irritated with being treated as if she were helpless, but she tried not to complain. As she was wheeled down the long, colorless corridors with Jason and Karen strolling by her side and Dr. Horton leading the way, Bree tried to imagine what Daniel would look like. Would she be able to tell which baby was hers right away, by instinct? Would she be able to hold him? Was he going to be ok now? When would she be able to take him home? She gave voice to none of her questions, assuming that this information would be given to her without solicitation when the time was right.

Bree didn't have to guess which child was hers when she was brought into the NICU. Daniel was the only baby in there at the moment. A flood of contradictory feelings overwhelmed Bree when she beheld Daniel for the first time. She was filled with joy, love, and adoration for him instantly, but when she saw how tiny and pitiful he looked in his clear plastic box, and how many wires and tubes were hooked to his miniscule body, her heart shattered. She did the only thing she seemed to know how to do anymore – she cried.

"Are you ready to hold him?" Dr. Horton asked Bree.

"Absolutely," she replied without hesitation.

When she finally held Daniel for the first time, which was a moment that had been delayed for far too long, she didn't want to ever let him go. She, Jason, and Karen marveled at his tiny face and pug-like features. He was so small and fragile that Bree was in constant fear of hurting him, yet she had no desire to put him down. As she proudly admired her son, Dr. Horton told her about the great responsibilities that came with caring for a premature baby. He then informed Bree that she would be getting a lot of practice with caring for Daniel, as the general policy was to have the parents perform as much of the daily care for their infants as possible during the infant's stay in the NICU.

"Babies who spend more time with their parents tend to do better, and may even have shorter stays in the NICU," Dr. Horton said. He then encouraged Bree to be at the hospital as often as she could after she was discharged.

"I'll be here as much as the hospital will allow," Bree declared resolutely. "I wouldn't leave Daniel's side at all if I didn't have to."

In the ten weeks that Daniel was in the NICU, Bree spent every day at the hospital. Though caring for him in the beginning was sometimes a nerve-wracking experience on account of his fragility, she soon became accustomed to handling and moving her tiny son. She watched proudly as he grew heavier and stronger each day until the day when she and Jason finally got to take their tiny baby boy home.

When Bree carried Daniel into the house for the first time, she was surprised by a sudden feeling of foreboding. She ignored it, as she couldn't think of any logical reason for feeling that way. This should be a joyous moment, and she quickly let her happiness drown out any fears or doubts.

Jason carried Daniel through the house, introducing him to his new home. He and Bree spent the entire day fussing over the little bundle and taking turns holding him while he slept, which was a good portion of the day. It had been over two months since Daniel's unexpected arrival into the world, but Bree still had a hard time believing that she was a mother. She credited her disbelief to his long stay at the hospital which robbed her of much of the average experiences of a new mother. She quickly discovered, however, that some new-mother experiences were more frustrating than heartwarming.

When Jason and Bree were ready to go to bed, Daniel suddenly decided that he was going to wake up and be cranky. At first, Bree laughed about it and sent Jason to bed, assuring him that she would take care of Daniel and enjoy spending some time with him while he was awake since he had slept most of the day. By one o'clock in the morning, however, she brought the screaming child upstairs to Jason, waking him from his slumber.

"I can't do this!" Bree announced as she presented Jason with his howling son. She was wiping her tears of frustration on her shirt sleeve and sniffling.

Jason sat up and took the baby from her. "Has he been crying this whole time?"

"He hasn't stopped for even a second! He doesn't want to eat or sleep and he has a clean diaper. I don't know what the hell his problem is, but I've never been so angry at something so little and cute and innocent!" She was on the brink of a meltdown.

"It's alright, honey. Why don't you relax for a little while and calm down. I'll take him downstairs for a bit," Jason offered.

Bree gladly accepted his offer, but within ten minutes of lying in bed and listening to Jason try to calm Daniel downstairs, her guilt got the best of her. Jason had to get up and go to work in four hours, and she didn't. As much as she hated to, she felt compelled to relieve Jason of the fussy baby so he could go back to bed. All she wanted to do was sleep, but she knew she wouldn't be able to with her martyr-like conscience nagging at her. She reluctantly climbed out of bed and went downstairs.

Jason was pacing back and forth through the living room with the unhappy infant when Bree came down the stairs. He gave her a puzzled look.

"I thought you were going to rest for a while," he said.

"I know, but I think I'm a little better now. I just needed to get away from the screaming for a few minutes. You can go back to bed. I'll just sleep whenever Daniel does."

Jason handed the baby over to Bree without further hesitation. "Ok, but don't be afraid to wake me up again if you need another break. I don't want the little guy to drive you crazy all night."

Jason kissed her and Daniel and went back upstairs to bed. Bree sat on the floor with a baby blanket spread before her. She laid Daniel on the blanket and leaned over him, putting her face close to his.

"What am I going to do with you?" Bree asked Daniel in the sweetest baby-talk she could muster given the circumstances.

Daniel stopped crying for a second, as if to listen to her, and then carried on with his wailing. Bree tried talking quietly to him some more, and she got another brief moment of silence. After talking nonstop about absolutely anything that popped into her head, Daniel had fallen silent and then let out a burp of a volume quite disproportional to his size. He was asleep within minutes.

Relieved, Bree carried Daniel to the master bedroom and put him in the bassinette. When she climbed into bed, Jason rolled over and whispered to her.

"You got him to go to sleep?"

"Yeah. Apparently he screamed for three hours because he had gas," she replied. "And now he's probably going to wake up in an hour and want to eat so he can do it all over again."

"Fun," Jason sighed.

As Bree pulled the covers up to her ears and closed her eyes, she heard Daniel stirring in his bassinette. *Please go back to sleep,* she prayed as she savored the comfort of the soft bed and warm, heavy blankets. Daniel began to cry.

"You've got to be shitting me," Bree said, exasperated.

***

As the weeks went by, Bree's nights were as sleepless and frustrating as the first night Daniel had spent at home. When Daniel did finally begin adhering to a schedule, Jason and Bree found that he was such a light sleeper that sometimes he was awakened simply by the rustling of the comforter when one of them rolled over in their sleep. Once Daniel was awake, he cried about it and made everyone's life miserable until he was rocked back to sleep. By the time June came around, Daniel had been home for over two months and Bree was about two months behind on sleep.

On a warm, sunny Saturday morning, Bree sat at the table looking over her hospital bills with tired eyes. When Jason came downstairs after putting Daniel into his bassinette for his morning nap, Bree began venting her financial frustrations to him.

"My God! Can you believe these bills? How the hell do they expect us to pay these? Our health insurance didn't pay for shit, it seems!" Bree slammed the bill she was holding onto the table in anger.

"We'll make payments," Jason suggested. "We might never get Daniel paid off in this lifetime, but it's not like they can take him back," he joked, trying to lighten Bree's sour mood.

"Sometimes, when he's howling at 2 AM, I would gladly hand him over," Bree retorted. She meant it as a joke, but it surprised her at how serious she sounded when she said it.

Bree sighed and rested her head on the table. As her eyes wandered aimlessly over the growing pile of bills, something suddenly caught her attention. It was the date of her admittance into the hospital. It seemed somehow significant, but she couldn't place its importance.

"Jason, is there something special about January 11th?" Bree queried.

"Isn't that when you fell down the stairs?"

"Yeah, but it seems like something else about that date is important, or at least familiar. That's really going to bug me now," Bree said with furrowed brows.

Later that evening, after pondering it all day, Bree finally thought she had figured out the significance of January 11th.

"Jason," Bree whispered as she fed the dozing Daniel a bottle, "I think I know why that date jumped out at me."

"What date?"

"January 11th! Don't you remember talking about it this morning? Anyway, I think that was my great-grandmother's birthday." She waited to see if Jason understood the significance.

"Your great-grandmother's — oh," he said as he comprehended who Bree was talking about. That was followed by a more drawn out, "Oh...," as he realized who else might find that date to be significant - Gregory. "I don't want to talk about this right here," Jason said uneasily.

When Daniel had drained his bottle, Bree carried the sleeping baby outside, inviting Jason to join her on the porch. They sat in their comfortable wicker chairs and watched the daylight dwindle.

Bree began the conversation that she knew would make Jason uncomfortable. "Why do you think I fell down the stairs on the day that I did? Do you think it's merely coincidence?"

"Bree, I don't think this is the right place to have this discussion," Jason replied, looking around warily.

"We're *outside*. If we aren't safe outside, then where are we safe? I really need to talk about this," Bree pleaded.

Jason considered her reasoning. "Ok, fine. But let's keep it quiet and brief, alright?"

"Deal. Now, don't you think it has to be significant that I would fall or be pushed down the stairs on the exact same day that a certain woman had her illegitimate child – the birthday of my great-grandmother?" Bree spoke in a whisper for both Jason's sake and the sleeping baby's.

"It's undeniably strange, to say the least," Jason replied in a nearly inaudible whisper. Bree could tell that he was truly afraid to speak of such matters. "I don't know what to make of it, though. Cora came in that very day and said she didn't feel anything in the house."

"That's true, and I believe that she didn't feel anything. But what if...*he*...figured out how to hide himself the way that...*she*...did," Bree postulated.

"But Cora was still able to find her when she was trying to hide. She didn't sense *him* at all," Jason pointed out.

"Maybe he's just become better at it than she was."

"I'll agree with you that the date of the fall is a very strange coincidence, but I see no real reason to believe that it is anything we need to be overly concerned about. Hell, we've been living here for almost a year without incident – other than your fall. Maybe we should just chalk this one up to fate rather than...*him*," Jason suggested.

Bree could see the appeal of his logic. She wanted to believe he was right. Her brain easily accepted his reasoning, but her gut was unconvinced. She felt that there had to be more to it than just coincidence, but she couldn't argue with the evidence (or lack thereof). She decided to try to forget about the date for the time being.

As the Wilson family prepared for bed that night, Jason suggested that Daniel try sleeping in his own room. "I think we would all sleep better that way. Every little noise we make wakes him up, and then he wakes us up. If he's in his own room, he won't have any disturbances."

Bree was hesitant. "I don't know, Jason. I think he may be ready to sleep in his own room, but I don't know if I am. He'll be so far away!"

"It's not *that* far. He'll be across the hall, and we'll set up the baby monitor so you can hear every little squeak and fart he makes. We can just try it for tonight, ok? If you don't sleep any better, then he can move back into our room for a while longer," Jason persuaded.

Bree finally gave in and got his crib ready. After Daniel's bedtime bottle, she put the sleeping child into his crib and put the baby monitor on the changing table right next to the crib. When she climbed into bed shortly thereafter, she was already suffering from mild separation anxiety.

"Don't you feel even a little bit badly for him?" Bree asked Jason. "He has to sleep in a room all by himself, the poor little guy."

"He'll be fine, honey. Don't worry. If he gets upset, we'll hear him over the monitor."

Bree didn't easily fall asleep. Every time Daniel grunted or hiccupped, she was put on full alert. She turned on the television, which was one luxury she'd had to do without while Daniel slept in their room, to try to distract her from her unease. She kept the volume low, however, and turned the closed captioning on to avoid missing any little noise coming through the monitor.

Bree awoke in the middle of the night. She didn't remember falling asleep. She looked over at the clock and saw that it was a quarter after three in the morning. When she looked down at the baby monitor next to the bed, she was horrified to find that it was turned off. Had she done that before falling asleep? She quickly switched it back on and immediately heard Daniel coughing. He then began to cry. As she started to climb out of bed to go check on her son, she heard an eerie laughter coming from the monitor. Her heart froze in her chest.

"Hush, little piss ant," a quiet male voice spoke in a sing-song tone through the monitor as Daniel wailed. "It will all be over soon. Mommy's not coming for you."

It was Gregory.

Bree dropped the monitor and yanked Jason's arm violently to wake him. She then dashed from the room, hoping he would come along right behind her. She ran blindly across the hall in the dark toward Daniel's nursery, and when she tried to run through his doorway, she collided abruptly with the door. His door hadn't been closed before she went to bed, but it was now. Her hands fumbled to find the door handle, but when they finally closed around it and tried to twist it, the handle wouldn't turn.

"Oh my God, oh my God!" Bree cried in panic and began shaking the handle violently and throwing her shoulder into the rigid door. "Jason! Jason! Help me!"

Jason was behind her in an instant. "What the hell's going on?!" He was in panic as well.

A deep, sadistic laugh resonated from beyond the door.

"He's in there! Gregory is in there with our baby and I can't get the door open!" Bree shouted as she ferociously fought to bust the door from its hinges.

Jason unceremoniously shoved her aside and began ramming the door with all his weight.

"What terrible parents!" Gregory shouted. "You failed to check the closet and under the bed for the boogeyman! You'll pay dearly for that mistake!" Another terrible laugh.

Bree's heart was in the pit of her stomach. She could hear Daniel shrieking and coughing in his room, and it was tearing her to shreds. Her breath suddenly caught in her throat, and it took her a moment to realize that the reaction was not a purely psychological one. She was inhaling thick smoke. As Jason continued to work the door, Bree ran to the staircase and switched on the hall light. What she saw when the lights came on horrified her.

Thick, gray smoke was rolling into the hallway from beneath the nursery door.

"His room's on fire!" Bree shrieked at Jason as tears streamed down her face. "Get him out of there!"

Jason began kicking the door furiously, and it began to splinter.

Suddenly Gregory appeared next to the door, leaning casually against the jamb.

"I've barricaded it. You'll never make it through before your precious little bastard is burnt to a crisp," Gregory taunted, seemingly amused.

Bree rushed the apparition with a guttural roar of rage erupting from her throat. Gregory disappeared before she reached him and reappeared near the stairs where she had just been.

"It's about time Liz's kin felt the same pain and anguish she caused me. None of you will make it out of this with your lives," Gregory said calmly as he stood by the stairs. He was in his regular form, undamaged by fire or decay.

"Fuck you, you worthless piece of shit!" Bree screamed.

"Ignore him! Help me!" Jason shouted at her. He had managed to break the door from its hinges, but Daniel's dresser was obstructing the door from falling and it had become wedged in such a way that they could not pull it outward.

Jason and Bree worked together to shove the entire obstruction back into the room far enough to make a space large enough for Bree to slip her small body through. She squeezed through and ran into the burning room. Flames licked up the walls and the carpet was a sea of fire. Unconcerned for her own wellbeing, Bree rushed to Daniel's crib, which was miraculously unaffected by the inferno. She snatched up her choking infant, and as she lifted him over the rails of the crib, a woman in an old-fashioned blue dress suddenly appeared. She was curled up inside the crib with her arms encircling the area in which Daniel had been lying. The woman looked haggard and beaten. Bree knew instantly that it was Elizabeth.

"I kept him safe. Now get out of here!" Liz shouted urgently.

Bree had already run back to the door before Elizabeth had even finished speaking. She handed Daniel to Jason through

268

the small opening and then slid through herself. She was amazed that she had suffered no burns, but she was choking on the smoke.

"Is he ok?" Bree asked Jason anxiously.

Jason was looking Daniel over thoroughly. The baby was coughing, but it appeared to Bree that he was unscathed.

"I think he's fine, but we need to get him out of here," Jason replied quickly. "Here, take him outside and I'll get the fire extinguisher," he ordered authoritatively as he handed Daniel to Bree. When she had the child cradled in her arms, Jason reached up and ripped one of the sleeves from his t-shirt. "Keep this over his face to help with the smoke," he said as he gave her the sleeve.

As Bree loosely covered Daniel's face with the cloth, she told Jason, "Forget the extinguisher! Let's just get the hell out of here! I don't care if the whole place burns to the ground!"

She grabbed Jason's arm and pulled him toward the stairs. He resisted briefly, then followed obediently. They hurried to the staircase, but just before they reached it the lights went out. As they groped around in the dark, trying to find the top step while their eyes adjusted, they were halted abruptly by Gregory's apparition. He appeared before them, completely engulfed in flames. The skin on his face was bubbling and oozing down his neck.

"Where do you think you're going? You don't want to go down there," Gregory warned ominously.

"Move it, you sick fuck!" Jason growled. He tried to move past Gregory, but he was suddenly thrown violently backward onto the floor. He grunted painfully when hit the floor.

Bree cried out, "Stop it! Leave us alone!" She rushed to Jason, no longer having to fumble in the dark as the flames from Daniel's nursery had spread into the hallway and illuminated the entire upstairs. She helped Jason to his feet. As he rose, Bree readjusted the cloth over the baby's face.

"Why can you not accept that you are not meant to live, Bree?" Gregory hissed. "Not you, nor any rat that crawls from your womb."

Bree frantically tried to think of any way to get past Gregory. She thought of what her mother might do, and an idea came to her.

"Our Father, who art in Heaven, hallowed be thy name," she began reciting the Lord's Prayer.

Gregory laughed viciously and said, "Fine. If you really want to go downstairs, be my guest. But I've been down there, and, well..." He disappeared.

Jason and Bree rushed down the stairs. When they reached the last few steps, however, they found that Gregory's warning had not been an empty threat. The living room was ablaze. Gregory had apparently ignited the entire first floor while they were rescuing Daniel.

"Shit, Jason, what now?!" Bree shouted.

"Make a run for the door!" He barked.

As he began to propel his body forward, the blazing couch slid forcefully across the living room and came to a crashing halt across the entrance to the hallway. A wall of flames now blocked their path. They hesitated, dumbfounded.

"I've been building up my power, as you can see," Gregory's voice spoke from behind them. Bree whirled around and found him standing at the top of the stairs, still on fire. "Liz unwittingly taught me a neat trick, and I perfected it. I've been here all along, shielding myself from that annoying medium's invasive mind. Oh, and by the way, Bree, you were right. Your fall down the stairs was no accident." The staircase echoed with laughter.

It was at that moment that Bree realized that all of her nightmares had been premonitions. A new wave of panic flooded through her as she remembered that Daniel hadn't survived in one of those nightmares. She began to feel an empty hopelessness envelop her.

"We aren't going to make it, are we, Jason?" She sobbed as she dropped to a seated position on the stairs. "My poor, sweet baby." She lifted the cloth from Daniel for a moment to gaze at his precious little face. It was red and scrunched up as he howled his misery to the world, but it was still beautiful to her. She kissed him and held him tightly to her chest. Her heart was in tatters, her mind in shambles.

A voice suddenly broke through Bree's thoughts, speaking directly into her mind. *Get to the widow's watch. It's your only chance. Go!* It was Liz.

A sense of calm and reassurance washed over Bree, but it wasn't her own. Elizabeth was somehow *making* her feel that way. When Bree wondered how Liz could do that, she heard the voice once more. *He isn't the only one who's been reserving his power.*

"We need to get up to the widow's watch," Bree whispered to Jason. "Elizabeth said it's the only way out." She started up the stairs toward Gregory.

"How will we get past him?!" Jason shouted.

I will take care of him. Now go!

"Just run!" Bree shrieked.

They ran up the stairs, straight toward Gregory. His melted, hideous face was contorted in a sadistic smile as they rushed toward him. Just as they reached the third step from the top, Gregory's smile turned to a look of confusion, then of alarm. He was suddenly thrown backward, flailing through the air all the way through the doorway into the master bedroom. The bedroom door slammed shut behind him.

Neither Jason nor Bree stopped to marvel at what had just taken place. They continued around and began to ascend the stairway to the attic and widow's watch.

"What just happened?" Jason wondered breathlessly as he followed Bree up the stairs.

"Justice, long overdue," she replied as she reached the widow's watch.

They stood in the tiny room, coughing and hacking, trying to catch their breath with their smoke-filled lungs.

"We need to get out onto the roof," Jason said.

The entire room was walled with giant windows. Bree looked around and could see that the ground and trees outside were bathed in a flickering light, illuminated by the flames through the downstairs windows.

"Do any of these windows open?" Bree wondered.

They checked each one, but none of them had that capability.

"How the hell do I break through one of these without cutting myself and bleeding to death?" Jason panicked.

Everything you need is there.

Bree looked around in the dim, moonlit room and noticed a huge pile of sheets in the corner with the large, heavy vase she had purchased from the Gypsy's Treasure Chest sitting next to them.

"Use this," Bree said as she grabbed the vase and gave it to Jason.

"How did this get up here?"

"Liz. Now hurry up!" Bree urged.

"Get back and cover Daniel," Jason instructed, cocking his arm to throw the vase.

Bree turned her back to the window and huddled protectively over her squirming, crying baby. She heard a loud crash and the sound of shattering glass behind her. When she turned, she saw Jason kicking jagged pieces of glass from around the opening the vase had made.

"We can fit through, but be careful. We're probably going to get cut on our way out," Jason warned. He went to Bree and took Daniel from her. "You go through first and I'll hand him out to you."

Bree began to cautiously climb through the small opening. As she made it part of the way through, she heard, *Hurry! He's coming!* In her rush to get out, she gouged her back on a chunk of glass and hissed at the sharp pain.

"Are you alright?!" Jason fretted.

"Yes! Give me Daniel! Gregory's coming! Grab the sheets!"

Jason quickly but carefully maneuvered the tiny bundle through the glass and into Bree's outstretched arms. As he turned to grab the sheets, the room was suddenly filled with a bright orange glow. Gregory's flaming form appeared at the entrance to the room, and his face bore an expression of pure fury. Bree shouted at Jason to get out of there and watched in terror as Jason scrambled to the window with Gregory looming behind him. Jason tossed the sheets out the window, but as he began to climb through, he was pulled back into the room and fell onto the floor. Gregory was on him in an instant, and he reached down and lifted Jason up off the floor by his neck. Gregory slammed him against the unbroken window next to their escape route. His flaming hand was wrapped around Jason's neck, and Jason's feet were dangling in the air, at least a foot off the floor.

"Let him go!" Bree pleaded helplessly from the roof.

"She is the reason you are going to die," Gregory growled. "You do realize that, don't you? If it weren't for her, you'd be a happy bachelor, blissfully unaware of the nightmares that exist beyond the realm of the living."

Jason tried to speak, but all he could do was make gurgled noises.

"Just as well," Gregory said nonchalantly. "I really don't care what you have to say."

Bree frantically looked around, trying to figure out a way to distract Gregory so Jason could escape. She saw a portion of the vase poking up from the gutter. She carefully scooted toward it with Daniel cradled in one arm. Precariously perched at the edge of the roof, she slowly reached for the vase. When her fingers finally made contact, she carefully grabbed it by the rim and pulled it out of the gutter. To her dismay, all she had retrieved was a shard of the vase. She crawled back up the slope of the roof, clutching the vase shard in her free hand.

As she raised her arm to throw the shard at Gregory through the broken glass, however, something strange happened. The fire enveloping Gregory's apparition suddenly began to dim, the flames growing smaller and less brilliant. Jason slipped out of his grasp and crumpled to the floor. Gregory looked at his hands and arms while the fire engulfing him fizzled, and he began to fade.

"No, no! Not yet!" Gregory roared in frustration and anger. As his apparition slowly dissolved, he shouted, "This isn't over yet!"

Bree rushed to the broken window. "Jason! Jason!"

Jason sluggishly rose to his hands and knees, coughing and gasping. He crawled to the window and clumsily climbed through it, gashing his forearm and shin on his way out.

"Jason, are you ok?"

"I'll survive," he croaked. He grabbed the sheets and began tying the end of one to the end of another. "We have to hurry...before the roof caves in."

Bree assisted him by tying a third sheet to the other end of the one upon which he was working.

"What do you think happened to him?" Bree asked as she worked. Daniel was crying in her lap.

"I think he ran out of juice," Jason replied simply.

Once the sheets were all tied together, Jason tried to find something off of which to tie their makeshift rope.

"What about the chimney?" Bree suggested, pointing across the roof to the old brick chimney protruding from the rooftop.

"Perfect."

They scurried across the roof to the chimney. Jason tied one end of the sheets around the base of the chimney and tossed the other end over the edge of the roof.

"How will we get Daniel down? I can't carry him while I'm climbing down," Bree stressed.

"I'll carry him, but I'll need you to hand him to me once I get over the edge and into position. That means you'll have to wait for me to get down before you can go. Are you ok with that?"

"Of course. I just want to make sure Daniel gets down safely," Bree assured him.

Jason grabbed the sheet-rope and lowered himself over the edge of the roof. He clamped his legs tightly around the sheets and held out one arm for Daniel. Bree carefully rested the baby in the crook of Jason's bulky arm and watched anxiously as he slowly made his way down the side of the house. At that moment, she was more thankful than ever for Jason's immense muscles and strength. When he reached the end of the sheets, he was still several feet from the ground. She held her breath as he let go of the sheet-rope and dropped to the ground. When he landed, he landed hard and lost his balance, rolling onto his back. Bree gasped.

"Jason!" She shouted in panic.

Jason quickly checked Daniel over before he got to his feet. "We're ok! Hurry, Bree!"

Bree's heart pounded as she grabbed the sheets and hoisted herself over the gutters. She hadn't climbed down a rope since her middle school physical education class and was unsure of her upper body strength. She wrapped her legs around the sheets and slowly slid down. The muscles in her arms began to shake from exhaustion before she had even made it halfway down the sheet-rope.

"I don't think I can make it!" She looked down, and when she saw how far away the ground was, she began to panic. "Jason, I can't do it!"

"Yes you can! You have to! Just GO!"

Her hands were cramping painfully as she willed herself to keep going. *Just a few more feet, just a few more feet,* she chanted in her mind. She tried to ignore the fire in her limbs and hands as she slid further and further down the sheet-rope. Suddenly, she didn't feel the sheets between her knees anymore, and her weakened arms were forced to support the entire weight of her body. She looked down just as her strength gave out and saw the ground quickly rising up to meet her. She bent her knees slightly and braced herself for the landing. When her feet hit the ground, a small rock jutting from the earth rammed painfully into her bare heel and her legs buckled beneath her. She landed in a heap.

Jason had tried to catch her when she fell, but since he had to be careful of the baby in his arm, he was unsuccessful. He was already next to her when she collapsed to the ground.

"Honey! Bree! Are you hurt?" Jason touched her gently.

Her heel was throbbing, her muscles were on fire, and she knew she was scraped and bruised, but she didn't think she had been seriously injured. She slowly rose to her feet, trying to keep her weight off of her bruised heel. Jason put his hand on her back to guide her away from the house, and the instant his palm made contact she yelped in pain.

"Oh my God! Your back is covered in blood!" Jason exclaimed, horrified.

"It was the glass. I cut my back on my way out the window. How bad is it?" She lifted her shirt for his inspection.

When Jason looked at her wound, he inhaled sharply through his teeth. "That's going to need stitches, but I think you'll be ok. That's got to hurt like hell!"

"I didn't even notice it hurt until now. Everything hurts." She looked back and saw the house from the outside for the first time that night. The entire house, even the widow's watch, was ablaze. She then looked over at her frightened son, and was overwhelmed with love for him. "Well, almost everything," she corrected.

"We need to get to the hospital," Jason said as he took Bree's hand and led her to his truck.

"We don't have Daniel's car seat. It was in the house. And you're in boxers and a ripped t-shirt."

"After what we've been through, I doubt anyone will care. Just hold Daniel. I'll drive slowly and carefully," Jason assured her.

When they climbed into the truck, Jason grunted when he sat in the driver's seat, apparently having sat upon something which caused him discomfort. He reached under him and pulled out his cell phone. It must have fallen out of his pocket when he was getting out of the truck yesterday after work.

"Shouldn't we call the fire department or 911?" Bree asked when Jason just looked at the cell phone blankly.

He continued to sit in silence for a moment, contemplating, and then threw the phone in the back seat of the club cab.

"What are you doing?"

Jason looked at her conspiratorially. "I think the battery is dead. I guess we'll just have to let the place burn to the ground." He gave her a meaningful look.

Bree understood. "I think you're right. We'll just have to let it, and everything inside of it, *burn*."

Jason opened the ashtray under the dashboard and withdrew his keys. As he guided the truck slowly down the driveway, Bree looked at the house one last time in the side mirror. She was just in time to see part of the roof collapse into the fiery carnage below. Watching this scene filled her with a sense of justice and, unbelievably, peace. She never thought she would be so calm while watching flames consume her home. She was happy to watch Gregory burn again within that house, which he had made into a nightmare for the occupants living within it while he was alive, and a hell for the occupants living within it after he died. It seemed only fitting that his reign of terror would end in a blazing inferno. He had made his bed, and now he must sleep in it.

Epilogue

The Journal of Bree R. Wilson

September 12, 2010

Well, here it is. I've decided to take up a hobby of my great-great grandmother's and I've begun a journal. Perhaps someday far into the future this journal will be read by one of my descendants and help them to get to know me as Elizabeth Barry's journal helped me to get to know her. I do hope, however, that the circumstances surrounding that event will be better for them than it was for me. Maybe someday I will record what exactly has transpired over the past year-and-a-half, but not today. I still find it stressful to even think about it, and I don't know if that will ever pass.

Jason, Daniel, and I have just moved into our new home. After our old place burned down, we rented a tiny, one-bedroom apartment to get by until we got our insurance money and found this place (we decided to buy a newer house this time – one without such a history). It was kind of a hairy ordeal, as the police suspected arson when our house burned down and conducted an investigation to make sure we weren't the ones who did it. We obviously couldn't tell them what had actually happened to us, and we led them to believe that it was as much a mystery to us as it was to them. They're still looking for our arsonist. I'm not sure what I'll have to do if they ever do present us with a suspect. They'll never believe who the real arsonist was. They'd throw us in an institution if we told them the truth – that a deranged psychopathic entity bent on revenge lit our house on fire in an attempt to extinguish the last "viable" blood-relatives of his wife. I never could have imagined that one man could destroy so many lives, even long after his death. He may have died on the burning side, but it didn't stop his reign of terror. Now I hope he goes to the burning side to which he belongs...Hell. How I wish I had known what would happen when we bought that house. I would have left a cloud of dust and agitated gravel in the driveway and never looked back. Alas, I didn't see the would-be assassin until I was already within his crosshairs.

I'm just glad that it is all over now. Daniel is safe and growing more robust all the time. That little man overcame more than any baby should ever have to. He survived a fall down the stairs while still in the womb, a premature birth resulting from that fall, and a house fire, which started in his nursery. God must have great plans for him.

I'm still baffled at how Elizabeth managed to save us all. I think she must have felt an obligation to us, as she was the catalyst that started this series of events over a century ago. But if it weren't for her betrayal so long ago, I guess I wouldn't be here today. I just wish I could've had an actual conversation with her. I wish she would've appeared to me, or at least let me speak to her through Cora. I never did get a chance to thank her for saving our lives. Maybe she's found her way into Heaven now that the house is no longer there to bind her to this world. She may have made some mistakes in her life, but she's spent her afterlife trying to make sure that no one else has to pay for what she did. She has finally succeeded at that. I had asked myself many times throughout our ordeal why God would stand idly by and let Gregory torment us, but I think maybe I've figured it out. He had a plan all along. Liz was the one who was meant to save us. Perhaps that was her shot at redemption. It may sound silly, but I like to believe that that was the case. She was foolish for doing the things she did when she was alive, but I hope God will see all the good in her now.

It has been three months since the "hell house" burned. It has been stressful, of course, with living in the tiny apartment and trying to prove our innocence to the police in the arson case, but it has also been a relief knowing that the house is gone from our lives forever. Gregory is gone from our lives forever. We never have to go back there. We still own the property, but I don't foresee selling it because I would never be able to live with myself if someone bought it and built a house on it. I wouldn't feel right about it. We'll just pay the taxes and let it sit dormant.

I've been thinking lately about whether or not to tell Daniel about our experience in that house when he grows up. We'll obviously have to warn him about the property someday, as he may very well inherit it. But what would we tell him? When would we tell him? How would that make him feel? I know I shouldn't be so worried about it now since that's a long way down the road, but I think it will always be gnawing at the back of my brain until the moment actually comes. He's such a sweet little guy. It kills me to even think of telling him that there was once an entity that wanted to take his life. I want to protect him from that knowledge, but I don't want his innocence and ignorance regarding the matter to put him in danger as it did us. And then there's the matter of whether or not he'll truly believe our story. Oh, why can't he just stay a baby forever?

Well, it is late, and Jason is already fast asleep beside me. I suppose I should retire my pen for the night. I just have one final thought before I end this entry: for any possible future readers of this journal, let it be known that there really are things that go bump in the night, whether you believe in them or not. As much as you might try to ignore them, they are there. I know this because one of those things tried to kill me and my family. I hope that you will believe my words, but if you don't, then I hope you never have to find out otherwise. Just know this: your disbelief won't save you.

Bree tucked her journal under the bed and turned off the bedside lamp. She double-checked the new baby monitor to be sure that it was on before curling up next to Jason. Daniel was sleeping soundly in the bedroom right next to theirs, and she was grateful that she didn't have to worry about any vengeful spirits tormenting him. When she closed her eyes, she enjoyed the feeling of peace that now resided within her. Finally, after more than a year of terror and anxiety, she felt that they were all safe.

That night, for the first time since the old house burned down, Bree dreamt of Gregory.

THE END

About the Author

I was born and raised in Michigan. I have spent most of my life in the Upper Peninsula, where I currently reside with my husband and our two children. I earned my Bachelors of Science degree from Grand Valley State University in 2008 and started my first book in early 2010. When I'm not writing, I teach painting classes, read, and enjoy being active.

I have been inspired by the works of a variety of both fiction and nonfiction authors, including Brian Greene, Michio Kaku, Carl Sagan, Stephen King, and Dean Koontz.

If you enjoyed *The Burning Side*, check out some of my other books: *Dream Jumper, Beyond Reason, The Time Thief,* and *The Time Thief: A Change of Face.*

Special thanks to my family and friends who have been so supportive and given me constructive criticism and ideas along the way. I couldn't have done it without you.